Who Can You Trust

Susan Lewis is the internationally bestselling author of over fifty sensational novels across the genres of family drama, thriller, suspense, crime and romance – including the Richard and Judy picks *One Minute Later*, *I Have Something to Tell You* and *Don't Believe A Word*. She is also the author of *Just One More Day* and *One Day at a Time*, the moving memoirs of her childhood in Bristol during the 1960s. Following periods of living in Los Angeles, the South of France and the Cotswolds, she currently lives in Somerset with her husband, James, and their beloved, naughty little dog, Mimi.

To find out more about Susan Lewis:

www.susanlewis.com
/SusanLewisBooks
@susanlewisbooks
@susanlewisbooks
@susanlewisbooks

Also by Susan Lewis

A Class Apart
Dance While You Can
Stolen Beginnings
Darkest Longings
Obsession
Vengeance
Summer Madness
Last Resort
Wildfire
Cruel Venus
Strange Allure
The Mill House
A French Affair
Missing
Out of the Shadows
Lost Innocence
The Choice
Forgotten
Stolen
No Turning Back
Losing You
The Truth About You
Never Say Goodbye
Too Close to Home
No Place to Hide
The Secret Keeper
One Minute Later
Home Truths
My Lies, Your Lies
Forgive Me
The Lost Hours
I Have Something to Tell You

Who's Lying Now?
No One Saw It Coming
I Know It's You
A Sicilian Affair

Books that run in sequence
Chasing Dreams
Taking Chances

No Child of Mine
Don't Let Me Go
You Said Forever

Featuring Detective Andee Lawrence
Behind Closed Doors
The Girl Who Came Back
The Moment She Left
Hiding in Plain Sight
Believe in Me

Featuring Laurie Forbes and Elliott Russell
Silent Truths
Wicked Beauty
The Hornbeam Tree
Intimate Strangers

Featuring Cristy Ward
Nothing to See Here
Don't Believe a Word
Never Look Back

SUSAN LEWIS

WHO CAN YOU TRUST

HarperCollins*Publishers*

HarperCollins*Publishers* Ltd
1 London Bridge Street
London SE1 9GF

www.harpercollins.co.uk

HarperCollins*Publishers*
Macken House, 39/40 Mayor Street Upper
Dublin 1, D01 C9W8, Ireland

First published by HarperCollins*Publishers* Ltd 2026
1

Copyright © Susan Lewis 2026

Susan Lewis asserts the moral right to
be identified as the author of this work.

A catalogue record for this book is available from the British Library.

ISBN: 978-0-00-873425-1 (HB)
ISBN: 978-0-00-873426-8 (TPB)

This novel is entirely a work of fiction. The names, characters and incidents portrayed in it are the work of the author's imagination. Any resemblance to actual persons, living or dead, events or localities is entirely coincidental.

Set in Sabon LT Pro by HarperCollins*Publishers* India

Printed and bound in the UK using 100%
Renewable Electricity at CPI Group (UK) Ltd

All rights reserved. No part of this publication may be reproduced, stored in a retrieval system, or transmitted, in any form or by any means, electronic, mechanical, photocopying, recording or otherwise, without the prior written permission of the publishers.

Without limiting the exclusive rights of any author, contributor or the publisher of this publication, any unauthorised use of this publication to train generative artificial intelligence (AI) technologies is expressly prohibited. HarperCollins also exercise their rights under Article 4(3) of the Digital Single Market Directive 2019/790 and expressly reserve this publication from the text and data mining exception.

Prologue

Most people walked a little faster when passing 42 Randall Lane, picking up the pace as if something about the house might somehow be rotten or contagious or was waiting to spring out and get them. It was entirely different to the others on the street, had been on its plot far longer than the sprawling new estate that had sprung up around it in more recent years. It could be described as a grand dame surrounded by ambitious courtiers, although it wasn't that grand, just bigger and older and definitely sadder. Out of place, even though it had been there the longest.

Late Victorian in style – red-brick, double-fronted with two windows either side of its rarely-used front door and three more windows on the upper floor. A kid's drawing of a house, really, with a waist-high dry-stone wall protecting its apron of a front garden, a rusty iron gate at the end of a straight, flagged path, where weeds had pushed their way up through cracks and tree roots were buckling the edges. The back garden, not visible from the street, sloped in gentle tiers down to a stream that circled a small woodland. It was here that one of the worst deeds was said to have happened back in the day.

Everything was quiet over there now – as still as a painting, seeming untouched by winds or weather. Occasionally, someone used the bus stop outside the front gate either to get on or off the bus, but Megan Whitmore, who lived opposite, had never seen anyone go into the house – apart from the postman, but even he passed it by more often than not. This made Megan sad at Christmas. Did Mrs Ivorson never receive any cards or visitors? Did she ever speak to anyone on the phone or in the supermarket when she went to do her weekly shop?

Had everyone in the world shunned her?

Maybe she had shunned them.

Megan had been ten years old when she and her parents moved into their semi on the Randall Lane edge of the new estate, twelve when it all kicked off at number 42: sirens and flashing lights, helicopters, screams, search parties, news cameras, more police than she'd ever seen in one place before or since.

And *blood*.

She hadn't seen the blood herself, but she'd heard about it. All over the place, apparently, in the hall, the kitchen, up the stairs and in the bedrooms. She used to picture it in her mind's eye, dripping from banisters, smeared over wallpaper, pooling on carpets. The other kids around had said evil lived in the house, that anyone who went near it would be cursed forever.

Megan was thirty-two now, and the house still creeped her out a bit in spite of how sorry she felt for Mrs Ivorson. None of it was Mrs I's fault.

Or was it? What did Megan know? What did anyone, come to that? So many rumours, wild and terrifying speculation involving cults and ghouls, sacrifices and mass murder. Everyone had heard something; the whole estate had been bursting to share what they knew about Mrs Ivorson's daughter, Nicole, and the kinds of things she got up to. Twenty years ago, no one could talk about anything else. Friends, neighbours, the media, Megan's own family and indeed Megan herself – they couldn't get enough of it. And the more lurid the tale, the more gripping and real it was made to seem.

For a long time, Megan had more or less forgotten about the events of July 2005, but now she was back in her childhood bedroom at number 39, right opposite, waiting for the flat above her new hair salon to be ready. Number 42 The Mane Collective, as it was to be called, due to open at the far end of Randall Lane in a few weeks' time.

In the years while Megan had been living elsewhere, she'd only been reminded about the Ivorsons when she came home for visits, although nothing much was ever mentioned then really. Time had passed, people had moved on with their lives, and Megan guessed Mrs Ivorson must have too, in her way, although given what a recluse she'd become how would anyone know?

It was literally freezing outside today, minus three factoring in the wind-chill they'd said on the local news. Frost was glistening its wintry loveliness over pavements and gardens, while icicles dripped and dropped from frozen gutters. The gritters had been out earlier, so traffic was flowing – not that Randall Lane was especially busy, not since they'd made it one-way and put in sleeping policemen to stop speeders.

Megan was all snug in a fleecy onesie, curled up in an old wing-backed chair in her childhood room – too cold to be right up by the window today – iPad in her lap, phone within reach as she worked on updating her accounts. She'd heard that Mrs Ivorson used to be a book-keeper, before everything, working for lots of local small businesses, but that was so long ago it wasn't relevant now, and anyway, Megan would never have the nerve to ask for her help.

She wondered, as she gazed idly across the street towards the lonely looking house, if Mrs Ivorson would like to have her hair done. She used to have a lovely head of coppery curls, kind of carefree and yet stylish, one of those looks that made it seem like nothing had gone into it when probably a lot had. The last time she'd seen Mrs I, she'd been wearing a bobble hat and woolly scarf, her hair all covered up, though Megan knew she'd cut it short a long time ago. It was as if, Megan had thought when she'd first noticed the dramatic change, Mrs Ivorson had decided that her flamboyant curls were in some way to blame for what had happened, so they'd had to go. Now, Megan felt it was probably sadness that had made Mrs Ivorson want to change her look. Her mood, her heart, simply couldn't live up to the cheerful image created by her lively hair.

Should she go over and offer a freebie? How weird would that seem when she hadn't been over once in the last twenty years? Her mum had gone, a few times, after Mr Ivorson had passed, just to ask if everything was all right and was there anything she could do. Mrs Ivorson had never invited her in or taken her up on her offer. She obviously just wanted to be left alone to sort out her own shopping, tend her garden, go to her appointments and carry on doing whatever she did inside those dark grey walls.

Spooky or what?

Had she cleaned up the blood by now? Must have, surely.

How dearly Megan would love to chat with Mrs Ivorson, have her tell everything about what had really happened in July 2005. There was definitely more to it than the press had reported. Everyone knew that; even the papers admitted it. They'd made a big deal of it at the time, actually. No one had the real answers, the proper explanation, the inside story on what had actually gone down and why. Not even the police had been able to answer all the questions, and chances were they still couldn't – although the daughter was definitely paying for what she'd done.

And so she should.

Megan frowned slightly as a van pulled into the bus stop outside number 42's gate and a youngish-looking man in a padded coat and leather hat with earflaps got out. A moment later, another man all wrapped up against the cold went to open the back doors of the vehicle and began taking something out: a steel case the size of a boot box, and another case, long and plastic-looking, that could easily contain a gun, but it turned out to be . . .

Megan sat forward, her heart starting to race with excitement. Another van was pulling up now, this one grey with blacked out windows. Its insignia left no doubt as to which TV station it had come from.

More vehicles arrived, more people got out, all of them shrouded against the wind. She couldn't quite believe it. It was like watching ghosts morphing back into life, a rerun of what had happened before, except now it was in winter; the last time had been the middle of summer.

'Mum!' she shouted, getting to her feet. 'Something's going on over the road.'

'What?' Ella Whitmore asked, coming into the room, still in her dressing gown and carrying a cup of tea. 'It's a bit hot in here, Megs.'

'Look,' Megan cried, pointing to the window. 'Tell me I'm not seeing things.'

Puzzled, Ella went to check and gave a small gasp of surprise.

'They just turned up,' Megan told her. 'Oh my God, Mum! What if . . . You don't reckon it's happened again, do you?'

Ella's eyes widened before she collected herself. 'Don't be silly,' she scolded. 'It can't happen twice. But maybe . . .'

'Maybe what?' Megan urged.

Ella looked at her. 'We need to turn on the news,' she said. 'I heard something a few weeks ago . . . Oh, Megs . . . They must have let her out, and if they have, does it mean . . . ?' She pressed a hand to her mouth. 'I don't even want to think it,' she said, 'not after all these years.'

Understanding what was in her mother's mind, Megan stared at her in disbelief. Eventually she said, 'If they've found them – oh my God, it could be bodies.' She felt sick.

'Or maybe,' she added tentatively, 'they're still alive and someone's found them.'

Could that even be possible after all this time?

No way! It couldn't be.

It just couldn't.

CHAPTER ONE

'We're going to make you an offer you can't refuse.'

'What kind of an offer?'

'You'll find out soon enough. I'll have my PA reach out to make an appointment. I think you're going to like it. Confidential for now, though. OK?'

That short, totally unexpected phone call, coming out of the blue as it had, just before Christmas, was still resonating with Cristy Ward two weeks later as she boarded the train to London. She had already spent far too many hours trying to second guess what might lie in store today, letting all sorts of scenarios run away with her, although she felt quietly certain that the podcast she produced, *Hindsight* was going to be at the heart of it all.

It would be something big – she was sure of it, because the great Paul Kinsley wasn't someone to waste her time, or his own.

It must have been ten years or more since they'd last met in person, at a party to celebrate the publishing of his book, *Staying Tuned* – a first-hand account of his journey through local and national media to become the head of a European-wide network of news and entertainment channels. Back when Cristy was fresh out of UCL, he'd given her her first big break as a researcher for a London based current-affairs show. That was where she'd met Matthew, her now ex-husband, and father of both her children, who'd been an associate producer at the time. Kinsley had orchestrated their move to Bristol – her hometown, to set up *The News Agenda*, which Matthew presented to this day. She'd been a senior producer on the programme until just over five years ago when her marriage had ended. Since the divorce she'd reinvented herself as a true-crime podcaster, and now, thanks to some early successes, she felt that all was right with the world.

A dangerous conclusion for someone with a fiftieth birthday coming up and the menopause looming.

She was definitely no longer the bright young thing Kinsley probably remembered. However, she now had experience and maturity on her side, and according to her astutely loyal nineteen-year-old daughter, Hayley, she carried off glamour as easily as if no effort went into it at all. It did, although Cristy had to admit that she wasn't as focused on her looks as some. However, for today, her lively and magnetic – Hayley's word – blue eyes were subtly enhanced by liner, and her normally scrunched up shoulder-length curls were falling loosely, hopefully stylishly, around her oval face. Beneath her long padded coat, she was wearing a navy suit from The Fold, and since, at five foot nine, she didn't need the discomfort of extra height, her matching ankle boots were low-heeled. She simply wanted to look smart and elegant without appearing to have tried too hard.

She'd do that later today for the man in her life: the one she'd once tried, through her podcast, to expose as a triple-murderer.

David Gaudion. The man who was living proof that she didn't get everything right, and in this case she couldn't be happier for it.

Simply thinking about him caused her heart to skip a beat. They'd been together for over a year now, and she still experienced teenagerish flutterings of pleasure at the prospect of seeing him. Apart from being drop-dead gorgeous, at least to her mind, he was a Guernsey-based wealth manager, a father of three, a skilled yachtsman, a powerful and passionate lover, and though he was never around often enough, he somehow managed to feel like a constant and always welcome presence in her life.

Knowing that he was going to join her later today made her even happier about being in London, and as the anticipation of seeing Kinsley began to build, she found herself almost wanting to laugh.

It was just after eleven when she jumped into a cab at Paddington, and after giving the driver directions, she took a call from her podcast co-producer, Connor Church. 'Hey, Con. Everything OK?'

'I'm guessing you haven't seen the news,' he said, 'or you'd have rung by now.'

'What is it?'

There was a crackling on the line as he said, '. . . knew you'd want . . . Trying to remember . . .'

'Hang on, you're breaking up,' she interrupted.

'Sorry, in a bit of a dodgy area,' he told her. 'Any better now?'

'I think so. Carry on.'

'OK. Did you get the bit about Nicole Ivorson being released? Not sure about any of the conditions yet, but apparently it's happened.'

Cristy's eyes rounded as her heart skipped a beat. 'We knew it was going to after she confessed . . . Did she confess? Do we know that for certain yet?'

'All accounts say she did. The nation's press has already flocked to Randall Lane apparently, but no sign of her yet – or her mother.'

'Does Maeve still live there?'

'My sources say, yes, but as of right now, no one knows where she is.'

Cristy's mind was already reeling back to the time when

she, as a thirty-year-old TV reporter, had stood outside 42 Randall Lane, reporting on the tragic and mysterious events that had happened inside the house. 'Where are you now?' she asked Connor.

'On my way back from Devon. I can drop off Jodi and the baby and go on to the office to start pulling up old files.'

'Great, and try to get more background on the release. Is she on temporary licence, or parole? Has she confessed? I should be on an early train back tomorrow. Let me know if you hear anything meanwhile.'

After ringing off, Cristy sat with the case for a while, selecting different parts of it from her memory, each one firing up as much eagerness as it did apprehension about going there again. It had to be done; there was no doubt about that. It was a mystery – an aberration almost – that still cried out for answers, which made it a perfect investigation for her crack team of podcasters: a brand-new series for *Hindsight*.

She just hoped that, this time around, it wouldn't mess with her head the way it had back then, but she was a different person now, older, wiser and very definitely not pregnant.

At last, the cab turned into the exclusive, cobbled enclave of Soho's Ham Yard, where a uniformed doorman was outside the hotel, ready to greet her.

After paying the driver, she followed the doorman into the hotel's uniquely styled lobby and slipped him a ten-pound note. Too much, probably, but who knew in an establishment like this? It was so high-end it might actually not be enough.

'Hi, I'm Ellie.' A petite, smartly dressed hostess smiled as she came to greet her. 'Welcome to the Ham Yard Hotel. Are you staying with us?'

'I am,' Cristy replied, looking around at the hugely excessive but beautifully artful flower displays, the arrestingly funky art on the walls and a curious bank of fast-moving clocks. 'The booking should be in the name of David Gaudion. He'll be coming later. I have a meeting at eleven with—'

'Cristy! You're here!'

At the sound of the voice she remembered so well, Cristy broke into a delighted laugh as her old mentor appeared from an open door at the other end of reception. His arms were open ready to greet her, and she all but ran into them. He was large in just about every way: tall, wide, loud and effortlessly charming, and being swallowed into his embrace had the feeling of coming home.

'You look fantastic,' he told her, holding her back to study her face. 'More beautiful than ever, I see.' His fleshy, crinkled face broke into a happy grin as he chuckled delightedly. 'I've missed you,' he told her. 'You need to be in town more often. Dinah would love it.'

'How is your lovely wife?' Cristy smiled, enjoying his arm around her as he led her into the room he'd come from. It was clearly a library given its high, book-lined walls and the cosy nest of sofas and armchairs grouped around a grand fireplace and coffee table. 'It seems so long since I last saw her.'

'She's on great form and I know she'd love to see you. Now, let me introduce you . . .'

Two grey-suited men got to their feet.

'Carl Finsberg, my CFO,' Kinsley told her, as the shorter and older of the two came to shake her hand. 'You guys might remember one another?'

'Of course we do,' Cristy replied, pulling Carl into a hug. 'How are you? And how's James?'

'We finally got married,' Carl told her, pushing his glasses further up his nose. 'And he's great. Wanted me to send his love.'

'And this,' Kinsley said, steering her to the other man, whom she recognized instantly in spite of never having met him in her life, 'is Vikram Rathour.'

'Not to be confused,' Rathour said, reaching for her hand, his dark eyes suffused with irony, 'with the famous cricketer. It's a pleasure to meet you, Cristy.' Cristy knew he'd been born and raised in the sub-Continent and had later relocated his growing empire to the US, it would account for why he sounded more American than Indian.

'I'm afraid I've never heard of the cricketer,' she told him, 'but of course I know who you are, and it's a pleasure to meet you too.'

What on earth was he doing here? Why did Kinsley want her to meet *Vikram Rathour*, one of the world's leading businessmen? Just wait 'til she told David – and Connor. It was going to blow their minds. It occurred to her as she settled into one of the elegant cream-and-coral upholstered sofas that there might be something Kinsley and Rathour wanted her and Connor to look into. That would be pretty mind-blowing in itself, given the stature of both men – also insane even to think it, when Kinsley alone had an army of people at his disposal to carry out all his investigative needs.

'Will you have coffee?' Kinsley asked, lifting a large silver pot ready to pour.

'Black, thanks,' she said, and settled her handbag between her feet, wondering if she should take out her laptop and mobile phone to join the others on the table.

'How was your journey here?' Rathour enquired politely, folding one long leg over the other as he relaxed back in an armchair with his cup and saucer. 'Did you come by train?'

'I did,' she confirmed. 'It was fine, very smooth.' Could she get any more banal? She almost asked how he'd got here but stopped herself just in time. It didn't seem the sort of question to ask someone who'd very probably flown in on a private jet and been stretch-limo-ed right to the door.

'Are you working on any investigations at the moment?' Carl asked chattily as he reached for one of the delicious-looking cannoli.

'We're digging into a few cold cases,' she told him, aware of Nicole Ivorson leapfrogging the others straight to the front of her mind, 'but nothing's ready to go just yet.'

'Pity. James and I are always so gripped by your podcasts – we never want them to end. We were very moved by the last one. Terrifying what AI can do in the wrong hands. That poor woman.'

'It was an excellent series,' Rathour declared, putting his cup down. 'As were those that came before. There's an intriguing mix of the personal and professional in your work that makes it both unique and compelling.'

'She's the real deal,' Paul assured him. 'An actual investigative journalist with a lot of kudos behind her.'

Embarrassed and of course flattered, Cristy said, 'I have a first-class team supporting me, and my co-producer, Connor Church, is also an experienced journalist. We worked together in TV before setting up *Hindsight*.'

'He doesn't hanker for the screen?' Kinsley asked. 'Most guys his age still see it as the holy grail. Or am I wrong about that?'

'It's changing,' she replied, knowing he was fully aware of that – in his position, how could he not be? And he knew Connor's age. Interesting.

'But you do have ambitions for your series?' Kinsley prompted. 'I know you do because I know *you*, so let me come to the point of why we've asked you to meet us today. Nothing's been announced yet, and probably won't be for a while, but Vikram and I are looking into creating a joint podcasting enterprise. We can go into the detail another time – still a lot to be ironed out – but in principle, the new company would have a significant global reach, thanks to our existing media networks, and could greatly expand exposure for the established podcasts we take on board. It will also generate opportunities for strong, innovative and creative minds to gain full recognition in a crowded marketplace with the advantage of having been brought on by RK Media. The name is under review.'

Cristy's mind was spinning as she tried to get a full grasp of what he was actually saying.

Before she could speak, he continued, 'Vikram is keen to run operations out of New York. I would prefer them be centred in London, so I'm hoping you'll help me to convince him I'm right. As someone who knows the podcasting business, who has a wealth of media experience and a knack for building a great team, you are my number one choice to head up the new venture.'

There was a beat before her mouth almost fell open. Her eyes darted between the two men, as though seeking assurance she'd just heard right.

'You'll have Vik's backing,' Kinsley assured her, 'if you do decide to join us, but don't worry, we're not asking for a commitment at this stage. We just want you to know that the top job could be yours, plus a place on the board, if you want it.'

Cristy simply stared at him, unable to think of a thing to say. This was so beyond her wildest imaginings that she hadn't even begun to consider such a leap, never mind a monumental change to her world.

'Naturally, it will be up to you how you run your team – or teams, plural,' he continued. 'As the executive producer of all podcasting output, structure and strategy will be in your hands. We'd love for you to bring *Hindsight* with you, and personally, I'd encourage you to continue presenting where you can. Our focus groups show that people respond well to you—'

'You've already focus-grouped me?' she spluttered, knowing she shouldn't be surprised – this was Kinsley, after all – and yet she was.

Clearly amused, he said, 'You came out well, so don't be offended.'

Not sure whether she was or wasn't, she said, 'I'm sorry, but this . . . It's a lot to think about . . .'

'Which is all we want you to do at this stage,' Rathour reminded her. 'As Paul said, we're still a good while away from launch, so take a few weeks to think it over – hell, take a few months if you need it. For obvious reasons, we'd like to launch with you on board, but there's still plenty of time. Incidentally, do you have ownership of *Hindsight*?'

Certain he must already know the answer to that, she said, 'I do, but Connor, who I mentioned just now, is heavily invested both professionally and personally. As are the Quinns – Harry and Meena – who own the harbourside studios in Bristol where *Hindsight* is based. They're fully involved in running the business side of things.'

'I'm sure you have great loyalty to your colleagues,' Kinsley commented, 'and if it's your ambition to continue working out of the premises you're in, with a team of four and limited back-up, in a technical sense, then we, of course, will respect that. Our aim here is simply to open your mind to further possibilities – greater scope, shall we say – and everything is on the table.'

Cristy looked at Rathour again, feeling seriously wrong-footed without exactly knowing why.

'Carl has drawn up a financial package for you to consider,' he said. 'I'm sure you'll find it generous.'

She looked down at the envelope Carl was pushing towards her, not sure if it was feeling like thirty pieces of silver or not.

Kinsley said, 'Take your time with this, Cristy. It's a great opportunity, but obviously it needs careful consideration given the many changes it could call for.'

Swallowing, she said, 'Leaving Bristol being one of them?'

He crooked an eyebrow. 'As I said, take your time with it, and contact me any time with any questions you might have. I am anticipating a lot,' he added with a smile.

Her eyes returned to the envelope. It wasn't sealed, and there was no name on the front, but it looked to contain several folded pages that could, if she wasn't dreaming this, be outlining the next chapter of her life.

It was a moment before she realized Kinsley was speaking again.

'... so we'd like everything to remain confidential for the time being. I know that'll be hard when you'll naturally want to discuss it with someone.'

'Yes, I'm sure my team will—'

'Can I suggest before you go there that it might be more beneficial to you, in the long run, to know exactly what you want to tell them before you start upsetting the status quo?'

She knew he was right, while hating the mere thought of keeping it from everyone when it was already starting to feel like betrayal. 'I'm sorry, I should probably be thanking you for even considering me—'

'As far as I'm concerned,' he interrupted, 'you're the right person for the job, but it seems you still need to convince yourself of that. Perhaps it will help if I say we'd like you to consider approaching Andee Lawrence with a view to her co-hosting *Hindsight* with you, should you decide to stay in the presenter's chair. If not, I think she could be a perfect lead on her own, don't you?'

Cristy's eyes widened in shock. She really hadn't seen that coming. Andee Lawrence wasn't only a dear friend and an ex-detective – she was an exceptional woman in so many ways. How could she possibly not want to work with Andee? She'd be brilliant at true-crime podcasting, if she wanted to do it.

But why weren't they talking about Connor?

'I didn't realize you knew Andee,' she said cautiously. 'Have you already spoken to her?'

Kinsley shook his head. 'You're the one calling the shots, but I know you're already seeing the potential of the suggestion: two highly intelligent women with a myriad of talents between them, most of which will lend themselves perfectly to moving everything forward in a way to benefit us all.'

'But what about Connor Church?'

Kinsley's failure to answer told her exactly what she didn't want to know, that for them at least, Connor wasn't being seen as a major player.

For her, this could be a deal-breaker, but now wasn't the time to challenge it.

CHAPTER TWO

'Wow!' David muttered two hours later as he finished reading the offer Cristy was still having some difficulty digesting.

She'd thrust the paperwork at him as soon as he'd walked into their hotel room a few minutes ago, and after sitting him down in one of the wing-backed armchairs, she'd gone to pour them both a drink from the mini-bar while he went through it.

He looked up, his acute yet gentle navy eyes showing how impressed and apparently amused he was. Her heart tripped with a rush of unsteadying emotions: desire, because she always felt it when she hadn't seen him in a while; elation at this incredible recognition; guilt for wanting it; fear of taking it . . .

'They're giving me time to think,' she told him, 'which, at the moment, is the only part I really seem able to get my head around.'

Drolly, he said, 'Well, they obviously want you, but then again, who wouldn't?'

She shot him a look and said, 'It all feels so bloody big-time in comparison to my little world in Bristol – which, let's not forget, I happen to love.'

Putting the offer down on the table next to him, David picked up his wine glass and saluted her. 'You're right, it is big-time,' he agreed. 'Or it could be, if you end up deciding it's what you want.'

Sighing, Cristy sank down into the other chair and stared moodily at the enormous bed, with its six-foot high padded headboard and luxury pillows, where in normal times, they'd already be deeply into the throes of a joyous reunion. Right now, she was too distracted to think straight, let alone make love.

Doing her best to refocus, she said, 'How did your lunch meeting go?'

'It was good. All fintech IPOs and business models – follow-up first thing tomorrow. Now, stop trying to change the subject.'

Smiling, she sipped her wine and felt overwhelmingly relieved that he was here. David was just about the only person in the world she actually wanted to discuss this with, and not only because he was such a good listener, with a far greater understanding of all the nuances and ramifications of the offer than she could claim to have right now. It was also because he wouldn't bring his own agenda to bear on her final decision. In fact, she was pretty certain it would make no difference to him, or to their relationship, where she lived or how she decided to proceed. All he'd care about was her. At least that was the vibe he always gave off, and apart from a little misunderstanding here and there, she never had any reason to doubt him.

She turned to look at him and could tell right away that his dark eyes were seeing straight to the heart of her dilemma – her conscience even; how could she not love that about him? 'It's really thrown me,' she admitted.

'I know,' he said, 'which is why Kinsley's given you time to think. If you'd had to make a decision today, you'd most probably have turned it down.'

Certain he was right about that, Cristy looked away and caught her reflection in the large, gilt-framed mirror over the glass-topped desk. She could see, even from this distance, how bright her eyes were and how pale her complexion. It was the look of someone trying very hard to keep her feet on the ground while wanting to shout with amazement and joy and . . . triumph? Was that how she felt: triumphant? Certainly flattered, maybe even a tad smug. How horrible was that?

What she really felt, she decided, was out of her depth and unforgivably disloyal towards her team – Connor most of all.

'When are you speaking to Kinsley again?' David asked, going to refresh their glasses.

'Nothing's in the calendar, but I have his mobile number. He told me to call any time.'

'OK, then I recommend you start now with a list of everything you want to ask or discuss when you do speak. Chances are, he'll contact you fairly soon just to check on the direction of your thinking, so best to be prepared for that.'

Taking that as good advice, even finding it a little easier to breathe at the prospect of space, she said, 'Have you ever met him?'

Bringing their drinks back to the table, he said, 'Once or twice. A long time ago, during my lobbying days. I never got to know him – he was someone else's client – but he always struck me as an impressive, no-nonsense sort of guy.'

'He's that, all right: definitely not someone you want to be on the wrong side of, but a great ally if you ever need one.'

She took a sip of wine and felt it turn suddenly sour on her tongue as her thoughts returned to Connor and what this could mean for him. Four years ago, when she'd been at her lowest ebb and in need of finding her way again, he'd abandoned his assured climb up the TV ladder to start *Hindsight* with her. And what a great job they'd made of it so far. They were a terrific partnership in spite of the age difference – or maybe because of it. They could almost read one another's minds when it came to producing, so why on earth would she want to risk losing that?

Maybe she wouldn't lose it. Kinsley had said the decisions

would be hers, and Connor was only thirty-one, so there was a chance, being as ambitious as he was, that he'd want to move to London with her. Even as she thought it, she felt her heart sink. He was as settled in Bristol as the SS *Great Britain*. His wife and baby daughter were there, most of his friends, his contacts . . . It would devastate him if she decided to give it all up to come and pursue her dream – if it *was* her dream, and she had no idea yet if it was.

'Kinsley didn't actually say this,' she said, 'but here's what's bothering me the most at the moment: I got the distinct impression that no one was seeing a good role for Connor in this new venture. I mean, Kinsley insisted I'd get to call the shots, so presumably if I wanted to bring Connor on board I could, but if Kinsley is serious about approaching Andee Lawrence – and why wouldn't he be, when she's such a great choice – where would that leave Connor?'

After giving it some thought, David said, 'He could present with Andee, if you decide to run the show from behind the scenes?'

Cristy nodded slowly. 'That could work, but right now, today, I'm not at all sure I want to take that sort of step back. I like being on the front line. Anyway, there's no doubt Kinsley and Rathour are keen on the idea of me and Andee leading the pod.'

'Anything wrong with a three-hander to include Connor?'

She considered it and sighed. 'I'm not sure. There's a good chance he'd see himself as a third wheel, and I really don't want that for him. We work brilliantly together as we are. We love getting stuck into an investigation, planning the episodes, revealing new information, turning conventional wisdom on its head, exposing the bad guys . . .' Her eyes twinkled. 'Falling for the good ones.'

David's eyebrows rose as he took a sip of wine.

'Anyway,' she continued, sobering again, 'there's not only Connor to consider. What about Harry and Meena? Losing

Hindsight would mean a big hole in their business. How on earth could I do that to them when they're the ones who took a chance on me with the podcast in the first place? They've worked as hard as anyone to get it established, pulled in all sorts of favours and even got a sponsorship liaison team going. Basically, it's thanks to them and all the effort they've put in that *Hindsight* has got the exposure it has.'

Sitting back in his chair and stretching out his legs, David let the silence run for a while until finally he said, 'As I see it, the main thrust of your conflict is between loyalty and ambition – both massive drivers in their own right, especially for someone like you who values friends as highly, perhaps even more highly, than success. We'll see if that's true as you work on your decision. In the meantime, something you've yet to mention is family. I get that Hayley's at uni in Edinburgh . . .'

'She'll definitely want me to do this, I'm sure of it,' Cristy said, 'and you know how chilled Aiden is about everything. And he's seventeen now, kind of independent . . . Actually, knowing him, he'll probably see it as an opportunity to take over my harbourside flat while he finishes up Sixth Form, except neither Matthew nor I would let that happen.'

'The point is, he has his dad right there in Bristol, and being Mr Supercool, he's not likely to beg you to stay. More likely, he'll be so pumped – to use his word – about you moving to London that he'll probably want to come with you.'

Laughing and groaning, Cristy said, 'God spare me. Letting him loose in Bristol is risky enough; here would be inviting disaster.' Her smile faded. 'It'll happen though, if he gets into UCL next year, so perhaps having me around to keep him focused and out of trouble will be a good thing.'

'But we both know he's smart enough to take care of himself, in spite of the front he puts up of having next to no relationship with the concept of consequence. Anyway, as

I said, while he's in Bristol, Matthew will be there, and for all your ex's faults, no one could accuse him of not being a hands-on dad.'

'Unless he's in LA with his soon-to-be ex-second-wife and their baby son.'

'But that's not often.'

Her eyes were unfocused, her mind still racing as she ran through scenarios as exciting as they were daunting. In the end, finishing her wine, she said, 'Please let's talk about something else for a while? Maybe go for a walk or decide on the show we want to see later? Is that still the plan?'

'Up to you,' he replied. 'I have a few calls to make before we go anywhere – one to home, and I'm sure Rosie will want to say hi.'

Warmed by the mere mention of his dear, thirty-two-year-old daughter, Cristy broke into a smile. Rosie's Down's Syndrome had never held her back, if anything it seemed to make her sweeter and livelier with each passing day, and she was every bit as adorable as her grandmother, Cynthia, who'd played such a big part in helping to bring her up. David's other daughter, Anna, who was in her mid-twenties and his twelve-year-old son, Laurent, the girls' half-brother, also lived at the big house in Guernsey, and what a wonderfully chaotic and happy place it was to spend time.

Deciding to check emails as David connected with Rosie, she reached for her phone just as Connor rang. 'Hi, what news?' she asked with no preamble.

'Still no sign of Maeve or Nicole Ivorson,' he told her. 'I've sent Clove and Jacks over to Randall Lane to keep an eye on the press guys still hanging around over there, but it's looking like the Ivorson women have gone to a secret address.'

'Of course they have. Why would they want to face a lynch mob? Any details on the terms of release yet?'

'Full parole, apparently, but still working on the conditions.'

'Do we know if she confessed?'

'Some are saying she did, but no statements providing clarity so far. I've put in a request for your old TV reports on the case.'

'They should be . . . interesting,' she said wryly. 'But good call. If there's any push back, Matthew should be able to help.' Her ex-husband still had a lot of clout at the TV company she'd once been a part of. 'I really think this is going to be a good one for us,' she said, meaning it in spite of how disloyal she was feeling. It wasn't as if she'd made a decision yet, and nor would she before the next series was over.

'Agreed,' he told her. 'Got to go – another call coming in. Say hi to David.' And he was gone.

As she put her phone down, David said, 'Sounds as though you've got something interesting brewing?'

She nodded pensively, once again caught up in the past. 'Nicole Ivorson's just been released,' she told him.

He frowned. 'I recognize that name. Isn't she the teenager who was sentenced to life for murdering her baby twins in some sort of ritual?'

'Twenty years ago, so she's no longer a teen. I covered the story at the time . . . It was . . . There was so much about it that was . . . *off*, for want of another word, even at the trial. I don't have all the details in my head now – as if any of us ever had them at all – but one thing I do know is that Nicole was charged and convicted in spite of no bodies ever being found.'

CHAPTER THREE

Connor was waiting at Temple Meads station when Cristy's train arrived the next morning. Standing in the main concourse, engrossed in his phone, his North Face padded coat open, scarf wrapped loosely around his neck, he barely seemed to notice the crowds swarming about him. He was tall, slender, dark-haired and frequently teased for being the perfect embodiment of Clark Kent, thanks to his large, black-framed glasses and chiselled good looks.

He was also, Cristy thought, experiencing a wave of tenderness (threaded with guilt), like a brother to her – or even a son. Certainly not just a co-producer or business partner. She could only feel thankful that this news about Nicole Ivorson was – potentially – providing them with something major to focus on over the next few weeks as she tried to come to a decision regarding Kinsley's offer.

'Hey you,' she said, reaching him and wanting to laugh when he gave a start of surprise. 'Remember me?' she mocked, and linked an arm through his to steer them out into the rain.

'It'll come to me,' he promised, and shooting up an umbrella, he kept them both covered as they jaywalked through traffic over to the short-term parking.

'So, good trip?' he asked, when they were buckled into their seats and starting down the station slip road. 'How's David?'

'He's great, thanks. Says hi. Good new year in Devon?'

'Bracing.' He grinned. 'Jodi's aunt is pretty non-stop where fine wines and exotic foods are concerned. And boy does she love a walk on the beach when the wind's howling. She's a creature from another world, I swear it. Anyway, if you're up for it, I thought we'd take a drive over to Randall Lane, get the lie of the land. Most of the press should have cleared out by now, so there might be a chance to ask around, see if anyone has a clue where Maeve is, which is presumably somewhere with Nicole.'

Since that was exactly what she'd been about to suggest, Cristy said, 'I've been checking social media updates all the way here, and it doesn't seem like anyone's tracked them down yet. But give me what you've got on the parole conditions.'

'I can go one better than that,' he announced, turning left at the lights, and left again to head along the Feeder. 'Julian Hargreaves has agreed to meet with us on Friday at four.'

Impressed, Cristy said, 'Her defence lawyer, no less. How did you manage even to speak to him? He's never wanted to talk about this case, at least not on the record.'

'I dropped your name, and he called me right back. Well, his PA did, but we got the right result, so let's not be picky. Turns out Nicole's definitely on parole, but surprise, surprise, very tight-lipped on where she is. Do you reckon this guy in front is lost? Because if he turns next left, he's going to end up in the canal.'

Cristy was frowning thoughtfully. 'I'm trying to remember Nicole's father's name . . .'

'Ronnie. He died ten years ago, after a stroke, poor guy. As far as I can tell, Maeve's been on her own since.'

'But she has a sister, as I recall, and a brother? She and Nicole could very well be with one of them.'

'That's what I thought, so I've put our trusty researchers on the case to try and turn up some addresses.'

Cristy instantly pictured Clover St Jean and Jackson Caine at work in the *Hindsight* offices over on the Harbourside. They completed the perfect dynamic of their team, and she knew how fortunate she and Connor were to have two such remarkable investigators on board. If – and it really was a big if – she went to London, she'd definitely want to take them with her, and being young, ambitious and unattached as they were, there was a good chance they'd leap at the opportunity.

She hated herself for even thinking about taking them from Connor, actually felt slightly sick at the prospect of leaving Connor herself, so pushing the thought away she went back to Maeve and Nicole Ivorson. 'Have you spoken to Matthew yet about getting access to the TV archives?' she asked.

'I sent him an email last night – no reply so far this morning.'

Quietly confident that her ex would get them what they needed, Cristy said, 'Did you bring a recorder with you?'

'I did, because I thought it might be a good idea to lay down some background on the case for those who might be new to it. For everyone actually, given how long ago it happened. I was only a kid at the time, so I have no memory of it myself, and with it happening only days before the 7/7 bombings in London, it doesn't seem to have received the kind of coverage it might have in more normal circumstances.'

Cristy remembered only too well how so many of her colleagues – and the police – had completely switched focus to the horrific terrorist attacks and the frenzied search for the killers. She said, 'It's almost certainly the reason Nicole's case was left with so many unanswered questions. Everyone wanted it wrapped up, out of the way, no longer a drain on valuable resources, and sorry as I was about what had happened in London, those baby twins deserved so much better. And don't let's forget Nicole has always maintained her innocence . . . Except, of course, she's now confessed. It's the only way she'd have got parole.'

'Still no bodies,' he countered. 'That's what I can't get my head around. She fesses up, they let her go, and as far as I can tell, no search for remains. Big question marks there, if we're reading it correctly.'

As Cristy turned to look out at the rain-soaked, easterly suburbs of Bristol, she felt the reawakening of a twenty-year old unease coming over her. 'Why on earth would she confess now,' she said, 'when she could have done so at any time since she was sent down, not least of all at her last parole hearing? And like you say, it's bizarre that they'd grant her parole without knowing where to find the twins.'

'Everything about this case is bizarre and always has been,' he commented. 'But maybe they're tracking her now, hoping she'll lead them to the bodies. Do they do that?'

'I don't know, who can say what kind of deals might have been done, or subterfuge put in place, but I can tell you this: I'm not letting go this time until we've finally got to the bottom of what really happened to those babies.'

Eventually, they were in the vicinity of Randall Lane, and as they joined a one-way system that definitely hadn't been there in the mid-Noughties and rocked gently over speed bumps – all new – Cristy noticed how dated the erstwhile brand-new estate was now looking. The exterior of number 42 seemed different in its way too. They might even have passed it by, given how much smaller it seemed than the house Cristy remembered. It was the lay-by outside that she recognized first, home to a bus stop and wastebin now, and just past it was the garage where Maeve and Ronnie used to keep their car.

'Bringing back memories?' Connor asked, as he searched for somewhere to park.

'Kind of,' she admitted, actually feeling as though an old dream was trying to break through in small, elusive pieces:

Nicole's lovely face; Maeve's horror; Ronnie's confusion; press vans everywhere; reporters' feverish excitement. 'Why don't we use the space next to the garage?' she said. 'We can always move if asked.'

After steering carefully into the sparsely gravelled, overgrown plot of wasteland and squeezing out of the driver's side, Connor said, 'I'll leave you to go and find out if anyone's at home while I unload the gear.'

Starting along the narrow pavement next to the crumbling dry-stone wall, Cristy glanced at the houses opposite, and felt thankful the rain had eased off. Nevertheless, it remained a dull and dreary day. Everything was damp and dripping, cold and lifeless – so very different to when she'd come as a much younger reporter in the middle of summer, when the gardens had been bursting with colour and the neighbours had grouped around their front doors, appalled and fascinated by what was going on across the road. Number 42 had been cordoned off, of course; no one had been able to see past the forensics tents or even get close to the house. For days, press and public alike had been left to speculate on what was happening inside. All they'd known for certain was that Nicole Ivorson's eleven-month-old twins were missing and that search parties were quickly being formed.

Clanking open the old iron gate, Cristy picked her way along the broken path that led to the front door, which didn't appear to have been painted since that terrible time back in 2005. It hadn't been repaired either, if the scratched and damaged panels were anything to go by. Those particular scars, she recalled, had been inflicted by angry neighbours wanting to show their disgust, and by thugs who got a kick out of terrorizing the people inside.

Raising the stained brass knocker, she rapped three times and leaned in to listen for the sound of someone moving around.

Silence – apart from the passing traffic and a siren somewhere in the distance.

She knocked again and stood back to survey the windows. The curtains were pulled – all of them, upstairs and down – but there was a chink in what she guessed might be a sitting room, so she went to peer inside. It was too dark to make anything out, although she couldn't escape the sense of forlornness that seemed to emanate from the place in waves.

'Nothing?' Connor asked, coming up behind her.

She shook her head and led the way past an untamed holly bush around to the back of the house. 'It's hard to tell when anyone was last here,' she remarked, opening up a black wheelie bin and finding nothing but dirty rainwater inside, 'presuming no one's hiding out in the attic or basement, but I'm not feeling it, are you?'

'Just a tad creeped out and bloody freezing,' he admitted, zipping up his coat. 'Was it like this the last time you came?'

'Not a bit. It was much more . . . lived in and colourful, but obviously, it was summer then.' She stopped on a cracked and weed-filled back patio, where half a dozen tubs containing bedraggled plants and undrained water formed a balustrade of sorts between the unfurnished seating area and the long, sloping garden beyond. Things seemed to be growing: onions, parsnips, brown slimy rhubarb leaves, and a small greenhouse on the second tier appeared to be in fairly good nick, as was the rotary washing line: no laundry, just a couple of wet rags and a pair of gardening gloves dangling from plastic pegs.

She turned to gaze up at the back of the house. It seemed taller from this angle, even slightly grander. The back door was locked, and all the windows, curtained and firmly closed, seemed fixed like unblinking eyes over the tops of the trees below.

'I guess those are the woods that were dug up during the

search,' Connor said, gazing down over the desolate garden to the stream and small wilderness beyond.

Nodding, Cristy found herself caught in the past, listening to the echo of voices shouting, a helicopter roaring overhead, dogs barking, more sirens, radios squawking and someone yelling.

Pulling herself back to the present, she looked around as she said, 'It's obvious no one's here, so let's do a recording.'

Dumping his heavy shoulder bag onto the wet ground, Connor pulled out a small device and much larger, fur-wrapped mic. 'Do you want me to kind of interview you,' he asked, settling his headphones around his neck, 'or just roll with it?'

Still feeling oddly haunted, she said, 'Come in where you feel it's right.'

Moments later, levels checked and mic tilted from the wind, he gave her a cue to begin.

> CRISTY: 'We're outside number 42 Randall Lane, made infamous twenty years ago by the events believed to have taken place inside. Some of you might remember, but for those of you who don't, Noah and Abigail Ivorson, eleven-month-old baby twins, disappeared one summer's day back in 2005.'

She paused, giving herself a moment to get past the images her own words had brought to life: the babies' sweetly smiling faces and chunky little bodies; their tangles of golden curls and the sound of their laughter, which she'd never heard of course, and yet it seemed to be coming to her now as if they were somewhere nearby, playing hide and seek.

She continued.

> CRISTY: 'Noah's and Abigail's bodies have never been found, in spite of extensive searches at the time and

heartfelt pleas from the family for someone to come forward if they knew anything.

'Nicole, their mother, aged only nineteen, was charged with their murder just days after the police were first called in. She was tried at Bristol Crown Court ten months later and found guilty of the crime. She's now out on parole after serving nearly twenty years of her life sentence.

'So what happened back in 2005, when those tiny twins vanished? How many of the rumours, half-truths, conspiracy theories and horror stories are actually true? I can tell you that most of us who remember the trial were left on the final day with more questions than answers.

'Not so the jury. Their guilty verdict was unanimous.

'So what did they know that the rest of us didn't? Or were they simply persuaded by a brilliant prosecutor who outclassed the defence on just about every level?'

She stopped again, wanting to get her memories straight, to stop them clashing or falling over one another and stumbling into territory she couldn't be certain was real or imagined or simply distorted by time. She guessed she wouldn't know for sure until they'd done the research and brought it all back into the light. Funny how she felt slightly unnerved by that, resistant even, as if the past was going to reveal truths that maybe ought to remain hidden.

CRISTY: 'Something I've long wanted to know was why the prosecution never asked Nicole about the rumours of sacrifice and ritual. There was plenty about it in the news, both before and after the trial: reports of how she had joined a cult that demanded the life of a firstborn child. It was said by some that she, unable to make a choice between the twins, had offered up both.'

Cristy stopped again, as her heart contracted with an inextinguishable sense of horror.

'Are you OK?' Connor asked. 'You've gone pale.'

Distractedly, she said, 'I was pregnant with Hayley when the twins went missing . I didn't know until after Nicole was sentenced, but the whole thing had a kind of . . . destabilizing effect on me. I kept thinking about Nicole and wondering if she'd really faced that sort of choice. I started having nightmares about being in her position, having to give up my baby . . .' She gave a small, self-conscious laugh. 'Hormones can make you crazy at the best of times, especially when you're already spooked by the brutal murder of two innocent little souls.'

'So you believed in the sacrifice thing?'

She shook her head. 'I'm not sure what I believed, given what a weird headspace I was in. But nothing was ever found to substantiate the claims, so that'll be why it never got mentioned in court. The rumours, though . . .' She cut herself off and gestured to the mic, ready to begin again.

> CRISTY: 'Nicole always insisted they'd been abducted, and she was taken seriously in the first few days. The trouble was: no one ever came forward to say they'd seen or heard anything to make a case for abduction, and then everyone was thrown off-course by the 7/7 terrorist attacks in London. After that, almost immediately, every force in the country was focusing on the chance of repeat attacks and the hunt for terror suspects. There was hardly any space for anything else, until suddenly we learned that Nicole had been charged with the double murder.'
>
> CONNOR: 'On what grounds?'
>
> CRISTY: 'It was the blood, apparently. They said it was

everywhere, all over the house, although I think the accounts were exaggerated, quite often by the press, especially the tabloids who like nothing better than a gory story. In the end, it turned out that most of the blood belonged to birds, rodents, all kinds of creatures, but there was also some from one of the twins. That's when it all really kicked off and the rumours of ritual sacrifice got going.'

CHAPTER FOUR

It was Friday morning, two days after Cristy's return to 42 Randall Lane for the first time in nearly twenty years. Since leaving the house, she'd experienced a few unsteadying moments when it had felt as though the past was trying to draw her back into a dark and threatening place and hold her there. Of course, it was easily escaped: she had only to remind herself that she was no longer her thirty-year-old self, that she was in fact a very different person today, albeit hormonally challenged for rather different reasons.

What a joy the run up to fifty was turning out to be.

Whatever, pregnant or peri-menopausal, it was definitely unsettling to find herself so fixated on the case again.

Right now, she was at her desk in the *Hindsight* office, a large, high-ceilinged room full of original character at the front of a classically Georgian house a stone's throw from the SS *Great Britain* and the busy harbourside. The usual sounds of construction and footsteps on the cobbles just beyond their small car park were muted by the closed sash window – or, more accurately, drowned out by the hammering rain. There was no doubt the bad weather outside made it seem cosy and safe inside, especially with everyone around her.

Clover St Jean, dressed in an electric-pink polo neck that matched half the beads in her lively dreads, was in front of the whiteboard she'd already begun for the Ivorson case, while Jackson Cain, with his trendy ponytail, wispy goatee and gold-rimmed specs was, as usual, stuck into something on his computer.

Harry and Meena Quinn, the trusted business brains behind the podcast – and Cristy's dear friends of many years – were seated comfortably on the battered leather sofa as they listened to a playback of the recording Connor had made at number 42 on Wednesday. They were intrigued; she could see that as clearly as she could Meena's beautiful Indian heritage and Harry's charming public-school Englishness – and who wouldn't be when the Ivorson case remained one of the great unsolved mysteries of its time.

As Connor clicked off the recording, Meena's eyes remained on the whiteboard, where Clove had attached headshots of Nicole, Noah and Abigail Ivorson – the three figures at the centre of it all. Here, Nicole was still only nineteen and was so like a Millais muse, with her luscious, coppery curls and creamy pale skin, that she could surely inspire any artist of any generation. She was a true beauty, with wide, cerulean eyes, a perfect heart-shaped mouth and the look of a child in the process of becoming a woman.

Her babies, with their erratic caps of golden curls and innocent blue eyes, were as strikingly similar to each other as they were to their mother. In his shot, Noah was full of smiles, showing his sweet little teeth and a dimple in his left cheek. In hers, Abigail was gazing curiously at the camera as if trying to figure out what it was.

Cristy could sense how unsettling Meena was finding it to look at the children, to be reminded all over again of how those tender little souls might have met their end. It had disturbed everyone when these very photos had first been made public, especially after Nicole's purported attachment to a cult had come to light. And there was no doubt that all the murmurings of evil, demonic practices and curses that had swirled around the case at the time were beginning to resonate again all these years later – not only in the press coverage of Nicole's parole and the ongoing mystery of what had happened to the twins, but right here in this office.

Turning to Cristy, Meena said, 'Does Matthew know you're looking into this case?'

'What on earth has it got to do with him?' Cristy replied, startled.

Meena's eyes were resolute as she put down her coffee. 'I remember how much it upset you when it was happening, especially around the time Hayley was born and you went through a crazy period of thinking you had to give her up because she was Abigail really and didn't belong to you.'

Stung and embarrassed, Cristy tried not to notice the others' curious glances as she cried, 'That was nearly twenty years ago, and I thought it *once*, when I was still drugged up after a very difficult birth.' She was furious with Meena not only for mentioning it but for humiliating her in front of her friends, her colleagues, the team who looked up to her. She was tempted to ask her to leave or at least to apologize. However, sensing that would only make things worse, she forced herself to say, 'As my state of mind twenty-odd years ago has no more bearing on this meeting than what my ex-husband might think about anything, shall we get to confirming that this is going to be our next series?'

'Already on it,' Connor announced, throwing a scowl at Meena.

'I'm all in,' Jacks piped up.

'Me too,' Clove said, gesturing to the board.

Meena shifted uncomfortably as she turned to her husband.

'That makes you outnumbered,' Harry told her, 'but if you want my input, this case is tailor-made for *Hindsight*, and no one's going to tell the story better than these guys. Hell, knowing them, they'll turn up all sorts of stuff that didn't come out at the time . . .'

'Please don't say they'll probably end up finding the twins,' Meena warned. She turned back to Cristy, making a better show of hiding her concern this time, although Cristy knew it hadn't gone away. 'Is that what you're hoping for?' Meena asked. 'To discover them alive somewhere, living a whole other life that no one's ever known anything about?'

'It would surely be better,' Clove interrupted, 'than finding their bodies.'

Halted by that, Meena sighed as she sat back and said, 'OK, so talk us through the detail of what Nicole said happened the day her children . . . *disappeared*.'

'Her story at the time,' Cristy replied, keeping an edge from her voice, 'was quite simple in its way. Apparently, the family cat had died that morning, so she waited until the twins were having a nap and went down to the woods to bury it. When she got back, they'd gone.'

Harry nodded, as though remembering. 'Just like that. Two kids vanished into thin air, and no one saw a thing. Did anyone ever find the cat?'

'No,' Cristy replied. 'They dug up the woods, but there was no sign of it.'

Meena fanned her hands as if to say, *guilty as charged*.

'Anything from a vet to confirm the cat was put down that day?' Harry asked.

'Apparently, it choked on something,' Cristy told him. 'Or maybe it died in its sleep. It was very old – eighteen, from memory – so it wasn't exactly a shock.'

'How long after she claimed she'd buried it did they start digging up the woods?' he wanted to know.

'Five days,' Jacks replied, reading from his screen.

Harry nodded. 'So maybe a fox went off with it. Would a fox do that: dig up a dead cat?'

'I checked and it could,' Jacks confirmed.

'The other theory,' Cristy told them, 'was that she, Nicole, took the cat and the twins down to the woods and handed them over to someone who was waiting there.'

Meena shivered. 'Back to the cult thing.'

'Which no one's ever been able to make stand up,' Connor put in, 'but back then, a lot was said about it.'

'Anything of substance?' Harry asked, clearly searching his memory.

'Not really,' Connor replied, 'but we're hoping Julian Hargreaves, Nicole's defence lawyer, might help us with that when we see him later.'

'Definitely feeling cultish to me,' Clove muttered to no one in particular.

Casting her a glance, Harry said, 'Let's go with the abduction claim for the moment. Tell me how anyone could have got them out of the house, which I recall is on a main road, and into a waiting vehicle, without anyone seeing? Is that what Nicole wanted us to believe, that someone drove off with them?'

'She claimed never to have known what actually happened,' Cristy reminded him, 'only that the twins were gone when she got back to the house.'

'Wasn't the place covered in blood when the police arrived?' Meena asked.

'I don't know about covered,' Cristy replied, 'but there were definitely traces found all over the place, mostly belonging to wildlife – hence the rumours of sacrifice.'

'But some of it belonged to one of the twins, didn't it?' Meena persisted.

Cristy nodded. 'Abigail.'

Meena took this in. 'So what did *you* believe at the time? Before you went a bit . . .' She circled a finger at the side of her head.

Wanting to slap her, Cristy said, 'To be honest, I changed my mind about it so often – we all did – that I can't tell you now what I did or didn't believe at any given time, but what

I do know is that Nicole never had any witnesses to stand up for her. No one, apart from her mother, could say that the cat had died; no one saw her go down to the woods or come back again. No one saw the twins being taken from the house, and no one came forward with any solid evidence to say she belonged to a cult.'

'Where was her mother that morning?' Meena asked.

'At her sister's,' Cristy replied. 'Apparently, Nicole was at home alone with the twins from the time her mother left the house at just after nine o'clock.'

Reading from her notes, Clove said, 'There was a neighbour who came forward to say that he'd noticed Ronnie, Nicole's father, leaving for work around seven, as usual. And Maeve's sister confirmed that Maeve was at her house in Chippenham from around ten until two o'clock, when they got the call from Nicole to say the twins were gone. Same for Ronnie, who was alibied at his office all day until two.'

'Remind me what he did,' Cristy said. 'From memory, he was some kind of an engineer, working at British Aerospace in Filton?' She looked to Jacks for confirmation and received it.

'Guidance, navigation and control,' he said. 'That was his thing. And it was BAE Systems by then, although I think a lot of locals still refer to it as British Aerospace even now.'

'One of the glaring questions for me,' Clove said, 'is who was the twins' father? I know he was never named, but . . . any thoughts?' she asked Cristy.

Cristy shrugged. 'Take your pick – the mystery cult leader was, unsurprisingly, the favourite theory, but with no proof of his existence . . .' She simply shrugged. 'There was also talk of a random rapist for a while – no, she didn't ever report an attack – even Ronnie's name was in the frame at one point.'

Meena's lip curled. 'Was he ever ruled out?' she asked.

'Not by the tabloids as far as we can tell,' Jacks replied.

'But he was by the police,' Connor added. 'Obviously, they had the twins' DNA, but no match was ever found to identify a father . . .'

'Nicole always said she didn't know,' Cristy told them.

Meena frowned in confusion.

'She was a promiscuous girl,' Cristy explained.

'But she must have known who she slept with,' Meena protested.

Cristy suddenly found herself half-overcome by a flush of heat starting to build inside her. 'All I can tell you,' she said, looking around for something to fan herself with, 'is that she was assessed for post-partum depression before the trial . . . It wasn't as big a thing back then as it is now, I mean obviously it was, it just wasn't recognized in the same way. Anyway, the defence psychiatrist claimed she had it and what do you know, the prosecution leans in heavily on all the stereotypes of mental instabilities and irrational behaviours that can come with it. It was pretty misogynistic actually, not to mention insulting and insensitive.'

'Was it generally believed that she really did have it?' Clove wanted to know.

Flapping a useless Post-It back and forth, Cristy said, 'Much depended on who you spoke to, and what their preconceived opinions of the condition were. I don't suppose much has changed there, actually, although on the whole I think people are more sympathetic even if they don't really understand it. Anyway, moving on,' she said to Jacks, 'have you found addresses for any of Maeve's family yet?'

'Doing my best,' he assured her, 'but there's a lot to go through, and trying to pick out their names . . . Her sister's married, apparently, so no longer a Reynolds – Maeve's maiden name – and for the moment, nothing on the brother.'

'That makes me suspicious right off the bat,' Meena declared.

Cristy didn't disagree, although she didn't recollect

anything in particular about Nicole's uncle coming up at the time. 'Remember,' she said, 'everyone, even Maeve herself, was under suspicion for a while. It was held by some – I never found an actual source for it – that both she and Ronnie could have been part of the same cult or sect that wanted the babies for sacrifice.'

Wrinkling her nose, Clove said, 'Are we talking actual sacrifice here, as in killing them? Or as in like, you know, giving them up for . . . like adoption or something?'

'I guess it could mean anything,' Cristy replied. 'But once again, no actual evidence of them being involved in a cult.'

'Although it's kind of speaking to me,' Clove confessed, 'but maybe I've read too much of that stuff.'

'Going back to the blood in the house,' Harry said. 'The fact that some belonged to one of the twins is what led to Nicole being charged?'

'And tried and found guilty,' Jacks pointed out, once again reading from his screen. 'I mean, there were other factors, but that was the main one. During the trial, her defence barrister made a big deal out of how regularly small children fall over and graze or cut themselves, so no house in the land with kids living there could be free of blood traces . . .'

'So it really was only traces?' Meena interrupted.

'That's what it says in this report,' Jacks replied. 'It's from the *Western Daily Press*, dated halfway through the trial. Same date, different paper, says there was a "bloody scene" in the children's bedroom. This line was taken by the nation's sweetheart – *not* – Molly Terrance, never known to let facts get in the way of a good story. There's also a report of hers claiming that Nicole was soaked in blood when she ran screaming out of the house to raise the alarm, but no mention of a source. And here we have a statement from Julian Hargreaves's office calling the exaggerations and misinformation in certain sectors of the press "shameful".'

'That still doesn't tell us how much blood there actually was,' Harry pointed out.

'How did the prosecution describe it at trial?' Meena asked.

Taking the question, Clove said, 'We don't have a transcript of the trial yet. I've put in a request, but given how they work, I'm not expecting to hear back this side of next Christmas.'

'We'll hope to get more out of Julian Hargreaves when we see him,' Cristy said. 'Now, as I think it's a given that we're moving forward with this, here are our next moves—'

'Hang on, don't we want to run it past Iz first?' Meena asked.

Cristy stared at her, while Connor glared. Isabel "Iz" Penny – and the Sponsorship Liaison Group who employed her – were their main source of funding, and Iz had been known to kick back on some of their ideas in the past. Connor, in particular, was deeply resistant to the money men having any say at all regarding editorial input or final content. Although Cristy was of a similar mind she was perhaps less hostile, but bringing this up now was, for her, an untimely reminder of how much bigger and better financed the series could be if they turned it into a flagship for Paul Kinsley's and Vikram Rathour's RK Media.

Pushing the thought aside, she said, 'I don't think anyone here expects Iz, or any of her team, to push back on the story, but I'll call her this evening to talk it through with her. So, our next steps . . . Jacks and Clove, I know you're still info gathering from the archives. Anything back from Matthew yet about my own reports?' she asked Connor.

'Yep, he's on it, says we should have something soon.'

Cristy shot a quick glance at Meena, who was undoubtedly expecting, or hoping, Matthew would come back with a reminder of how the case had affected his now ex-wife back in the day. When Meena said nothing, Cristy continued. 'We're going to need a list of all the main players: lawyers, police officers, witnesses – I'm talking forensics, psychiatrics, anyone else who was put on the stand – also, try to find out if Nicole made any particular friends in prison. If they're out now and willing to engage, they might have some insight on who visited her, who she talked about, if she ever mentioned the twins.'

'Where did she serve her time?' Harry asked.

'She was at Bronzefield for most of it,' Clove informed him, 'but ended up at Eastwood Park until she was paroled.'

'So not too far away,' Connor commented, bringing the prison up on a map. 'Could that mean she's staying nearby? Isn't that how it works where parolees are concerned?'

Reading from his screen, Jacks said, 'It depends on the risk assessment and the conditions imposed, so it's not mandatory that she stays local to the prison. What are the chances of Julian Hargreaves telling you where she can be found?' he asked Cristy.

'Small, I'd say,' she replied, 'and I'm afraid it's not going to be this afternoon.' Looking as fed up as she felt, she said, 'I've just had an email from his PA. Apparently, he's been called into court so he has to reschedule. Will four o'clock next Thursday work for us?'

'Shit!' Connor muttered under his breath. 'He's kind of key to everything.'

'Only if he's willing to tell us what we want to know,' Cristy pointed out. 'For now, let's focus on the detectives who worked the case and hope that at least one of them has retired by now – surely a good chance of that – and is ready to share.'

'Sending a few names your way,' Jacks told her. 'Something else we need to do is go door to door over at Randall Lane, see if anyone there has an idea where Maeve might be – unless she's come back in the last couple of days.'

Cristy said, 'We knocked on a few doors while we were there, but it was a working day, so maybe you and Clove could try again over the weekend?' To Connor, she said, 'We have a lot of reading and viewing to do, so maybe not such a bad thing that Julian Hargreaves has bumped us. We'll have more to go in with next week this way.'

Getting to her feet and stretching luxuriously, Meena said, 'You won't forget to call Iz, will you? It's not just polite to keep her up to speed – it's necessary if we want her to bring the right sponsors on board.'

Such a horrible put-down flashed in Cristy's mind that it almost made her head spin. *Remind me again what you and Harry do now that Iz controls the funding?* Thank God the words hadn't escaped her – and nor would they, *ever*. Hurting the people she cared about was not who she was, and besides, she knew very well that Harry and Meena worked closely with Iz and the SLG, always with *Hindsight*'s best interests at heart. So where the hell had that nastiness even come from? Was this the kind of person she was about to turn into via hot flushes, sleepless nights, weight gain and hair loss?

*

Later, as she walked along the Harbourside towards home, umbrella up, ankle boots splashing in puddles, she quizzed herself again over that awful moment. Though she knew she'd been irritated with Meena over the untimely reminders of her mental health issues back in the day, not helped one bit by the fluctuation of hormones now, there was also the underlying stress of Kinsley's offer. It was undoubtedly playing its own part in skewing her reactions to things, and if it was going to assist in changing her into the sort of person who turned on her friends, then maybe she ought to refuse it now. She had Kinsley's number; it would be the easiest thing in the world to connect to him or even to send an email saying thanks, but no thanks. No hard feelings.

So why didn't she? There was nothing to stop her, and no harm would be done because no one even knew about it yet. The fact that she didn't want Kinsley to think less of her was an ego-driven pathetic excuse – or was she actually seriously considering accepting? Was her conscience – her sub-conscious – already trying to create a distance between this life here in Bristol and a new one in London by taking the gloss off treasured and established relationships by hardening her heart?

Deciding there was no point tormenting herself any further over one random – and, thank God, unspoken – thought that wasn't even meant, she pushed it aside and refocused on the Ivorson case.

There was a time, maybe a year or so into her sentence, when Nicole had agreed to a visitor request from Cristy, only to turn into a no-show when Cristy had got to the prison. After that, she'd never replied to any of Cristy's letters; nor had Maeve. It was Ronnie who'd finally got in touch, not with her but with Matthew, to ask him to persuade Cristy to let things go.

She'd forgotten that until now: Ronnie had actually rung Matthew to get her to back off. By then, she'd just given birth to Aiden, and because Matthew had been afraid that she'd start imagining Noah Ivorson was reincarnated in their son, he'd literally ordered her to stop. She actually hadn't suffered any such craziness after Aiden; his had been a much easier delivery. However, after a fight with Matthew over his offensive manner, she had decided it was time to move on, in spite of still feeling quietly desperate to know what had really happened to the twins.

That feeling was back, that burning need to find out what had really taken place that hot July day back in 2005, when

Nicole had gone out to bury a dead cat and returned to find no sign of her twins.

It had been implausible then, and remained so now, but what was just as intriguing, unsettling even, was why Nicole had decided to confess to the killings after all these years. And why was nothing being said about the bodies?

CHAPTER FIVE

Cristy's ground-floor flat was at the Redcliffe end of Bristol's Harbourside, tucked into the far corner of a leafy quadrant close to the magnificent landmark of St Mary's Church and a mere stone's throw from the offshoot of waterfront beyond the swing bridge. With its two generously sized bedrooms, spacious open-plan kitchen-dining-sitting room and beloved walled garden, it was as special to her as anything she'd ever owned. She'd initially bought it as an investment, with money inherited from her mother: a place she could rent to carefully selected barristers who came to Bristol for cases at the Crown Court. Following the break-up of her marriage, it had become nothing short of a sanctuary, a kind of return to her mother's comforting arms. Even now, simply being inside the flat, or enjoying the patio on warmer days, made her feel closer to her mother, whom she continued to miss ten years on from losing her. She knew it was the same for her brother, Tom, and the place he'd bought with his inheritance.

It was late on Sunday afternoon, already dark outside, and Cristy was – very generously, she thought – preparing a full-trimmings, no-wicked-ingredient-spared, Sunday roast for Matthew and Aiden, who'd just returned from the rugby at Ashton Gate. Although it wasn't unusual for her to entertain her ex, she preferred not to make a habit of it, mainly because she didn't want to encourage him to think they could make a go of things again. She knew it was what he wanted – he never made a secret of it – but though she still cared for him deeply and actually cherished his friendship, there was simply no going back on his betrayal or the subsequent divorce. Especially now David was in her life.

Fortunately, Matthew was coming to accept that. In fact, they were even starting to morph into something akin to a blended family, given how well he got along with David and the rest of the Gaudions over in Guernsey.

As she started to dish up, while Matthew and Aiden continued a noisy rehash of their team's crushing defeat, Cristy let her own thoughts drift to their daughter's plans to travel around Canada this coming summer. She must remember to bring it up with Matthew before he left to find out how much she needed to contribute to the cost when the time came.

'Wow, Mum! You've done us proud,' Aiden declared, rubbing his hands together as she carried two over-loaded plates to the table. Thick slices of medium-rare beef, massive crispy Yorkshire puddings with fluffy interiors, succulent cauli-cheese, crispy roast potatoes and side dishes of parsnips, greens, garden peas and Tenderstem broccoli.

'I hope there's enough for seconds,' Matthew teased, sitting down next to his son and shaking out a paper napkin.

Cristy couldn't help the rush of pleasure she often felt when seeing them together. Aiden was as tall as his father now, his shoulders almost as broad, his hair virtually the same shade of dark brown, although his was fashionably shorter at the sides and much longer on top – and their shared passion for most sports and some music meant they were as easy in one another's company as they were with any of their friends.

Joining them with a much smaller plate, Cristy reached for the horseradish as Matthew poured the wine and said chattily, 'So how was your trip to London this week?'

Wondering if he knew about her meeting with Paul Kinsley, she said, casually, 'Thanks for taking Hayley to the airport on Tuesday so I could make my train. Have you spoken to her since she got back to Edinburgh?'

'I did, yesterday,' Aiden said, through a mouthful of food.

Cristy scowled at him, and he reached for his drink.

'Sorry,' he said after swallowing. 'She's got this plan to drive across Canada with Hugo in the summer,' he announced. 'Sounds really cool. I asked if I could go with, and she said no. What kind of sister is that, I want to know.'

'A wise one,' Matthew replied, helping himself to more gravy.

'Hah!' Aiden scoffed. 'You'd give anything to go anywhere with me – we all know that – and I'm good to you, Dad. I let you tag along whenever you want, no embarrassment with my mates, no trying to lose you in town . . .'

Archly, Matthew said, 'I won't remind you who made you his guest at the rugger today, or who blew off a date last night so I could pick you up from Cardiff—'

'You had a date?' Aiden cut in, all interest. 'Tell us more.'

Cristy watched Matthew flush and almost laughed.

'OK, not a *date* exactly,' he confessed. 'I was supposed to be having dinner with friends, but I let them down because *you*, idiot that you are, had maxed out on your credit card and lost your rail ticket home.'

Frowning, Cristy said, 'Couldn't you just have paid for his ticket over the phone?'

Matthew grimaced. 'Why would I pass up an opportunity to spend some drive-time with my son and two of his fascinating friends . . .'

Cristy laughed. 'Someone set you up on a blind date last night and you bailed. That's the real story here.'

Matthew didn't deny it, simply looked helpless and long-suffering as Aiden launched into all the apps he could try, to get himself a 'bit of action, no strings' or someone to take him on 'long walks, and even longer shags . . .'

'Why does everything come down to sex with you?' Matthew groaned. 'It sounds to me as though you're the one who's not getting enough, the way you keep going on about it.'

'No problem here,' Aiden assured him, 'but that's because I come at things kind of differently to you. I get we're a different generation, and you're, like, recognizable – don't want anyone posting about your performance on social media if you're no good, I get that – but think what it would be like if someone described you as a tiger. I'd share that – could reflect well on me as your son.'

As Cristy laughed, Matthew said, '*Is* he my son? Because if not, now would be a good time to tell me.'

Loving their banter, Cristy sat back in her chair and thought fleetingly of how much she'd miss it if she weren't here in Bristol any more to share it.

'So how was David?' Matthew asked. 'Is it still on between you two?'

Used to the jibe, she said, 'Still on, and he's great, thanks for asking.'

'Well, there's a relief,' Matthew stated, 'or the party next weekend would be a bit awkward.'

How true that was. 'I take it you're going to be there,' she said, picking up her wine.

'Are you kidding?' Aiden cried. 'No way are we going to miss your fiftieth in Guernsey. We love it there. Hayley's definitely coming – did she tell you?'

Cristy nodded. 'And Hugo and his parents, by all accounts. Plus the whole *Hindsight* team . . . Have you seen the guest list?'

'Not since Friday,' Matthew admitted, 'but I noticed Andee Lawrence's name is on it. It'll be really good to see her and to meet her partner, Graeme – is that right?'

Cristy nodded and wondered again if he knew something about Paul Kinsley's offer. Maybe he'd brought Andee's name up to make a point, although it didn't seem to be the case.

'No one's spilled any detail about the big surprise yet, have they?' Aiden wanted to know.

As Cristy's heart flipped, Matthew groaned, saying, 'Why did you even bring it up? You're such a tosser at times . . .'

'Do you hear what he just called me?' Aiden demanded of his mother.

'So who's the surprise?' she interrupted, trying to conjure up an answer and getting nowhere. Unless it was Paul Kinsley. No – surely to God it wouldn't be him. She was overthinking things, unable to get the offer out of her head.

'If we told you that, we'd ruin it,' Matthew pointed out.

'But is it someone you've invited, or David?' she insisted.

'Let's just say we agreed it would be a great idea. Now, change of subject: I've put in a request for archive material on the Ivorson story, but I have to ask if you're sure you want to go into it again. I get that it was a long time ago and we're all a bit older and wiser now, but it kind of messed you up a bit back then.'

'What was it about?' Aiden wanted to know.

'A couple of twins, murdered by their mother,' Matthew told him. 'Babies, they were. It was a horrible case, got us all on edge with the strange way it played out.'

'Strange in what way?'

Matthew looked at Cristy.

'A lot of ways,' she conceded, not really wanting to get into this now, but going with it anyway, 'which is why we're taking a look into it again, to see if we can come up with a clearer perspective or even some new information.'

'The mother, Nicole Ivorson,' Matthew explained, 'has just been released on parole, and no one knows where she is right now . . . I'm guessing you still haven't tracked her down?' he said to Cristy.

'Not yet, but I'm sure we will. Any thoughts on when the archive stuff might be coming our way?'

'I'll chase it tomorrow.' He took a mouthful of food and, after a while, said, 'It's likely to be pretty weird seeing yourself as a thirty-year-old when you're about to be fifty – a proper trip down memory lane to a time when you were fresh and young, kind of radiant . . . Of course, goes without saying you're even more beautiful now.'

'Nice catch, Dad,' Aiden chuckled. 'That hole was only getting deeper. Pass the gravy please.'

*

It wasn't until later, after Aiden had disappeared into his room to do whatever he did there, and Cristy and Matthew had finished clearing up, that they sat down on the sofas with fresh glasses of wine to accompany their coffee.

'Am I going to like this surprise you and David are planning?' she asked, putting her feet up on the coffee table. 'I mean, if it's someone I haven't seen for a while, I guess it's occurred to you that might be because I don't want to see them.'

Clearly amused, he said, 'You'll be fine with it. Promise.'

Still worried, she had another go. 'Male or female?' she prompted.

'Stop.' Matthew laughed. 'No one's even said it's a person, but you have my word you're going to love it. Now, tell me about Andee Lawrence and what she's doing these days. You two were great friends when we were all still in London. God, that takes me back. Good to know you're still in touch.'

Cristy sipped her drink and wished she could get his thoughts on Kinsley's offer and how he saw it playing out for the future. She might not agree with anything he had to say, but she wouldn't mind hearing it anyway.

'In the end we just talked about Andee,' she told David on

the phone later. 'Then it was time for him to leave – Aiden's here tonight – and I'm still no closer to knowing what I want to do than I was when the offer was first made.'

'Will you mention it to Andee next weekend?' he asked. 'Maybe Kinsley already has.'

'I don't think so, but I'll check beforehand, and then, well, to be honest, I can't really see her signing up for it. She might want to – actually, I have no doubt she will – but she's pretty involved in her local community, Graeme's business is there, and her mother's not well. She won't want to be far from her these days.'

'Well, I guess that's for her to decide if and when you finally put it to her. You might find she'll seize it with both hands and organize a work-from-home system that covers all bases.'

Intrigued by the idea, Cristy said, 'Maybe I could do that and stay in Bristol?'

'Maybe, but as the big boss, you'll have to have a place in London, and it seems likely you'll be back and forth to the States a lot . . .'

'Then how will I ever find time to see you?'

'A question I've been asking myself, but we'll work it out, and I definitely don't want you letting it get in the way of things.'

'That sounds as though you think I should take it.'

'Does it?' She could hear the smile in his voice and for no explicable reason it annoyed her.

Forcing herself to get a grip, she tuned back in to what he was saying.

'What I do know is that plans are heating up for the big party next weekend . . .'

'Tell me about the surprise,' she broke in eagerly, the absurd flash of bad temper gone as quickly as it had come. 'Are you certain it's one I'm going to be happy with?'

Laughing, he said, 'Matthew assures me it's a perfect idea,

and frankly, I trust him on this. Now, that's all I'm going to say, or it won't be a surprise. So, maybe tell me how much you're missing me now.'

Laughing softly, she said, 'You're assuming I am.'

'I can feel it, in all the right places, but before you start, if Aiden's nearby, you might want to go into the bedroom and close the door.'

CHAPTER SIX

The Mane Collective, a hair salon on the corner of Randall Lane and Holly Drive, smelled as strongly of fresh paint as it did of a pungent mix of lemony shampoo and instant coffee. The place was clearly in the process of being fixed up ready for business, with mirrors, basins and a reception desk already installed, while wires still hung out of walls and plastic sheeting covered the floor.

'Sorry about the mess.' Megan Whitmore grimaced, whisking a paint tray from a styling chair for Cristy to sit down and quickly moving to the next to clear an Amazon box out of the way for Connor. 'I meant to get here earlier, but my brother went off with the keys last night . . . I already told you that. Are you sure you're OK with instant? We haven't had our machine delivered yet . . .'

'Instant's fine,' Cristy assured her.

'I can easily pop out for some milk. The Co-op's right . . .'

'We both take it black.' Cristy smiled, trying to put the young woman at her ease.

Megan smiled too and gave a little shudder of excitement. 'I've never been interviewed before,' she confessed. 'I mean, apart from on Saturday when your guys knocked on our door to ask about Mrs Ivorson. They didn't record what I said or anything – they just talked me through what would happen today if I was up for it . . . You get that I was only twelve back then, don't you? So I don't remember much, but Clove said you'd probably still want to talk to me.'

'Would you mind if I pinned this mic to your collar?' Connor asked. 'It just clips on, won't do any damage.'

'Oh, this is an old jumper,' Megan assured him, 'no need to worry.' She looked down, watching his fingers at work, and seemed to flush slightly, which made Cristy smile. Young women were often attracted to Connor, and the most amusing part of it was that he almost never seemed to notice.

As he stepped back, Megan's long-lashed eyes rose to his face and fluttered slightly, but he was already turning away.

She looked at Cristy, seemed to realize she'd been sussed and blushed again. 'Great hair!' she suddenly gushed. 'What do you use for the waves?'

Wryly, Cristy said, 'It's how they fall . . .'

'No way! I know women who'd pay fortunes to get that look.' Her attention switched to the door. 'Oh, here's the postman – I'll be right back.'

As she rushed to let him in, Connor attached mics to himself and Cristy, while she quickly scanned the notes Clove had typed up following the door-to-door enquiries at the weekend. There was only a short list of questions for Megan, but the answers she'd given on the day were interesting enough to get on record for possible future use.

Finally, they were ready to record, with Megan perched on the edge of a basin chair, her small hands folded over one knee, her big brown eyes fixed on Cristy as she delivered her usual preamble to set things up.

Suddenly, Megan gasped.

MEGAN: 'There's something I need to tell you. Oh God, I nearly forgot. It was after Clover and Jacks left on Saturday, when my mum got home. She wanted to come this morning, to see you herself, but she's had to take my nan to the doctor's. Anyway, she said to tell you that Mrs Ivorson usually goes to the churchyard on Thursday afternoons to visit Mr Ivorson's grave. She takes flowers and sits there for a bit . . . I don't know how my mum knows that – she must have stalked her . . .'

She laughed nervously.

MEGAN: 'Not really, my mum's not like that. I expect she just happened to be passing.'

CRISTY: 'Is your mum a friend of Mrs Ivorson's?'

MEGAN: 'No, I wouldn't say that, but she tries talking to her every now and again. Mrs I is always polite but prefers to keep herself to herself. I suppose people have been that mean to her over the years . . . We've always wondered why she never moved away – that house must have such horrible memories for her . . . It used to spook the hell out of us when we were kids. To be honest – actually, I hate saying this – but she can come over as a bit creepy too, the way she never looks at you or bothers to say hello or answer if you ask how she is. We used to shout that out to her when we were young, you know, *How are you, Mrs I? Tell us, how did they die?* Isn't that terrible? I feel so ashamed now, wish I could tell her I'm sorry . . .

'You know what's strange though – or nice, really – is she puts veg from her garden out in boxes for people to buy when they're passing. And people do: tomatoes, rhubarb, onions, potatoes, strawbs in summer . . . She grows it all herself . . .

'Of course, back when she started doing it, we used to think she was trying to poison us all, but my mum and dad were having none of that nonsense. They made us eat it, wouldn't let us leave the table until we did... And now, here we are, all these years later, still eating her stuff and still here to tell the tale.'

Megan seemed so delighted by this that Cristy dutifully smiled, while picturing boxes of fresh, muddied produce perched on the wall of number 42 with, presumably, an honesty box somewhere nearby. She guessed people must have paid up, or it was unlikely Maeve would have continued to do it – at least it sounded as though Megan's parents were the decent sort.

It was making her feel sad, Cristy realized, to think of Maeve's tentative contact with the outside world. Did she watch from the window as passers-by helped themselves to her offerings?

How are you, Mrs I? Tell us, how did they die?

CRISTY: 'Can you remember when you last saw Mrs Ivorson?'

MEGAN: 'Mm, Clove asked me that at the weekend, and I've been trying to think. It was probably about two weeks ago, I'd say, on the Wednesday or Thursday. She came out of the house in her burgundy coat – she always wears it in winter with a black bobble hat and checked scarf – and she walked up the road to her garage. I suppose she drove off. I wasn't looking any more... It was pure chance I even saw her, so I can't tell you when she came back or if she did, but I'm pretty certain I haven't seen her since. The only action there's been over there is when the press turned up last Tuesday because Nicole had been let out.'

Cristy was watching her closely, trying to get a sense of

how she might feel about the release, but for the moment at least, Megan seemed unbothered by it.

> CRISTY: 'Nicole would be – what, seven years older than you? Do you remember her very well from when you were young?'
>
> MEGAN: 'Kind of. I mean, we weren't friends or anything – the age gap was too big – but obviously I saw her coming and going. She had, like, this amazing hair, all red and curly, right down her back . . . And loads of friends . . . I remember them sitting on the wall outside her house waving at drivers as they passed and laughing their heads off if someone beeped. She was probably about fifteen or sixteen at the time, and my mum always used to say, "They'll get themselves in trouble, those girls, carrying on like that."
>
> 'I used to think they were pretty cool, especially as they got older and seemed more . . . sophisticated, I suppose. That was kind of when all the rows started, between her and her mum. She had a right temper on her, did Nicole. You could hear her screaming from across the street, telling her parents to mind their own business, they weren't the boss of her, that sort of thing.
>
> 'Then the next time you saw her, she'd be like all sweetness and light with her mum, and they'd be laughing about something. Come to think of it, I guess it wasn't much different in our house when I was a teen.'

Cristy made a quick check of her notes, feeling thankful that she and Hayley had never gone through such dramas. She'd probably never have survived it, given those difficult years had coincided with the break-up of her marriage.

> CRISTY: 'Do you remember if Nicole had a boyfriend?'

MEGAN: 'What I do know is that all the boys had a thing for her, but I never knew about anyone in particular before she dropped everyone from round here and started hanging out with this crowd up in Redland, or it might have been Clifton. I suppose they were more her type – private school and all that . . . The Ivorsons were always a bit more *la-di-dah* than the rest of us, if you know what I mean. The big house, smart car, lots of dosh . . . Nicole went to a school in Bath . . . I wouldn't call them snobs or anything, just a step up from the rest of us, if you know what I mean.

'The friends Nicole had round here will be able to tell you more about her. I gave Clove the names I remember . . . Most of them have moved on by now, of course, but Becky Rawlings is living in one of the flats over on Peck Lane with her kids. They have different fathers, according to the gossips. I don't know her myself, so no idea if that's true.'

CRISTY: 'Have you ever heard who the father of Nicole's twins might have been?'

MEGAN: 'Hah, six-million-dollar question that everyone asked back then, and I heard that many stories . . . some lowlife rapist who attacked her in Bethalls Park; an older bloke who was married and lived somewhere in Wiltshire; one of the Clifton crowd – no one ever knew their names, but I think a few of them were foreign. Even the local vicar was mentioned a couple times. If you saw him, he was Robbie Williams in a dog collar – everyone had the hots for him, and quite a lot of girls started going to church when he took over. I don't know if Nicole was one of them. Course, he's long gone now – don't ask me where.

'There was an awful time when people started saying it was her own dad . . . That was later, after she'd gone to prison . . . It was horrible, because Mr I was such a lovely bloke . . . Or that's how he always came across to me. My mum was certain he'd never lay a hand on his girl in that way, but my mum never really sees the bad in anyone. I say you never can tell with blokes, can you? Present company excluded, I'm sure.'

Cristy's eyes moved to Connor, and she smiled to see how startled he appeared to have gained attention.

Returning to the list Clove had laid out, Cristy skipped the next couple of questions and asked if Megan had ever heard anything about a cult?

MEGAN: 'Oh God, yeah. Everyone said there was one, or they used to, anyway. I guess they will again now she's back in the news. I'm not following it much myself – too busy trying to get this place up together. Anyway, the only thing that made me believe in it, a bit, was all the blood they found in the house at the time it happened. They said it was all over, up the stairs, in the bedrooms – the cots were soaked in it . . . It makes me feel sick to think of it, even now. Why the heck would you do that to your own kids? That's what I'd like to know.'

CRISTY: 'But we know it wasn't the twins' blood.'

MEGAN: 'But I thought some of it was? That's what everyone was saying.'

CRISTY: 'It sounds as though you think Nicole really was guilty.'

MEGAN: 'To be honest, sometimes I did and other times I didn't. I mean, she's confessed now, so we know that she did it. So I suppose we can say she did the crime and served her time. Seems weird to think of her being out. I keep wondering what she's like now, what sort of things might have happened to her when she was inside. They say it's pretty tough for people who hurt kids, don't they? Might have turned her into an even worse monster . . . That's not something we want to think about really, is it? Sorry I said it now.

'Funny, because with all that hair and the lovely face, she looked a bit like an angel.'

CHAPTER SEVEN

After thanking Megan and asking her to be in touch if she saw or heard anything she thought might be of interest to them, Cristy and Connor left the salon to head for their next appointment further along Randall Lane. It was at number 50, apparently: a double-fronted, Fifties bungalow just past the Ivorsons' house, where they were due to talk to a Mr Wilson at eleven o'clock.

They hadn't gone far when Clove rang.

'Did you get my message?' she asked, when Cristy answered.

'We've only just left Megan,' Cristy replied, putting the call on speaker and stepping back from the spray of a passing car. 'Why? What's happened?'

'Jacks has managed to get a number for the friend, Becky Rawlings – she gave evidence in court, by the way – and as luck would have it, she's at home now. She has to go out at twelve, so I've bumped Wilson to one-thirty – I'm sure you can get to him earlier if you end up not needing so long with Becky. Jacks is sending the address to Connor's phone. How did it go with Megan?'

'It was interesting. Definitely stuff we can use as part of the first episode. Great soundbites.' She stopped as Connor raised a hand.

'We're going in the wrong direction,' he told her.

As they turned, Cristy said to Clove, 'Have you already briefed Becky Rawlings? Does she know what to expect?'

'More or less. I'll whiz over some notes, but basically, she hasn't been in touch with Nicole or Maeve since before the trial – she told me the same as Megan did, that Nicole more or less dropped her local friends about a year before it all happened. She, Becky, was one of them.'

'So she has no idea where Maeve and Nicole could be now?'

'Her guess was with someone in Maeve's family, but she doesn't know their names or where they live.'

'OK – seems we're a ten-minute walk away and, joy of joys, it's just started to rain.'

Twenty minutes later, boots in the corridor outside the front door and damp coats hanging in a cramped hallway that smelled of scented candles and something foodish, Cristy and Connor were seated on a sagging faux-leather sofa in a small sitting room. The house exuded the same worn-down air as the woman they'd come to see. Becky's tired eyes were sad and shadowed, her lank hair fell randomly from a grip behind her head, and the exposed flesh between her crop top and baggy joggers revealed the kind of stretch marks most women strived to conceal. She looked about as fed up with life as she surely must be with the clutter of toys and dirty dishes scattered about the floor.

'Sorry about the mess.' She sighed, sinking into a battered armchair and reaching for her cigarettes. 'Do you mind?' she asked, holding up the pack. Before anyone could answer, she put it aside. 'Of course you do, everyone does. Clove said you don't pay anything for interviews.' She shrugged dejectedly. 'Shame. I could do with a bit extra, so if you can see a way to changing your rules . . . ?' Her eyes came to Cristy's, and for a brief moment, Cristy felt the dejection coming off her in waves.

'Thanks for seeing us,' Cristy said, 'and I'm sorry about not paying. It's just that it could be viewed as a bribe, and we can't allow ourselves to be in that position.'

'Sure, I get it. Credibility and all that. Makes sense. So,

anyway, you want to talk about Nicole? There was a time when everyone did – seems we're there again. I guess it's true she's out?'

'She is,' Cristy confirmed, 'but at this stage there will probably be certain conditions attached to her parole.'

Becky nodded absently. 'So free, but not free,' she stated. 'Kind of like me, though I guess her situation has to have been a whole lot worse than the one I've been struggling through all this time. God, who knew having kids could be so hard?' She gave a mirthless laugh. 'Maybe Nicole had the right idea back when she got rid of hers.' Her eyes darted to Cristy's. 'I don't mean that, obvs. Stupid thing to say. It's not their fault they're pains in the backside and their mother has a lousy taste in men, is it? I'm talking about myself now, not Nicole, although her taste was no better, was it? He never stood by her, whoever the fuck he was – left her to cope on her own. Sure, she had her parents, and mine are pretty good, but it's not the same as having someone hands-on all the time, is it? Do you have kids?'

Cristy nodded, and realizing Becky wanted her to expand, she said, 'Mine are grown now. Still a handful, but . . .'

'Don't tell me – they've got a great dad and more advantages than he's got cash in the bank. What about you?' she said to Connor, resentfully. 'Any little chips off your old block?'

'A daughter,' he replied. 'She's just turned one.'

Becky pulled an upside-down smile. 'So about the same age as Nicole's twins when they . . . left the party, I suppose you could say.'

'Do you mind if we start recording?' Cristy asked.

Becky waved for them to continue. 'Thought you already were,' she said, staring at the mic although probably not really seeing it.

CRISTY: 'Unless I misunderstood, you don't sound convinced that Nicole really did harm her children?'

BECKY: 'I've got no idea what she did or didn't do. All I can tell you is what I said in court: that she blew hot and cold about being a mother – loved them to bits one day, wanted her life back the next. Much like all of us, I guess. Anyway, they found her guilty, didn't they? And now she's admitted it, so I don't understand why you're asking.'

CRISTY: 'As far as we know, she still hasn't said where the bodies are.'

BECKY: 'No, that's weird, isn't it? But don't look at me – I've got no idea where they might be. Anyway, I wasn't really seeing much of her by the time she had them. None of us were. I mean, now and again, but she'd kind of moved on. She had other friends she was really into who didn't live around here.'

CRISTY: 'Did you ever meet any of them?'

BECKY: 'No. They were student types: brainy, monied backgrounds, that sort of thing – I don't know any of that for sure. It's just the impression we got. I think some of them were foreigners – not that I've got anything against foreigners – just saying is all. They hung out in Redland or Clifton, that sort of area – up by the university, anyway. She told me once that she was getting into all the intellectual stuff, learning things she couldn't explain to us, but it was opening her mind . . . I remember her saying that. It was opening her mind to a whole other world and way of living.

'Hah! She was full of it, like you are at that age, I suppose. We're all guilty of it one way or another, saying shit to try and impress. She just had more of it about her than most, and I guess some of us were kind of in awe of her. She was clever, you know, daring, and in a class of her own when it came to looks. Plus, her parents weren't short of a few . . .'

She sat quietly with that for a moment, clearly gathering up old memories and impressions as they came back to her.

BECKY: 'She had all these airy-fairy ideas of being some kind of dancer at the Moulin Rouge in Paris or an artist on the French Riviera. Like I said, she was full of it, although I think she might have tried it out, eventually, if she hadn't had the twins and . . . Well, we know how things turned out from there. God, who'd ever have thought she'd end up the way she did?'

She reached for her cigarettes, shook one out of the pack and put it back again.

BECKY: 'I'll tell you what I think might have happened – it's just me who thinks it, right? Or maybe others do too . . . I don't know. Anyway, that set I mentioned – there was this bloke, he was part of it . . . I never met him, or saw him, but I remember her telling me once that he wasn't like anyone she'd ever met before. She used to say that the rest of us wouldn't understand someone like him, that no one did, apart from those he allowed to get close to him. She was kind of besotted – do you know what I mean? But it went deeper than that, like she . . . I don't know the right words for it, but she was seriously into him.'

CRISTY: 'Did she ever tell you his name?'

BECKY: 'If she did, I don't remember it, but I can check with some of the other girls if you like and get back to you if one of them knows.

'You're going to ask next if he was the twins' father, aren't you? So here's what she told me when I asked . . . She said, "They are in a world of many fathers and are loved by them all." Now if that's not weird, I don't know what is.'

As her mind drifted again, Cristy let the silence run, knowing better than to interrupt when Becky was clearly and quietly on a roll.

BECKY: 'You'll have heard about the cult?'

Cristy nodded.

BECKY: 'I honestly don't know if there was one, but when she said stuff like that, it made you think there might have been. How could it not? But then she'd say all sorts of stuff to make herself seem more interesting, more sophisticated than the rest of us, and we never knew how much of it was true.'

CRISTY: 'Did you ever hear of her being raped?'

BECKY: 'Yeah, I did, in Bethalls Park. I never knew anything about it. None of us did, and I can't see her keeping something like that to herself, so we always put it down to more BS. There was so much of it back then, in the press, you know – stuff none of us had ever heard about, but hey, maybe some of it was true.'

CRISTY: 'We've heard mention of a local vicar? And an older man, living in Wiltshire? Possibly married.'

BECKY: 'Hah! Vicar Robbie Williams? You've heard about him. His real name was Nick Hopkins – or it might have been Neil. Yeah, that's right. Neil. He was a nice bloke, too good-looking for his own good, if you ask me, but do I think he was the one who knocked her up? No, I don't. For one thing, she never seemed as interested in him as the rest of us, and for another, he was too clever to get mixed up with a bunch of teenage girls.

'As for the older bloke in Wiltshire . . . I know someone

mentioned it back then, but I can't tell you who he was, or even if he really existed.'

She glanced down at her phone as it buzzed, read the message and sighed while putting it aside again.

BECKY: 'This is what's always bothered me . . . *If* she was telling the truth about burying the cat . . . Well, first up, what the hell happened to it after – that's what I'd like to know? But second – and here's the thing no one's ever answered – if someone came into the house when she was down at the woods, how the heck did they get a couple of year-old babies out without anyone seeing?

'You know where the house is, right on the main road, and there was two-way traffic back then. Cars and buses would've been passing, neighbours coming and going, so surely someone would have spotted something . . . Plus, how did they know no one was in the house when they went in? OK, they could have been watching, waiting to seize their chance, but you can't see the back from the front, so how did they know when she went down to the woods?'

Cristy watched Becky blink slowly, sadly, clearly puzzled by her own thoughts.

BECKY: 'Maybe she'd arranged it with someone to come in and get them so she could say they'd been stolen, but even if that's true, how come they found blood in the house?'

CRISTY: 'There was only mention of traces in court . . .'

BECKY: 'I know, and most of it belonged to animals. Really weird that, don't you think? Takes you straight back to thinking about a cult. Or it does me, anyway.

'And now tell me this: if she was as innocent as she claimed at the beginning, how come she never appealed against her sentence? If it were me, I'd have fought tooth and nail for my liberty – wouldn't you, if you hadn't done it? But she never did, and now, according to the news, she's finally confessed to it, so what's going on there? Answer me that.'

CRISTY: 'We agree things aren't adding up, but without being able to talk to her ... Do you have any thoughts at all on where she might be?'

BECKY: 'Me? Not a clue. The person who could probably help – if they're still in touch that is – is her cousin, Lauren. Those two were pretty thick back then. She'd be able to tell you a lot more than I can.'

CRISTY: 'Do you know where we can find her?'

BECKY: 'After all these years, wouldn't even know where to start.'

CRISTY: 'Was she Maeve's sister's daughter? Or from Ronnie's side?'

BECKY: 'I never asked, but at a guess I'd say she was Maeve's sister's kid. She was younger than Nicole by a year or two, looked up to her, you know, wanted to be like her – hah, didn't we all with those looks? No, Lauren's your best bet if you want a more inside look at what went on back then. I'm not sure if she was part of the "Clifton set" – that's what we called them – but it's likely she was, given how close she was with Nicole and how she'd do practically anything to please her.

'Sweet girl. You've got me thinking now, I wonder what ever happened to her.'

CHAPTER EIGHT

Clove's messages came up as soon as Cristy and Connor turned their phones back on.

> *Serious leads to whereabouts of bodies. Call when you get this.*

'I tried getting hold of you before you went in,' Clove told them when Connor got her on speakerphone. 'Molly Terrance broke the story online.'

Cristy winced. Her nemesis from the time of the twins' disappearance was apparently all over the case again. *Great.*

'What sort of leads?' Connor demanded. 'How credible are they?'

'She's citing her source as an "official spokesperson",' Clove replied, 'which as we know means sweet FA without a name or at least a department. It hasn't made any bulletins yet, but it's on a couple of news websites: BBC, Sky, LBC . . . They're attributing it to the *MailOnline*, which is where the Terrier hangs out these days, so they're obviously covering their backs in case it turns out to be false.'

'She's got nothing,' Cristy stated. 'Anyone can run a headline like that – what does she say in the piece?'

'Basically, that she's been told the search for bodies continues and the police will, I quote, "surely be acting on the serious new leads that have come in." She can't reveal what they are at this stage, but she's promised to share more as soon as she has it. So yeah, looks like you could be right, Cristy: she's sensation-seeking, trying to stay relevant.'

'OK, but dig into it a bit more, just in case,' Cristy said. 'We'll discuss further when Con and I get back to the office. Now, I'm wondering if this neighbour Mervyn Wilson is still worth talking to in light of our chat with Becky. She gave us quite a lot to work with, and if this guy's profile is anything to go by – late seventies, lives alone, lot to say . . . I don't remember him coming forward back in the day. Did he?'

Joining the call, Jacks said, 'Nothing on record that we've found so far, but where backstory's concerned, he's a must. You'll know what I mean when you get him talking.'

'OK, great,' Connor said, directing Cristy into the pub they were passing. 'It's still early, so time for a quick bite. We should be back mid-afternoon,' he told Clove and Jacks before ringing off.

By the time they both had drinks in hand and had found a corner table, Cristy was reading a message on her phone. She didn't immediately respond when he asked what she wanted to eat.

'Something I should know about?' he asked, trying to get her attention.

She looked up, focused on him and quickly shut the message down. 'Nothing important.' She smiled. 'What did you say? Oh, just a sandwich for me – ham and cheese? I'm going to pop to the loo while you go and order.'

Once in the ladies, Cristy took her phone out again and reread the text from Paul Kinsley.

No pressure from this end, just wondering if you'd like to have another chat. Sure you have questions by now or thoughts on how you'd like to take things forward. You have my number. PK

Knowing she couldn't simply ignore the message, much as she might like to right now, she quickly hit reply and said:

Sorry for radio silence, a new series underway. Would love to chat, will call next week when I've figured out how to make you an offer you can't refuse. CW

Knowing it would amuse him to have his own words quoted back at him, particularly in this way, she pressed send and immediately regretted it. God only knew what her offer was going to be when she wasn't even close to making a decision. Or maybe, given that response, it was already made and she just needed to find a way to make it work without hurting – or feeling as though she was *betraying* – some of the people she loved most in the world. Would she actually do that? Put herself and this once-in-a-lifetime offer ahead of her loyalties and precious friendships? Was that who she really was?

Yes and no. Her heart, her soul, was in *Hindsight*, with Connor and the team, with Meena and Harry, Matthew and Aiden, and everything that was special in her hometown of Bristol.

Time to fly, Mum, she could hear her children saying. *Fifty next week, and this could be a fantastic new start to the rest of your life. All you have to do is get out there and live it.*

*

Mervin Wilson's bungalow, bright yellow with green window frames and matching front door, turned out to be all polished dark wood inside, and cabinets stuffed with Matchbox cars and Airfix planes, flowery carpets that clashed with the bulky chintz furniture. A massive crucifix hung over the old-fashioned tiled fireplace. the open-mouthed agony of Christ sending a shiver down Cristy's spine.

Wilson himself was clearly well into his seventh decade: tall but stooped, squint-eyed, and as softly spoken as he was borderline creepy.

Declining his offer of tea and madeleines, Cristy waited until he'd settled into an armchair next to the TV and said, 'Are you happy for us to record right away?'

The older man's eyes slid to Connor and stayed there. 'Go ahead,' he said, and he still didn't look away as Connor began setting up the equipment.

Wanting to laugh at the way Connor was gaining some sort of fan club today, Cristy checked her notes, and once she'd received the thumbs up, she began by describing Wilson as a dapper gentleman in his later years who'd lived on Randall Lane for as long as the Ivorsons.

WILSON: 'Since before the estate was built and all them depressing flats went up over on Peck Drive. The Ivorson's house was a farm back then – a small-holding, I suppose you'd call it now – that belonged to Ronnie's parents. They used to keep all sorts, even had a cow at one point, I recall. Anyway, everything changed when the developers moved in; they were lucky to keep as much land as they did, although I believe they were offered a tidy sum for the bottom plot, next to the woods.

'They turned it down, and Ronnie and Maeve never sold when they took the place over after the old folk passed on – that must have been after all the building started. Or maybe it had finished by then. I can check if it's important...'

CRISTY: 'Don't worry, it's not something we need to know at this stage. We're more interested in the "incidents" you described to our researchers when they came at the weekend. You mentioned something about activity in the woods...'

WILSON: 'Saw it with my own eyes, all that gallivanting about down there, chanting, wailing, setting sticks on fire, dressing up like brides and animals. There was all sorts going on, and I mean *all sorts*. It was like watching the Kama Sutra come to life some nights . . . They had no shame . . . She was a proper little tart, that Nicole, strutting down through the garden, not a stitch on her back . . . It's no wonder she could never name the father of those poor twins – it could have been Lucifer himself, and believe me, he was there, all horns and pitchfork and phallus as big as a horse. Sorry, is it OK to say that? Just trying to tell it like it was.'

Already getting a measure of this man, Cristy took the decision to play along for a while, mainly to be polite, but also to see how far he might take things.

CRISTY: 'So it was some sort of Satanic cult?'

WILSON: 'Couldn't see it any other way. I mean, I'm no expert, but I can tell you this: it frightened the life out of me, and I can't remember how many times I complained to the council to get them to stop. There was proper evil afoot down there. You could feel it like it was coming off the trees and oozing up through the ground. That's why I've got so many crucifixes in the house – I needed something to protect myself, didn't I? To ward off all that devilry. It's just a shame none of the local vicars had the guts to do their jobs properly – having quiet chats with the Ivorsons was never going to do anything, was it? Then young Hopkins came along, and he did go down there with the intention of breaking it all up, or that's what I thought until I realized he was bloody one of them.'

CRISTY: 'The local vicar became part of the cult?'

WILSON: 'That's what I'm saying. One of the randiest of the lot, from what I could make out.'

Realizing they really were dealing with the neighbourhood nutter – actually, pervert might be a better description – Cristy was on the point of wrapping things up, when Wilson began speaking again.

WILSON: 'I reported it all to the police. I wasn't going to keep something like that to myself, was I? Not when I found out those poor little mites had been sacrificed. I always knew something terrible was going to happen. I could sense it right through to my bones, and for all I know, they weren't the first kids to end up on one of those disgusting altars.'

CRISTY: 'Do you know if the police looked into it?'

WILSON: 'They told me they did, but by then they'd disbanded, hadn't they? The cult, I mean – not the police.'

CRISTY: 'Did any of your neighbours also witness what was happening?'

WILSON: 'You'll have to ask them, but as far as I know, none of them ever came forward. Too scared, probably, and who can blame them? It takes real courage to stand up to that sort of evil, and even when you do, you end up not being believed.

'But I know what I saw. I've never forgotten it, and now, finally that wicked girl has confessed to her sins. May the Good Lord forgive her and have mercy on her soul, because I can't see who else she's going to get it from. Certainly not me or those poor twins.'

CHAPTER NINE

'I'm guessing you didn't believe any of that shit,' Connor remarked as he and Cristy returned to the car.

'Not a word,' she replied, and lowered her hood as she slipped into the passenger side. 'You could tell he was getting off on it . . . All those naked cavortings, horns and phalluses . . .' She shuddered. 'In his dreams . . . I feel like I need a hot shower now.'

Backing out of the space next to the Ivorsons' garage, Connor said, 'I can't believe Clove and Jacks didn't see straight through him.'

'It's my guess they did and decided to share,' Cristy said dryly. 'To return the favour, we'll get them to check with the local authority whether there were any similar complaints at the time. That should be fun, trying to explain a satanic cult to a Gen Z connectivity specialist from the perspective of a local pervert.'

Laughing, Connor said, 'Connectivity specialist? Is that what they call telephone operators these days?'

'Something like that.' After checking her phone and finding *Can't wait* from Kinsley, and a flurry of chat between her children on WhatsApp, Cristy closed her eyes and let her head drop back against the seat. She felt so tired all of a sudden, so incredibly weary, as if everything in her was shutting down . . .

When she looked up again, they were minutes away from the studios.

'You didn't hear a word I said, did you?' Connor challenged as he turned along the cobbled lane and into the car park.

Embarrassed that she'd dropped off, especially as her mouth had clearly fallen open, she straightened up too quickly and immediately felt dizzy. What the heck was wrong with her? Groaning inwardly as she recalled her fluctuating hormones, she said, 'Sorry, I . . . What were you saying?'

'I was telling you about my daughter's latest teeth,' he replied. 'As her godmother, I thought you might be interested.'

'I am. Definitely. Why, what's happening to them?'

'Well, they just keep showing up. She must have at least forty by now.'

Laughing, Cristy flipped his arm and climbed out of the car. 'Looks like she's here,' she commented, spotting his wife's car next to her own. 'Were you expecting them?'

'Not this early, but Jodi's working later, so chances are she's come to remind me that I'm in charge tonight. You could join us if you like. Me, you and Aurora. I'll cook.'

'While I do the nappies and bath-time? Count me in. I might ask Aiden if he wants to join us. Matthew's in Davos this week, as is David actually, and the last I heard, they're meeting for dinner tonight. Strange world, isn't it?'

The instant they walked into the office, Aurora gave a shriek of delight and waved her little fists in the air as Cristy went to scoop her into her arms.

'My angel,' Cristy cooed into her silky soft baby neck, acutely aware of the two other babies whose images were on the whiteboard behind her. 'It's lovely to see you.'

'Da, da, da, da,' Aurora chortled, grabbing Cristy's cheeks and blowing bubbles against her lips.

'Lovely.' Cristy laughed and held out an arm to hug Jodi as she came to join them, supermodel figure and glowing looks fully restored a year after giving birth. 'I hear you're leaving Daddy in charge tonight?' she said.

'I've got a meeting for a story in Weston,' Jodi explained,

dabbing drool from the baby's chin. 'Green shoots and new piers – don't ask, but the contributor's fantastic, a real eccentric the audience is going to love.'

'For your pod or for a news insert?' Cristy asked, trying to keep out of Aurora's grasp. She needed to remember that Jodi had returned to making her *Happy* pods now and loved what she did – right here in Bristol, her hometown. What right did she, Cristy, have to try and tempt her husband into changing their world? Where was it going to leave them if she, Cristy, bailed and left them to fend on their own?

Belatedly spotting Iz, their sponsorship liaison rep, watching and beaming from her little desk in the corner, Cristy handed the baby to Connor and shrugged off her coat. 'Hi. I didn't realize you were coming today, Iz. How are you?'

'Yeah, I'm great thanks,' Iz gushed, starting to get up, sitting back down, then finally launching herself awkwardly at Cristy for a hug. 'I've missed you guys since the last series ended. Now, with a real biggie in the works for the next, I thought I'd come and check out progress in person.' With her shiny round face, multicoloured hair and fast-blinking eyes, she was so guilelessly keen and desperate to be liked that Cristy hugged her twice.

Connor said, 'We don't need checking up on, Iz. We'll call when we're ready to discuss—'

'Sorry,' Iz broke in hastily, 'I didn't express myself well. Not checking up, just touching base, and Clove and Jacks have been filling me in on what's been happening since my initial chat with Cristy. The Nicole Ivorson case, no less. Wow!' She danced a little jig, shoulders hunched, fists pumping. 'And you have history there, Cristy. This is going to be amazing – I know it. We'll have sponsors falling over themselves . . . Any thoughts on when you might start the uploads?'

'Give us a chance,' Connor protested. 'She only got out a week ago, and we're still pretty scant on details of conditions etc, including where she is.'

'And whether she'll talk to us if we do find her,' Cristy added, turning to Clove and Jacks. 'Any news to share?'

Clove shook her head. 'Still no official confirmation that there are leads on the whereabouts of the bodies,' she replied. 'I've been in touch with Julian Hargreaves's office; his PA said they haven't heard anything about it and advised that I shouldn't believe everything I read online.'

'Kind of her,' Cristy retorted. 'Is her boss still up for meeting on Thursday?'

'Apparently yes.'

'Great. Now, before we get into the delightful little sideshow you set up for us with Mervyn Wilson, you must surely have tracked down at least one of Maeve's siblings by now?'

'No actual phone details yet,' Jacks replied, 'but the sister – Bridget Hawkes – is over near Chippenham, so not millions of miles away, although not particularly close to the prison. No idea at this stage if Maeve and/or Nicole are there.'

'But you've got an address?'

'Sure, so we could – Clove and I – go stake the places out, see what's going on and report back. Or we could—'

'Put a couple of supersleuths to use,' Iz interrupted excitedly, 'and send them. We were just discussing it as you came in the door.'

Cristy turned to Connor. Although their back-up team of social media scrutineers, all of whom worked from home, were excellent at what they did, sending them out on field work was a different ask altogether. They weren't journalists or detectives, or in any way trained for surveillance. However, the task could be time-consuming, and getting someone with the proper experience on board could take forever and a sizeable chunk of the budget.

Wouldn't be a problem if they were being bankrolled by RK Media.

These sorts of rogue thoughts really weren't helpful in spite of being true.

'I reckon it's such an obvious place for them to hide out,' Connor said, 'that they won't be there, so no harm in sending a couple of supersleuths to check the place out.'

'What we don't want happening,' Cristy said, 'is Molly Terrance finding them first and signing them up for an exclusive. They don't call her the Terrier for nothing, and she'll have some big bucks to throw their way, so we need to stay focused on this.'

'With the kind of sums the Terrier can call on,' Clove said dubiously, 'I don't see how we can ever compete.'

Cristy sighed. 'Then we definitely have to get there first, presuming we're not already too late. You don't need me to tell you that the Terrier is as loathsome as she is relentless, and no way can we let her snatch this from under our noses.'

'She could have them holed up in luxury somewhere, even as we speak,' Jacks pointed out.

'God forbid,' Connor growled, 'but you're right: money could already have changed hands, not only with Nicole but before that, with someone on the inside – a probation officer, maybe. Even her lawyers could have brokered a deal. We're not frontline media – no one's coming to us first.'

Would they, if *Hindsight* had a wider reach and a globally recognized name? Could she achieve that with Kinsley and Rathour? It was possible.

Turning to Iz, Cristy said, 'We might need to make a counteroffer to get an exclusive with Maeve and Nicole, so if I send you some figures, can you work on it?'

'I'll do my best,' Iz promised, 'but I should probably remind you that some of our regular sponsors have interests in the big media outlets, so it could be tricky.'

Clove said, 'If worst comes to worst, we could always interview the Terrier after she runs her exclusive, if she has one.'

'Bollocks to that,' Connor scoffed.

'If she already had Nicole on board,' Cristy said, 'she'd be crowing about it by now, getting everyone worked up for the big splash. So let's carry on as if we're in with a chance, at least until we know we're not. Have you received any archive material from my TV coverage?' she asked Jacks.

'Not yet,' he replied. 'I messaged Matthew to ask him to chase it.'

'He promised to do that before he left.' She grimaced. 'Now that he's hobnobbing with the superrich in Switzerland, I don't expect he's giving us a second thought. I'll put in a call myself and see how I get on. Are you OK?' she asked Jodi, noticing her staring at the whiteboard, seemingly oblivious to what was going on around her.

Jodi nodded. Her eyes were fixed on the twins. 'They're more or less the same age as Aurora in these shots,' she said soberly.

Turning to study them herself, Cristy felt an unsettling sensation inside. Their sweetness seemed to shine out of the images, and the tragedy of their lives once again pulled her back to that terrible time. They looked so happy in these photos, so healthy and full of life, but she knew only too well how deceptive a single captured moment could be. So, had they been loved and cherished . . . ? All the dreadful rumours that had swirled around their disappearance, the horror of what could have happened to them, had fuelled her postnatal derangement and was even seeming to unsteady her now . . .

'I should be going,' Jodi said, reaching for her coat. 'Traffic could be bad, and I don't want to be late.' Going to drop a kiss on Aurora's head and Connor's lips, she added, 'I should be back by nine, ten at the latest. Just tell me before I go, Cris – are you looking forward to the weekend?'

Cristy frowned, until, remembering her own birthday party, she broke into a smile. 'Yes, I think so,' she replied. 'I'm just not sure whether or not to be worried about this so-called surprise. Are you up for giving me some clues?'

'That would be a no,' Jodi assured her. 'When are you flying?'

'Friday afternoon, with Aiden and Hayley, if she gets here in time. Her boyfriend, Hugo is coming on the same flight as Matthew on Saturday. What about you guys?'

'Friday, same as you,' Connor told her. 'Harry and Meena have booked for Saturday.'

'We're doing the Saturday flight too,' Clove told her. 'I just hope the weather isn't bad and we end up being cancelled. I'll be proper gutted to miss the big event.'

Noticing Iz watching them awkwardly, Cristy said, 'Please tell me someone remembered to invite you?'

Iz smiled in a way that said no one had.

'For God's sake, we can't leave you out,' Cristy cried. 'Get yourself on a flight to Guernsey this weekend – just make sure you're there by Saturday night, and if you have a problem finding somewhere to stay, let me know.'

Beaming all over her face, Iz said, 'That's amazing. Thanks so much. I'll definitely be there, and I can get some really great publicity if you want it? *Hello, OK* . . .'

'No!' Cristy broke in sharply. 'Just you, and a plus one if you like – definitely no press.'

'Got it,' Iz assured her. 'Um, what should I wear? I mean, is it formal . . . ?'

'Black tie,' Jodi told her, 'so ballgown, cocktail dress, sparkles – you get the picture. Now, I'm off. See you all later.'

After she'd gone, Cristy took Aurora back from Connor and went to snuggle with her on the sofa while he and the others listened to the playback of Megan's and Becky's interviews, making notes for an edit.

When they'd finished, Clove looked up innocently and said, 'So don't we get to hear what Mervyn Wilson told you?'

As Cristy's eyes narrowed, Connor said, 'You seriously want to take a roll in all that crap again?'

Laughing, Clove said, 'He's the worst, isn't he? But

I've been thinking about it, and you know what *could* be interesting is not so much what he said as when he first started saying it. In other words, did his fantasies come out of nowhere except his own sad head? Or did he actually see *something* that he's expanded on over the years?'

'That's exactly what you're going to find out when you contact the local authority,' Cristy told her. 'Were there ever any other complaints from the neighbours, as he claims?'

'His property is actually the only other one that overlooks the woods,' Jacks came in. 'I mean, a lot could have changed in the last twenty years, but going by today and the fact that the stretch that covers number 42 and its immediate neighbours hasn't been developed, it's possible no one else did see what was going on. I mean, *if* something was.'

'If it was, others would have known about it,' Cristy assured him. 'You can't have something like that happening in the middle of a community, remote as that wood might seem, without word getting out or people sneaking in to find out more.'

'We need a timeline on the rumours of a cult,' Clove declared, 'because I wouldn't be surprised to learn that he's the source that kicked it off in the press. Did you ever run the story, Cristy?'

'Not personally, although I knew it was being talked about before the tabloids picked up on it, so it was definitely out there pretty early on. And you've just heard Becky talking about the bloke Nicole was involved with – he sounds kind of mesmerizing to me, although she didn't mention anything about woodland orgies or sacrifices, and I'm sure she'd have known if they'd been happening. Give her a call to check, Clove. Or you could drop in and chat with her again when you're over there on Thursday?'

Clove blinked. 'I'm there on Thursday?'

'We need you and Jacks to go and stake out the churchyard on Randall Lane. Apparently, Maeve visits every Thursday.

Con and I would go ourselves, but I don't want to miss the meeting with Julian Hargreaves.'

'And if she does show?' Jacks asked. 'Do we approach or follow?'

'I'd say keep well back, watch what she does, and if it feels right to approach, give her my card. With any luck, she'll remember that unlike some, I didn't trash her and her daughter after the trial. Now, let's take Becky's advice and get to work on finding cousin Lauren. She could be the one to open up avenues to this "Clifton set", who I have no recollection of ever being mentioned either at the time of the arrest or during the trial.'

CHAPTER TEN

On Thursday afternoon, after being kept waiting an hour past the scheduled time, Cristy and Connor were finally shown into Julian Hargreaves's office. It was a large, musty space on the first floor of a nineteenth-century merchant's house, as cluttered with law books, case files and old steel filing cabinets as it was devoid of visitor comfort. Two hardback chairs had been placed in front of the old-fashioned oak desk, where the lawyer himself remained intent on whatever he was reading. He was a harried, impatient looking man in his mid-to-late sixties, with a shock of white hair, a florid nose and a jutting lower jaw.

'Hi, I'm Honey Blackwell.' A much younger, far friendlier-looking associate smiled as she gestured for them to sit. She had to be around thirty, was smartly dressed and wore her extra weight well. She was quite probably, Cristy thought, related to Jeffrey Backwell, the other half of Hargreaves Blackwell, given their shared ethnicity and same workplace. 'I hope you were offered refreshments while you were waiting?' Honey asked.

'Thanks, we were,' Cristy told her, and after Honey seated herself at the edge of Hargreaves's desk, taking a kind of umpire position, Cristy turned back to the man himself.

Finally deigning to look up, he said gruffly, 'Cristy Ward. You reported on the Ivorson case back in the day.'

'I did,' she confirmed, and deliberately held out a hand to

shake. 'It's good to meet you, Mr Hargreaves. Thank you for sparing us the time.'

Taking the hand, he half rose from his chair and fixed a stare on Connor, who also reached out to do the polite thing.

After dutifully accepting the formal greeting, Hargreaves sat back down, saying, 'I'm not sure how much I can help you. You must have all the background you need on the—'

'From a press perspective,' Cristy interrupted, 'and of course, we hope to have the trial transcript soon. What we'd like to discuss with you today is Nicole's recent release.'

Before Hargreaves could respond, Connor said, 'Would you be OK with us recording this?'

'No,' Hargreaves replied bluntly.

That was it. No qualifier, no attempt to soften the refusal and certainly no smile.

Cristy glanced fleetingly at Honey Blackwell, who at least had the decency to look embarrassed.

Hargreaves said, 'I will confirm that Nicole has now accepted responsibility for her actions and has been granted parole, but if you're going to ask me to reveal her whereabouts, I'm afraid you're wasting your time.'

'Actually, I was going to ask if the twins' bodies have been found,' Cristy informed him. 'Or if there have been any leads as to their whereabouts.'

He eyed her warily. 'Not as far as anyone in this office is aware,' he retorted.

Connor said, 'We understand you can't give us any information on where Nicole is, but would you be willing to pass on a message from us?'

As Cristy pulled a small white envelope from her bag, a note already prepared, Hargreaves stalled her with a raised hand.

'It won't do you any good,' he said. 'One of her parole conditions is to stay away from the media – social and mainstream. Of course, there's nothing we can do about the former, although she's been strongly advised for her own sake not to engage, but you . . . *mavericks* from the old school trotting out your modern-day podcasts and—'

Deciding she'd had enough of this windbag's insufferable condescension, Cristy cut in smoothly, 'That was offensive, Mr Hargreaves, and if it's how you feel, I have to wonder why you agreed to see us.'

Hargreaves stared at her hard, clearly not used to being challenged in his own office – or by a woman. He allowed several chilling moments to pass before apparently realizing she was just as good at playing the silence game as he was. He backed down first.

'I apologize,' he said, his manner slightly less hostile now. 'I should probably tell you that you're only here because Honey is a fan.'

Cristy glanced at the associate, who rolled her eyes. Apparently, she had a little more sway around here than Cristy had given her credit for – good to know – and so was almost certainly related to the firm's other senior partner.

Hargreaves was saying, '. . . after the way Nicole was treated by the press, both before and after the trial – you were there, so you know, although Honey has assured me you weren't as bad as some – you can't be surprised to hear that she actually doesn't want anything to do with any of you now. Besides, as I've already pointed out, it would break the terms of her parole, and she naturally has no desire to find herself back in prison.'

Unable to argue with that, Cristy said, 'Would you be willing to tell us why she's confessed now when she could have done so at any time over the past twenty years? Her previous parole hearing, for example.'

Once again, Hargreaves stared at her, tapping the desk with a forefinger as he seemed to calculate how much or how little he was willing to share. 'She was found guilty at trial, so I'm not sure why you're seeking to cast doubt on her confession.'

'Do you believe she did it?' Connor jumped in.

Deflecting, Hargreaves said, 'As her lawyer, it was my duty to provide as full and robust a defence as we could, so that is what we did.'

Cristy was starting to remember him in court, seated behind the barristers he'd appointed, occasionally talking to them, mostly scribbling on a notepad and seeming, at least to an observer's eye, to have virtually no connection with the girl in the dock at all.

He wasn't doing much to change that opinion now.

'Can we ask how Nicole came to be your client?' Cristy ventured.

Hargreaves's thready eyebrows arched. 'I was on duty at the time of her arrest.'

Of course, he would have been part of his firm's rotating team of on-call lawyers back then, obliged to advise and represent anyone who didn't already have someone to reach out to. She wondered if he thought he'd lucked out with the Ivorson case – quite probably, considering how heavily companies like his depended on legal aid for income.

Connor said, 'Just to be sure we've got things straight: Nicole thought she could get away with a plea of not-guilty if she – or her lawyers – could convince the jury that someone had stolen the twins? That was the thrust of her defence, wasn't it?'

Hargreaves eyed him coldly. 'Where exactly are you going with that, Mr . . .'

'Church, but you can call me Connor. I'm just trying to get a handle on why there was never a search for a potential abductor. Or maybe there was?'

'All I can tell you,' Hargreaves said tersely, 'is that neither we, at this firm, nor the police, had anything to go on; no evidence of abduction. We would have carried out a search if we had.'

'So Nicole had no theories?' Cristy asked. 'She claimed at the time that some random person or persons must have entered the house and taken the twins while she was down at the woods burying the cat.'

'Correct. This is all common knowledge, so I'm not sure—'

'What about the blood?' Cristy interrupted. 'Traces were mentioned in court—'

'Correct, traces. The way you lot reported it, anyone would have thought the place was awash with it.'

Barely suppressing a surge of irritation, Cristy said, 'There was animal blood, we know, which might have been what led to rumours of a cult?'

He shrugged. 'There was mention of a cult, yes, but neither we nor the police ever found anything to corroborate the claim.'

'So how did the animal blood get there?'

'They had a cat.'

His tone was so scathing that it made her feel foolish simply for asking – and actually, she was, because she remembered now that this very point had been made at the trial. The cat was known to bring in small creatures and kill them.

What was wrong with her? How had she forgotten that?

Taking over again, Connor said, 'As far as we know, Nicole never appealed her sentence . . .'

'We had no grounds for appeal – no new evidence to present to the court and, frankly, no instructions from our client to try and find any.'

'How much contact have you had with her since she went to prison?' Cristy asked, starting to suspect that he'd cut and run as soon as the legal aid tap had been turned off.

'Honey here covered the recent parole hearings,' he replied, 'so she has been in touch during recent times and still is, of course.'

In other words, he hadn't been in contact at all himself. So no post-conviction work, no more advice on how they might be able to turn up new evidence. Even if Nicole *had* done it, she'd surely have played along with that, given her continued claims of innocence.

Unprompted, Hargreaves said, 'You seem to have reached certain conclusions concerning this case that aren't in keeping with the facts. She has confessed, Ms Ward, and now, finally, she's convinced a parole board of her remorse, which has led to where she is today.'

'Has she changed her name?' Connor asked.

Hargreaves's tone was snarky as he said, 'If she has, you surely can't think I'd tell you.'

'You don't have to say what it is, only that it's happened.'

Getting to his feet, Hargreaves said, 'I'm afraid I'm already late for my next meeting, so if you'll excuse me, Honey will see you out.'

Minutes later, they were on the street, a stone's throw from the Crown Court, where a trial of interest was clearly breaking for the day given the press presence.

Completely unexpectedly, Honey Blackwell said, 'I'd like to join forces with you regarding Nicole's case, although I'm afraid there's a limit to what I – or you – can do, given her parole conditions.'

Surprised and encouraged by this, Cristy said carefully, 'Does that mean you're not entirely convinced by her confession?'

Honey's warm, amber eyes met hers. 'Let's just say it concerns me, but you have to understand that she can't personally engage in an attempt to prove her innocence or the licence will be instantly revoked.'

Picking up on the nuances, Cristy said, 'So what are you suggesting?'

Honey said, 'I've familiarized myself with just about every aspect of the case since taking it on, and I've found no record of you labelling Nicole "The Face of Evil", the way so many did back in the day. Unfortunately, some are doing it again.

Others are angling for "inside stories", as they call them, or "exclusives", so are choosing to forget how they treated her before. I believe, if anyone will give her a fair hearing, you will, so I'm prepared to act as a go-between with a view to clearing her name.'

Quietly stunned, Cristy turned to Connor.

'So you *do* think she's innocent?' he asked Honey.

Honey said, 'Let's just say, I share your doubts about her guilt, in spite of her confession.'

Watching her closely, Cristy asked, 'During the parole hearing, did she offer any detail on how or why she did it?'

'No, she simply accepted responsibility and said she was sorry. I'm précising, of course.'

Cristy allowed a moment to take that in. 'So they've let her go without knowing *how* the twins died or where to find their bodies?'

'Correct.'

Stunned all over again, Cristy said, 'Don't you find that odd?'

'Of course, because it is, but there isn't always logic attached to these decisions, or none that's obvious anyway. I wasn't there to try and change their minds, only to advise on how she should express her remorse. Naturally, they also took into account the fact that she's been a model prisoner all this time.'

'I guess you're not going to tell us where she is?' Connor ventured.

'I really can't, but she's with her mother in a place she's unlikely to be found that's within the forty-mile radius set for this early stage of her release.'

'OK,' he responded, drawing out the word, 'so where do you suggest we go from here?'

'I'm going to tell Nicole that you – and I – are keen to help her prove her innocence. I don't know how she'll respond – it obviously contravenes her licence conditions to engage with you in any way, even through me, and she might be too afraid to do that. If she is, I'll have to respect her decision. Also, let's keep in mind the fact that she hasn't asked for help. It's simply that I know, right here in my gut, that she's holding something back.'

Having no problem believing in the instinct, Cristy said, 'What does her mother say about her confession?'

'Maeve won't talk about it, but if I can convince them both that we're on their side, maybe they'll start to open up.' Honey paused and sighed quietly. 'Or maybe we're all wasting our time and she really did do it.' As her eyes came to Cristy's, it was plain to see how reluctant she was to believe that.

'What is Julian Hargreaves's real take on it all?' Cristy wanted to know.

Honey dropped her head and inhaled quietly before looking up again. 'I'm sure you know that many in the legal establishment find it hard to admit to getting things wrong,' she replied evenly.

Reading what she could into that, Cristy said, 'You mean he never believed in her innocence, in spite of defending her?'

'It happens all the time,' Honey reminded her. 'It's our duty as lawyers to provide a defence for someone—'

'But how does he feel about you looking into the case again?' Cristy interrupted. 'Particularly when Nicole hasn't requested it.'

'He's not willing to put any resources into it – hence me coming to you – but he won't stand in my way. My uncle will make sure of that; he's a more reasonable man.' She checked the time. 'I'm sorry, but I have to go. I'll be in touch as soon as I've seen Nicole, which should be some time in the next couple of days.'

And after they'd set up a WhatsApp group between them, she disappeared back inside.

Minutes later, as Cristy and Connor headed for the

waterfront to take the cross-harbour ferry over to the office, Cristy said, 'Tell me your thoughts.'

'As this stands, we don't have much of a series,' he responded, 'because no way can we reveal that we're in touch with Nicole, albeit at one remove, or use anything that suggests we're talking to her. So any information we might get is likely to be unusable.'

'Exactly,' Cristy agreed. 'However, if we take the long view and work with Honey Blackwell, who knows what we might uncover. So I'd say, for now, let's delay uploading anything until we have a clearer sense of where things are going. Meantime, we record whatever we can, where we can, and I reckon there's a good chance we'll end up with a seriously mind-blowing series on our hands.'

Connor broke into a grin. 'Especially if she turns out *not* to have done it in spite of the confession. Actually, either way, it'll be sensational, but after the chat with Honey, I'm definitely leaning into Nicole's innocence.'

'Mm,' Cristy responded thoughtfully. 'If Nicole Ivorson was a journalist or politician, I'd say she's been gaslighting us all this time, given it's what we do to deflect from the main story: "throw a dead cat on the table" – or in this case, bury it in the woods. It's too serious for that, though. However, as an alibi, it hardly stands up at all, which in its way almost makes it more credible.' She checked her phone as it rang, saw it was Clove and put the call on speaker.

'No sign of Maeve at the churchyard,' Clove told them. 'We're still here, but—'

'Don't worry, come on back now,' Cristy replied. 'We've just been put in pole position to find out what actually happened in July 2005, so there's a lot to fill you in on.'

CHAPTER ELEVEN

David's grand, Italianate-style villa, with its black filigree veranda and balconies, towering windows and extensive grounds, was in the high parishes of Guernsey. Secluded and stylish, it was a triumph of architectural and interior design, mostly overseen by his extrovert and talented younger daughter, Anna.

On Friday afternoon, as Cristy drove herself and both her children in through the electric gates, closely followed by Connor, Jodi and Aurora in their own rental car, the estate – named Papillon by David's eldest daughter, Rosie – was a still and beautiful midwinter landscape. The frosted trees, evergreen and leafless, glistened in the early burn of sunset, while the fields each side of the meandering drive flowed and dipped like a wonderland out to the distant boundaries.

Cristy had grown to love the place almost as much as its owner, who, having released the gates for their entry, was now coming out of the front door to greet them as they reached the house. He looked so Lord of the Manor-ish in his cream chunky-knit polo neck and dark green cords that Cristy almost laughed. Seeming to reflect her humour – maybe it was simply pleasure on both their parts to see one another – he pulled open her car door, and as she stepped out into the cold, she found herself wishing they could have a few moments alone before the craziness began.

Already too late. Rosie was barging past him, whooping with delight as she yelled everyone's names in excitement, and watching her, as she flung her arms around Hayley and Aiden, Cristy felt her heart swelling with emotion.

'We've made biscuits and cakes and hot chocolate and all sorts of things for the party,' Rosie gushed, her adorable round face gazing eagerly up at Hayley, more than ten years her junior, but one of her 'favourite heroines'. 'I wanted you to sleep in my room, but Dad says I snore, so you and Aiden can be in one of the cottages with your dad when he comes. And I don't snore,' she informed her father, treating him to her most ominous scowl. 'Aiden, Laurent said to tell you that he'll be back soon and if you're up for some Xbox, he is too.' Thirteen-year-old Laurent, David's youngest child and Rosie and Anna's half-brother, lived right here on the island with his father, grandmother and half-sisters, while his mother preferred to stay in Paris.

'Sick.' Aiden grinned, and giving Rosie a giant hug, he said, 'You're so cool, I think I might have to start dating you.'

'Oh yes!' she exclaimed excitedly. Rosie was big-time into dating. 'I'd like that. And then we can dance together tomorrow night. I've got a lovely new dress for the party that Grandma helped me to choose.'

'She so did not,' Anna protested, coming out to join them. 'It was me who took you shopping and me who paid for it.' Anna, at twenty-seven, was almost as chaotic in nature as her sister and so incredibly like her dead mother, with her exquisite heart-shaped face and mass of dark curls, that Cristy felt sure David must think of Lexie every time he looked at his middle child.

Hayley, very like her own mother with her natural blonde waves and shining blue eyes, went straight into Anna's embrace, while Cristy moved into the circle of David's arm and watched as Connor, Jodi and Aurora were treated to their own Rosie-welcome.

'You're staying in one of the cottages,' she informed them, 'but Grandma wants everyone to come inside first so she can see the baby . . . Can I hold her, please?'

Stepping in before Rosie could make a grab, Anna said, 'She's sleeping, but I'm sure Jodi will be happy for you to hold her when she wakes up.'

'Any chance we can go inside now?' Cristy asked. 'It's freezing out here.'

'Dad lit all the fires,' Rosie announced as they started for the door. 'The kitchen, the sitting room, the orangery . . . Oh no, not the orangery – we don't have one in there. That's where the main party is going to be. We've already installed an amazing bar where you can get anything you want to drink . . . I'm going to have champagne, or I might have some of my special cider . . . Dad's really excited; he's even got a jazz band coming and a magician and . . . somebody else . . . I can't remember who . . . Oh, and we've got a really big surprise for you—'

'OK, enough,' David cut in, pulling her into a gentle headlock and pretending to zip her mouth.

'It's a secret,' Rosie said, 'and everyone says I'm not very good at keeping them, but I am. We're going to have dancing in here,' she declared, waving her arms to indicate the spacious entrance hall with its double-height ceiling, fascinating collection of artworks and mirror-image staircases climbing each curved side wall.

'Ah, here you all are.' Cynthia, David's mother, smiled, coming out of the kitchen to greet them, her age-crumpled face and warm grey eyes almost as dear to Cristy as her own beloved mother's. 'I see Miss Chatterbox is filling you in on everything, but let's get you in by the fire now and some refreshments going.'

The aroma of fresh baking, burning pine logs and Golden Retriever was as welcoming and familiar to Cristy as the L-shaped kitchen itself, with its large, open workspace, big round table and fireside sofas. Henry, the dog, leapt up gleefully at the sight of visitors, waggling his furry body and whipping his tail so hard his feet left the floor.

Grabbing Henry's collar, David said to Connor, 'I'll take you down to the cottages when you're ready. The heating's been on since yesterday, so everything should be good. Hayley and Aiden, you're in the house with us tonight, unless you'd rather go and settle yourselves . . .'

'We don't mind either way,' Hayley assured him, going to slip an arm around her mother. 'Are you excited?' she whispered.

'Very,' Cristy murmured, watching Aiden getting stuck into the brownies as Anna began filling mugs with hot chocolate. Rosie gazed adoringly at Aurora, who was still sleeping in Jodi's arms.

'We have various plans for tomorrow,' Cynthia announced, going to take a small cake from the oven. 'Walks, a spot of sailing, shopping for anyone who fancies going into town; there's a table booked for lunch at Pier One . . . David, are you collecting Matthew from the airport?'

'I think he's renting a car,' David replied, finally managing to press the dog back down on its bed.

'He is,' Cristy confirmed. 'He's bringing Hugo, Hayley's boyfriend, and Harry and Meena. I'll probably go to pick up Clove and Jacks . . .'

'I've already arranged for them to get here,' Anna told her. 'We can't have you playing taxi service on your big day. And Iz is coming in from London? There's a car booked for her too. We're putting her in the top room here – a bit of a squeeze, but maybe better than banishing her to a hotel on her own. Oh, Hayley, we're in for a blow-dry at ten in the morning, Jodi and Cristy same time for manicures . . . Grandma, did you want to come with us? I'm sure they can fit you in.'

'I'm with caterers and planners most of the day,' Cynthia

reminded her, 'and I've already had my hair done – thanks for noticing.'

Since it was scrunched into a jaunty clip on the top of her head, with stray strands doing their own thing in every which way, they all laughed, and David went to give her a hug.

'Always the belle of the ball,' he told her. 'Now, go sit while I take over here and make sure everyone has whatever they need.'

*

An hour later, after David had driven down to the cottages with Connor and Jodi, Cristy was helping Cynthia to clear up while the others slumped on the sofas or sat around the table, checking their phones.

'I'm not going to tell you what the surprise is,' Rosie failed to whisper to Cristy.

'Rosie,' Anna warned.

Rosie giggled. 'Do you want to know?' she asked Cristy.

'No, she doesn't,' Cynthia told her. 'Remember, you promised to keep it to yourself.'

'Will she like it?' Aiden asked mischievously.

Rosie nodded eagerly, then gasped. 'What if she doesn't?' she asked her grandmother.

'Don't worry, she will,' Cynthia assured her.

'You will,' Rosie confirmed to Cristy. Then, speaking from behind one hand, she shout-whispered, 'Dad's going to ask you to marry him.'

As Cristy blinked, Anna leapt up from her chair and planted a hand over her sister's mouth.

Cristy was so stunned that she couldn't even smile. David was going to propose? In front of everyone? And they already knew? She was too shocked to even work out how she felt about that.

Anna was furiously shaking her head while keeping a

tight hold on Rosie. 'It's what we told her,' she confessed, 'to make her stop asking. Sorry, it's not true . . . I mean, it might be, for all I know, but it's not part of the plan.'

Rosie turned to her sister. 'Did you tell me lies?' she asked accusingly.

'Not really,' Anna answered, throwing a pleading look her grandmother's way. 'Just a little one . . .'

'You've just proved you can't keep a secret,' Cynthia scolded. 'And now look what you've done – got everyone into a state of confusion over nothing.'

Rosie looked upset now. 'But I want Dad to propose,' she grumbled. 'I thought he was going to.'

'Oh God,' Anna groaned. 'He's going to kill me for this.'

Finally managing to laugh, Cristy said, 'Rosie, why don't you show me your dress for tomorrow night? I'm sure Hayley would like to see it too.'

'Dying to,' Hayley agreed, going to slip an arm around Rosie's plump shoulders. 'What colour is it?'

'Blue,' Rosie replied, and allowing herself to be led out of the room, she chattered on about ribbons and pearls and matching shoes . . .

'Sorry again,' Anna said quietly to Cristy. 'I hope you didn't . . . I mean . . . Oh God, what a disaster. *Please* don't say anything to Dad . . .'

'Don't worry, your secret's safe with me,' Cristy assured her with an ironic smile, and helping herself to a chocolate, she went off to see the dress, thankful that David – or Matthew, come to that – hadn't been in the room for Rosie's big reveal.

*

'You looked totally shocked,' Hayley told Cristy when they were alone in the villa's master suite a little while later.

It was dark outside now, so the heavy silk drapes were

closed, and the room was lit by soft creamy lights and the warming glow of a touch-button faux-log fire. This was David's private space (tell that to Rosie) where he came to read newspapers, watch sport on TV or make phone calls he'd rather weren't overheard. It was a sumptuous suite dominated by an enormous bed, with twin sofas flanking the fire and a small bar set up in one of the armoires. Naturally, he had an office downstairs for when he was working at home, but up here, he could properly relax and, when she was here, be alone with Cristy.

'What would you have said if it had turned out to be real?' Hayley asked, stretching out on the bed as Cristy sank into one of the sofas with a gin and tonic.

'I'm not sure,' Cristy replied, feeling suddenly edgy and way too hot. 'I mean, being married again isn't on my agenda.'

'Not even to David? I thought you were nuts about him.'

'I am, but that doesn't mean I'm ready for that sort of commitment.'

'You're fifty tomorrow – not getting any younger.'

'Only someone your age would think fifty was past it.'

'Teasing!' Hayley laughed. 'You're definitely great for your age. You don't look much over forty, but you can't want to grow old on your own. I mean, obviously me and Aiden will be around, but that's not the same. And we won't mind – you know we love David. And imagine being here all the time, in this gorgeous place . . .'

'Will you stop? If you knew what was really going on in my life, you wouldn't be writing me off quite so soon.'

Immediately fascinated, Hayley said, 'Oh! Do tell.'

'Not now . . .'

'Hang on, you haven't met someone else, have you? Is that why . . .'

'I have not met someone else.'

'So what's going on?'

'You'll find out when I'm ready. Now, if it makes you

happy, I'll admit that if I was going to marry anyone, it would probably be David.'

'Probably? That would hardly fill him with confidence.' Hayley frowned worriedly, her eyes studying her mother more closely now. 'What's going on with you?' she asked. 'Obviously something is . . .'

Sighing, Cristy deflected away from Kinsey's offer with an excuse about the new podcast series taking up a lot of head space, which was true: it really was. However, she couldn't get into the details of that either, and nor did she want to admit to being menopausal. So, switching the subject back to where they'd started, she said, 'Tell me, do you think Anna or Cynthia noticed that I didn't look thrilled?'

Hayley shrugged. 'I don't know. It all happened so fast, but I'm glad David wasn't there to see it. If he knows you as well as I do, he'd have picked up right away that the surprise, if it was real, was going to backfire.'

Would it have?

She couldn't say for certain, only knew that she was glad it wasn't in the plan – and was it going to seem strange to Hayley if she opened a window when it had to be close to zero outside? 'Thankfully he wasn't there,' she said, tugging off her jumper, ' and as it's no longer an issue, maybe you'd like to tell me what the surprise *actually* is?'

Hayley laughed. 'Nice try, but no deal. I can tell you this, though: it's not a great big fat diamond . . . well, it might be – I've no idea what David's got for you – but the real surprise is from all of us and is definitely something you're going to love.'

CHAPTER TWELVE

The following evening, after a hectic day spent bringing everything and everyone together, Cristy gave herself a quick last appraisal in the mirror before, satisfied she was neither glowing nor perspiring, she sauntered out of David's dressing room, keen to get his reaction to her floor length, figure-hugging silver gown.

When she saw him standing in front of a long mirror in his tux, fixing his sapphire blue bow-tie, she found herself so distracted by how damned gorgeous he looked that it was a moment before she registered the way he was looking at her reflection.

'Jesus,' he murmured, and turning to her, he let his eyes sweep her from top to toe in a way that actually made her heart beat faster. 'You are sensational,' he told her gruffly. 'Now I want to know how I got to be so lucky.'

Loving his response, she gave him a twirl to reveal the gown's exquisite drop-back, right down to her waist, and had the satisfaction of hearing him groan.

Coming to her, he pressed his mouth gently to her bare skin and said, 'Can we cut to later, after the party's over and I get you all to myself?'

'Already counting the hours,' she replied, keeping her voice low.

Clearly amused by her answer, he reached into his pocket and pulled out a small red Cartier box.

Her heart somersaulted. So he *was* going to propose! *Jesus.* What was she going to say? It couldn't be no, obviously – it would ruin the evening – but so would anything other than yes.

'We can always change them,' he said, opening the box to show her what was inside. 'If you think . . .'

'Oh my God, David,' she cried, unravelling with relief and dazzled by the exquisite diamond stud earrings. 'They're beautiful. I've never . . .' Her voice faltered as she looked into his eyes. 'I've never owned anything like this,' she said truthfully.

He smiled. 'I'm glad you like them. Will you wear them tonight?'

'Of course.' And quickly unfastening the fakes she was wearing, she watched him watching her in the mirror as she replaced them with the most expensive and subtly stunning jewellery she'd ever worn. 'Thank you,' she whispered, as he cupped a hand gently around her face. 'I love them.'

'I hope you don't mind that I stole a lead on everyone else with my gift,' he said, 'but I didn't want them to be upstaged by the surprise.'

'What on earth could be better than Cartier earrings?' She laughed incredulously.

With a playful arch of his brows, David tucked her arm through his and led her out of the room.

Fifteen minutes later, they were in the spaciously exotic environs of the orangery, drinks in hand, family close by as guests who'd come from all over to celebrate her big day began arriving. They all looked so happy and glamorous in their tuxedos and cocktail dresses that Cristy was delighted to see Connor taking shots for her to keep and cherish.

'Hey you,' a familiar voice whispered, coming up behind her. 'Happy birthday. You look stunning.'

Turning, Cristy cried, 'Andee!' and quickly putting aside her champagne, she gave her dear friend a bruising hug, determinedly pushing away all thoughts of Paul Kinsley and RK Media. Now definitely was not the right time for it. 'Thank you for coming all this way,' she gushed. 'It's wonderful that you're here, and you look amazing.'

Laughing, Andee gave a quick twirl to show off her clinging black jersey dress, with diamanté detail around the wrists and collar that matched the sparkling clip holding her curly dark hair. Her mesmerizing aquamarine eyes and infectious smile always had set her apart as a beauty, and seeing her now, all dressed up and glowing like a movie star, made it hard to believe she'd once been a detective investigating some of the nation's most violent crimes.

Would she want to go back to that?

She wouldn't be anywhere near as hands-on with RK . . .

'Cristy Ward! At last, I get to meet you.'

Cristy turned to be greeted by an extremely distinguished-looking man with neat silver hair, deep-grey eyes and an ironic sort of smile.

'Graeme Ogilvy, my partner,' Andee quickly explained.

Liking him on sight, Cristy said flirtatiously, 'I kept wondering why she was hiding you away. Now I know.'

He laughed. 'I'm lucky I get to see her at all; she always has so much going on. You look stunning, by the way – and this is a beautiful party.'

'We're very honoured to be invited,' Andee assured her, 'and this house . . . We were just talking to David's daughter, Anna, who I believe built it?'

'She had a lot of help.' Cristy laughed. 'But she was very involved in the design . . . Oh, David,' she cried, noticing him pressing a path towards them, 'have you met Andee and Graeme yet?'

'I have,' David told her, and leaned in slightly as Graeme said something in his ear. 'OK, everyone's here now,' he declared, 'so let's get you in position . . .'

Intrigued and not a little apprehensive, Cristy allowed David to lead her through the crowd as Connor and Harry gently ushered everyone to clear a space in the middle of the room. At the bar, David turned her around and called for everyone's attention as Matthew, Hayley and Aiden came to stand the other side of her – and if it were possible for Hayley to look more excited or Matthew more pleased with himself or Aiden more chilled, she didn't know how.

'What's going on?' she whispered to Matthew. 'What have you done?'

'You'll see,' Hayley interrupted, and grabbing her brother's arm, she gave it a vicious squeeze.

'What the . . . ?' Aiden cried, shrugging her off.

Laughing, Cristy turned back to David as he began to address the gathering.

'I know it's a little early for speeches,' he said, 'so lucky for you, that's not what this is. However, I'm sure you'll agree that we can't possibly allow the party to continue without the guest of honour being present.'

Cristy turned to him curiously.

'I know you think that might be Cristy,' he continued, 'but there's someone else here tonight who she certainly will consider just as important, perhaps even more so . . . OK, you can come join us now.'

As everyone turned to the door, Cristy watched a tall man in his early fifties step into view. He was slightly balding, had a close-shave beard and was dressed in a stylish black dinner suit – and her hands flew to her mouth in shock.

'Oh my God!' she cried, unable to believe her eyes. 'Tom? Is that . . . ?' And sobbing with joy she rushed across the room, straight into her brother's open arms.

'Happy birthday, sis,' he murmured into her hair, his voice thick with emotion, his embrace as encompassing as he could make it without crushing her. Almost six years might have passed since they'd last been together, but in this moment it felt like no time at all. 'You didn't think I was going to miss this, did you?' he teased.

'No. Yes! I mean . . . Oh God, I can't . . . You look . . . wonderful. When did you get here?'

'Yesterday. I've been lying low at a hotel in town.'

'I told you you were going to love it.' Hayley laughed, coming to hug them. 'Uncle Tom, you're amazing for coming all this way . . . Thank you . . .'

'It was my idea to invite him,' Aiden interrupted, grabbing his uncle's hand.

'It was mine!' Hayley protested.

'I don't care whose it was – it was brilliant,' Cristy declared. 'Oh, Tom, just look at you. I swear you're more like Dad than ever . . .'

'I'll take it,' he twinkled, 'and you, of course, are the image of Mum with a little bit more height and bluer eyes. Matthew.' He grinned, hugging his ex-brother-in-law as he joined them. 'It's good to see you . . . It's been all of four hours since we last shared a drink?'

Cristy laughed. 'So that's where you all were this afternoon,' she scolded Matthew. 'I wondered what had happened to you. Oh, Tom, there's so much I want to ask you – I hardly know where to begin. Where's Sandie?' she demanded, looking around for her sister-in-law. 'Did she come too?'

'Long story,' he replied wryly, 'not for tonight, but she sends her love and . . . David! I think we pulled it off.'

Grinning, David passed Tom a glass of champagne. 'I wondered a couple of times if she'd guessed. Did you?' he asked Cristy.

'No, not at all. I mean, it's such a long way to come from Canada, and you're always so busy,' she ragged Tom.

'Unlike you,' he responded dryly. 'But here we are now, and you've got all these guests dying to talk to you . . .'

'I see them all the time,' she protested. 'How long are you staying?'

'We'll discuss tomorrow – go on, scoot now. Everyone's

here to celebrate you, and I'm told Cynthia's expecting us all for breakfast in the morning, so we can . . .'

'Oh no, I'm not letting you go that easily,' she protested. 'Come on – let me introduce you around. Connor, you already know, and his wife, Jodi . . .'

She was beaming with pride as she took him around the room, enjoying the banter while wondering how on earth she was going to continue with the new series now that he was in Europe. Feeling a small tug on her arm she turned to find Iz beside her.

'Oh, I'm sorry, have I not introduced you?' Cristy cried, actually certain she had.

'It's fine,' Iz said and leaned in close to make herself heard above the hubbub of voices and music. 'I hear you're planning to delay the start of the new series. If true, I just wanted to let you know that the sponsors won't like that, so . . .'

Cristy drew back in astonishment. 'This is hardly the time, Iz,' she said sharply.

Looking shocked, Iz said, 'No! Of course not, I'm sorry. I just thought . . . Oh God, I'm so bad at parties . . . Please just shoot me.'

Apparently sensing a problem, Clove sailed in, saying, 'Hey, Iz, come and meet one of David's cousins. She's a hoot.'

Shooting her researcher a grateful look, Cristy turned back to her brother, to find him play-flirting with Rosie, who'd apparently ditched Aiden in favour of the 'guest of honour'.

'Your reaction was perfect,' David told her as they danced a little later. 'I think it meant a lot to Tom.'

'Not as much as it did to me to see him.' Cristy smiled, watching Tom chatting with Andee and Graeme now and thinking of how much she wanted to catch up with him herself. 'I have to admit,' she continued, 'I had a mad theory you'd invited Paul Kinsley.'

Surprised, David said, 'Seriously? With your whole team around you and Andee here . . . Will you mention anything to her before she leaves?'

'I can't until I've made a decision, although I have to admit I'd love to talk it through with her. If I knew she was up for it . . . Well, that's why I can't mention it, because if she is and I end up deciding *I'm* not, that would leave us in a very bad place.'

David conceded the point and allowed Matthew to cut in, before disappearing in the direction of the bar.

'Has Tom shared his news with you yet?' Matthew asked, moving her around the floor.

'What news?' she asked, instantly worried. 'Is he OK?'

'Sure. He's fine. Sorry, I shouldn't have . . . I assumed he'd have told you by now.'

'What is it?' she urged when Matthew didn't continue.

'It's not for me to say, but . . . Go ask him,' he said, and turned her to where Tom was now dancing with David's mother.

She was already part way there before she realized that if it was that big and he wanted to discuss it now, he'd already have told her. 'Maybe he's saving it until we're alone together?' she suggested, turning back to Matthew.

Matthew nodded. 'That would make sense. He won't want to make this evening about him, when obviously it has to be all about you.'

She eyed him suspiciously, not sure if that was a barb or not. 'Maybe time for me to dance with someone else,' she said, and leaving him rolling his eyes, she went to grab Connor.

'Enjoying it?' Connor asked, expertly twirling her around.

'I think so,' she replied. 'I mean, yes, of course . . . It's just that Matthew . . . Actually, don't let's talk about him. Did you tell Iz we're delaying the first upload?'

'No, but I think Clove did. Why?'

'She's just told me that the sponsors won't like it.'

His eyebrows shot up. 'Great timing, Iz,' he muttered, 'but I guess we are going to have that battle on our hands if they've already got dates in their schedules. And I'm presuming from this that they do.'

'We're the ones in charge,' she reminded him.

'But we also need a budget, and if Harry and Meena have committed us to a timeline . . .'

'They wouldn't without telling us first.'

He shrugged. 'What matters right now is whether or not Nicole is prepared to accept our help, because if she isn't, we won't have much of a series anyway.'

'I hope you two aren't talking shop,' Jodi complained, coming to plonk the baby in Connor's arms. 'Cristy, I'm in love with your brother, always have been, so I think I'm going to run off with him. Do you reckon his wife will have a problem with that?'

'Never mind her, what about me?' Connor demanded, rocking Aurora back and forth. 'Hayley, fancy a spot of babysitting? I pay well.'

'Give her to me,' Cynthia insisted, coming to take over. 'Cristy, David was looking for you a moment ago.'

'I'm right here,' Cristy declared, laughing. 'Where is he?'

Snaring another glass of champagne, and spotting Tom engrossed in a chat with a couple of David's cousins, she decided to go and join in.

By the time midnight came round and David lit the fireworks outside, Cristy was ready to kick off her heels and sink into the nearest comfy chair, but somehow, she kept going until just past one, when Tom's taxi turned up to return him to his hotel.

'Walk on the beach at dawn?' he suggested.

'You've got to be kidding!' she cried, and laughed when she realized he was.

'I'll be here by ten for brunch,' he told her, 'and at some point in the day, I'll tell you all about my plans to move back to London.'

CHAPTER THIRTEEN

As it turned out, Cristy, David and Tom were all up in time for a pre-brunch walk in the morning, so after checking tide times and collecting Tom from his hotel, David drove them all over to Cobo Bay. It was gloriously sunny, freezing cold and windy, but the beautiful, elongated curve of the beach was quiet and calm at this hour, with no one else around apart from a couple of dog walkers and a solitary jogger.

'So, looks like we could be roomies.' Tom was laughing as they trod the wet sand, arm-in-arm, with Cristy in the middle and Henry the Retriever racing ahead. 'Or I guess we should say flatmates being British and all. Whatever, this is an amazing opportunity for you, Cris, to set up a major new podcast company . . .'

'What about you, moving to UCL, my alma mater? My brother, Professor Ward, the head of history. You won't miss Canada?'

'Of course, but hey, we're neither of us getting any younger – time for us both to seize the day and make our marks on the world. I'm keener than ever now I know you're going to be in London too.'

'I haven't accepted the job yet,' she reminded him, 'but obviously having you around is going to be a huge sway. How does Sandie feel about the move? Aren't all her family in Toronto?'

'Or nearby, but that's my other news. We've decided to split . . .'

'Oh God, Tom!'

'It's all amicable,' he assured her. 'We've been growing apart for some time, different interests, unshared goals . . . Lucky, I guess, that we don't have kids, although I'd have liked them as you know, just that she was never keen . . . Well, as it turns out, I've met someone who is.'

Cristy came to a stop. 'Jesus, Tom!' she exclaimed, as he and David turned to face her. 'This is . . . mind-blowing! Who is she? I want to know everything.'

Laughing, he said, 'Her name is Serena, she's thirty-six, so a little younger than me, Belgian, a lecturer in fine arts at Sint-Lukas in Brussels, and the plan is for her to try and get a position in London at some point in the next couple of years.'

'So when do we get to meet her? You should have brought her to the party . . .'

'Of course David invited her,' Tom assured her, 'but she was keen for us to talk without you having to meet her at the same time. She felt it would be overload: new job, marriage break-up, move to London, possibly kids on the horizon, and I guess she had a point, especially after we decided to spring me as the big surprise last night.'

Loving the memory of it, Cristy linked his arm again and hugged it hard as they walked on, while David threw sticks into the waves for the dog. 'So what's the immediate plan?' she asked. 'How long have I got you for?'

Tom laughed. 'Knowing you as I do, I'm sure you're in the middle of some project or other, so my immediate plans are not to disrupt yours.'

'But . . .'

'Which means I'll fly to Brussels on Tuesday, and from there, Serena and I are planning to go to Paris, our first stop on a two-to-three-month tour of Europe and perhaps the Far East. I've already quit my job, so I was always planning to make it over for your birthday, and Serena's sabbatical has been agreed, so hopefully, by the time we come back, the four of us will have worked out how to spend a good amount of time together.'

Shaking her head in mock despair, Cristy said, 'That's so like you to have everything all worked out then just announce how it's going to happen.'

'Is there something you want me to change?' he asked.

'No, not at all. It sounds perfect to me . . . I just don't want to let you go so soon.'

'Says the woman who's already booked on a flight tomorrow morning . . .'

'Which could be changed . . .'

'But doesn't have to be.'

'I could delay until Tuesday.'

'Your decision, but we'll have most of the summer to catch up on everything, and we – David and I – have already arranged a day's sailing tomorrow.'

Astonished, Cristy laughed, 'Well, please don't let me stand in the way of that.' Hearing a phone ring, she fished in her pocket, before realizing it was David's.

'Connor,' he announced and turned away from the wind as he clicked on. 'Hey, good morning,' he said, pressing a finger to his other ear to hear better. 'Everything OK at the cottage?' He listened, looked at Cristy and said, 'Yeah, she's right here, I'll put her on.'

Taking the phone, she automatically put it on speaker in time to hear Connor saying, '. . . if you don't have your phone, you won't have seen Honey Blackwell's message.'

With a jolt of surprise, Cristy said, 'She's been in touch already? What's she saying?'

'Apparently, Nicole's seriously considering letting us help her, so Honey is keen for us to keep going.'

CHAPTER FOURTEEN

CRISTY: 'It's a bleak, sleety Tuesday morning in January, and Connor and I are in the car on our way to doorstep Nicole Ivorson's aunt, Bridget Hawkes. We have an address for her near Chippenham, and we know she's been there over the past weekend because our supersleuths have seen her, so we're hoping to find her at home today.'

CONNOR: 'To explain, she's Bridget Hawkes's aunt whose daughter, Lauren, is the cousin who was apparently close to Nicole back in 2005. At this time of recording, Nicole has confessed to the murder of her twins and has recently been released on parole, but we have reason to believe that there's much more to the story than ever came to light at the time of the twins' disappearance and Nicole's trial.'

CRISTY: 'It's possible Lauren can fill us in on some, if not all, of the detail, so we're hoping she's either with her mother at this address or that perhaps Bridget will be able to point us in her daughter's direction.'

CONNOR: 'I want to mention here – no idea where we're going to use it, but use it we must, and we'll also put it on the website – that we, as a team, spent some of yesterday viewing a much younger Cristy's reports from the time of the arrest. She couldn't bear to look while the rest of us had a few laughs at the fresh face and earnest style.

'Curiously though, neither Cristy, nor other reporters whose footage we've got hold of from back then, made mention of Lauren Hawkes.'

Stopping the recording as the satnav announced they'd reached their destination, Cristy looked around to take in their surroundings. They were at the end of a small, balloon-shaped cul-de-sac in front of a neat, brick-built semi with a single-car garage to one side, solar panels on the roof and vertical blinds at the windows. There was no garden to speak of, just a small patio open to the street, where a doll's pram and a child's tricycle shared the space with a couple of empty planters.

It looked quite sad, Cristy thought. Then again, didn't everything when the weather was so dreary?

Leaving the recorder in the car, they walked the short distance to the front door, where Connor rapped the knocker three times as Cristy pressed the bell. It played the sound of a train hooting.

As they glanced at one another, eyebrows arched, someone shouted from inside, 'Coming! Hold your horses!'

A moment later, Bridget Hawkes – easily identified from the shots the supersleuth had taken – tugged open the door and gave a blink of surprise. She was a short, plump woman with neat grey-blonde hair, tired eyes and a rosy, faintly lined complexion.

'Oh,' she exclaimed. 'I was expecting the plumber. You're not him, are you?' she asked Connor. 'There's a leak under the sink—'

'I'm Cristy Ward,' Cristy interrupted, 'and this is my colleague, Connor Church. We were hoping to talk to Lauren. Is she here by any chance?'

Bridget Hawkes eyed her in astonishment. It turned rapidly to suspicion. 'Are you the police or something?' she asked carefully. 'Is she all right?'

'We're podcasters,' Cristy quickly explained. 'We're putting together a series about your niece, Nicole . . .'

'Oh Lord!' Bridget cried, clapping her hands to her cheeks in apparent distress. 'Have you seen her? I've been trying to call Maeve, but she never rings me back. They'll be together somewhere, and I reckon I know where, but I can't get a response . . .' She stopped abruptly and eyed them warily again. 'Who did you say you were?'

'We're making a podcast looking into what happened back in 2005,' Cristy explained, 'and we're hoping Lauren will be able—'

'Lauren's not here,' Bridget interrupted. 'I haven't laid eyes on her in over sixteen years. Just a card at Christmas and on my birthday – nothing to say where she is or how we can get in touch with her. I don't even know if anyone's told her her father's dead. It broke his heart, the way she went off like that, and properly screwed up our poor Julie. She was only fourteen at the time, idolized her sister, kept thinking Lauren would come back for her, but it never happened. She's over it now, or I suppose she doesn't think about it much any more. No time to, with two small kids on her hands and a husband who can't find himself a decent job.' She inhaled deeply and looked more flustered than ever as she said, 'Gosh, it's thrown me, hearing our Lauren's name . . . I don't suppose you know where she is? No, you're here looking for her.' Guarded again, she said, 'What exactly is it you want to talk to her about?'

Cristy said, 'We think she might be able to tell us something about what happened to the twins.'

Bridget gasped and took a step back. 'We know what happened,' she cried. 'They were stolen, and it didn't have anything to do with Lauren.'

Cristy said gently, 'Nicole's confessed to killing them. It's how come she got parole . . .'

'Oh yes, that's right,' Bridget said, flustered. 'It's hard to keep up with it all sometimes. Those poor little souls – so sweet they were, little angels – and Nicole . . . sorry, but she . . . I don't like speaking ill of my own niece, but she was a wild one at times. No controlling her. She used to drive her parents out of their minds with worry, and she was forever leading my Lauren astray . . .' As her words dried up, her eyes slipped away into sadness. 'She wasn't a bad girl, though, not at heart. She was just young . . . I can't make myself believe she really hurt them. I mean, she didn't like having the reins put on her much, but half the time she took them with her when she went out to see her friends. And credit where it's due, she was a better mother than most of us expected. She kept them clean and fed, used to dress them well too, but of course Maeve had a lot to do with that.'

'Do you happen to know who the twins' father was?' Cristy asked, sorely wishing they were recording this.

Bridget shook her head and looked at her again.

'Do you think Lauren knows?' Cristy pressed.

'If she does, she never let on. I don't know why it had to be such a big secret . . . Actually, that's not true, I do know, because I don't think even Nicole knew who the father was – not for certain anyway.'

'Were any names ever mentioned?' Connor prompted.

Bridget appeared more desolate than ever as she said, 'The only one I remember is Claude . . . Major, I think? He was French – or foreign anyway. That's who Lauren will be with now, I'm sure of it, but don't ask me where – they could be on the moon for all I know.'

'Is there anything else you can tell us about him?' Cristy asked.

Bridget regarded her blankly. 'We never met him, her dad and me, but Lauren used to talk about him a lot, back before she went off with him. That's what we've always assumed happened. She thought the sun shone out of him, he could do no wrong, and everything about him was better than anything we could ever understand. That's what she used to say. He was special, different, someone to be looked up to.'

'How did she know him?'

'Nicole introduced her to him, before everything, obviously . . .' Frowning, Bridget peered at them again and said 'You know, it's not very nice of you to come round here raking it all up again, especially if you don't know where she is. It was a terrible time for our family, and we've tried hard to put it behind us . . .' She shrugged helplessly. 'I suppose it was to be expected you'd turn up again now that Nicole's . . . Are you in touch with Maeve?'

'Not directly,' Cristy replied. 'But we can get a message to her if you'd like us to.'

Bridget clearly gave it some thought but ended up shaking her head. 'She'll get in touch with me when she's ready.'

Needing to come right to the point, Cristy said, 'Do you think there's a chance Lauren might have gone to join a cult?'

Bridget frowned as colour rushed to her cheeks. 'We heard rumours there was one,' she confessed, 'but I'm sure . . . No, I'm not sure about anything. You know what teenage girls are like, up for anything – or most things anyway. So yes, she might have, but I'm sure someone looked into the rumours when they started, and nothing ever came of it.'

'Do you know if Lauren ever gave a statement to the police about what happened to the twins?' Connor asked.

Bridget nodded. 'We all did, but none of us knew anything that could help find them. Lauren was as shocked and upset as the rest of us. Traumatized, she was, actually. Went into a terrible depression for a while – wouldn't talk to any of us about it. Well, we all found it hard to put into words. I mean, what do you say when two innocent little children just disappear off the face of the earth? Makes me feel sick to think of it even now.'

Judging by Lauren's reaction to the abduction, or murder, Cristy felt certain that Lauren had known more about it than her family ever had.

Connor said, 'Can you think of anything else Lauren told you about this Claude?'

'You mean apart from him being foreign and something special? We racked our brains over that after she left, but we could never think of anything to help us to find him or her. Even with the internet, we've never got very far.'

'Did you ever talk to Maeve about Claude?'

'Oh yes. She knew him and never had anything but high praise for him. Same went for his friends, the ones Nicole and Lauren got so involved with, but like the rest of us, Maeve was left wondering what happened to them all after the twins disappeared. I mean, I heard that this Claude spoke to the police, but apparently he wasn't in the country at the time it all kicked off, so it didn't go any further. And Lauren was certain he'd never hurt a fly, that none of them would.'

Cristy said, 'You told us just now that Lauren left around sixteen years ago, so it would have been three years after the trial ended?'

'Nearly that,' Bridget confirmed. 'She was never the same after her cousin went away. Like I said, it tore the heart out of her, and she wouldn't let any of us comfort her, or try to get her some help. She just kept saying Claude was the only one who understood her and the rest of us should leave her alone.'

'So she was still in touch with him?'

'As far as I know, right up until the time she walked out on us.'

Cristy was about to speak again when Bridget looked past them, saying, 'Ah, this must be the plumber, and not before time. Sorry,' she said to Cristy, 'I have to deal with this now and then get to work. My manager's only allowed me a couple of hours off. You were lucky to catch me.'

'Thanks for talking to us.' Cristy smiled past her frustration. 'We really appreciate it.'

Bridget blinked sadly. 'If you manage to find Lauren, maybe you'll let me know?' she said hopefully.

'Of course,' Cristy promised, and after moving aside to allow the plumber through, she followed Connor back to the car.

CHAPTER FIFTEEN

An hour and a half later, Cristy and Connor were with Honey Blackwell in a crowded, steamy coffee bar adjacent to Bristol's Justice Centre, a stone's throw from the waterfront. The noise and heat were making Cristy, in her menopausal state, want to scream but she somehow managed not to.

'I don't have long,' Honey told them, stirring sugar into her latte. 'I'm due back in court at twelve, but you've spoken to Lauren's mother, and . . . ?'

'During your chats with Nicole,' Cristy said, 'has she ever mentioned anyone by the name of Claude Major?'

Honey frowned as she shook her head. 'I'd remember if she had,' she replied. 'Why? Who is he?'

'Does he get a mention anywhere in your case files?' Cristy persisted.

'I'll have to check, but tell me, who is he?'

'We already have our team working on it,' Cristy assured her, 'but Lauren's mother seems convinced that her daughter ran off with him when she left the family home sixteen years ago.'

Appearing mystified now, Honey said, 'And how does this relate to Nicole?'

'Apparently, she introduced Lauren to this guy, and Bridget thinks he was interviewed at the time of Nicole's arrest. Others might have been as well – we don't have any names for them – but we're thinking they were part of this so-called "Clifton set", and we're hoping you might have some disclosure records you can share.'

Honey appeared thoughtful. 'I'll certainly take a look,' she promised. 'There are a lot of them, and some are still in the archives, but I'm happy to dig through when they've been retrieved.'

'Great. Anyway, as far as Bridget remembers, this guy – she thinks he might have been French; the name Claude clearly is – she's fairly certain he wasn't in the country when the twins disappeared. However, Lauren stayed in touch with him during the years after Nicole went to prison. I don't know what we should draw from that right now, but taking into consideration the kind of things both Nicole and Lauren are known to have said about him, there's a possibility that at least some of the rumours about a cult could be true.'

Honey looked concerned.

'We think the nutty neighbour is responsible for the Satanism crap,' Connor put in. 'No one else has mentioned anything like it, but the way some have described this Claude – my words here – he sounds a pretty charismatic character. Requirement number one for a cult leader.'

Still frowning, Honey said, 'Did Bridget Hawkes suggest he might have harmed the twins?'

'No, she didn't say that,' Cristy replied, 'but if he was interviewed by the police . . . Actually, if he was, they must surely have swabbed him, so I guess he was ruled out as the father?'

Connor nodded. 'A reasonable assumption.'

Honey was checking her watch. 'I'm sorry, but I have to go . . .'

Cristy said, 'Apparently Maeve knows – or knew – this guy, so do you think she'd speak to us about him?'

'I can but ask,' Honey replied, 'and I will the next time I speak to her. Not sure when that'll be right now, but I'll be in touch as soon as I've had an opportunity to check the files.

Just bear in mind that getting things out of the archives takes time, so it might not be this week.'

'Meanwhile,' Connor remarked, after she'd gone, 'we need to redouble our efforts into finding someone from the police who worked the case and more crucially, is willing to talk.'

CHAPTER SIXTEEN

Over the next two days, the team remained office-bound, cosy and safe from the storms outside, as they dug even deeper into the Ivorson case. This meant scrutinizing every frame of footage they could lay their hands on from 2005 and 2006, every audio report, each print story – those that were digitized and many that weren't, the latter acquired from the cuttings libraries of both local and national newspapers and TV stations.

Much was made of the post-partum depression when the diagnosis was revealed at trial, although the salacious possibility of a sex-cult was given more coverage, especially by the tabloids. So far, they'd found no mention of a Claude Major in any of the reports, and there were so many individuals with the same name listed on the various social media platforms that it was like diving into an impossible warren of rabbit holes and never finding the right way up again.

'The three big problems,' Connor declared on the second day, after spending another fruitless few hours on several LinkedIn profiles that had led him precisely nowhere, 'we're not even sure it's his real name, or if he actually is French, never mind where on the entire planet he might be now—'

'Or if he's even still alive,' Cristy finished with a sigh, and pushed back from her desk retying her hair. She hadn't managed much sleep last night thanks to her very first night-sweat – what a joy life was at fifty – so she was feeling slightly detached today, kind of spacey. Thankfully no one seemed to have noticed. 'Given that Bridget Hawkes is only certain about Claude, not the surname,' she said, 'unless we can get something out of Nicole or Maeve – or Honey when she comes back with the files – you're right: we're wasting our time.'

'How are you getting on with the cults?' Connor asked Jacks.

Looking up, Jacks said, 'Which ones in particular? Doomsday, political, religious, health. There's even one devoted to female orgasm that I'm thinking of joining.'

Laughing, Cristy said, 'Maybe don't rule it out. What about Satanic? I know we're not believing Mervyn Wilson's fantasy world, but nevertheless . . .'

'Yeah, they're here,' Jacks confirmed, 'creepy as fuck, but same as with the social media stuff – without knowing if Claude's group was actually demonic, or if it's still operational, or even it ever was, I can't see how I'm going to get to sign up for the "About Us" page.'

Clove's eyes were fixed on the screen in front of her. 'I might have something here,' she said. 'Not about cults . . . I'm going through some outtakes from your early reports, Cristy, and I reckon this girl in the background here could be Lauren.'

'Share,' Jacks commanded.

Moments later, a mid-shot of Cristy, aged thirty – a clear-eyed, very blonde and unsweaty version of her fifty-year-old self – was on their screens, announcing to camera that Nicole Ivorson had just been led from the house and taken into custody. 'We can't get close enough to see what's actually going on,' she was saying, 'everything's cottoned off . . . Did I just say cottoned? Shit, cut!'

Clove froze the image and said, 'See her? Just over your right shoulder at the edge of the crowd . . . Is that her?'

'How do you know what she looks like?' Jacks challenged. 'We don't have any shots of her. Do we?'

'Sorry.' Cristy grimaced. 'Bridget sent a couple through this morning. They should be on the board by now – I forgot to do it.'

'Other things on your mind?' Connor enquired, seeming to tease although she couldn't be sure.

'Something like that,' she responded irritably. Had he clocked the text she'd received earlier when he'd returned her phone from where she'd left it next to the coffee machine? Even if he had spotted Kinsley's name, it surely wouldn't have triggered any sort of alarm, only interest in why her old mentor might be in touch.

And feeling annoyed with Connor because he was irking her conscience was pretty shameful.

'Could be her,' Jacks agreed, comparing the images he now had in front of him. 'And what about the bloke next to her, the one with his hand on her shoulder? Tall, longish dark hair . . . He's kind of turned away, so can't really see his face, but could we be looking at the infamous Claude?'

Peering closer, Cristy said, 'With no reference shots, we'd have no way of knowing, even if he was looking straight at camera.'

Connor turned to consult the whiteboard. 'According to Bridget, he wasn't in the country when it all "kicked off", so we need to find out when the police actually spoke to him. Was it at the time of the disappearance, or after Nicole was arrested? Five days between the two. No idea right now how the timing's relevant, but it might be useful to know.'

'Well, if it is him, or Lauren,' Jacks said, 'feels a bit weird that they're standing on the sidelines watching what's going on, doesn't it?'

'Just a bit,' Clove agreed. 'As Nicole's cousin, why wasn't she in the house with Nicole? Or at home with her parents? Or anywhere except in the crowd watching events like some sort of . . . I'm struggling to come up with the right word . . .'

'Perp?' Jacks suggested. 'That's what it's making me think of: perpetrators hanging about the scene of a crime? Maybe a bit extreme? Anyway, leave it with me. There might be a way of pulling up an ID for this bloke using some facial recognition software . . .'

'But you don't have anything to compare it with,' Connor reminded him.

'Apart from a million social media profiles,' Clove said helpfully.

'It's a start.' Jacks grinned. 'And AI's a lot faster than you think.'

Returning to her thirty-year-old self on the desktop, Cristy sat staring at the image for a while, feeling almost as though she was seeing a stranger. She hadn't known on the day they'd shot this item that she was pregnant – that had come later, eerily followed by the bouts of paranoia and confusion over who Hayley really was.

Even now, it unnerved her to think of that bizarre dysmorphia, how deeply she'd been affected by the twins' disappearance, the possibility that their own mother had somehow been involved in harming them. She remembered how desperate she'd been to believe Nicole's claims that she knew nothing about what had happened to the twins, how conflicted she, Cristy, had felt by the suggestion that someone had taken them while Nicole was burying a cat – a cat that had never been found but that could so easily have been responsible for the animal blood in the house.

Then and now, it was all so surreal, so oppressively macabre and disturbing it was making her head spin.

She closed her eyes.

'Even when Nicole was professing her innocence,' she said, apropos of nothing as far as the others were concerned, 'she never put forward a theory as to who *might* have taken the twins. I remember that striking me as odd at the time, even though it obviously could have been complete strangers. Also, if she really is guilty as she now claims, do the police accept that she acted alone? I mean, how credible is it that she could actually kill her own children and get rid of the bodies with no one's help? I'd say not credible at all, but there's been no mention of questioning anyone else since she confessed, has there?'

'These are questions for Honey,' Clove said, adding them to the clipboard.

'Could she have been covering for someone?' Cristy wondered aloud.

'For killing or at least stealing her children?' Clove cried, aghast. 'Why would she do that? Why would anyone?'

'No one would, if they were in their right minds,' Cristy replied pensively, 'but if you've been brainwashed, fallen prey to someone who knows exactly how to manipulate you, how to get what he wants out of you . . . It's how cults operate, don't forget. Coercive control, abuse dynamics, stripping away your ability to think rationally, making you dependent . . .'

'OK, I get that she could have been under some sort of influence back in 2005,' Connor said, 'possibly even during her trial, although it's a stretch given they were almost a year apart . . .'

'From your perspective, of course it's a stretch,' Cristy told him, 'because you've never been in that position. No one on the outside ever understands how anyone can fall under the spell of a cult leader, how ready or willing someone can be to do anything to prove their loyalty, their worth, their devotion.'

'I guess I can see how it might keep going for a year, maybe two,' Connor declared, 'but she's been inside for a couple of decades, she can't have been drinking the Kool-Aid all that time – at least not without some sort of contact, surely?'

'How do we know she didn't have any?' Cristy challenged. 'Maybe he visited her, or Lauren did, if Lauren's also in the cult, presuming there is, or was, one and it's looking possible, wouldn't you say?'

'And what, they suddenly stopped showing up a year ago?' Clove put in dubiously. 'At which point, Nicole comes to her senses and confesses?'

'Maybe they told her to,' Cristy suggested, not quite believing it herself, although they couldn't rule it out – not yet anyway. 'Whatever,' she said, 'we need to find out from Honey who went to see Nicole while she was in prison, and how often they were there.'

They all looked up as a small voice said, 'Knock! Knock!'

Iz was standing in the doorway.

'Hope I'm not interrupting,' she said awkwardly, lowering the hood of her bright-yellow raincoat. 'I know I'm early, but I didn't much want to hang around out there.'

Having totally forgotten she was coming, Cristy said, 'Come in, come in. We're just brainstorming a few things, so feel free to join in.'

'Tea or something stronger?' Clove offered, going to their well-stocked corner kitchen.

'I guess it is five o'clock,' Iz replied, shrugging off her coat and hanging it next to Cristy's, 'so if everyone else is up for a glass, I won't say no.'

'Open a bottle of the Picpoul,' Cristy instructed, and switching screens, she began a quick search of the latest news, just in case anything else had broken about Nicole Ivorson's release. Finding nothing new, she remarked to Connor, 'Do you think we should be concerned that Molly Terrance hasn't posted anything for over a week?'

He frowned, considering it. 'It's hard to believe she's given up that easily.'

'Christ, you don't think she's found Nicole and they're working on some sort of exclusive even as we sit here trying to piece it all together, do you? Even if they are, she still can't run it or according to the terms of her parole Nicole will be straight back to prison.'

'Would the Terrier care about that?' Connor asked.

Cristy shook her head. 'Of course not – Molly Terrance has never been much troubled by something as inconvenient as a conscience.'

'And would Honey Blackwell actually play us all off against one another like that?' Connor wondered dubiously.

Not seeing why Honey would, Cristy looked around as another visitor came into the room.

'Ah, Iz, you're here,' Meena declared, looking up from her phone as if she might have been tracking the publicist. 'Oh, I'll have one of those,' she told Clove, who was filling five glasses with wine, now six.

'Is Harry joining us?' Cristy asked, going to open another bottle.

'He's stuck at a meeting in Clifton,' Meena replied. 'He'll get here as soon as he can. So, Iz, have you shared the bad news yet?'

Cristy's eyes went to Iz.

Cheeks aglow, Iz said, 'It's not disastrous . . . It's just not what we'd hoped for at this stage.'

Before Cristy could ask, Meena said, 'One of the main sponsors is threatening to pull out thanks to your decision to delay the upload of a new series.'

Cristy stiffened.

Connor said, 'Aren't you running cover for us on that, Iz? I thought it was supposed to be your job.'

'Don't try to shift the blame to her,' Meena snapped. 'She works damned hard for you guys, and there's a lot of competition out there. If you can't deliver for the sponsors when you say you will, they're bound to look elsewhere.'

'We didn't actually give any dates,' Cristy reminded her tightly.

'Sorry,' Iz wailed. 'It's my fault. When I knew what you were planning for the series, I assumed you'd start uploading right away – you know, with backstory – so I said the start of February . . .'

Cristy's eyes flashed as she said, 'You should have checked first, and it's not your place to give out that sort of information . . .'

'She has other people to answer to, as well as you,' Meena cut in sharply.

Cristy felt ready to strike back hard, but she somehow managed to rein it in as Connor took over.

'They're not the only sponsors in town,' he pointed out, 'and they could also come back on board when we're ready to go. It's not as if their products are time-sensitive, any of them.'

'I wish it was as simple as that,' Iz told them, 'but these guys have already allocated their budgets for the next six months – they want placement now . . .'

'Then let's find others,' he interrupted. 'We can't be short of interest given our ratings—'

'Which actually fell off during the last series,' Iz reminded him, with an apologetic grimace. 'I'm sorry, but I've been instructed to tell you that unless you can begin the uploads in the next two weeks then the Sponsorship Liaison Group will consider withdrawing their support . . .'

'What the fuck!' Connor raged. 'They sent you here to deliver ultimatums as if we have absolutely no say in our own schedule! Well, you know what you can tell them—'

'Calm down,' Meena interrupted. 'It's not unsalvageable – not yet anyway. We just have to come up with something that's going to work, and if it means putting your current investigation on hold, then it's what you have to do.'

'Says you,' Connor spat, 'who actually has no say in anything—'

'Stop!' Cristy came in loudly. 'Before this meeting gets

completely out of hand, I'm ready to make an executive decision. As I see it, we actually need to start uploading something straightaway or we might never find Claude Major – sorry, Jacks, I still have faith in your tech skills, but even if you can get some background on him, it might not lead us to where he is today.'

'And you're certain he's key to taking this forward?' Jacks asked.

'As certain as I can be, at least until we get some answers from Nicole.'

'Does that mean you've found her?' Iz exclaimed. 'That's amazing . . .'

'We're communicating through her lawyer,' Cristy explained, 'and if Nicole confirms that Claude Major was involved in the twins' murder or disappearance, and she doesn't know where he is today, then we need to get the public involved.'

'But how do we do that without compromising Nicole?' Clove wanted to know.

'By doing what Iz herself has already suggested,' Cristy replied. 'We make the backstory multi-episodic for at least the next three weeks, adding commentary as we go, such as the rumours about a cult leader called Claude Major. We probably shouldn't refer to him as that, but the name doesn't have to have come from Nicole. In fact, it didn't, so no worries there. And we could get ourselves some useful feedback without putting her licence in jeopardy.'

Cristy allowed a moment for everyone to take this in, then continued.

'If we don't do it this way, then someone out there, from the media or another podcast, is going to get to the heart of the story first, and if that happens, it could seriously screw with our series. So the timing of our uploads really does matter, and thankfully it means we'll no longer be in conflict with our sponsors.'

After a stunned moment, Iz broke into a delighted grin, while Meena looked profoundly relieved, and the others – Connor most of all – were clearly already assessing what this sudden turnaround was actually going to mean for them over the next few days and weeks.

*

'And that's why,' Cristy told David later, at home by now, snuggled up on the sofa with him on video link, 'they are the world's best team. One hundred percent support, no dissent, total trust and full immersion in the story.'

Clearly amused, he said, 'So you've decided to turn Kinsley down?'

She grimaced as her heart jolted with unease. 'We're due to speak in the morning, and right now, I'm ashamed to admit that I still haven't actually made many notes, never mind reached a decision. Obviously, if I knew I could take Connor, Clove and Jacks with me, there wouldn't be a problem, but there would still be Harry and Meena to consider, and I'm no closer to feeling OK about leaving them in the lurch than I ever was. Although, Meena really pissed me off today, not sufficiently to start considering abandoning her as some sort of petty revenge, but it wasn't easy biting my tongue.'

Sipping his drink, David said, 'The hardest choices almost always end up with someone feeling disappointed or let down, and if you do take up Kinsley's offer, you're likely to be facing a lot of that. So maybe get used to it?'

She eyed him balefully. 'Is that your way of telling me to man up?'

He laughed. 'What I'm saying is what you already know: life is all about winning and losing, opportunities taken or lost, people who come and go.'

People who come and go. That was the hardest part.

Sighing, she reached for her drink as she said, 'I know I'm repeating myself, but Connor and I work so well together. We've had each other's back since I hired him as a young researcher straight out of uni. He gave up a perfectly good career in TV to come and start the podcast with me and he feels like family. So, if we want to talk about loyalty, let's look at his to me. I owe him big-time for taking the risk he did to help me get my life back on track after my marriage broke up, so the idea of bailing on him now is unthinkable – unconscionable. Sorry, I just keep going over and over it in my mind, and I know it's a sign of madness, doing the same thing and expecting a different outcome, but I seem to be on that wheel.'

'OK, let's look at it another way,' David said. 'How do you feel about leaving Bristol now that you know your brother's going to be in London?'

'Well, obviously having Tom nearby, or even sharing an apartment with me for a while, makes me want to pack up and leave right away. And if Aiden does end up getting into UCL . . . Oh God, let's stop – it's all so confusing. Just when I think, *yes*, it's what I'm going to do, I see Connor and the team without me in Bristol and I feel so wretched I'm right back at the beginning.'

'So what *are* you going to say to Kinsley?'

After finishing her drink, she said, 'I have a few things I'd like some clarity on, but that's for tomorrow. Let's drop it now and talk about you. We haven't spoken since you and Tom went sailing on Monday. How did it go?'

'Actually, we had to call it off in the end. The weather turned crazy right after you flew out. So we spent the day getting to know one another at home, and I have to say, I'm a fan.'

Laughing, she said, 'I'm sure the feeling was mutual. I'll let you know when I finally catch up with him. You know, I was thinking, if it works out with our diaries, we might join him and Serena somewhere for a few days while they're travelling Europe. Would you be up for that?'

'Sure. Is that Aiden I just heard shouting for his mother?'

Groaning, she said, 'He's just come back from rugby training, so he'll be stuck at the front door, filthy, wet and starving.'

David laughed. 'I'll let you go. Good luck with Kinsley in the morning; don't forget to let me know how it goes.'

CHAPTER SEVENTEEN

As it turned out, Paul Kinsley had to reschedule the call the next morning, so after putting together an email outlining everything she'd like to discuss when they did get to speak, Cristy headed to the office. The focus now was on structuring Nicole's backstory in a way to cover three half-hour episodes, the first launching next Tuesday. She'd already drafted some proposals on how the three would break down, and knew that Connor had too, so the rest of the morning would be spent creating a comprehensive outline for everyone to work from.

'Big news!' Clove announced as soon as Cristy walked in, unravelling her scarf (hand-knitted by Rosie) and peeling off her gloves. 'Well, potentially big,' Clove modified, apparently realizing she might have oversold it. 'Becky Rawlings has been in touch following the message I sent her last night. Here – I'll play you the voicemail and record it into the system at the same time, so we'll have it ready when we need it.'

Gesturing for her to go ahead, Cristy went to pour herself a coffee, while listening to the tired, unmistakably West Country drawl of Nicole's old friend from the Peck Lane flats.

BECKY: 'Hey, Becky Rawlings here. I got your message about this Claude guy. So, I checked with some of the other girls we were friends with back then, and it turns out the name rang a bell for a few of them. Actually, after we chatted about it, I realized it kind of did for me too.

'We were all agreed he was French, and he might have had a blue Ford Escort, because Kylie Clarke said she saw him picking Nicole up from number 42 or bringing her back quite a few times. She also remembers seeing him and some woman – not Nicole, not Lauren either – lifting the twins out of the back of the car once and carrying them down the street into the house. So, not stealing them, bringing them back from somewhere.

'Oh, and we all remembered how much Lauren idolized Nicole, really looked up to her, but none of us are in touch with her now, so afraid we can't help with where she might be.

'Um, I think that's it. If we come up with anything else, I'll call you back. Hope this is helpful. See ya.'

Cristy looked at Connor, who'd arrived in time to hear the message. 'Shame she didn't give us a surname for Claude,' she said, 'but at least it's further confirmation that someone of that name was on the scene back then.'

'And yet he's not appearing in any of the reports,' Connor commented. 'I'll take one of those,' he added, indicating the coffee as he made for his desk. 'I guess no news from Honey about the archived files?'

Clove shook her head. 'No court transcript yet, either,' she said, 'but Jacks has made some headway on the detectives who worked the case. We've got lots of names from the news reports, and apparently, he's narrowed it down to a workable list. He should be here any minute.'

'Great,' Cristy responded. 'Meanwhile, there's a lot to get through if we're going to drop the first episode on Tuesday. Your main task today, Clove, will be to collate media coverage from the time the twins were first reported missing. That means pre-arrest, pre-rumours even: just the alarm being raised and the search. Once that's sorted, you'll need to work on copyright permissions. Jacks, here you are.

Clove informs us that you might have something to share about the detectives involved in Nicole's case?'

'Good morning,' he responded brightly. 'Yes, I'd love a coffee, thanks, and by the time you've fixed it, I should have my computer ready to fire off darts of useful information.'

Amused, Cristy did the honours, and after turning on her own desktop while Connor did the same, she said, 'I guess you guys realize we're going to be working all weekend, so if any of you have plans to be elsewhere, now would be a good time to rearrange.'

'Already done,' Connor told her. 'We need to know if Iz has alerted the supersleuths, and if so, one of us – probably you, Clove – should put some time aside tomorrow to brief them.'

'OK, detectives!' Jack announced. 'After sifting through an amazing amount of shit, I can now cut straight to the chase. Our man – or woman I should say – is one Elizabeth Patten, ex-DC with Avon and Somerset circa 2005 to 2006. She was one of the arresting officers, and she gave evidence at the trial. She's retired from the force now, so freer to speak to us than if she was still with them. No guarantee she will, of course, but we'll find out when we get hold of her.'

'So where is she?' Cristy prompted.

'If my information is correct and up to date, she now lives in Cumbria, where she runs a local Leisure Centre . . .'

'I'm up for a trip to the Lake District,' Clove hurriedly put in. 'I've always wanted to go there.'

As Clove volunteered for all location assignments, near or far, Cristy simply said, 'Let's see how willing she is to share first. Go ahead and set up the contact, Jacks.'

'Will do. Just a quick update first on facial recognition for the bloke with the girl who could be Lauren in your old TV footage – turns out, not enough to work with. However, I've passed it on to my team in the outstanding Creative Computing department at the University of the West of England, and they're looking into it.'

'You need to listen to the message we received from Becky Rawlings,' Cristy told him. 'Clove, can you print out a shot of a blue Ford Escort from that time and put it on the whiteboard? No idea at this stage if it's going to be helpful, but let's have it all up there.'

'Actually, we need to start colour-coding the board,' Connor declared, getting to his feet. 'Red for the backstory, black for where we are with the investigation.'

By the time he'd finished reorganizing, Jacks was ready to connect to ex-DC Elizabeth Patten.

'OK, Clove, you should lead in gently with this,' Cristy instructed. 'If you manage to speak to her, simply say that we're doing a podcast about the case as it unfolded back in the mid-Noughties, nothing about the investigation we're conducting now.'

'I know the drill,' Clove reminded her, and as soon as Jacks had the number ringing, she sat forward, closer to the mic.

FEMALE VOICE: 'Hi, you've reached Lizzie Patten's mobile. Please leave a message and I'll get back to you when I can.'

CLOVE: 'Hi, Ms Patten, my name's Clover St Jean. I'm calling from the podcast *Hindsight.* Our presenters Cristy Ward and Connor Church would really appreciate having a chat with you about the Nicole Ivorson case, which I believe you worked while you were with Avon and Somerset Police.

'I'll text all our contact details to this number as soon as I ring off. Hope to hear from you soon. We're around all weekend – weekdays too, obviously. Thanks. Once again, my name is Clover St Jean.'

*

They heard nothing back from Elizabeth Patten either that day or the next two, as they continued to script, brief, view, edit and research ready for Tuesday. Meena brought in supplies both days and generally made herself useful, while Harry entertained himself with a deep dive into UK cults and Iz organized a video chat with the supersleuths for three o'clock on Sunday.

As soon as that particular briefing was over, Cristy and Connor drove to her flat to meet Honey Blackwell. It was still just about light when they got there, but the sky was low and grey, the air damp and unpleasantly warm for the time of year.

Almost as soon as Cristy had turned on the lights and they'd taken off their coats, the doorbell rang, announcing Honey's arrival.

'Thanks for meeting us here,' Cristy said, leading her through to the sitting-room-cum-kitchen. 'There's a lot going on at the studios today . . . You got my WhatsApp about us starting uploads on the backstory this Tuesday?'

'Yes, yes,' Honey assured her, looking around admiringly. 'I've always wondered what these places were like inside,' she said, 'and it turns out they're much bigger and lighter than I expected.'

'Even better when there's some sun,' Cristy said wryly.

'Actually, meeting here saved me unlocking the office and putting the heating on,' Honey said, settling comfortably at one end of a sofa. Noticing the recording equipment on the coffee table, she said worriedly, 'If you're planning to record this . . .'

'Only if you've got something we can use,' Cristy assured her. 'Otherwise, ignore it – it's just something we never go anywhere without.'

Seeming to accept that, Honey opened up her briefcase and pulled out a legal pad along with three sharpened pencils.

'Have you had anything back from the archives yet?' Cristy pressed, disappointed not to see some files.

'Some,' Honey replied. 'I'm afraid I can't hand anything over to you, but I can tell you that there's nothing so far about Claude Major or anyone of similar name.'

Frustrated, Cristy said, 'So are you saying he might *not* have been interviewed by the police?'

'I still have a way to go, so it's too early to be definitive. At the same time, we have to keep in mind that the CPS might not have handed everything over. It happens sometimes – actually more often than it should. Nevertheless, I'll keep looking.'

'Do you have any idea yet,' Cristy asked, 'when you're next seeing, or speaking to Nicole?'

'We don't have anything in the diary at the moment,' Honey confessed, 'but Maeve has asked me to call her on Tuesday or Wednesday. She's going to let me know what works best for her.'

'Do you know if there's anything in particular she wants to discuss?' Cristy queried.

'She probably wants an update on what you guys are doing – and I'll take the opportunity to ask if she'll speak to you directly.'

'OK, great.' Cristy grimaced as she considered what had to come next. 'I'm afraid I have a slightly awkward question for you before we go any further,' she said. 'We need to be certain that you – on behalf of Nicole – aren't in discussions with one of the major newspapers or TV stations to speak exclusively to them further down the line?'

Honey looked up from her notepad in surprise.

Cristy waited. Catching her off-guard like this wasn't kind; however, it was a pretty foolproof way of finding out if there was any double-play going on that they needed to know about.

Fortunately, Honey showed no signs of artifice or hedging or even embarrassment, only pique as she said, 'I'm sorry you felt the need to ask that. I'd have thought me being here would have put your minds at rest, but as it hasn't, let me assure you that neither I, nor anyone at my firm, is talking to anyone else about this case. As you know, any suggestion of press contact, or of trying to row back on the confession, could have disastrous results for Nicole.' She paused, eyes still flashing. 'I will admit, however, that we've been approached by one or two organizations with some startling sums.'

Accepting the rebuke as well deserved, Cristy said, 'Have you passed the offers on to Nicole?'

'I have to, but I can tell you that money is the least of her concerns. She's too relieved to be starting the journey towards freedom to have the process sabotaged now by getting involved with someone trying to buy her story. What matters to her, to all of us, is finding out what really happened to her twins.'

'Has she finally shared any theories on what might have?' Connor asked.

'Not yet, but I think she will once she's convinced you can be trusted.'

Wondering exactly what they were supposed to do to make that happen some time soon, Cristy said, 'That might be easier to achieve if we could meet with her in person. But OK, I understand why that can't happen. However, it would be good if Maeve or Nicole could tell us something about this Claude guy – such as, is his surname actually Major? What is his nationality, and do either of them know where he might be now?'

'And has he been visiting her in prison?' Connor added. 'If so, how often and how recently?'

Making a note, Honey said, 'Do you have a reason for thinking he might have been going to see her?'

'To be frank,' Cristy replied, 'we're wondering if he still has some kind of hold over her.'

Honey frowned. 'Are you thinking he could have influenced her recent confession?' she asked carefully.

'Anything's possible,' Cristy responded, 'but we won't know for certain until you've asked her, or until we find him. If he does have some way of triggering her . . . Well, let's take it a step at a time and find out first if they are still in touch.'

Honey returned to her notepad, only looking up again when Cristy said, 'Please don't take offence at this, but is it looking to you as though no one from Nicole's defence team – i.e. your firm – tried to track this Claude down either before or after the police spoke to him? Presuming they did, and OK, I get that we only have Bridget's word on that.'

'At the moment, the name isn't only missing from the CPS files,' Honey replied evenly. 'It's not showing up on ours either. That might change as more comes to light. Meanwhile, I'm not here to make excuses for anyone; they'll have to do that for themselves when – if – the time comes. What's striking me about it most, right now, is that it's taken you guys less than three weeks to get his name as a person of interest. So why *isn't* it all over the files? And what was the press doing at the time, given there doesn't seem to be any mention of him there either?'

'Bloody good question,' Connor retorted with a sideways look at Cristy, a reminder that she'd been there at the time.

'The only answer I can give,' Cristy replied, annoyed at being made to feel responsible for the omission, 'is that, as you well know, the press generally report what they get from the police, especially during early stages of an investigation. And let's not forget there was a big distraction with the 7/7 bombings coming so soon after. For obvious reasons, it sucked the air out of everything else, so it seems that some pretty basic stuff was either overlooked or simply not followed up on.'

Nodding her understanding, Honey said, 'OK, let's go over what you've found out about this guy so that I have an idea of what to look or listen out for next time I speak to Nicole. Actually, first, what's your current thinking on the whacko a few doors down who told you about satanic gatherings in the woods?'

'He's still written off as a fantasist,' Cristy told her. 'However, something might have triggered him, so it could be useful to find out what it might have been. Leaving him aside for now, Lauren's mother told us her daughter thought this Claude was something special. A bit different . . . Her exact words . . . ?'

Reading from his phone, Connor said, '"She thought the sun shone out of him, he could do no wrong, and everything about him was better than anything we could ever understand. He was special, different, someone to be looked up to."'

Cristy said, 'So we could say he was charismatic, charming, educated, persuasive, reassuring . . . essentially, all traits of a cult leader. Of course, there's no definitive proof that there was a cult, but something we know about the men who lead them is how secretive they can be – and frighteningly influential. So, until we can rule out the possibility of Claude being a master manipulator of some sort, he very much remains a person of interest.'

Honey said carefully, 'I guess you don't need me to tell you the other typical characteristics of cult leaders?'

Rising to it, Cristy said, 'They're generally viewed to be exploitative, paranoid, messianic . . . Depending on their levels of self-aggrandizement and their need to control, they can also be psychopathic in their tendencies as well as their actions.'

Honey's eyes remained fixed on hers.

They were all thinking of the twins.

'So, what are you going to do next about finding him?' Honey asked.

'Well, *you*,' Cristy replied, 'are going to talk to Maeve, and through her, Nicole, while we do what we do best – and that's put out a podcast.'

CHAPTER EIGHTEEN

On Tuesday evening, everyone was gathered at the office by six, excited for the first episode of a new series to drop. By now, Iz hadn't only brought the worried sponsors back on board: she'd worked miracles whipping up last-minute publicity for the launch, not only with regular multi-platform announcements but with mainstream promos and down-the-line interviews.

Now, they all sat quietly listening to the first twenty minutes of the episode as if it were a live broadcast show – a ritual they'd always adhered to, in spite of technology making everything available at all times. Jodi, Connor's wife, moved quietly about the room, topping up glasses with champagne while Jacks handed out nibbles. Matthew and Aiden were also there, not wanting to miss out on 'the big event', as Matthew had called it during his own news bulletin earlier. Even David had flown over to join in marking the occasion.

Playing now was the big scoop that had come their way only this morning, when Jacks had managed to get hold of Maeve's 999 call to report the twins missing. Though the audio wasn't always clear, he'd managed to clean up some of the more salient parts.

MAEVE: '. . . they're my grandchildren. Twins. We don't know where they are. My daughter came home, and they were—'

OPERATOR: 'How old are they, Mrs Ivorson?'

MAEVE: 'They'll be one next month. They're not even walking ... Please, you have to help us find them.'

OPERATOR: 'I've got your address. Someone will be right there. Can you tell me when you last saw them?'

MAEVE: 'I – me? Early this morning. I went to my sister's and got back ten minutes ago. We've looked everywhere. My daughter's in a terrible state—'

OPERATOR: 'Is she with you now?'

MAEVE: 'She's outside searching ...'

OPERATOR: 'When did she first realize the children weren't in the house?'

MAEVE: 'When she came back from the woods ...'

OPERATOR: 'Who was in the house while she was out?'

MAEVE: 'No one. Oh God! It's not like it sounds. Please, just get someone here ...'

OPERATOR: 'A police car should be arriving any minute—'

MAEVE: 'Oh! Yes, yes, I can see it ...'

As the call ended, Cristy was staring at the twins' images on the whiteboard, still listening as her recorded voice took over the narrative.

CRISTY: 'Here's an excerpt from one of my own reports filed that day:
"... Everyone is being kept well back from the house right now, but we can see a lot of activity going on around it: uniformed police and plain-clothed officers

standing about in groups; some are swarming down the hillside into the woods . . . A helicopter arrived a few minutes ago, and apparently a canine unit is being deployed. In talking to some of the neighbours, we've learned that Nicole was heard screaming around two o'clock this afternoon, but so far, we haven't found anyone who responded to her distress . . .'"

CONNOR: 'Nobody knew then exactly what had caused Nicole to scream – was it the twins' disappearance, as she claimed at the time, or could she, as was later claimed by the prosecution, have been faking a frenzy to cover up what she'd done to her children?'

CRISTY: 'Over the next few days, all kinds of rumours started to fly about what kind of mother Nicole was, how concerned some people were over her neglect, even possible abuse, while others wanted to talk about how well she'd seemed to settle into motherhood . . .

'There were a lot of conflicting opinions, and looking back, I can see that an element of hysteria was creeping into the situation even before Nicole was charged. I found it profoundly disturbing myself, even more so during Nicole's trial the following May, but we'll come on to that in a future episode.

'Staying with the events of July 2005, I'm still not sure exactly when the mutterings of cult worship started to take hold. I can only tell you that the whispers and gossip seemed, for a while, to take on a life of its own.'

CONNOR: 'No one was ever able to prove anything – indeed, we can't be sure at this stage to what extent the police even followed up on it. We're hoping to talk to someone who was involved in the investigation any day now, but for the time being, we'll leave you with this . . .'

CRISTY: 'The name Claude Major has been mentioned to us a few times recently by people who were close to Nicole back in 2005, including her aunt. Apparently, he was involved with both Nicole and her cousin, Lauren Hawkes, around the time the twins disappeared.

'We're still working on a more comprehensive description of him, but his name suggests he's probably French, and we believe he drove a blue Ford Escort back then. He's thought to have been connected to Bristol University, most likely as a student, maybe as a member of staff, and we believe he lived in Clifton or Redland. He was understood to be part of a group of friends also living in the area.

'So, if you are Claude Major, or someone who knew him then or knows him now, we'd love to hear from you.'

CONNOR: 'Thanks for listening . . .'

As the sign-off continued, with various contact details and thanks to the sponsors, Connor killed the sound and everyone broke into a round of applause.

'Long live *Hindsight* and all who sail in her,' Iz exclaimed tipsily.

The others raised their glasses, and as Cristy caught David's eye, she knew he was thinking about her plan to jump ship in the not-too-distant future. It was for another time, definitely not now, when the mere idea of it was making her feel even worse than she had during several sleepless hours last night.

'Am I allowed to ask this?' Meena said awkwardly. 'Would it have been better to wait and hear what Nicole might have to say about this Claude person before putting his name out there?'

Trying not to be irked by the implied criticism, Cristy said, 'We had the discussion and decided that a) we don't know how long it might take for Nicole to give us an answer; b) can she be relied on to tell the truth about him if he has managed to brainwash her . . .'

'After all these years?' Meena broke in incredulously. 'Really?'

'And c),' Cristy persisted, 'it was a great way to end episode one by getting the audience involved.'

'And if he turns out not to exist?' Meena queried.

Taking over, Connor said, 'Not sure why you're asking that when Nicole's aunt obviously didn't conjure him out of thin air and her friends remember him. As Cristy said, the important thing right now is to build intrigue—'

'And the murder of eleven-month-old twins at the hand of their own mother doesn't do that on its own?'

Cristy swallowed more irritation. 'It's a compelling story, Meena, but an old one with no new angles – yet. Apart from the confession, of course, but that's been all over the news lately. Reminding everyone about the cult rumours of 2005 will almost certainly reignite interest in the original case.'

Harry said, 'So you have no issues with leading people up the garden path? I mean, given you have no evidence of a cult? Not a criticism,' he hastily added, when Connor looked about to cut up rough, 'just a question.'

'If you can show me an investigation that doesn't get caught up in false leads at times,' Cristy responded, not quite through her teeth, 'then I'll show you one that isn't doing a good job.'

'And we do know,' Clove added supportively, 'that even Nicole's defence team might not have dug in as deeply as they should have before the trial, although Honey Blackwell's trying to make up for that now.'

'Well, I for one,' Iz declared happily, 'am completely on board for this series, as is everyone on my side of things. In fact, speaking on their behalf, Cristy, Connor and team, we have no problem trusting your judgement on how best to unfold the story.' She looked puzzled for a moment. 'Did that make sense?' she asked Jodi.

'We got it,' Jodi told her reassuringly. 'And I'm with Iz,' she added, raising her glass. 'Let the guys who know what they're doing get on and do it.'

Meena bristled, and Harry's colour deepened.

Aiden groaned. 'I'm starving. When are we going to eat?'

Loving her teenage son for his typical, timely interruption, Cristy said, 'We have a booking at the Ritorno Lounge across the water, but it's too late to take the ferry, so we either drive or walk.'

As everyone began peeling off into various vehicles or heading down to the harbourside, Cristy hooked an arm through David's, setting their pace towards Prince Street Bridge.

Glad to be alone with him she said, 'It's at times like that I want to throttle Harry and Meena. First, they push us into starting the series early, then they criticize the way we're handling it.'

Squeezing her arm against him, David said, 'You wouldn't respect them if they didn't express their views, and by the sound of it, they touched a nerve.'

'Don't you start,' she grumbled. 'OK, the cult thing might not end up going anywhere, but frankly, both Connor and I have a hunch it will, at least on some level, and right now, it'll be doing its job in sparking interest.'

Accepting that, he said, 'So, have you rescheduled your call with Kinsley yet?'

She sighed as her heart clenched with unease. 'Apparently he's back from the States on Friday, so it'll probably be sometime next week. I keep thanking God he's not rushing me on this – I guess if he were, I'd cut and run.'

'The man's not where he is today without knowing how to play the long game.'

Knowing that to be true, she dug out her phone as it buzzed. Text from Hayley:

Brilliant start, Mum. Loved hearing thirty-year-old you. So cool. Is there really a sinister cult behind it all? We're all dying to find out. H xxx

PS Really sad about the twins, maybe focus on them a bit more?

CHAPTER NINETEEN

'She makes a good point,' Cristy declared the next morning, as the team gathered with their hangovers, large mugs of coffee and some delicious pastries that Cristy had picked up on the way in. David had left on an early train to London, with a wry reminder that it might be easier on their relationship if she were to move to the capital, given how often he had to be there himself. Something else to throw into the decision making-mix – but right now, she was more focused on Hayley's critique that they weren't paying enough attention to the twins.

'The problem is,' she continued, 'with them being so young when they disappeared, there's not much we can say about them apart from the fact that they were tiny human beings totally dependent on their mother and vulnerable to just about everything the world could throw their way.'

'Such as being used in some grotesque sort of ritual,' Clove put in, with a grimace of distaste. 'Or maybe they were handed over to some psychotic visionary, if that's who Claude Major is, in order to . . . what . . . ? What would he have done with them?'

'Instead of speculating about that,' Cristy said, 'we should focus on trying to get some less salacious detail about them from Maeve or Nicole, even if it's matching dimples in their cheeks, making one another laugh or cry, some sort of bond between them, the way there often is with twins.' She turned to Jacks. 'We wouldn't be able to use it now, but if by some miracle we discover they might not have died back in 2005, would you and your UWE guys be able to run some facial enhancement to give us an idea of how they might look today?'

'No probs,' he responded, calling up the babies' images on his screen.

'Just make sure no one else gets hold of them,' Connor cautioned. 'It could backfire on us horribly if it turns out they really are dead.' To Cristy, he said, 'No news from Honey Blackwell yet today.'

'Give her a chance,' Cristy responded, checking the time. 'She was due in court first thing, so we're not likely to hear anything from her until later. I guess it's also too early for feedback from the supersleuths?' she asked Clove.

'A brief initial report,' Clove said, bringing it to her screen. 'The usual nutters haven't wasted any time – obvs already discounted. An anonymous bloke claimed that Claude Major is John Major's illegitimate son currently transitioning. They obviously put that in for its amusement factor. Apparently, someone saw Lauren Hawkes in Strasbourg last week pushing two babies in a pram. I guess this person hadn't worked out that the twins would be twenty-one by now, so most likely walking, although it does bring us back to a question we haven't yet explored: was Lauren involved in the twins' disappearance?'

'You mean working together with Nicole and/or Claude Major?' Cristy said, trying to get a sense of how she felt about that. 'It's a definite possibility, although we know Lauren was questioned at the time, and clearly nothing came of it.'

'Weird that Lauren ran off three years after Nicole was sent down,' Clove mused. 'I know her mother said she was depressed, took the whole thing really hard, but she also said Lauren was in touch with Claude Major during that time. What about Nicole? Was she in touch with her too?'

'Shit!' Connor muttered under his breath.

Cristy turned to him.

'You're not going to want to see this,' he told her, 'but you probably better had.'

He sent her the link and as Cristy read Molly Terrance's online article aloud, she felt her insides tightening with outrage and fury.

> Were we all glued to our tablets and smartphones last night in high anticipation of Cristy and Connor's first episode of a new Hindsight series? I'm sure many of you had better things to do, but yours truly decided to bite the bullet and dutifully downloaded on your behalf. And what a lark it turned out to be. All that self-adulation on Cristy's part, using her own reports from back in the day to tell the story of Nicole Ivorson and her baby twins, when others were far more informed than she ever showed herself to be.
>
> I know, because I was there, and I can tell you that Hindsight's laughable attempt to whip you up into a lather of horror concerning cults and missing cousins and mysterious Frenchmen driving blue cars isn't only nonsense – it's highly irresponsible. I expected more from a couple of journalists who actually have a pretty decent track record, but it seems on this occasion, they've decided to compromise their own standards and reputations by spinning baseless rumour into purported fact and trying to haul the rest of us onto their sensationalist bandwagon with an invitation to take part in a search that will inevitably lead nowhere. I, for one, will be sitting this series out.

'Bitch!' Clove spat disgustedly. 'It'll be because we didn't use any of her sorry-ass material from back in the day.'

'Also because we've stolen a march on her by launching

the series now,' Jacks put in. 'She hasn't run anything since she broke the non-starter "leads to the bodies", so it's my guess she's been working on a massive spread of what happened back then, because it's all she has.'

Still fuming, Cristy said, 'We just have to hope that Nicole is as committed to maintaining her freedom as we're told she is, because obviously any interaction with the Terrier stands zero chance of ending well for her.'

'This piece has had a ton of views already,' Clove grumbled, checking the screen.

'Everything does on that website,' Connor reminded her. 'But come on, guys – this is hardly career-ending. Everyone knows what a lame-ass liar she is, especially those of us in the business. I wouldn't be a bit surprised if this provokes a serious backlash of high praise from other sources, given how unpopular she is. So, ratings-wise at least, she could end up doing us a favour.'

'I don't believe it!' Cristy exclaimed in shock as her phone rang. 'She's actually bloody calling me.'

'Cut her off,' Clove instructed. 'Why the hell would you want to speak to her?'

Cristy almost hit decline, until, realizing it was a video call, she decided to hell with it, and clicked on.

Moments later, the detestable Molly Terrance with her luxuriant cascades of mousey-brown hair, ludicrous lash-extensions and ever-so-slightly buck teeth was filling all their screens. 'Cristy!' she cried cheerily, as if they were old friends reuniting after a lengthy time apart. 'How wonderful to see you, and you're looking terrific as always.'

Since she was hungover, un-made-up, and her hair was scrunched into a ponytail, Cristy almost gagged on the shameless obsequiousness. 'Hello, Molly,' she said coolly, 'what can I do for you?'

'Oh dear.' Molly grimaced playfully. 'Methinks you've already seen my piece. Sorry, didn't mean to offend, but you know how it is: us girls are dependent on clicks and shares these days, and telling it like it is doesn't always work out so well. I'm sure you'll find your pod last night will prove my point. Going with a rehash of what everyone already knows will earn you more yawns than likes. You have to get the punters worked up somehow, and facts are so yesterday, aren't they? I guess that's why you fixed on the cult. I don't blame you, but we know it isn't going anywhere, don't we?'

Biting out the words, Cristy said, 'Still waiting for why you're ringing.'

Terrance smiled, showing her white buck teeth. 'Always straight to the point – that's what I love about you. Well, I was going to ask if you'd like to meet for a coffee, but I'm getting the impression you might not be up for it.'

Appalled, Cristy said, 'You're in Bristol?'

'I could be if you wanted to meet.'

'And why would I want to do that?'

Tilting her head, the Terrier said, 'Maybe you'd like to discuss how we can go forward together on this story?'

Cristy could only conclude she'd lost her mind.

'Think about it,' Terrance said, swiping her copious locks over one shoulder. 'A collaboration could generate more coverage, more prestige *and results* than either of us might otherwise manage.'

'Prestige?' Cristy repeated incredulously. 'You are joking, of course.'

'Not at all, and you really should try to get over your prejudice where tabloids are concerned – it's not useful. Think about *The Sunday Times* and *Channel 4 News*; *BBC Panorama* and the *Observer* . . .'

'Neither of which are tabloids . . .'

'But they are examples of successful collaborations. You could break new ground for a podcast by linking up with a major newspaper. New media merges with mainstream to deliver high quality and in-depth reporting to the masses.'

Cristy almost laughed. 'And exactly how does that work with facts being so yesterday?' she wanted to know.

Apparently unfazed, Terrance said, 'There are many ways to approach a story, as we both know only too well . . .'

'Ours is not to make things up or disregard the truth if it doesn't fit the preferred narrative, and why the hell you think we'd work with you after what you ran this morning . . .'

'Clicks and shares.' Terrance's tone was condescending to the extreme.

'For God's sake, do you even care about your own credibility?' Cristy cried. 'If you moved forward with *Hindsight* now, after the way you trashed us . . .'

'People have short memories. All they want to know about are the gory details, and if getting to those details means taking a bullhorn to the whisper of a sinister cult – as you have already – they'll leap on board, no matter who's running the show. Hell, half of them – no, most – don't even know our names.'

'This conversation's over,' Cristy told her abruptly. 'We're really not interested in collaborating with anyone – I could say least of all you, but that would be rude . . .'

'It would, but I deserve it given what I said about you in my piece. Please just give it some thought. I know you wouldn't want to let anyone down.'

Cristy hesitated, sensing a kind of undertone to those last words.

Terrance's eyebrows rose. 'Our mutual friend, Vikram Rathour, asked me to send his best when I spoke to you. He's very keen on the idea of us working together.'

And a beat later, she'd gone.

CHAPTER TWENTY

There was a moment of bemused silence as Cristy inwardly raged at Terrance and struggled for a way to handle this.

Connor said, 'I'm guessing she wasn't talking about the cricketer, Vikram Rathour?'

Cristy briefly shook her head.

Clearly confused, and concerned, he said, 'I didn't know you knew the other one.'

'Who is he?' Clove and Jacks asked in unison.

'He's an American – well Indian by birth actually,' Connor told them when Cristy didn't answer. 'He's head of one of the world's biggest media companies.' He was still looking at Cristy, clearly waiting for her to explain. 'What's going on?' he said warily. 'Why did she bring him up at the end like that?'

Needing more time to think before addressing this, Cristy said, 'You know what a name-dropper she is . . .'

'But she said he was a mutual friend.'

Realizing she was on the brink of being too defensive Cristy measured her tone as she said, 'We met once, by chance. I doubt he even remembers my name. So God knows why she mentioned him . . . I guess to let us know that she has friends in high places. Well, big deal – let her go have coffee with them. We don't need her on this, and we certainly don't *want* her, so let's look at what we actually learned from her today, which is that she hasn't ruled out the possibility of a cult either.'

'I was thinking exactly that,' Clove told her.

Connor was still staring at Cristy.

Throwing out her hands, Cristy cried, 'Christ, Con, you know how devious she is. Lobbing grenades is what she does – yet another reason why she's coming nowhere near us. She'll end up finding a way to expose the story, whatever it turns out to be, and take all the credit while leaving us high and dry.'

'That's definitely her MO,' Jacks asserted.

'Con, please stop looking at me like that,' Cristy implored. 'Or are you thinking we should accept the offer and bring her in? Is that—?'

'No, of course not,' he replied. 'I'm just . . .' He shrugged, seeming unsure of what he was thinking.

After a beat, Clove said, 'Well, I guess we should brace for more bad press now we've knocked her back. She's not going to like it, but do you know what I say? Fuck her. We're already moving ahead with this, and for us, it's not about clicks and shares, FFS! It's about those two little babies, their mother and the *truth*, no matter how alien a concept that might be to the Terrier, or how *yesterday* it is in her sorry little world.'

Finally turning back to his computer, Connor said, 'You're right, Clove. For us, it's about integrity and honesty, and as long as we know we can count on one another for that, we're not going to go far wrong.'

*

'Ouch,' David muttered, when Cristy repeated the remark to him later during a video call. 'Did he say anything after that?'

Sighing, she said, 'No. The subject was dropped, and we got on with the day more or less as if nothing had happened. But he's not stupid – he sensed something was going on, and

I'm sure he saw Paul Kinsley's name on my phone the other day.'

David's concern showed. 'But would he have any reason to connect Kinsley to Rathour?' he asked. 'This is a new venture for them, still very much under wraps, today's call notwithstanding, so why would Connor think you're holding something back from him?'

Hating herself, she said, 'Maybe because I *am*, and we're actually pretty good at reading one another. Anyway, he was quiet for the rest of the day, and when he left, he told me that if I did want to rethink the Terrier coming on board, he'd be up for discussing it.'

David's eyes widened. 'Seriously? But of course you're not?'

'Hell no! Not in a million years. What concerns me though is that Rathour seems to be putting her forward as someone he wants involved in RK Media.' That couldn't be true, it just couldn't.

'In what capacity?'

'I've no way of knowing without talking to Kinsley. Obviously, I've left messages, but he hasn't got back to me yet.'

'OK. So I guess it's a deal breaker for you if they are talking to her?'

She was about to answer but stopped and let her eyes slip from his face out to the dark night, where a crescent moon was shining so brightly it was lighting up her small garden. 'It ought to be,' she said in the end, 'but if I do turn it down, she'll be right there, waiting, and the thought of her taking an opportunity that should have been mine . . .' She looked at him again. 'I haven't felt this competitive in a long time,' she admitted, 'and I'm not sure how much I like it.'

'When it used to be something you thrived on?'

'How do you know that?'

'Wild guess.'

She smiled. 'I wouldn't be surprised if Kinsley is actually behind this,' she said. 'He's a great mentor, no doubt about that, and a fantastic ally if you need one, but he can be a manipulative bastard when he sets his mind to it, and he doesn't like to lose.'

David's eyebrows arched with interest. 'If you're right, then perhaps this is a timely reminder of who you're going to be dealing with?'

She nodded slowly. Being Kinsley's number-one choice for a high-profile media position was beyond ego-boosting – but if she was being controlled, played like a pawn in one of his carefully calculated power games . . . that didn't feel good at all.

'I'm going to have to ring off,' David told her. 'Mum's about to serve supper, and Rosie wants me to run lines with her for the new play she's in.'

Smiling, Cristy said, 'What time did you get home?'

'Just after six. I took the four o'clock plane, but I had a meeting in St Peter Port . . . Tell me before you go, has Claude Major been in touch since last night's drop, or anyone to give you a lead?'

'Nothing credible.' She sighed. 'But if he's in France, which is highly possible, or anywhere else in the world, actually, it could take some time to get to him – or someone who's keen to talk about him. Some good news, though: we finally got a call back from Elizabeth Patten, the ex-DC who worked the case? She's not available until next week, apparently, but she'll be happy to talk to us on Tuesday if we email her some times that work for us. Actually, I'm thinking of sending Clove up to Windermere rather than do it by video link. She's always keen to travel, and it might be good for her to start taking on more of the main interviews.'

'Ready for when you're no longer around? Unless you take her with you, of course.'

Her insides lurched at the mere suggestion of such treachery and how it would affect Connor.

After ringing off, she went to run herself a bath and sat on the side for a while, staring absently into the cascading water. She hated feeling this way, so torn and disloyal and wretched about keeping things from Connor, while knowing that she might be about to shatter his world. He deserved so much better, especially from her.

As she turned off the taps and went through to the bedroom to start undressing, she heard the tell-tale warble of a WhatsApp message dropping into her phone in the sitting room. It was probably Aiden confirming that he was at his father's tonight or Hayley sharing some news that could easily wait. She got no further than stripping off her jumper before the phone began to ring.

When she went to retrieve it, she saw it was Connor and felt a horrible jolt of unease. Had he decided to challenge her away from the office? He'd almost certainly have discussed things with Jodi by now, and between them, they'd no doubt agreed that the air must be cleared. She was tempted to let the call go to voicemail, but detesting herself for such cowardice, she clicked on.

'Hey, have you seen Honey's WhatsApp?' he asked right away.

'No. Why?' She was already scrolling to find it. 'Oh shit,' she murmured when she read it. 'Oh my God. Wow! I definitely didn't see this coming.'

'Me neither,' he admitted. 'So, what do we do?'

'We discuss it in the morning – hopefully with Honey. I'll message her now to find out if she's free.'

*

They met Honey the next morning in a small conference room adjacent to an empty office at the Hargreaves Blackwell premises. As it was still only eight o'clock, no one else was around, so no need to close the door or to speak quietly – and yet the door was closed, and their voices were low.

'Why would she take the risk?' Cristy was asking worriedly. 'Obviously we want to talk to her, but she knows what it could mean . . .'

'I haven't spoken to her yet,' Honey said. 'I only got the message from Maeve last night that Nicole wants to speak to you in person. I should say right here that I will be strongly advising against it. I've already told Maeve as much, so by the time I'm in touch with them again, it's possible Nicole will have changed her mind.'

Knowing how disappointed they'd be if she had – although they'd understand of course – Cristy said, 'Do you know *why* she's suddenly made this decision? Was it something we said in the podcast?'

'Possibly. I mean, it seems likely, given the timing, but I've no idea what it was.'

'I'm guessing it was the mention of Claude Major,' Connor stated. 'Maybe she's ready to spill the beans on him?'

Honey frowned as she said, 'I've no idea why she'd do that with you, now, and not with me before her parole hearings, but we are where we are. Maybe this is a good time to mention that if she remains determined to go through with this, then you – and I – will need to do everything we can to make sure the authorities know nothing about it. This will mean, of course, no use of anything she tells you, on or off the record.'

'Goes without saying,' Connor assured her, 'but naturally, if she gives us information to act on, we'll be doing so, obviously without naming our source.'

'And no direct quotes or allusions that could be linked to her,' Honey added. She looked up as the old-fashioned wall clock behind her chimed the half hour. 'I'm afraid I have to go – I'm due in Taunton at ten – but I'll be in touch as soon as I've spoken to Maeve.'

'When do you think that'll be?' Cristy asked as they stood up to leave.

'I'll try her tonight when I get home.'

'One quick last question,' Connor said, 'just so we're prepared: how far away are they?'

'Not very,' Honey replied, putting on her coat. 'I'll take you there myself when – *if* – I hear that Nicole still wants to go ahead.'

CHAPTER TWENTY-ONE

The following Monday, the second episode was finally close to being ready for the next day's upload, the team having spent the entire weekend prepping it. This time, the focus would be on Nicole's arrest and the storm of horror and outrage that had followed, through to when she'd been charged with her children's murder. They'd decided to make no further mention of Claude Major until after they'd spoken to Nicole – should they ever get to speak to her. There was still no word from Honey on that.

'I'd be more confident of it happening,' Cristy said, sighing, as the day drew to a close, 'if Honey was actually on our side, but I get that her priority is to protect her client, not to give us an exclusive.'

Looking up from his computer, Jacks said, 'Are we definitely not running anything about the cult? Only, I've got a perfect slot for one of the anonymous calls, if we want to use it?'

'Which one did we single out in the end?' Cristy asked, as Clove swore under her breath at something on her screen. 'Everything OK?' Cristy asked, going to fetch them all an end-of-day beer.

'Elizabeth Patten's just pushed me to Wednesday,' Clove explained. 'I guess it's no big deal – we were never going to have her input in time for tomorrow anyway.'

'And that's presuming she has something to say that can

be included at this stage,' Cristy pointed out. 'Remember, we can't use anything that might suggest we doubt the confession until such time as we get the go-ahead from Nicole, and that obviously won't be any time soon – in fact, it could be never, if it turns out she actually did kill her children.'

'OK,' Jacks said, 'are you ready to hear from Claude Major himself – keeping in mind that this guy is probably as nutty as all the others. On the other hand, he *does* have a foreign accent.'

'Go,' Cristy said, and after passing around the beers she returned to her chair.

> ANONYMOUS CALLER: 'Hello, **Hindsight** team. I've heard that you might be looking for me. My name is Claude Mailer, not Major, and I knew Nicole Ivorson back in 2005. We became very good friends a year or so before she murdered her children. Needless to say, I had no idea she was going to do that or why she would. I was as shocked and upset as everyone else. There was much talk following her arrest that she had fallen under the influence of some very bad people. If that is true, I do not count myself amongst them. I am not someone to cause harm to anyone...'

Pausing the playback, Jacks said, 'This is where he goes off on a little rant about his inherent goodness and belief in karma, then he gives details of how we can contact him. As of ten minutes ago, he's still not picking up. The number is a French mobile, if I haven't already told you that.'

'This doesn't add or prove anything,' Connor declared, 'so I say we save it until we can at least get hold of the bloke.'

'I agree,' Cristy said. Her phone rang, and seeing it was Paul Kinsley, she declined and sent a quick text to let him know she'd call in ten minutes. 'I need to go,' she announced, starting to pack up. 'I guess no word yet from Honey?' she asked Connor.

'No, but time to start drafting some questions just in case it all goes ahead with Nicole,' he suggested.

'I'll work on it as soon as I get home,' she promised.

After she'd left, she waited until she'd driven out of the car park before connecting to Kinsley via the handsfree. 'Did you get my email about Molly Terrance?' she asked, as soon as the niceties were out of the way.

'I did.' His tone was impossible to gauge, although it suggested amusement. 'I take it, from what you said, that you wouldn't consider some kind of partnership with her?'

'I would not,' she confirmed. 'Anyway, I thought you wanted Andee Lawrence?'

'She is indeed the first choice. Vikram's simply exploring possibilities should Andee not be interested. He has some sort of connection to Terrance's uncle, I believe – that's how her name came up. Of course, if you have any suggestions yourself for an alternative—'

Anyone but Terrance, she inwardly seethed. 'You know I want Connor Church—'

'But you don't know if he'll join you, and besides, we don't consider him the right fit for the flagship pod we're hoping that you and Andee will create.'

'That's new. I thought you wanted *Hindsight.*'

'Nothing's set in stone, just putting it out there. Two strong female leads is what we're after, with you in charge, as discussed, and you get to decide on any other podcasts you want to bring into play. *Hindsight* of course can be one of them, with Connor at the helm if you so wish. It's just hard for me to see how you'd find the time to work with him if he remains in Bristol and you're in London or New York – or who knows where else in the world you might be as you build your team and delve into your own investigations.'

Avoiding the issue of shape-shifting that was clearly going on, she said, 'Before we go any further, let me be clear about Molly Terrance. She isn't someone I'd ever want on my team in any capacity. She's smug, spiteful, mendacious and has absolutely no regard for the truth on any level, unless it suits her. She said as much when we spoke last week. So, if Vikram Rathour really is rooting for her, you need to count me out, because I won't have my name or my reputation associated with hers.'

Kinsley laughed. 'There's my girl – as feisty as ever, and boy, have I missed you . . .'

'Cut the flannel – I want your reassurance, Paul.'

'OK. Leave it with me. I'll get back to you the minute I can tell you what you want to hear.'

As soon as she was in the door, Cristy tore off her coat, kicked off her boots and was about to call David to report on Kinsley's maddening response when a hot flush bloomed out of nowhere, just as Connor rang.

'I'm guessing you were driving so haven't picked up Honey's WhatsApp?' he said when she answered. 'We're on! With Nicole. Wednesday at four. Honey's going to drive.'

Cristy's surprise turned to irony as she struggled to strip off. 'Has she asked us to wear blindfolds?' she asked.

He laughed. 'She didn't mention it, but don't let's rule it out.'

CHAPTER TWENTY-TWO

No blindfolds. No recording either, as Honey drove them out of Bristol on Wednesday afternoon, heading for an unknown destination that appeared to be west of the city and north of the M48. Connor was in the front passenger seat, Cristy in the rear, exchanging messages with a behavioural psychologist who'd finally got back to her for a paid consultation on the potential issues someone like Nicole Ivorson might be dealing with now. This 'expert in her field' could be good for the pod at a later stage; today, she was advising on traits or cognitive patterns to look out for, and how long-lasting or damaging or deceptive they might be. As Cristy couldn't mention anything about the crime, or the twins, without making it obvious who the subject was, the information being received was at best conflicting, at worst misleading, although it could come into its own once they were face to face with Nicole.

Sensing they'd left an urban area, she looked up to discover they were travelling along a country lane surrounded by fallow fields and sorry-looking hedgerows, and guessed they were probably a couple of miles inland from the River Severn. It was a dank, mizzly February day with the cloud so low and thick there was no earthly chance of the sun breaking through, only the potential of more, heavier rain on the horizon and an upsweep of the bitter southwesterlies. It was so miserable it was enough to make even the birds weep, as her mother used to say.

After a while, Honey slowed the car in what seemed to be the middle of nowhere and turned in through a wide-open five-barred gate. There was no signage to speak of and no particular road markers either, as far as Cristy could tell.

For the next minute or so, they bumped awkwardly and slowly along a potholed track, running like a vein through the heart of a forest of soaring pines, until, eventually, they turned off the trail and came to a stop outside a long, low red-brick building. It had probably once been a stable block, but with its ornate French doors, twin chimney pots and small, surrounding garden, it was now clearly a residence.

'Maeve's brother, Harold, owns everything hereabouts,' Honey told them. 'His house – one of his houses – is further along the trail. You can't see it from here, but it's an old manor.'

'So what does Harold do in this out-of-the-way nirvana?' Connor asked, taking it all in.

Climbing out of the car, Honey said, 'He usually lets the whole place for corporate or private events. He actually lives opposite his car dealership over on the A38: Strummonds – I don't know if you've heard of it. He took his wife's name when they got married. They're away on a Caribbean cruise at the moment, so no chance of running into them, and they've cancelled the rest of their bookings so that Nicole can be here in peace.'

Once they were all gathered next to the car, Cristy said, 'So, Nicole has a concerned uncle keeping her safe from the public eye? Can we assume he doesn't believe in her confession either?'

'It's not a conversation I've had with him,' Honey replied, 'but given where we are, I'd say there's a good chance you're right. His only condition to them staying here is that he isn't dragged into any unwanted publicity, so please keep that in mind as we go forward. Maybe leave it there,' she said to Connor as he opened the boot to take out the recording equipment.

As he complied he nodded for Cristy to look behind her. She turned to see an older woman, wearing an Aran knit sweater and baggy blue jeans, coming out of a set of French doors to greet them. In spite of her dignified bearing, her face was drawn with weariness, and her short, auburn hair seemed unsure of its style. Her deep-brown eyes were shadowed and sad.

'Maeve,' Cristy said, moving forward to take her hand. 'I don't expect you remember me—'

'I do, actually,' Maeve interrupted. 'You were one of the better ones, back when most in your profession were calling my daughter a monster fit to be hanged. It's the reason we've agreed to see you today – plus Honey here has convinced us you really do want to help. You must be Connor,' she said, turning to him and holding out her hand again. 'You're younger than I expected, but no harm in that, as long as you can be trusted.'

'He can,' Honey assured her. 'Shall we go inside? It's starting to rain.'

Maeve turned to lead the way, standing aside at the door to show them into a cosy kitchen with a plentiful number of oak cabinets, a double-front Aga and black stone worktops. A kettle was boiling, and some mugs were laid out on a tray, but Maeve seemed not to notice as she pushed open a door at the far end.

'She's through here,' she said, indicating for them to follow.

As they filed into a long, narrow hallway with half a dozen doors along one side and a large expanse of empty wall on the other, Cristy caught the pleasing scent of a diffuser blending with the warmth.

Stopping at the first door, Maeve said quietly. 'She's . . . Well, you'll see for yourself how she is. Just bear with her when you need to, and try not to scare her.'

Wondering what to make of that, Cristy glanced at Connor. Maeve pushed open the door, and moments later, they were in a small sitting room with an overstuffed corduroy sofa up against the back wall, an armchair angled inwards from the French doors and a beanbag slumped next to a freestanding TV. In the middle of the room, a square coffee table was laden with orange peel and sweet wrappers – beside it, seated on the floor with her back propped against the sofa, arms wrapped around her knees, was a small woman with her face turned away.

'Hi Nicole,' Honey said softly.

Nicole's head came around slowly, and Cristy felt a beat of shock hit her heart. Of course she was older now and had been through a lot, so Cristy hadn't expected to see the vibrant nineteen-year-old whose image was on the office whiteboard. Nevertheless, she was struggling to find a resemblance between the two versions of the same woman. Gone was the lustrous mane of golden-red hair, the glowing peachy complexion and dazzling blue eyes. This tragic, almost lifeless creature was pale, skeletal and hollow-eyed. And yet somehow, in some indefinable way, she retained a quality that held the eye.

'How are you?' Honey asked.

Nicole's eyes moved to Cristy. Before Honey could make the introduction, she said, 'It's good of you to come.' Her voice was scratchy and faint, as though she hadn't spoken in a while.

'They want to help you,' Honey reminded her, 'so you needn't be afraid to speak freely. Everything you say will be in confidence.'

Nicole's only response was to bite her lips and wince as she caught one of the sores.

'We appreciate your trust, Nicole,' Cristy told her, 'and to re-emphasize what Honey just said, we're completely on your side.'

Were they? Really? How could she mean that when they didn't know anything for certain yet? The artifice of a reporter aiming for an exclusive – in its way, it made her no better than the Terrier.

Nicole was looking at Connor now, her wary eyes taking him in as though trying to work him out.

'This is Connor,' Honey told her. 'I mentioned he'd be coming . . .'

'Yes, I remember. You look nice,' she told him. 'I don't get to see many men. Sorry if I was staring.'

'It's OK,' he assured her.

She smiled, and it transformed her face for a moment, as though a light had briefly flared, only to vanish again.

'Shall we sit down?' Maeve suggested, fanning out her hands for everyone to choose their seat.

Nicole rose to her feet and curled her skinny legs under her as she sank into one end of the sofa. 'Why don't you sit there?' she said to Cristy, indicating the other end. 'And you can go there,' she told Connor, pointing to the armchair. 'Do you mind the beanbag?' she asked Honey. She looked at her mother. There were no seats left for Maeve.

'I'm happy on the floor,' Connor insisted, and quickly gestured for Maeve to take the chair.

Nicole shifted and drew her knees back to her chest; it seemed to be a comfortable position for her. The sleeves of her navy sweatshirt were tugged down over her hands, showing only her bony fingers and painfully short nails. Moments ago, Nicole had seemed calm, engaged, yet now, as she stared at nothing, Cristy found herself recalling the psychologist's words: *it's very likely she'll be mourning the loss of twenty years and feeling a good amount of apprehension over what comes next.*

When no one else spoke, Cristy said, 'We'll be guided by you, Nicole. Tell us where you'd like to begin.'

Nicole shuddered and looked at her with confused eyes.

'Do you think they're still alive?' she asked. 'Do you believe it's possible after all this time?' Before Cristy could answer, Nicole tossed her head as though flicking away an image – a hope? She bunched her hands to her mouth and began to mutter, 'I didn't kill them. I didn't kill them. I didn't kill them. No one ever believed me, but I didn't kill them.'

'Shush,' Maeve soothed. 'It's all right – no one here is saying you did.' To Cristy, she said, 'This new arrangement – being here, coming to terms with the release – sometimes, it seems to throw her . . .'

Nicole's eyes returned to Cristy. 'You're wondering,' she said, her tone clipped, almost angry, 'why I confessed if I didn't do it? Well, let me tell you, it was the only way to get out of that place. I told them when they first locked me up that I was guilty so they'd reduce my sentence, but they didn't believe me. Can you imagine? It's never mattered what I said – I'm innocent, I'm guilty – they've never been interested. They don't care. I stopped being human the day they sentenced me. I'm a killer to them, a prisoner, someone who doesn't count . . . I can say anything, and it never makes a difference.' She stopped and stared anxiously at her mother.

'Mostly,' Maeve said, 'she continued to maintain her innocence, but eventually, with Honey's help, we got the parole hearings. The first wasn't successful. Fortunately, the second was, and so here we are, in this strange sort of limbo situation: freedom that doesn't actually feel like it. It's like restoring someone's sight with the underlying threat of plunging them back into darkness should they commit the smallest mistake.' She added, 'This, of course, could turn out to be a very big one.'

Feeling the discomfort of the position she and Connor had put Nicole on, in spite of having her permission, Cristy turned to look at her. She could hardly begin to imagine what kind of hell she'd been through these past years, or indeed what life felt like for her now. Attempting a reassuring smile she said, gently, 'What do you think kept you going through the worst of it?'

Nicole swallowed, and as her eyes filled with tears, she looked away. It was a while before she spoke, and when she did, it seemed she'd either forgotten the question or simply didn't want to answer it. 'I'm not right up here any more,' she said, tapping her head. 'I know it. I can feel how crazy I am, but I don't know . . .' She flinched as though something invisible had hit her. 'It's hard to understand myself, to get a sense of who I am now. I want to live my life again, but how can I do that when everyone . . . ?' A tear fell onto her cheek, and turning to Cristy, she said, 'You can record this if you like. I don't mind, as long as you don't use it against me.'

The offer was so unexpected that Cristy couldn't think how to respond.

Honey said, 'Nicole, you know that's not a good idea.'

Nicole continued to stare at Cristy. 'Would you like to record what I tell you?' she asked.

Torn between wanting to and her concern for how unstable Nicole clearly was, Cristy said, 'How about we set up to record, and then you decide whether you want us to carry on?'

Nicole nodded, seeming to like the idea, then she began nibbling her thumbnail as if it were something that needed to be done. It was as though, Cristy reflected, a part of her had never grown up, while another part had been unable to do so properly. What was it the psychologist had said about arrested development?

While Connor was at the car, Nicole suddenly and aggressively began scrubbing her short hair. 'I thought about dying it,' she told Cristy, 'so no one would recognize me, but the colour's all gone anyway.'

'Not entirely,' Honey told her. 'I've seen it looking better than it does today – livelier, redder.'

Nicole seemed to like that. 'Maybe it reflects my moods.'

She smiled, and there it was again: that tiny flash of radiance. 'But I'm scared of being recognized. No one will ever forgive me, no matter what I say or do.'

'Do you go out at all?' Cristy asked.

Nicole looked at her mother. 'We go for walks, here in the grounds, and sometimes we drive to one of the villages for a coffee. I have a cap, and I wear sunglasses, even when it's raining. Maybe I'm drawing more attention to myself by trying to hide.'

Maeve suddenly got up. 'Where are my manners?' she said. 'I made tea. Will you have some, Cristy? Honey?'

'That would be lovely,' Honey replied. 'I'll come and help you.'

After they'd gone, Cristy turned back to Nicole and felt a wave of pity come over her. If this poor woman hadn't harmed her twins – and it was easy to believe in this moment that she hadn't – then the level of heartbreak and injustice she'd suffered was off the scale.

'It's Meyer, by the way,' Nicole said out of nowhere. 'You called him Major in your podcast, but his name's Meyer.'

Stilling with surprise, Cristy let a moment pass, hoping she'd say more, but she didn't. 'Do you want to tell me anything else about him?' she prompted gently.

Nicole's eyes closed, and she seemed to hold her breath, maybe to stop words coming out, or was she waiting for them to gather? 'He's my reason to carry on living,' she said hoarsely. Her eyes opened again, and she stared vacantly into the middle distance. 'He's Swiss,' she said quietly. 'Not French.'

After a beat, Cristy asked, 'When did you last see him?'

Nicole frowned as she thought. 'I think it was about six or seven weeks ago.'

So before her parole hearing. 'Did he visit you often in prison?'

'Mm. Yes. As often as he could. All the time I was away.'

'Was that every month, or . . . ?'

'Yes, that was how it usually worked out.'

'Have you seen him since your release?'

'No, I can't. Not yet, but I will. He needs me to get through this . . . I can, because I have to. It's the only way we can be together again.'

Wondering exactly what that meant, Cristy said, 'He obviously matters a great deal to you.'

'He means everything. And I do to him.' She looked at Cristy, as though expecting to be challenged, but Cristy simply smiled, trying to convey an understanding she wasn't close to feeling.

They both looked up as Connor came back with the equipment.

'Are you sure you're OK with us recording?' Cristy asked Nicole.

Nicole rubbed her eyes, not seeming at all sure.

'You don't have to do anything you're not comfortable with,' Cristy assured her.

Nicole closed her eyes again and let her head fall back. 'I want to see him so much,' she murmured. 'He knows where they are . . . He hasn't told me yet, but he will. He'll take me to them . . .'

Cristy felt her heart contract. She had to be talking about the twins. 'Has he promised that?' she asked carefully.

'Yes. Yes, he has.'

'So they're still alive?'

Nicole pressed a hand to her heart. 'They've always been alive in here. My babies, my twins . . . I didn't kill them. I didn't. He knows . . .' She looked down at the mic Connor was unpacking.

Cristy said, 'What does he know?'

Nicole looked confused, and Cristy sensed her withdrawing. 'You're trying to make me say things that aren't true,' she accused.

'I only want you to tell me the things that are,' Cristy assured her.

Nicole blinked, as if she was losing track of what was being said.

'Did you give the twins to him?' Cristy asked.

Nicole nodded, then shook her head. 'Yes. No – not him. I didn't give them to anyone.'

CHAPTER TWENTY-THREE

Cristy looked up as Maeve and Honey returned, and over the next few minutes, as teas and sugar were handed around, she took the time to work out where she should go next in this complicated tangle of memories and emotions that Nicole was apparently trapped inside.

When everyone finally had their tea, Nicole said, 'Let's record now, shall we?'

Still not entirely comfortable with it, Cristy looked to Honey for guidance.

Maeve said, 'As long as you don't use it before we've found the twins.'

Cristy wondered if Maeve was aware that Claude Meyer might know where they were – presuming Nicole was to be believed, and right at this moment, Cristy had no idea what she thought about that. She gave Connor the signal to begin.

Her eyes were on Nicole as she considered the best way to continue their chat. In the end, she decided to go back a way, rather than pick up from where they'd left off – it would be interesting to see if she got the same answers.

CRISTY: 'We were talking about Claude Meyer just now...'

There was the smile again: a breaking through of the young girl she used to be, a connection with something inside that clearly made her feel good, even seemed to free her in a way. Her voice was warm and steady as she spoke; her eyes focused elsewhere.

> NICOLE: 'His visits were what kept us both going. We couldn't have carried on without them.'
>
> CRISTY: 'Can you tell me what you talked about when he came?'
>
> NICOLE: 'I can't use words the way he does, but everything he said . . . He could take me out of my surroundings, smooth away all the pain, so that I didn't see or feel where I was any more. When he's with me, all I see is him or what he's describing: the places, the people, the music, the paintings . . . He can be very funny when he talks about the animals. I'm longing to see them for real.'
>
> CRISTY: 'What sort of animals?'
>
> NICOLE: 'All sorts.'
>
> CRISTY: 'Do you know where they are?'
>
> NICOLE: 'For the moment, they're safely stored up here.'

She tapped her head, and the look in her eyes, though still distant, seemed oddly joyful.
Cristy glanced at Maeve, hoping she might say something, but she didn't. It wasn't even clear from her expression whether or not she was listening, but of course she was.

> NICOLE: 'Mum visited me a lot too, didn't you? And Dad before he died. That was the most awful time . . . I never got to see him, to say goodbye . . . There's a lot of cruelty in prison – rules that only hurt people and never do any good. That's one of the hardest parts . . . I don't want to go back . . .'

She began crying, and Maeve went to comfort her.

MAEVE: 'We're very grateful for her release, but there are still so many restrictions on where she can go, who she can talk to, how often she has to report to the authorities. It's really not possible for her to restart her life. Not yet, anyway.'

CRISTY: 'How long will it have to be like this?'

MAEVE: 'Possibly for the next two years – until her sentence is complete.'

CRISTY: 'Will you stay here the whole time?'

MAEVE: 'We're not sure yet. We just take one day at a time.'

CRISTY: 'What about Claude Meyer? Will you see him?'

MAEVE: 'He's not in the forty-mile radius.'

CRISTY: 'But you know where he is?'

MAEVE: 'Not exactly, no.'

Cristy didn't challenge her, although she did wonder if that was true.

NICOLE: 'If he wants you to know, he'll tell you.'

Cristy watched as Maeve dried her daughter's cheeks, pressed a kiss to her forehead and returned to her chair. What, Cristy wondered, were Maeve's feelings towards the man who'd clearly had such an enormous impact on her daughter's life? Cristy sensed no animosity, but it was hard to get a feel for anything when Maeve was giving off so little in the way of emotion – apart from great tenderness for her daughter.

NICOLE: 'Lauren comes to visit me too, now and again. When she can. Mum doesn't know that . . . Sorry, Mum, but you'd only tell Bridget, and Lauren doesn't want her mum to know.'

Maeve shook her head – more in exasperation, it seemed, than surprise. Whatever her true feelings about this news, she apparently wasn't going to share them now.

CRISTY: 'Do you know where Lauren is?'

NICOLE: 'Not exactly, but Claude does. She's happy, I think. It's nice to see her when she comes.'

She broke into a girlish laugh that seemed unrelated to anything or anyone in the room, and when she spoke, she sounded much as she might have as a playful teen.

NICOLE: 'You haven't asked how I met Claude, but I'm going to tell you anyway. It was at a nightclub in Bristol . . . You look surprised, but it's true. Lauren and I could hardly take our eyes off him . . . There was something about him that made it hard not to stare . . .
'He was older than us, not by much, and the way he was standing there, at the end of the bar on his own . . . He says he wasn't alone, but that's how I remember it. Everyone was trying to get him to dance, and he kept laughing, saying he was no good, but he danced with me, and we moved together like we'd been dancing forever.'

Cristy watched her closely and realized she could be witnessing something else the psychologist had mentioned: *some trauma victims show signs of being mentally stuck in the era before the trauma occurred. It's a safer space for them, where they don't have to think about or fear what comes next because they don't know. There can also be a lot of fantasy involved, a creation of how they want things to be rather than how they actually were.*

NICOLE: 'It was me who asked him if we could see one another again, but it didn't matter because we knew right away that we would. It was like we had to because ... We had to.'

CRISTY: 'You said he's Swiss, so what was he doing in Bristol?'

NICOLE: 'He was lecturing at the university, just for a year at first, but he ended up staying a lot longer than that.'

CRISTY: 'What was he lecturing in?'

NICOLE: 'Psychology.'

CRISTY: 'And he stayed. Because of you?'

NICOLE: 'And his other friends. They were special too, in their own ways, and I always felt as though I belonged with them. It's hard to explain that, but it's true. I want to go back to them.'

CRISTY: 'Are they all still together?'

NICOLE: 'Not all of them, no. Some have gone their separate ways.'

CONNOR: 'Maeve, how well did you know Claude Meyer? Do you still know him?'

MAEVE: 'I haven't seen him for years, but he – and his friends – used to come to the house back in the early days. They were a nice group to have around, always polite, a lot of fun ... Ronnie and Claude used to get into such debates, going on into the night ... They could talk about anything: politics, religion, rocket science – nothing was off the table for them. For any of them, actually.'

NICOLE: 'I used to say they could bore for England, and

Claude would remind me he was Swiss, so I'd tell him he had both countries covered. I've always loved being able to make him laugh. I still can.'

CRISTY: 'Did they carry on coming to the house after the twins were born?'

NICOLE: 'Of course. Everyone loved the twins.'

CRISTY: 'Is Claude their father?'

Nicole frowned deeply, as though trying to decide whether or not this was a trick question, or perhaps she was wondering whether or not to be truthful. More signs of traumatic effects: *sudden bouts of wariness, suspicion, an inherent need to self-protect even when no harm is threatened.*

Cristy waited and was starting to think no answer was coming when she was suddenly surprised.

NICOLE: 'We never had any tests done, but I was mostly exclusive with him. Not always, but mostly.'

Cristy glanced at Maeve and saw no surprise, so concluded this was something Maeve had heard before.

NICOLE: 'No one really understood who we were, how we liked to live our lives, but it didn't matter. We weren't interested in other people's judgement. There was no reason to be when we weren't causing harm to anyone else. What difference did it make who we slept with?'

She seemed to drift, maybe taking herself back to the heady, halcyon days of her youth that must surely feel more like a dream now than any sort of reality.

She started to laugh softly.

NICOLE: 'We used to have parties in the woods behind

our house. Lauren and I loved getting all dressed up just to go down the garden. Funny the things that excite you and make you laugh when you're young.'

CRISTY: 'Dress up in what way?'

NICOLE: 'Like we were going to a Sunday picnic or to pose for a painting. You know, the kind by Manet or Seurat or Renoir . . . We used to smoke a lot of weed at those picnics, and we never held onto much in the way of inhibitions – hah! Claude always used to say clothes were just shields hiding perfection, and why would any of us want to hide that?'

Realizing this must be what had sparked Mervyn Wilson's wild theories, Cristy glanced at Connor, wondering what he was making of all this. What sort of image did he have in his mind of Claude Meyer and the apparent influence he had wielded over his friends. A cult in plain sight? It was what it sounded like to her, and yet Maeve was showing no signs of having had a problem with it.

CRISTY: 'What happened when you found out you were pregnant?'

Appearing dreamy and reflective again, Nicole ran a hand over her abdomen as if she were pregnant now.

NICOLE: 'We stopped having picnics for a while because it was winter, but there was always someone's flat or house to go to. Claude was fascinated by my bump as it grew – he used to stroke and kiss it all the time. So even if he wasn't officially the father, he kind of acted like he was, and that was fine.'

MAEVE: 'He came to the hospital when she gave birth . . . He was the first to hold the babies, and he was so proud, very emotional . . . He said he felt like he was holding a pair of miracles . . . Well, I suppose he was, if you want to look at it that way.'

NICOLE: 'He used to call them the gifts instead of the twins. He even said prayers to them.'

CRISTY: 'What sort of prayers?'

NICOLE: 'Well, I don't suppose it was that exactly – more like he was honouring their creation. Those were his words: he honoured their creation, and he used to pour these lovely smelling oils over them, rubbing in so gently . . . They loved it. Always sent them right off to sleep.'

CRISTY: 'This was happening at the house on Randall Lane?'

NICOLE: 'No, at his place in Clifton, near the university. We were there a lot after they were born.'

MAEVE: 'Sometimes, you took the twins, but just as often you left them with me and your dad so you could go out and do the things you were missing out on . . .

'Nicole was no saint – we've never tried to say that she was – but Noah and Abigail, they were our sunshine, our joy . . . She loved them with all her heart and soul and did her best to take care of them. No, she didn't always get it right. Did you, Cristy, as a young mother? I'm sure you made mistakes too. I know I did, but we do our best, and that's what matters. Nicole was only nineteen, she wanted to start at university, and we were supportive of that right up until . . . well, until . . .'

Cristy saw the shadow of grief cross her face. Nicole seemed not to be paying attention, but then she muttered for her mother to stop or she was going to set everyone off. Her voice was slightly harsher than it had been a few minutes ago. Emotional detachment? More self-protection?

Eventually, Cristy judged it right to start again, but gently, cautiously. She was about to tread on very difficult ground now, and there was no way of knowing how Nicole might react.

CRISTY: 'Will you talk us through what happened the day the twins disappeared?'

Nicole eyed her curiously, as if she might not understand the question, but then she was talking in a toneless voice, recounting, as if by rote, something she'd long memorized that could be spoken without being felt.

NICOLE: 'Mum went to Bridget's like she sometimes did on a Monday. The cat had brought something in the night before . . . Sometimes, the place would look like a battlefield after he'd finished with his prey . . . He was a beast, that cat, and there was blood that morning . . . I promised to clear it up, but after Mum left, I saw that the cat . . .

'He was just lying there in the kitchen . . . He wasn't moving, and his eyes were open. It was horrible. He'd died, and no one had noticed. I remember it upset me a lot.'

CRISTY: 'What was the cat's name?'

NICOLE: 'We called him George, but we never knew what it really was. He'd adopted us a couple of months before . . . He kept hanging around our garden, so we started to feed him, and then somehow he kind of became ours.'

MAEVE: 'He was more of a stray, really, than the family pet.'

CRISTY: 'So when you realized he'd died, what happened then?'

NICOLE: 'I went back upstairs ... No, that was after ... I buried him first. That's right. I couldn't just leave him there on the kitchen floor. When I was little, Dad used to bury my guinea pigs in the woods, so I decided it was the best place for George.'

CRISTY: 'Where were the twins when you left the house?'

NICOLE: 'They were there ... Upstairs ... I should never have left them on their own – I know that – but I thought they were safe. How was I to know they weren't? And I was only gone for ...'

She broke off, seeming suddenly bewildered, and in the silence that followed Cristy felt the wrenching horror of what she, as a mother, might feel, or do, if she'd ever been unable to find her children. She glanced at Connor, and knew he was thinking of his little daughter and how he or Jodi would cope if anything so terrible ever happened to them.

Cristy spoke quietly and gently as she continued.

CRISTY: 'How long were you gone?'

NICOLE: 'I don't know. I had to find the right place to dig a hole and then fill it up again. I knew I should have left it for Dad, but I was doing it now ... It felt like it took forever, but it couldn't have been long ... Then I went back up to the house and I ... I didn't go upstairs straightaway. I can't remember what I did, but when I went, I remember ...'

Her breath caught, and she covered her mouth as she began to heave. Maeve went quickly to her side, held her firmly, assured her it was all right, that she didn't need to be afraid any more.

NICOLE: 'I couldn't think where I'd put them. I didn't understand . . . I started shouting their names like they might answer or come out from where they were hiding. I mean, I knew they couldn't – they weren't even walking yet . . . I panicked and rang Mum, thinking she must have taken them with her.'

MAEVE: 'I went straight home when she called, terrified out of my mind. I couldn't imagine what was going on . . . I didn't want to . . .'

NICOLE: 'I think I went outside to look for them. It's all jumbled up in my head . . . They were there, then not . . . I thought I must have taken them down to the woods with me and forgotten, so I ran back to check . . .'

MAEVE: 'As soon as I realized they weren't in the house, I called the police . . . We were so scared, terrified . . . You can probably imagine, but I don't think it sank in until later – maybe days later – that they really had gone.'

CRISTY: 'Were you in touch with Claude at that time?'

NICOLE: 'He was in Switzerland, but yes, I rang him . . . A few days after it happened, maybe it was the next day, I can't . . . It's all mixed up . . . now. I wanted him to come and he said he would, but then the police found some blood in one of the cots, and next thing, they were arresting me.'

CRISTY: 'Do you know how the blood got there?'

NICOLE: 'Abigail had nosebleeds sometimes . . . Her nails were too long – she could have scratched herself . . . I don't know, but I swear I never hurt them . . .'

CRISTY: 'Do you have any idea who might have taken them?'

NICOLE: 'No. I mean, I thought it might have been Claude at first, but obviously I wasn't thinking straight. He wasn't there. He was in Switzerland, but I carried on hoping it was him, because then I'd know they were safe. But he didn't have them, and no one saw anyone coming or going from the house. How can that be? We live on a main road, and no one saw *anything*. That's how they ended up blaming me.'

CONNOR: 'Did you tell the police about Claude?'

NICOLE: 'Yes. I told them about everyone who knew us.'

CRISTY: 'Did you mention that he was probably the father?'

NICOLE: 'I can't remember. I mean, it might have been in my statement...'

MAEVE: 'They made a big thing in court of her not knowing for certain who the father was... They painted her in a very bad light, as if she wasn't in a bad enough one already.'

CRISTY: 'So they didn't test anyone? Take their DNA?'

MAEVE: 'I don't know. You'd have to ask the police.'

CRISTY: 'Do you know if they questioned Claude?'

MAEVE: 'Yes, I'm sure they did, but he couldn't help – he had no idea where they were.'

NICOLE: 'He came to the prison after they took me there, and I got hysterical... I wanted to leave with him, but they wouldn't let me. The guard made him go, and I was terrified Claude wouldn't come again, but he did.

He said nothing would ever change between us, and it didn't – it hasn't.'

CRISTY: 'You gave me the impression just now that he might know where the twins are. Did I understand that correctly?'

NICOLE: 'No. I didn't say that. You must have misunderstood me. He doesn't know. None of us do.'

Nicole stared at the recorder for a hard, tense moment, then got up suddenly and knocked it to the floor. 'I've had enough of this now,' she sobbed. 'You have to go. Mum! I don't want to talk to them any more.'

Realizing there was no point in arguing, and feeling terrible for having brought Nicole to this point, Cristy got to her feet. If only there was a way to make up for the pain they'd caused, but of course there wasn't.

Minutes later she and Connor were out at the car with Honey. As they started to get in, Maeve came out.

'I'm sorry,' Cristy said, 'we didn't mean to upset her. Will she be all right?'

Maeve nodded. 'If there is such a thing for her any more. She needs to see him, but . . . Well . . .'

When she didn't continue, Cristy said, 'Do you think Claude knows where the twins are?'

Sighing, Maeve said, 'What I think is that he and Nicole tell themselves a lot of things that they want to believe, but they're not always true.'

'So he can't take her to them?'

'If she's given you that impression, it'll be because it's what she tells herself as a way to keep going. When there are no bodies, it's very hard to give up hope.'

Understanding that at least, Cristy said, 'Has Claude been here to see her since she was released?'

Maeve glanced towards the window where Nicole was

inside, maybe watching through the opaque curtain. 'He hasn't come yet,' she replied, making it sound as though she thought he would eventually.

'Do you have any idea where he might be?'

'Maybe in Switzerland?'

'With the twins?'

Maeve regarded her curiously. 'Of course we'd like to think so, but it seems unlikely, doesn't it? How would he explain them when everyone knows what happened back in 2005?'

'So what do you, in your heart of hearts, believe happened?' Connor asked.

There was a long moment, before Maeve said, 'All I can tell you is that I fear we'll die never knowing for sure where they are or who took them.'

CHAPTER TWENTY-FOUR

As they drove away from the secluded property, Cristy in the front now, Connor in the back, sending instructions through to Jacks, Cristy said to Honey, 'Clearly Claude Meyer played a much bigger part in everything than any of us in the press knew about back then.'

'Or than is showing up in the files so far,' Honey responded, 'but I'm not going to try excusing anyone from my office. We already know they didn't do a good job for Nicole, but if the police had been doing theirs properly . . . Well, there might have been a very different outcome to the trial.'

'Maybe there wouldn't have been one at all,' Connor muttered under his breath. Then, 'I think we can now dismiss the Claude Miller who rang in with his French accent and phony contact details, given no one's ever been able to get hold of him, as a fake. I'll get Jacks to run a search on Meyer, starting with Bristol Uni circa 2004/5. Interesting that his subject was psychology.'

Agreeing, Cristy said, 'A handy qualification for someone building a cult. I guess you registered that it was when I asked about him knowing where the twins are that Nicole threw a tantrum and shut us down?'

'Yes, I did pick up on that,' Honey responded thoughtfully. 'What did she actually say to give you the impression he might know?'

'While you were out of the room, she actually said as

much,' Cristy told her. 'Her actual words were: "he knows where they are". And apparently, he's promised to take her to them. I've no idea how truthful or fanciful she was being, but as far as I could tell, without really knowing her, she seemed to believe it.'

Honey sighed and took a left towards the motorway. 'Based on my dealings with her,' she said soberly, 'I can tell you that she's quite good at convincing herself, and others, of something she has going round in her head, before she suddenly changes her mind and starts telling another story altogether.'

'Such as, she killed the twins, she didn't kill the twins,' Connor put in.

Honey nodded. 'Not helpful, I know, but that's how she is, I'm afraid.'

Hardly able to imagine just how traumatized Nicole actually was given all she'd been through, Cristy said, 'Do you think she'll speak to us again?'

'I hope so, because I got the sense she was starting to trust you – until she suddenly wasn't. But maybe, for the time being, let's not count on it.'

Disappointed though not surprised by the answer, Cristy took out her phone and scrolled to Clove's number. 'We need to find out,' she said, 'why the police didn't consider Claude Meyer worthy of more attention back in 2005, and with any luck, ex-DC Patten might have given Clove some information on that.'

'She did,' Clove confirmed, when Cristy got through to her. 'His name's spelled M-e-i-e-r, by the way, not with a y in the middle, the way it sounds, and he *was* questioned at the time of Nicole's arrest . . . Just after actually, because he was in Switzerland when it happened and he had alibis to prove he was there the entire time.'

'Did he give a statement?' Cristy asked, glancing at Honey.

'There's an interesting answer to that,' Clove replied. 'I

can call the interview up and play it for you, if you like? There's no one else on the train, and it shouldn't take me long to find the most salient points.'

'Do it and get back to us,' Cristy instructed and rang off.

'OK, this is interesting,' Connor announced. 'Jacks has just forwarded a DM that came in earlier from someone with the name of Wilhemina – call me Willie – Miller. She's claiming to be an "ex-disciple" of Claude Meier's – interestingly, she's got the right spelling – although it was the ex-disciple thing that prompted the supersleuth to send the message through. Apparently, this woman's willing to talk to us if we want to take things further, but she doesn't want us to use her name.'

'Sounds interesting,' Cristy remarked. 'Tell Jacks to set something up.' And clicking on to take Clove's call, she switched it straight to speaker.

'OK, I'm not alone any more,' Clove announced, 'so I've sent a link that'll take you to where I've just asked Lizzie Patten about Lauren Hawkes. Playback starts with her answer.'

Calling it up, Cristy held out her phone so everyone could hear.

ELIZABETH PATTEN: 'I remember her as a slightly chubby, auburn-haired girl with bright-green eyes and a slight lisp when she spoke – quite cute, actually. Younger than Nicole, I think, by a year or two. Anyway, she was keen to be helpful, and certain her cousin couldn't have harmed the babies. She cried a lot when we talked to her – obviously upset about the twins and desperate for us to find them.'

CLOVE: 'Do you recall anything in particular about her statement that you can share with us?'

ELIZABETH PATTEN: 'Not after all these years, but she must have told us where she was at the time of the killings and it bore out, or we'd obviously have pulled her in again – and I'm pretty sure we only spoke to her the once.'

CLOVE: 'Anything else you can tell us about her?'

ELIZABETH PATTEN: 'Only that when it came to the trial, she seemed to have changed towards her cousin. I've no way of knowing what might have gone on between them during the intervening months – Nicole was in custody, of course – but when Lauren took the stand, she was . . . awkward, couldn't bring herself to look anyone in the eye . . . She carried on saying Nicole would never have hurt the twins, but she came over as a lot less sincere than she had when we'd first spoken to her. It could have been nerves – people often don't perform well in front of juries – but it stood out for me at the time.'

CLOVE: 'Did anyone else remark on it?'

ELIZABETH PATTEN: 'Not that I recall. I think we were all just glad when it was over and we could put the whole thing behind us. It was a horrible case, two tiny kids vanishing like that, and the mother still wouldn't tell us what she'd done with them.'

CLOVE: 'So you agreed with the verdict, that she'd killed them.'

ELIZABETH PATTEN: 'I wouldn't go as far as to say I agreed with it, but it was out of my hands by then, and from what I hear, she's finally confessed?'

CLOVE: 'She has, but tell me this, did you carry on looking for the bodies after Nicole was imprisoned?'

ELIZABETH PATTEN: 'Not me personally – I was reassigned – but yes, the search continued for a while.

To be honest, I don't think any of it was well-handled from a police perspective. You're no doubt aware the twins disappeared just before the 7/7 attacks and after the knee-jerk following all that I can't, hand on heart, say that we ever properly got back on track with it. Really sad that the bodies have never been found – unless you're about to tell me they have.'

CLOVE: 'Not as far as we know.'

ELIZABETH PATTEN: 'So she got parole based on a confession that didn't include telling anyone where to find her kids?'

CLOVE: 'Maybe she doesn't know where they are?'

ELIZABETH PATTEN: 'Well, she always claimed not to, so that obviously hasn't changed. But now it sounds as though someone in authority has decided it's time to let her start the long haul back into the community, regardless of what happened to her children. Pretty shameful, huh, but with the state the legal system's in these days, all sorts of decisions are being taken that never would have been twenty, even ten years ago.'

CLOVE: 'Were there any theories at the time of the investigation as to what she *might* have done with the children?'

ELIZABETH PATTEN: 'Well, the woods were dug up, as you know. No dead cat was found – no bodies either. It was rumoured that she'd given them up for some sort of ritual, but there was never any evidence of that, only of youngsters frolicking about in the woods some nights, getting up to all sorts, but nothing kids don't normally do when drunk or stoned.'

CLOVE: 'So you dismissed the ritual thing?'

ELIZABETH PATTEN: 'Not out of hand – we just couldn't find anyone or anything to back it up. If it had been up to me I'd have dug a bit deeper on it, because I always had a feeling it should have been explored. But I was a lowly DC at the time, no one was listening to me, and then it turned out she was lying about the cat, and when one of the babies' blood was found in the house... Someone at the top obviously decided it was an open and shut case.'

CLOVE: 'Do you recall anyone by the name of Claude Major being interviewed in connection with the disappearance?'

ELIZABETH PATTEN: 'No, I don't... Oh, hang on, there was a Claude Meier, I think his name was, not Major. Swiss, I believe. That's right. It's coming back to me now, how Nicole was really keen for us to speak to him at the time of her arrest, but it turned out he wasn't in the country. So a couple of officers, Ruby Trott and Pete Taylor flew to Geneva, I think it was, not Zurich, to interview him. I remember Ruby coming back declaring she was in love, and with that accent, he could have talked her straight into anything indecent or otherwise if only he'd asked.'

CLOVE: 'So was he ruled out of inquiries after that, given that he doesn't seem to have been mentioned anywhere in the press or in the disclosure documents sent to Nicole's lawyer?'

ELIZABETH PATTEN: 'The only way I can explain that is if his alibis checked out and I'm pretty sure they did. And presumably nothing came up subsequently to warrant talking to him again.'

'There's not much else,' Clove told them, when the playback ended. 'She's going to try and track down Pete Taylor for us –

apparently poor Ruby died in a car accident a few years ago, but Lizzie Patten thinks Pete's working as a security guard for a storage company in Hull these days. She'll get back to me if anything else useful comes to mind. Oh, something she mentioned before I left was that they checked all the landline records at the time – Nicole didn't have a mobile, which I guess wasn't unusual in 2005. Apparently the only person phoned from number 42 that day was Maeve's sister and the 999 call obvs.'

Cristy glanced at Connor as he said, 'Kind of chimes with what Nicole told us.'

'So, how did it go with her?' Clove urged.

Wryly, Cristy said, 'Where to start with that? The big takeaway is that Meier regularly visited her in prison, and there's a small chance he might know where the twins are or at least what happened to them. We'll play what we have for you when we're back at the office. Where are you now?'

'Probably about halfway between Manchester Piccadilly and Bristol Temple Meads. Train's not due in 'til seven. Will you still be there?'

'Maybe not, so let's meet early in the morning. Sounds as though we could be making some breakthroughs, but I'm still not sure where any of them are leading, although ultimately, hopefully to Lauren Hawkes and/or Claude Meier.'

'Not to mention to the truth,' Connor added.

Cristy turned to him. 'That too,' she agreed, and probably because her conscience wasn't clear, she couldn't be sure whether he was simply referring to the case or if it had been a deliberate dig at her.

CHAPTER TWENTY-FIVE

Cristy was lying in bed, staring at the ceiling, trying to remember what had happened the night before when she'd spoken to David on the phone. The tightness of apprehension inside her was enough to confirm that it hadn't gone well. She was aware that they'd snapped at one another over something to do with her never listening, being too distracted to consider what might be going on in anyone else's world. They'd even raised their voices at one point – well, she had, she couldn't be certain now if he had, only that he'd ended up telling her he was ringing off at which point he'd done just that right in the middle of whatever she'd been saying.

She'd been so angry at the time that she'd sent a text saying: *This long distance thing clearly doesn't work for either of us, so maybe time to rethink.*

Groaning aloud, she turned her face into the pillow trying to decide whether to call him now to apologize, or allow him more time to calm down. If she knew what she was supposed to be apologizing for she might have an answer for that. What the hell had she actually said to make him so angry? This was assuming it was her fault, but maybe he'd triggered it in some way . . . Hadn't he said something about not having the time to keep going over and over Kinsley's offer with her?

'Well, excuse me bothering you with my issues,' she'd snapped furiously. She remembered saying that, and he'd hit back with,

'If I thought you had time for mine I'd try changing the subject.' At which point she'd gone off about the privileged life he led over there in Guernsey with his perfect home and perfect family . . .

Was that when he'd hung up on her? Maybe, but she wasn't certain about that, and what an absolute shrew she must have sounded anyway.

Why the hell couldn't she remember all the vital details? It wasn't as if she'd had that much to drink, a couple of glasses, no more, and she hadn't been aware of feeling on edge before ringing him.

The trouble was these surges of mostly irrational temper kept sneaking up on her lately, along with the hot flushes and night sweats that had forced her up twice during the early hours to change the sheets and take a shower. If it didn't sound like such a lame excuse she might message him now to explain what was happening to her, but even the thought of it was making her feel ill.

Reaching for her phone she braced herself as she checked to see if he'd responded to her last text, all the time hoping she hadn't sent any others that she'd somehow forgotten about. She hadn't, thank God, but nor had he replied to her childish parting shot.

She closed her eyes as a wave of shameful emotion came over her. Just please don't let him be taking it seriously, because the very last thing she wanted was to lose him.

Deciding to try and make light of her ridiculous message, she tapped out another saying, *I've had a rethink and everything about you – us – works for me.* She read it several times, erased it and sent one that said, quite simply, *I'm really sorry. Please let me know when is a good time to talk. ILY, Cx*

By the time she got to the office she still hadn't received a reply.

*

'OK, so here we go on our mysterious Swiss guy,' Jacks announced as soon as everyone was at their desks and ready to receive. 'Recording, by the way.'

JACKS: 'Jean-Claude Meier, born 29th November 1978 – this makes him forty-six today – second son of Elias and Maria Meier, winegrowers from Lavaux – a UNESCO-listed region along the shores of Lake Geneva – thought I'd throw that in as a spot of scene-setting. Maternal grandmother married a Welshman later in life – might seem insignificant now, but we'll come back to it.

'Jean-Claude studied at the local school – they're all brilliant in Switzerland, so no need to go private – then went on to the Changins School of Viticulture and Oenology, before dropping out and enrolling at the University of Geneva to study psychology, with a focus on distorted beliefs through brainwashing. A really interesting reason as to why he changed courses... Not confirmed, but makes sense to me.

'Turns out his parents were members of the *Ordre du Temple Solaire* – excuse my French. For those who don't speak it, it means the Solar Temple. And for those who've never heard of it, it was a secret society back in the Nineties, claiming to be a continuation of the Knights Templar and other stuff that we don't need to get into here. It became famous – *infamous* – when it orchestrated a bunch of murders and suicides on two communes in Switzerland. Jean-Claude's parents belonged to one of them.'

CRISTY: 'You mean they were cult members who... what...?'

JACKS: 'Whether they were killed, or took their own lives, I can't say, but it's how they came to their end. Jean-Claude would have been eighteen at the time –

a traumatic experience for a son at any age, but I'm guessing it's what could have driven him to study psychology instead of viticulture things.'

Cristy looked around the office sensing that the cult theory was gaining some traction for them all. However it appeared no one had anything to say at this point – including Honey, who'd rearranged her schedule this morning to be able to join them.

JACKS: 'Moving on. Jean-Claude graduated in 2001 and went on to do an MA at the University of Bordeaux, in France. In the summer of 2003, he came to Bristol uni as a visiting scholar. His lecture series "The Psychology of Taste and Decision-Making" explored how sensory experiences, memory and social influence can shape choices. I guess you could call it a blend of his academic qualifications with his upbringing on the vineyards.

'Anyway, his gig must have been a hit because according to my source at Bristol uni, he was invited to stay on. He finally left in June 2005, when he returned to Switzerland, where he spent the next few years teaching at the University of Lausanne and also helping his brother, Julien, with the family business.'

CRISTY: 'How do you know all this already?'

JACKS: 'I have my ways – except I'm a bit stumped on where he went after he left his university job in 2012, because he's kind of dropped off the scene since then.'

CONNOR: 'So you can't tell us where he is now? Did he get married at all?'

JACKS: 'No mention of a wife. Or a husband.'

CLOVE: 'Maybe he's working full-time at the vineyard with his brother?'

JACKS: 'Doesn't seem to be, but still a way to go on that, which will probably include talking to said brother or someone close to the family, and I decided not to go there yet ... *because* ...

'One of the supersleuths pinged through a voice note late last night ... Hang on, it's here, so I can play it ... Can't make up my mind whether it's male or female, but definitely English. See what you think.'

VOICE NOTE: 'Greetings to whoever is listening to this message. I just took a look at your website ...'

Jacks hit pause. 'Sorry, forgot to mention that I posted the actual spelling of Jean-Claude's name on the website as soon as we knew it, with a little red flag to make sure it stood out.'

VOICE NOTE: '. . . If we are talking about the same person – and I feel certain we are – then I can probably tell you where to find Jean-Claude, but only if you can persuade me that you mean him no harm. He is an exceptional man who will welcome you into his world, but I will not lead the way until we've spoken and I am convinced that your motives are without malice. Thank you for listening to this. I wait to hear from you.'

Cristy and Connor exchanged wide eyed glances.

JACKS: 'We've also received an email from an Elaine Wilson-Jacobs who says, I quote, ". . . I've been trying to lay my hands on his actual address, but his farm is somewhere in the middle of Wales. No point googling him because he's totally off grid, but if I can find it, I'll let you know. All the best, Elaine."'

Cristy sat back in her chair as she digested all this. 'Well,' she said, 'I find myself becoming more intrigued by this man by the minute.'

'Don't we all?' Clove said. 'Definitely sounding culty to me.'

'OK, this is a reach,' Honey put in, 'but I'm thinking . . . Jean-Claude, J.C. . . .' She looked embarrassed. 'Am I going too far?'

'You mean as in Jesus Christ?' Connor asked.

Honey shrugged. 'I said it was a reach.'

'Can I bring us back to the Welsh grandmother?' Jacks suggested. 'She was Swiss, actually, but married a Welshman after her first husband died. I didn't pay much attention to her at first, but when Elaine Wilson-Jacobs said he's somewhere in Wales, I asked myself whether tracking Granny down might lead us to where he is now?'

'And you've found her?' Connor asked, clearly impressed.

'Just got started, but it turns out her husband's name is/was Gwyn Jones, and hers is/was Marie so that's how easy it's going to be to track her down.'

With a laugh, Connor said, 'OK, well good luck with that. In the meantime, we need to respond to these other guys and try to get them on record. Cris, why don't you take the voice note. I'll reply to Elaine . . .'

'There's more coming in from the supersleuths,' Clove announced. 'Maybe we should take a look at the new report in case there's something we need to know before speaking to anyone else?'

'Given there's stuff coming in all the time,' Cristy said, 'we shouldn't let anything hold us up.'

'But what's the rush?' Connor argued. 'It's not like Meier can disappear on us when we already don't know where he is.'

Failing to hide her irritation, Cristy said, 'I thought we wanted to get to the heart of this, so what's the point of delaying contact with two people who've already told us they might know where he is? Three if we include Willie Miller the "ex-disciple".'

Connor stared at her hard. She could tell her tone had been too harsh, had irked and confused him, and now she was angry at herself for the unnecessary show of bad temper. Maybe if David would get in touch she might relax a little.

'Sorry,' she said, 'let's do it your way,' and she reached for her phone. No one was calling or texting – she simply needed to break the moment and get herself under better control.

Leaving the office, she let herself into the meeting room across the hall and closed the door behind her. If someone needed to use the space, she'd vacate; meanwhile, it was somewhere private to make a call.

It was a long time since she'd felt so apprehensive about making a call, and the fact that she was so pent up and worried about it now must mean she had a bad feeling about how it was going to go. Nevertheless, she pressed to connect to David's number, trying to think what she'd say, or do, if she went straight to voicemail. He'd know it was her, obviously, so simply ringing off wasn't an option. 'Hi,' she said, a mix of relief and deeper apprehension tightening inside her when he answered. 'How are you?'

After a pause he said, 'I'm OK. How about you?' His tone wasn't friendly.

'I'm . . . When we spoke last night . . . Did I say something that maybe . . . I shouldn't have? If so . . .'

'You can't remember?' he cut in incredulously. 'You didn't sound as though you'd been drinking.'

'I hadn't. I just . . .' She really didn't want to get into anything about brain fog, much less mood swings, but what other excuse could she offer for not remembering what they'd argued about, who had started it, or even exactly how it had ended, apart from badly, obviously?

Realizing she had no choice but to deliver her embarrassing excuse, she simply said, 'I'm afraid it's my time of life.'

She waited, cringing when he didn't say anything, and was about to apologize again when he said, 'I guess it could explain why you jumped down my throat for asking how the decision-making process was going.'

Remembering how he'd said he didn't want to discuss it, over and over, her eyes closed. Maybe she'd imagined it, allowed her own guilt to conjure up an excuse to blame him. How could she be sure about anything when her mind was a blank? 'I'm sorry,' she groaned. 'I'm obviously not dealing very well with this offer business and taking things out on you and Connor is not acceptable.'

'You've had a fight with Connor?'

'Not exactly, just . . . We'll get past it. I hope we can too?'

'Sure, we all have our off days, just maybe don't tell me again that I'm overbearing and unsympathetic and have no idea how to deal with stressful situations when life is so perfect for me.'

'Oh my God, I'm sorry.' She knew she'd said something along those lines, and to a man who'd had to live through his wife's murder and all the horror it had brought to his world. Sure, it had happened a long time ago, but nevertheless . . . Where the hell had her head been? Who was she turning into, the way she was lashing out at people she cared for?

'I understand that you were stressed,' he said, coldly, 'but the words had to have come from somewhere, and if that is how you feel about me—'

'It's not! It really isn't. David, I'm sorry. I wish I knew what to say to convince you . . .'

'I can believe you're sorry, and I know you're not an insensitive person, but I've been thinking since . . . I've got a lot going on right now, so maybe we should take a pause for a while, think about things and how we actually want to go forward?'

She reeled at the shock of his words.

'I need to go now,' he said, 'and I'm sure you do too. I'll be in touch.'

As the line went dead, she stared down at her phone, hardly able to make sense of what had just happened. Had he just ended their relationship? Had he actually meant it when he'd said he'd be in touch? Or was it going to turn out to be an easier way of saying goodbye?

Barely knowing what to think or do, she tried again to cast her mind back to the previous night. She must have been a whole lot worse to him than he'd admitted to, or he'd surely never have done this, and it was half-killing her that she couldn't remember.

Dear God, surely this wasn't how it was going to be as she moved into her fifties and her hormone-tormented psyche struggled to cope? What kind of use was she going to be to anyone if that was the case? How the hell could she even think about taking a high-powered job at the helm of a new media company, when she might not even be able to run her podcast here? And now, thanks to some insane outburst last night, she had no one to talk to about it – apart from her daughter, maybe, but why on earth would Hayley want to be burdened with her mother's middle-aged problems when she was working so hard at uni and had her own life to lead?

There was always Meena, a dear and long-standing friend who'd stood by her so many times in the past, but she'd been so snappy with her lately, and considering how she was thinking of abandoning Quinn Studios, what sort of person did it make her even to think of using Meena that way now?

She looked up as someone knocked on the door, and her heart jolted as Connor put his head around.

'Hey you,' he said. 'Sorry if I'm interrupting – we've just been going through the supersleuth's latest report, and there's some interesting stuff I know you're going to want to see.'

Why was just the sight of Connor, and the friendliness in his tone, pushing her to the brink of tears?

For God's sake, Cristy. You have to pull yourself together, and the time to do that is right now.

CHAPTER TWENTY-SIX

Over the next few days, right up until Tuesday's drop at six, the team's main focus was on pulling together episode three of the series, featuring Nicole's trial. Having now received a court transcript, they had plenty to work with, although nothing to suggest the jury had reached a wrong verdict. It was surprising, that was for sure, given the lack of crucial evidence and the failure to produce any viable witnesses to the twins' abuse or neglect. It was the prosecuting barrister who'd won the day, with his brutal takedown of Nicole's character and her inability to produce a convincing explanation of what did, or didn't, happen that day.

Although Cristy hadn't been at the trial every day, being on maternity leave, she could remember how closely she'd followed the case and how frustrated she'd felt over not being able to see it through herself. The fact that neither the twins, nor their bodies, had been found by then, was what had disturbed her so much afterwards, making it hard for her, as a new mother, to think straight or rationally – or even at all, at times.

Demoralized and deeply worried by the thought of falling victim to hormonal imbalances again, Cristy vowed to keep a close watch on herself now, taking care not to overreact or read things into other people's behaviour or words that simply wasn't there. It might have been simpler if David would just call or message or do something to reassure her that this wasn't the end for them, but he'd made no contact since telling her they needed some time to think things through.

How long should she wait before calling him? Maybe he was just getting on with his life, satisfied he'd made the right decision to let her go and thankful that she wasn't putting either of them through the excruciating awkwardness of her trying to persuade him to change his mind?

Realizing how close she was to the edge again, how desperate she was going to feel if she did end up losing him, she quickly pushed him from her mind and forced herself to focus on where she was now and what was happening with the series.

Episode three was due to be uploaded in an hour.

They were currently assessing the growing number of messages coming in regarding Claude Meier, which were fascinating and conflicting, and in some cases pretty disturbing . . .

'What gets me just as much as the content,' Clove declared, scanning the list they'd compiled between them, 'are the sources: not just male, female, young, old, foreign, local, all the usual variants, but people clearly go to him in groups as well.'

Cristy said, 'You've obviously finished curating the input, so why not play us the selected highlights?'

'Sure. Just remember we're not naming anyone, mainly because we're not able to use it yet anyway. It's all for later, but here goes:'

> MALE (PLUMMY BRITISH): 'Giving myself over to Claude and his staff, becoming one with them for a while, has totally changed my life for the better. I think, dear *Hindsight* team, that you'll find the same if you are fortunate enough to be chosen to spend time with him.'

FEMALE (POSSIBLY AUSTRALIAN): 'Before I went, I was in a very bad place. By the time I left, I felt as though I was on a higher plane – do you know what I mean?'

FEMALE (MAYBE DUTCH): 'After receiving the recommendation and subsequently being accepted, I approached everything with a lot of nervousness and doubt. I need not have worried. I came away feeling that I could fly if I tried.'

MALE: (AMERICAN): '... I can't say it was for me. My wife seemed to get a lot from it, and everything's been great between us since, so maybe it was more for me than I realized... I probably shouldn't name anyone, not without their permission, but whoever he recommends for you, take it from me, you'll be in safe hands.'

MALE (IRISH): '... We'll go again. Exceptional therapies, lots to do, all kinds of activities, and when you come away feeling this great, why wouldn't you go again? Just hope we get accepted...'

FEMALE (BRITISH): 'I'm in love with Claude and everything about him.'

FEMALE (POSSIBLY GERMAN): '... They're charlatans, the lot of them, and should terrify anyone who goes near them or especially near him. He haunts me even now, and it's been over seven years since I was there. I've always kept quiet about it out of fear of retribution – that's why I'm not giving my name now. You don't know what you're messing with. If you take my advice, you'll stay away.'

MALE (ITALIAN): 'I end up shedding so many inhibitions when I am there that I discover I am a different man underneath, a better man, more confident and kinder...'

FEMALE (DANISH): 'Beware! Go there and you'll get hypnotized without your consent; I'm not sure even now what happened while I was under.'

MALE (AMERICAN): 'We saw and heard things that we'd never seen or heard anywhere else in our lives. A real eye-opener. People are not all the same; a good lesson to bring away. We hope to go again, next time with blinkers off and hearts fully open...'

Hitting pause, Clove said, 'There are more, obvs, and we've got more coming in, which is pretty amazing considering how little we've actually said about him.'

'What I want to know,' Cristy said, 'is where these people have been to see him? The farm Elaine mentioned in Wales? Somewhere else entirely? Everyone is speaking highly of him, or mostly anyway, but no one is giving us any concrete details on where to find him.'

'Interesting that no one's mentioned anything about Nicole or the twins,' Connor pointed out, 'the actual reason for the series.'

'Indeed,' Cristy agreed, and checked her phone as a text arrived. Hating herself for feeling disappointed it was her son, not David, she decided to get back to Aiden later and said, 'Let's have a listen to Nicole's selected highlights again. Have you got them handy?'

Finding them, Clove hit play.

NICOLE: '... Lauren and I could hardly take our eyes off him ... There was something about him that made it hard not to stare ... He was older than us, not by much, and the way he was standing there, at the end of the bar on his own ...

'No one really understood who we were, how we liked to live our lives, but it didn't matter ... What difference did it make who we slept with? ...

'We used to have parties in the woods . . . we never held onto much in the way of inhibitions – hah! Claude always used to say clothes were just shields hiding perfection, and why would any of us want to hide that?'

When the playback stopped, Jacks said, 'Right there is where the perve neighbour got his inspiration. Must have been getting his rocks off watching them, and over time, he's added his own set of mind trips – with horns.'

Not interested in the irritating neighbour, Cristy said, 'Personally, I'm not having a problem seeing Meier as a gifted sociopath who's probably been honing his talents over many years while building up a team of helpers, who could be called disciples if we're open to the Jesus-Christ delusion.'

'Works for me,' Clove told her. 'And there's a chance we know where to find him now – Elaine's sent through an address.'

'And it chimes with Meier's Welsh granny,' Jacks put in, happily, 'insofar as we've turned up a Marie Jones who was married to Gwyn Jones, a farmer of that particular part of Powys. He died back in 2005, and she continued to work the land before her time came back in 2012.'

'Which coincides with when J.C. disappeared from Switzerland,' Connor pointed out. 'So, we're guessing he left his brother to run the vineyard while he went to take over Granny's farm – and set up whatever he's got going on in the Welsh mountains now.'

'You'd think,' Cristy said, 'after what happened to his parents, he'd have a seriously bad view of cults.'

'I'm with you on that,' Clove told her, 'unless he was indoctrinated too. Anyway, from some of the feedback, you'd think it was a holiday camp he had going over there. Or a retreat of some sort.'

'The fact that it has no internet presence when people are obviously coming and going quite a lot makes it weird,' Connor stated.

'It seems to be word of mouth recommendation,' Cristy said, 'which could make it cult-adjacent at the very least. On the other hand, I'm not getting the impression anyone is going there to live permanently – more to be with him and to enjoy the therapy facilities, whatever they might be.'

'There's one way to find out,' Connor declared. 'Let's pay him a surprise visit.'

'We've got a phone number,' Clove reminded him.

'Which would open us up to being knocked back. So, I say we go in carefully, see if we can get the lie of the land before knocking on the door.'

'I agree,' Cristy said, and from the way Connor looked at her, she immediately wondered if she'd sounded too enthusiastic and perhaps needed to tone down a bit. 'But don't let's delude ourselves here,' she continued, hoping she sounded normal. 'I'm sure he already knows about the podcast; he's probably seen our website, and if he *is* some sort of master-manipulator, there's a good chance he's been directing at least some of the feedback we've had so far.'

After sitting with that for a moment, Connor said, 'Even if he's expecting us – and I guess that's what you're saying – he won't know *when* we're coming, so I still say we go.'

Not arguing, Cristy turned to Jacks. 'It's a shame we don't have some images of him. Any luck with that yet?'

'Still trying, but here's a link to Google Maps showing the farm, or whatever it is now . . . Copyright is listed as 2025, but the image capture dates back to 2016. Still, it's something to start with.'

They spent the next few minutes studying the satellite view of a sprawling old farmhouse in the midst of mountainous countryside, with several outbuildings around the main property, probably barns, maybe stables; it was hard to tell, as the closer they zoomed in, the more blurred the images became.

'What's that there?' Connor asked, pointing to a sandy

splodge of terrain fifty yards or so from the main house. 'Could be a building site?'

'Looks like it,' Cristy agreed. 'Are those cottages or animal pens next to it? Anyway, the river running through the heart of the valley is clearly the Wye, and those woods just beyond the barns . . .' She switched to street-view and dragged the image in a semi-circle until it showed a small, tight copse. 'We could head there,' she suggested. 'It's right next to the house and would give us some cover . . .'

'Hang on – we're looking at mid-summer images,' Jacks cautioned. 'There's no guarantee those trees are in leaf right now.'

'They're mostly Scots pine,' she said, 'so they'll be fine. And that enormous one between the house and barn is a yew, so definitely a friend.' She sat back and looked at the others. 'Of course, much could have changed since these shots were taken, but at least this gives us the start of a plan.'

Connor checked the time. 'We have less than an hour before this week's drop,' he warned them, 'so let's go back to the trial and Nicole's collapse in court when she realized she was going down for a crime she's always claimed she didn't commit – until suddenly she confesses, all these years later, and yet she still can't or won't say where the bodies are. We can use that last bit, can't we? It's not suggesting any doubt about the confession, just that there are still questions to be asked.'

Cristy was already shaking her head. 'Maybe end it with "until she suddenly confessed,"' she said. 'That way it's clean and gives no rise to ambiguity just in case anyone from the prison service is listening. I'm also thinking of Meier – and, of course, Nicole herself.'

*

Later, after the drop and usual drinks, Cristy was at home, already in pyjamas and curled up on the sofa, thinking so hard about David that when her phone rang, she actually expected it to be him.

It was Jodi, Connor's wife, who she'd said good night to outside the office less than an hour ago.

Pushing past the crush of disappointment, she clicked on with an affectionate, 'Hi. Everything OK?'

'Sure, we're good, thanks. Another great episode, and Con's keeping me abreast of what's coming down the line, so you must be pleased with the way things are going?'

'Absolutely, but I know you're not ringing about that, so what's really going on?'

'Well, I was hoping you might tell me. Con says you haven't been yourself lately, and I could see tonight that you were . . . Are you upset about something?'

'I'm fine,' Cristy insisted, doing her best to sound it. 'Just a lot on my mind – nothing for you guys to worry about.'

'But we do. You know how much you mean to us, and if something's bothering you . . .'

'Honestly, I'm good. It's just . . . Well, David and I . . .' In a rush of emotional frustration she suddenly blurted, 'I think we're splitting up.'

'What?' Jodi cried in disbelief.

'. . . But it's OK. I'm dealing with it, and having a new series underway is definitely helping.'

'I can come over,' Jodi told her. 'If I leave now, I'll be there in less than twenty—'

'No, please don't. I mean, thanks for the offer, I really appreciate it, but I've got a killer headache, and I was about to turn my phone off to try and get some sleep.'

Jodi was silent, and picking up on her confusion, Cristy felt tears sting her eyes.

'I should go now,' she said. 'Thanks for caring, but really, everything's OK. Tell Con I'll meet him at ten in the morning to drive over to Wales.'

She rang off, feeling wretched for cutting Jodi short, for

missing David so much, for feeling so helpless and pathetic... She sat staring at her phone, wondering if she should ring Jodi back or send a message asking her to come after all.

Maybe she should call David.

No, she couldn't do that. She truly didn't want to speak to anyone tonight – apart from him, of course, but only if things were OK between them, and they clearly weren't or he'd have rung her.

As for leaning on Jodi, she had absolutely no right to do that when Kinsley's offer was still on the table.

She started as a WhatsApp message arrived, and seeing it was from Honey, she clicked on.

I'm with Nicole. She wants to speak to you. Are you able to take the call now?

After immediately messaging back to say yes, Cristy poured herself a drink and set her phone to record, just in case.

By the time Nicole connected, sounding tired and anguished, Connor hadn't joined the group chat, so guessing he'd turned his phone off for the night, Cristy went ahead on her own.

NICOLE: 'Hi, Cristy, I just heard the latest podcast. It was horrible, being reminded of the trial.'

CRISTY: 'I'm sorry, I thought you realized we were going to—'

NICOLE: 'It's OK. I'm just saying, it brought it all back and made me feel... No one's ever going to believe I didn't do it, are they?'

Cristy waited, sensing – hoping – there was more to come, because it was difficult to give reassurance when Nicole was probably right.

NICOLE: 'You didn't mention Claude tonight.'

CRISTY: 'He wasn't a part of the trial.'

NICOLE: 'No, that's right. He wasn't. Honey says you know where he is?'

CRISTY: 'I think we do. Yes.'

NICOLE: 'If you see him . . . Will you ask him . . . Tell him I need to see him.'

CRISTY: 'Of course.'

NICOLE: 'Thanks.'

Cristy started to speak again, but the line had already gone dead.

She half-expected Honey to ring back, but she didn't, so Cristy replayed the call and ended up deciding not to send it to Connor tonight. If he happened to pick up, he'd only want to discuss it, and really, there was nothing to be said that couldn't wait until morning. Besides, Cristy didn't feel in a good enough place to deal with much else today.

CHAPTER TWENTY-SEVEN

'So what I want to know,' Connor stated as they drove across the Severn Bridge the next morning, 'is how, in less than a month, you get from an amazing birthday party, Cartier earrings and a seriously convincing together-forever vibe, to splitting up. Explain it to me like I was five.'

Gazing down at the river's wide, sludgy banks, and hearing the echo of David's *I'll be in touch* ringing in her ears, Cristy said, 'What can I tell you? I've clearly royally screwed up somehow . . . I mean, I know how, although the details are . . .' She took a breath, suppressing an upsurge of emotion that could as easily burst into tears as anger. 'Actually, any chance we could change the subject?' she asked. 'There's a lot I need to sort out in my head, and I appreciate your concern, I really do, but right now we should be focusing on where we're going and why.'

He glanced at her, as if to make certain she truly did want to move on. 'OK,' he said slowly, 'but you know if you want to talk—'

'Thanks, but honestly, getting into it now won't help. So, tell me what you think of Nicole's call last night. Most particularly of her needing to see Meier.'

Speeding up to overtake a slow-moving tour bus, Connor said, 'I'm going to guess we're on the same page with it – in that it's not feeling like something we should be facilitating, at least until we know more about him and whether or not he's exerting some kind of control over her.'

Glad to have her own instincts confirmed, she said, 'I don't expect you've seen Honey's WhatsApp since we set out, but here's what she's saying, I'll read it out: *Until we know what sort of role he's really playing in her life, never mind inside her head, we need to protect her. Are you going to enter the lion's den today or just stake the place out?*'

'Good question,' Connor commented, reaching for his Costa coffee. 'Have you answered yet?'

'Just about to,' and voice-dictating into her phone, Cristy said, '*If it feels right to go in, we will. Otherwise, we're just getting the lie of the land. Will keep you posted.*'

They drove on quietly for a while, each with their own thoughts, although Cristy was trying hard to escape most of hers. Much better to stay focused on Meier and Nicole, or even Aiden and Hayley – actually, her brother was a good source of welcome distraction. Knowing he was having a ball in Europe with the not-so-new love of his life, Serena, was both cheering and, Goddammit, making her tearful. Why was she always on the brink these days? What the heck was there to cry about in wishing she could be with him?

Actually, what she really wanted was to turn back the clock to before she'd caused this ludicrous situation with David . . .

'The guy's almost certainly some kind of narcissist,' Connor declared, as they joined the road to Abergavenny, the halfway point.

Taking a moment to realize he meant Meier, Cristy said, 'I'm more than half-convinced he's behind most, if not all, of the feedback we've received. If I'm right, then he's definitely trying to mess with us. Question is, to what end?'

'Maybe it's how he gets his kicks, alongside playing Jesus?'

With a faint laugh, she said, 'I'm trying to figure out if there's some sort of underlying message to the feedback that we're not quite getting? Actually, I'm going to ask Clove and Jacks to take a closer look at it, see if there are any commonalities or pointers that might connect the dots. They always enjoy a good code-breaking mission.'

By the time Cristy had relayed instructions and dealt with messages from both her children, she looked up to discover they were passing through Raglan, where the ancient castle appeared bleaker than ever on this dull grey day. Then a few rays of sunlight found their way out of the cloud to light the centuries-old ruins, as if to remind her of how beautiful and mystical the place really was. Her brother, the great historian, would love it here; he'd probably even be able to tell her all about its heritage without having to look it up.

'I bloody love this place,' Connor declared warmly. 'I don't know why; it just gets me every time I see it.'

Remembering he had a Welsh father, she said, 'Did you used to come here as a child?'

'Sure, but I didn't really appreciate it then. It's funny, though, how every time I'm in Wales these days, I feel my spirits lifting.' He threw her a quick glance. 'Any chance it's happening for you?' he asked hopefully.

Tilting her head, she said, 'I'm thinking that the people who once lived in that castle thought their issues were all-important when they were happening, and now we don't even know who they were.'

'Wow,' he murmured. 'Not really getting the upbeat thing.'

Laughing, she said, 'It does put things in perspective though, doesn't it? The reminder that nothing's permanent, and no matter how bad things are today – or good – it won't last because it can't.'

'OK, definitely not cheering me up here. So how about a song?' And he promptly broke into a pretty good rendition of 'Up on Cripple Creek', simply because it was the name of the place they were now passing through.

'You do realize the Cripple Creek you're singing about is in Colorado, don't you? Or is it Virginia?'

'Who cares? It's just a great song, and now, as we drive around this magnificent curve in the road into the heart of the Welsh valleys, we find ourselves overawed by the spectacle of no less than three of this amazing nation's most stunning mountain tops. Are you not falling to your knees in adulation of nature's most resplendent creations?'

Loving him just because he was him, she said, 'We should be recording this.'

'What makes you think we're not,' he countered, and nodded towards the red light on his display screen, showing that he'd activated the built-in recorder.

'How did I forget you had that?' She smiled. 'Except, I seem to be forgetting everything these days.' And, after a pause, 'Remind me, where are we going?'

*

Two hours later, after pushing through fast descending swirls of fog and outbreaks of sleeting rain as they drove high into the mountains, they finally arrived at the destination they'd selected by using a satellite view on Google Maps. It was a small pull-in from a single-lane road that passed the other side of the wood next to Bryn Helyg Farm. This, Jacks had discovered, was the name used during Meier's grandmother's time; they had yet to establish what the place was called today.

Funny how no one had mentioned it in their comments, and yet several had provided contact details without any prompting.

As they got out of the car, a cloying mass of freezing air instantly dampened their coats and chilled their faces. Thankfully, there was no wind and for the moment, no rain – just a morass of low-lying cloud spreading out in a dense grey fug around them. Cristy took in what little she could see: thorny hedgerows across the narrow road and the towering copse behind her, not a single person, vehicle, bird or animal in sight. In fact, even Connor wasn't wholly visible at the other side of the car.

'Not much in the way of signal,' he muttered, checking his phone as he came to join her. He looked up, surveyed the ominous cluster of trees and said, 'You first.'

Stifling a laugh, in spite of no one seeming to be around to hear them, she took a step forward, only to be blocked by his arm as he gallantly took the lead.

The tight cluster of trunks, with needle-branches coated in frost and upper limbs reaching like skeletal fingers into the mist, felt both unworldly and menacing. They moved gingerly, holding back brambles and steadying themselves against peeling bark, careful not to trip on exposed roots or sink into hidden rabbit holes. Their breath filled the space in front of them with small clouds of warm air; the scent all around was heady and earthy and very soon started to become sweetly pungent.

On reaching the other side of the copse, they remained partly hidden to get their bearings before moving on. Across the track in front of them was a huge, metal barn, doors wide open, with a tractor outside but no sign of a driver, and from their current perspective, the outbuilding's interior appeared as black as night. Thanks to Google Maps, they already knew that the dry-stone wall sloping downhill away from the barn surrounded the farmhouse garden. It was a relief to see that in reality it was no more than four feet high and that the huge trunk of the yew they'd spotted during their online stalk was right next to a small, wrought-iron gate.

From here, they could only see the roof of the house – muted grey slate with chimneys either end, and a lazy trail of smoke curling from one into the dank, colourless sky. It was clearly large and gave the impression of being solidly settled into its place on the hillside.

After checking up and down the track, glimpsing further structures fifty or more yards away but still no people, they made their way over to the stone wall and peered through the tangle of old man's beard that ran along the top. The property was indeed big and sturdy, a classic Welsh farmhouse with at least a dozen deep-set, wood-framed windows and a heavy oak front door. It had clearly undergone some improvements over the years to add a huge, peak-roof front porch and a deep-set flagstone front patio, with a wide, wrought-iron gate at one end opening into a lane that ran between the garden and what appeared to be stables.

'Is that a hot tub?' Cristy whispered, pointing to a small construction in the middle of the right-side lawn.

'Looks like it,' Connor responded, 'and there's a fire-pit over there, excellent for outdoor dining – or midnight rituals?'

Intrigued by the mix of olde-worlde charm and modern luxuries, Cristy made her way along the wall to the small gate in order to get a better view. The place was clearly well taken care of; even the outbuildings appeared solidly constructed and highly maintained.

'I can hear cows,' Connor murmured as he joined her.

She listened, and sure enough, there was the distant lowing of cattle. No sign of them, but the fog patches were too thick to get a good sense of where any fields or livestock sheds might be.

They tensed as the front door suddenly opened and a young woman came out onto the porch, wearing an old wax jacket, a woollen hat and jodhpurs. After taking a moment to dig her feet into a pair of green wellies, she let herself out of the side gate and disappeared into the stables.

They waited a moment to see if anyone followed or for her to return. Nothing happened, until suddenly the front door opened again. This time, a tall, slender man with thick dark wavy hair and a close-shaved beard came out of the house. He was wearing an old Guernsey sweater, a black gilet and workmanlike jeans. From this distance, it wasn't possible to make out his features, and yet Cristy just knew, instinctively, that they were looking at Jean-Claude Meier.

He moved easily, almost gracefully, as he went to collect wood from a pile to one side of the porch, and unless she was imagining it, thanks to all she'd heard about him, there really did seem to be something about him that was . . . arresting? It couldn't be his looks, given how indistinguishable they were from here, and certainly not his typical countryside attire. However, he definitely emanated a sense of *something*.

Apparently, Connor thought so too, because he whispered, 'I reckon that's Jesus.'

Managing not to laugh, Cristy watched as presumed-Meier piled logs into a cardboard box and carried them into the house, closing the door behind him.

'Do you think the woman might be Mrs Jesus?' Connor asked drolly.

Throwing him a look, Cristy said, 'Let's find out what's going on further down the lane. There are cars just past the stables, and—'

'Shit, someone's coming,' Connor hissed, and grabbing her arm, he tugged her back along the wall, around the tractor and into the murky darkness of the barn.

Hearing the sound of a vehicle approaching, Cristy took another careful step back from the wide-open door, then another—

Her foot hit something soft, and suddenly she was sliding about in a pool of something that might not be mud.

Catching her, Connor held her up, then lost his own footing, and next thing, she was on her knees in muck and he was doing some sort of slapstick midair pedalling in an effort to right himself before he ended up flat on his back.

She was laughing so hard she almost choked trying to keep it in.

He was laughing too, straining to keep quiet while slithering about in useless attempts to get up.

It was so hilarious she thought she was going to burst. She was out of control, becoming hysterical, and the struggle to hold it in was only making things worse.

Suddenly, Connor was still.

She peered at him in the gloom, saw his eyes fixed on something over her shoulder and turned breathlessly to see what it was.

Her head reeled. Only feet away, staring right at them with wide golden eyes and fearsome nostrils, was a massive cow – with horns.

'No fast moves,' Connor cautioned, and tried to ease himself in front of her.

She made a guttural sound as laughter threatened to engulf her again. This wasn't funny. This colossus could actually kill them, and yet she was beside herself with mirth.

They rose together, an inch at a time, clinging to one another while staring at the beast, and finally took a first tentative step towards the door.

The cow suddenly bellowed, a bellicose deafening roar.

They froze and watched in stunned terror as it turned away, stuck its head in a water trough and slumped heavily down in the hay with a weary grunt and snort. Only then did they realize it was tethered.

'Fuck,' Connor muttered, and quickly checking if the coast was clear outside, he beckoned her to follow.

'Jesus, that was close,' he muttered, as they reached the tractor.

'The state of us,' she spluttered. 'We're covered in shit.'

He strangled a laugh and was about to cross the lane, back into the copse, when they heard the sound of piano playing.

Exchanging surprised glances, they made their way back to the garden wall and peered through the long, spiked leaves of a cabbage plant. The music was clearly coming from inside the house, but the mist had thickened again, making the delicate, rippling arpeggios seem almost ethereal as they floated out into the gloom. The harmonies became rich and fluid, growing in intensity, portraying drama and passion before softening again and fading away like the dying strains of a dream.

It was so hypnotic that, for a moment, neither of them moved or spoke, simply paused in the lingering aftermath of the beauty.

Cristy's eye was caught by a movement at the side gate. She watched as someone emerged from the mist and felt her heart stumble to a stop. It was surely an illusion; it simply couldn't be real . . .

She continued to stare, dumbfounded, as the apparition moved to the house and in through the door.

Connor turned to her. 'Tell me I didn't just see that,' he said hoarsely. 'That was *not* what I think it was, was it?'

Equally as appalled and totally unable to explain it, Cristy took his arm and hurried him back to the copse, all the way through it and into the safety of the car.

CHAPTER TWENTY-EIGHT

'I don't get it,' Aiden cried in frustration. 'What's so shocking about some bloke dressed up in flowing white robes—'

'You're too young to understand the significance,' his father interrupted. 'Go on,' he encouraged Cristy.

'It was the last thing we expected to see,' she confessed. 'A bold-faced white supremacist in—'

'I thought he was wearing a mask,' Aiden jumped in.

'Google it,' Matthew told him. 'Put in three capital Ks, see what you get.'

They were at the Côte Brasserie in Clifton, where Cristy had joined them as soon as she'd showered, washed her hair and stuffed her clothes on a super-hot wash. Connor's car was a serious no-go zone for the next few days, while a magician of a valet worked on getting the seats clean and the stench out.

'We have no idea what to make of it,' she said, picking up her wine. 'Of all the things we've heard about the man, nothing remotely political has come up, and certainly not like that.'

'Are you sure you were reading it right?' Matthew frowned. 'There was a news story recently about some Aussies on a cruise ship who dressed up as snow cones and shocked the hell out of everyone, not realizing what they actually looked like. Same as our son, they were too young—'

'What the . . . !' Aiden exclaimed, staring at his phone in shock. 'This is seriously messed up.'

'Those people are,' Cristy informed him. 'They're full of hate and prejudice and everything you can think of that's vile. We can only be thankful they don't live here.'

'Some do,' Matthew reminded her, 'and from what you're saying, at least one of them is on that farm in Wales. Unless, he or she was supposed to be a snow cone, of course.'

Managing a laugh, Cristy said, 'I'm going to hope that's all it was, because the alternative is . . . Well, apart from all the hideousness of it, I don't know how we'd handle it. Badly, is probably the answer, but now we've had time to think about it, we're wondering if it was actually staged for our benefit. It feels like the kind of thing this J.C. would do to freak us out – if he actually knew we were there, and I have a horrible feeling he did.'

Reaching for the bottle to refill their glasses, Matthew said, 'So where do you go with that, if it turns out you're right about any of it?'

'We have a team meeting in the morning to discuss.'

Aiden started to laugh. 'The bit I can't get past,' he said, 'is you guys sliding about in shit. I'd kill to have seen that. And staring down an actual *bull*. Kudos to you, Mum. You are like no other.'

'Kind of what I always say about her,' Matthew put in, 'but she never wants to hear it from me. So, moving on . . . Are we ready to? Sorry, is that—'

'Definitely moving on,' she confirmed. 'Tell me what's new with you and your second divorce?'

Matthew's eyebrows rose.

Realizing her attempt at humour was actually offensive, (her sensitivity radar was definitely off these days), she said, 'Sorry. What I meant was: how goes life with you, Marley and your baby son, Bear?'

Taking a sip of wine, he said, 'We seem to be at a standstill right now, but I'm assured the divorce is going through, and I should hear any time now about shared custody. Obviously, my share will be holidays and whenever I can get to LA. Speaking of which, has Aiden told you about his plans for the summer yet?'

Aiden looked up from his phone. 'They've changed again,' he informed his father. 'Hayley and Hugo have decided to let me join their tour of North America, which they're planning to end on the West Coast, Vancouver, San Fran, LA. Uncle Tom's giving us loads of advice for when—'

'You're in touch with him?' Cristy asked, surprised and pleased. Tom had lived abroad for a long time and there had been shamefully scant contact between them since their mother's death.

'Hayley set up a WhatsApp, so we've been messaging. He's in Istanbul right now, which sounds seriously cool. He said you and David are talking about meeting up somewhere with him and Serena – so any thoughts on where yet?'

Losing her appetite, Cristy put her fork down as she said, 'We can't go anywhere until this series is over.'

Aiden shrugged. 'I'd choose Prague, if it were up to me. Or maybe Budapest. Dad, didn't you meet the King of Budapest once?'

'I think you mean Hungary,' Matthew said, his eyes fixed on Cristy, 'and I wasn't around at the beginning of the last century. You're probably referring to Alexander Karađorđević, Crown Prince of Yugoslavia.'

'That's the guy. I knew it was someone royal from over that way.'

'All the money we've spent on your education,' Cristy sighed, wishing Matthew would stop looking at her like that, as if sensing something was wrong when she hadn't said anything was.

'It'll be worth it in the end,' Aiden assured her. 'Hey, just spotted my mate Jed over there. I'll be right back.'

As he left the table, Cristy deliberately avoided Matthew's

eyes as she attempted to eat again. 'Jodi's weekly spot on the news seems to be working out well,' she commented chattily.

'It is,' he confirmed. 'So, what's going on with you? I can tell something is—'

'You don't know anything,' she cut in snappishly. God, he was annoying! 'You just make stuff up to try and undermine me and create problems where none exist, so give it a break, will you? I've had a long day, I'm not sure how to take the series forward from here, and having you on my case over nothing at all is not what I need.'

His hands went up in surrender. 'No need to bite my head off,' he responded. 'I was just trying to be friendly—'

'No, you were trying to make mischief, because you always do, and I've had enough of it. If we're going to carry on seeing one another for the children's sake, then you need to back the hell out of my personal life where it doesn't concern you. OK? *OK?*' She could almost feel her eyes flashing.

There was a moment before he said, quietly, 'If that's what you want—'

'It is. It's exactly what I want. I don't need you or anyone else interfering in my life.' She'd already gone too far, and she knew it, but she couldn't seem to make herself stop. 'Making assumptions about me, telling me what to do, how to live my life . . .' She was trying not to shout and wasn't even sure what her point was any more. 'I don't need your input, thank you very much,' she muttered. 'In fact, I'm doing much better without it, so please keep your concern or advice, or whatever the fuck it is, to yourself, and leave me alone.'

When she finally fell silent, Matthew sat staring at her, clearly mystified and shocked by how, in a matter of moments, she'd managed to morph into a shrewish, deranged stranger who'd apparently gone off the edge. It was how she felt – alien to herself, as if she'd lost control of her wits, but the rage was there now, and it still felt all-consuming.

'Well, I guess I should get the bill,' he said in the end, and signalled to a waiter. 'Did you bring your car?'

'I can get an Uber,' she snapped without meaning to.

'Aiden's things are in my boot,' he explained, 'and as he's staying with you for the next few days, maybe I should drive you home. Don't worry, I'll leave as soon as I've helped him in, and I promise not to ask you anything personal – ever again.'

*

By the time Cristy got into bed an hour later, she'd managed to calm down and was now feeling wretched and guilty and actually quite lost. In spite of knowing, in her rational mind, that the damnable changes in her middle-aged psyche were most likely to blame for the unforgiveable outburst, she couldn't help wondering if she was just using it to justify how badly she was handling the fear of losing David. It had been five days now and they never normally went this long without speaking, so was this his way of trying to let her down gently? Of course, she could call him, but it didn't feel like the right thing to do when he'd said he would call her.

And just to add to her stress levels here she was still trying to make a decision about Kinsley's offer (although that felt more of an impossibility than a bright star on the horizon right now). It was as though everything – mind, body, hormones, the bloody world at large – was conspiring against her, turning her into a monster, robbing her of reason and sleep and blowing her perspective on even the simplest things right out of the water.

She couldn't go on like this or she was going to end up alienating everyone by doing or saying something she didn't mean and would instantly deeply regret – as if she wasn't already there. She needed to see a doctor. Obviously they wouldn't be able to do anything about the heartache or the torturous indecision, but a course of HRT might help alleviate at least some of the strain by taking the heat out of her erratic temper. It wouldn't undo any offence she'd already caused, unfortunately, but it might at least prevent her from making things worse.

If there *was* anything worse than losing David. Right now, she couldn't think of a single thing.

CHAPTER TWENTY-NINE

'Am I speaking to Cristy Ward?'

Cristy's heart skipped a beat. The accent alone – quite different to the hoax caller of a week or so ago – told her who this was, and for a stunned moment, she couldn't think what to say.

Quickly signalling for everyone to pay attention, she switched the call to speaker and said, 'Yes, it's Cristy. Who is this please?'

Sounding faintly amused, he said, 'I think you already know that, but I'm happy to confirm it's Claude Meier.'

Looking across to Connor whose eyes had widened she said, 'It's good to hear from you, Mr Meier. I must admit, this is a surprise.'

With a low laugh, Meier said, 'I know you were here yesterday. We were quite entertained by your visit, but really, all you needed to do was call and we'd have been delighted to welcome you.'

Cristy immediately felt as ridiculous as he no doubt intended, mostly for not having realized sooner that the place was probably rigged with cameras. She said, 'That's very kind of you. We'd love to take you up on the offer, if it remains open.'

'Of course. All I ask is you don't disturb Arabella again. She's a first-calf heifer, you see, and quite close to her time.'

Recalling the massive cow, while ignoring the smirks from

Clove and Jacks, Cristy said, 'We can probably be there by early afternoon tomorrow, if that works for you?'

'*C'est excellent,*' he declared. 'We will see you then. Oh, by the way, there is plenty of parking a few metres past the stables, so no need to enter through the woods. *À demain.*' And he was gone.

Suppressing a growl that was more of a laugh, she said, 'Well, I guess we've made contact.'

'Why didn't you ask about the Klanner?' Connor wanted to know.

Disappointed with herself for having momentarily forgotten it, she said, 'Because he's already laughing at us, and if it turns out that little stunt was staged, we'll only make ourselves look even more foolish – if that's actually possible, and I'm not sure it is.'

'I'd pay money to have seen the shitshow.' Clove laughed. 'I wonder if he recorded it?'

'Not one of your most successful stealth ops,' Jacks remarked dryly. 'But hey, at least he seems willing to talk.'

'We could have gone today,' Connor pointed out. 'It would have given him less time to come up with any more little sideshows.'

'I have an appointment at five,' she replied, returning to her computer, 'and I don't want to miss it.'

There was a moment before he said curiously, 'Something we need to know about?'

Experiencing a flash of impatience, she said, 'Nothing to do with the series.' Then, making an attempt to level off with irony, 'I do have a personal life, you know, and sadly it doesn't come to a stop just because we've got a great story on our hands.'

Connor continued to look at her.

She eyeballed him back, clocked the moment he assumed it was about David and felt horrible when he nodded reassuringly, before turning to pick up where they'd left off when Meier rang.

Cristy was only half-listening as they discussed Jacks's ongoing efforts to make contact with Meier's friends during his time in Bristol – so far, he had a couple of names: Johan Bauer, a German national, and Freya Jensen from Copenhagen. If he could track one or both of them down, it would be great to get their input – their perspective, even – on those colourful times. For her part, Clove was fixed on finding someone, somewhere, who might lead them to Lauren Hawkes.

'You know what bothers me most about Lauren's disappearance,' Clove remarked later in the day, 'is that her mother's only received cards or emails since she left – no calls or visits. So I keep asking myself: is someone else making contact *for* her? And if so, why isn't she doing it herself?'

The very same issue had been bothering Cristy. However, the only answer she could offer right now was, 'If she hadn't been visiting Nicole in prison all this time, we might have reason to think the worst, but apparently she has, and so I guess that tells us she's at least still this side of the Pearly Gates.'

'And possibly on that farm?' Jacks suggested.

'Not ruling it out,' Cristy assured him.

Connor said, 'It could be worth asking her mother if we can take a look at the cards and emails?'

'I'll get onto it,' Clove declared, and a few minutes later, after setting up a meeting with Bridget Hawkes for the next day, she went to write it up on the whiteboard.

'Have you let Honey know we're seeing Meier tomorrow?' Connor asked Cristy, as Clove added their return visit to Wales to the board.

'No, but we should,' Cristy replied. 'Can you do it? I need to leave now.'

It was still too early for the last-minute appointment she'd managed to grab with a menopause specialist – getting to see her GP could take weeks, and she didn't want to waste any more time – but she was suddenly overcome by an urge to call Matthew.

Waiting until she'd driven away from the studios, she instructed handsfree to connect to his number and was both relieved and nervous when he answered.

'I want to apologize for last night,' she told him. 'I shouldn't have flown off the handle like that so . . . I'm sorry.'

After a beat, he said, 'OK.'

Irked by the brevity of his response, she said, 'Is that it? Am I forgiven?'

His tone was terse as he said, 'Your apology is accepted, but forgiveness is a different ask, and frankly I'm not feeling it right now. So, thanks for the call, much appreciated, but I'm about to go into a meeting.'

As the line went dead, furious tears stung her eyes, and for one ludicrous moment, she wanted her mother so badly that she felt she might scream with it. She took a breath, swallowed hard, inhaled again and drove on towards the Downs, wondering if she could dare to call David's mother, or even David himself.

What the hell did she think she was going to say to either of them? *Cynthia, you remind me so much of my mother I feel I can talk to you about anything.* Or: *Hi, David, it's me, I'm perimenopausal, so please ignore everything I say?* Or, *Oops, sorry rang your number by mistake, but now we're here, how are you?*

She shuddered even to think of humiliating herself that way, so no! It was nearly a week now, and though there was no part of him needing time to think that she didn't understand, she couldn't help feeling desperate to speak to him. She'd call right now, or message, if pride weren't such a masterful thing. She wondered what he thought about her not getting in touch. Was he taking it that she needed time too? Was it even bothering him? Maybe he'd already moved on.

Someone who apparently hadn't was Paul Kinsley, because as she checked in to the doctor's reception, he texted asking if they could speak the next day and there went her stress levels again.

She messaged back:

Sorry, going to be in Wales on assignment and rubbish reception. Will Saturday work for you?

Why was she even entertaining this now when her constantly irritated self was going into meltdown?

Great. I'll call around eleven.

She considered replying with a thumbs up emoji but added a message instead:

No change of mind about Molly Terrance, so hope you're going to be telling me what I want to hear.

She waited – and waited – but no reply came, and then it was time to go in for her appointment.

CHAPTER THIRTY

The next day, having suffered a near-sleepless night, Cristy let Connor drive her car over to Wales as his hadn't made it back from the valet yet and she was too tired to be trusted at the wheel.

They spent much of the journey attempting to discuss their approach to the upcoming meeting, but she kept dozing off and waking up suddenly, trying to recall where they were in the conversation – until finally she fell into a kind of abyss, and the next thing she knew, they were bumping along a pitted track past the farmhouse and stables to the car park Meier had mentioned.

She straightened up slowly, easing a crick in her neck and noticing with relief that there was no fog today, though no sunshine either. The sky spread out ahead of them was vast and leaden, the landscape dull and rambling as it dipped for miles down into the valley bed, rising and swelling again into the opposite mountain. Sheep dotted many of the closer fields, and laid out just beyond the car park, perched like landed spaceships at the top of the hill, were at least two dozen domed structures quietly taking in the view.

'Definitely wasn't expecting a glamping site,' Connor commented, killing the engine. 'They look pretty . . . futuristic, don't they?'

Cristy nodded. 'And deserted,' she added. 'Where is everyone? Someone must have seen us arrive.'

Turning to her, Connor said, 'At the risk of getting my head bitten off, are you OK?'

Confused, she said, 'Why would I bite your head off for asking that?'

'You seemed to be having a few bad dreams on the way here.'

Embarrassed, she said, 'Did I say something . . . ? Sorry if I—'

'You don't have to apologize, I just thought . . . I guess it's David. I mean, obvs it's him, but if . . .'

'It's not just him,' she confessed, experiencing a sudden urge to be truthful. 'It's me and what's happening to me. Actually, it's what happens to most women at my time of life, but please don't worry. I've seen someone about it, and once the HRT kicks in, I should be as good as new. Meanwhile, if I start going of the rails about anything, please risk me biting your head off if you try to pull me back. Actually, no, I shouldn't be your responsibility, and you shouldn't have to suffer my mood swings—'

'It's OK,' he said gently. 'I'm here for you. Now, if you look over your left shoulder, you'll see we have an audience.'

She turned, started and gave a laugh. A hairy-chinned billy goat had its face pressed to her window and was watching them with beady, amber eyes. 'He's cute,' she said, 'although he does have horns, so are we stuck here being the lemons again?'

'Hey, Jasper,' someone called, 'where are your manners? *Recule!* Let the lady out of the car.'

As if understanding, the goat turned, took the carrot he was being offered and trotted on his way, munching happily.

Their rescuer – unmistakably Meier, she recognized his voice – was laughing as he pulled open the car door for her to get out into the icy drizzle of rain.

'Sorry,' he said good humouredly. 'He enjoys visitors but doesn't always understand the rules of early engagement. Hi, I'm Claude. And you must be Cristy. It's good to meet you.'

As she took his hand, warm and strong, she wasn't sure if she felt a small wave of something coasting into her. More likely it was the heat of his skin absorbing the cold of hers. He was taller than her, around six feet, his shoulders broad, his wavy hair rain-spattered and dishevelled, while his deep-set black eyes shone with humour. His smile was magnetic. There was certainly something about him, and it had taken her all of a few seconds to sense it.

'It's good to meet you too,' she told him. 'This is Connor, who you no doubt recognize from your home movies.'

Meier laughed, clearly enjoying the joke, and clasped Connor's hand with both of his. 'Welcome to Bryn Helyg,' he said. 'I think it probably is not what you were expecting, or maybe it is. We are, if you do not know this already, a farm-cum-retreat-cum-wellness centre, with many treatments and therapies to offer our guests, but that is not the reason you are here, of course. So maybe we should get out of this weather and take some refreshments up at the house?'

As he gestured for them to go ahead, Connor said, 'Shall I bring the recorder?'

Turning back, Meier said, '*Pourquoi-pas?* Do you need help to carry anything?'

'It's fine,' Connor assured him. 'Just one bag.'

Taking heart from Meier's apparent willingness to be interviewed, Cristy fell into step beside him as they walked past the stables and into the lane next to the farmhouse. At the far end, a lorry with the rear doors open appeared to be receiving whatever was being craned out of the large building behind it.

Meier paused at the gate to watch. His tone was sombre as he said, 'I'm afraid it's Arabella. She gave birth last night and suffered a prolapsed womb afterwards. We had to let her go this morning.'

Cristy felt absurdly sad given how the very same cow had scared the living daylights out of her forty-eight hours ago. 'I'm sorry to hear that. Is the calf OK?'

'Yes, he's doing well. Someone is feeding him and making sure he stays warm. He's with a couple of brood cows and their calves, so he's not alone.'

Sensing that Arabella's loss had actually touched Meier quite deeply, Cristy said again, 'I'm sorry she didn't make it.'

He nodded, seeming to appreciate the words, and as Connor joined them, he pushed open the gate. 'I'm not sure anyone is inside at the moment,' he said, leading them to the front porch, 'but we've made the place as welcoming as we can for you. Please excuse us if we seem . . . *un peu rustique*, but this is a quiet time of year. Not many guests, mainly those of us who live and work here twenty-four seven. And the animals, of course. Here we are.' And pushing open the heavy oak door, he gestured for them to go inside.

As Cristy stepped into a large, high-ceilinged, oak-beamed kitchen, it was the warmth that hit her first, quickly followed by the mouth-watering aroma of freshly baked bread, mixed with something slightly muskier. Realizing it was the roaring log fire in a large, inglenook hearth, she inhaled deeply and looked around to take in the rest of the room. It was as homely a kitchen as she'd ever been in, full of wooden cabinets and quartzite worktops, with brushed velvet curtains at the recessed windows. There were all kinds of modern gadgets, a refectory table to seat at least twelve against the far wall, and a capacious sofa with patchwork-covered armchairs either side of the fender.

'Please make yourselves comfortable,' Meier invited, taking their coats to hang in an alcove next to the door. 'If you don't mind, I need to slip outside for a moment to make sure everything is in order before Arabella is taken away. *Excusez-moi.*'

As he left, Connor went to set his bag on the table, before going over to the fire. 'He's right about this place not being quite what we expected,' he said, rubbing his hands together in front of the flames. 'Although, to be honest, I'm not sure what we did expect – are you?'

Cristy shook her head and looked around again. 'He's . . .' Finding herself unable to describe him, she simply said, 'What do you think of him?'

Connor shrugged. 'So far, I kind of like him, and even I can see, as a hetero bloke with no hidden agenda, that he has a lot of appeal. Maybe I should get myself one of those accents.'

Laughing, Cristy began to examine the various photographs and knick-knacks scattered about the place. No faces she recognized – apart from Meier's in a few – and nothing that smacked of idolatry or far-right tendencies, or any sort of mysticism, if she discounted the half-burned candles and assorted small fossils, presumably from the many quarries around these hills. She looked at the table and found herself imagining it full of noisy diners and drinkers, a lot of laughter and shared stories.

'There's nothing gloomy about the place, is there?' she said, going to join Connor at the fire. 'It kind of radiates . . . welcome? Do I sound like a twit?'

'Yes, but think of the comments we've received – didn't someone say they felt like they were on a higher plane when they were here?'

Someone had said that, although Cristy wasn't sure she'd go that far herself.

'There's definitely a good vibe,' Connor decided, and glanced up at the ceiling as though it might be emanating from somewhere above.

'Do you think we're being listened to?' she whispered.

They looked around. No sign of mics or cameras – only a few cobwebs clinging to the cornices and a small sprig of Christmas tinsel seeming to sprout from one of the beams.

'That is good; everything is fine,' Meier announced, coming through the door and kicking off his boots.

'Sorry, we should have done the same,' Cristy said, quickly going to remove her own.

'No, no,' he said, stopping her with a raised hand. 'We have flagstone floors and threadbare rugs for a reason, so we can come and go without fuss. I take mine off now because, inside, my feet are wet and cold. Time to get a new pair. Of boots. Not feet.'

Smiling, Cristy said, 'I feel we should apologize for coming to spy on you the day before yesterday.'

Clearly amused, he said, 'That is not necessary; we very much enjoyed your visit. Now, will you take tea or coffee or maybe something a little stronger?'

'Coffee will be great,' Connor told him. 'No milk or sugar.'

Going to start an impressive Breville Barista Pro, Meier said, 'Susanna has been baking, if you are hungry. I find myself unable to resist.' And pulling open a door of the eight-burner range, he unhooked an oven glove to bring out a tray of golden scones. 'Susanna is also our jam-maker, and the cream is from our cows,' he told them. 'It is for you to decide which comes first, if you would like to take one. Or two. Or more. As you see, there are plenty.'

In next to no time, they were seated at one end of the refectory table with large mugs of coffee and plates of crumbly, curranty scones – they were all jam first, Cristy noticed – when the door opened again and the woman they'd spotted two days ago came in. She was older than they'd first thought, probably mid-forties, blonde with a single plait draped over one shoulder and a friendliness in her blue eyes and crimson-lipped smile that was easy to warm to.

'Hi, welcome to Bryn Helyg,' she said, shrugging off her coat. 'I'm Maggi – with an i, not a y.'

Wondering if there was some sort of theme going on with the i's and y's, Cristy smiled as much at the woman as the melodic Welsh accent.

'Maggi more or less runs this place,' Meier informed them. 'Without her, we'd all be lost. Come and join us, *ma chère*; I know you're keen to meet our new friends.'

'Right with you.' Maggi smiled and went to pour herself a coffee.

Cristy clocked how feminine she appeared, in spite of the baggy overalls and man's plaid shirt. As she turned back to Meier, he said dryly, 'Am I allowed to ask what conclusions you drew from your last visit here?'

Cristy glanced at Connor.

'None in particular,' Connor replied. 'Only . . . actually, we saw something that kind of . . . alarmed us.'

Meier nodded his understanding. 'Arabella really is – was – as gentle as a lamb,' he assured them, 'but of course you weren't to know that.'

As Connor blanked, Cristy realized he had no idea of the cow's name. 'Actually, it wasn't the cow that we thought was a bull,' she said, glancing at Maggi as she sat down the other side of Connor. 'It was someone we saw coming in here just before we left. Unless we were mistaken they seemed to be wearing long white robes and a conical sort of masked hat that—'

'Ah, our friend Ray Johnson from Alabama,' Meier interrupted, appearing both amused and concerned. How did he do that? 'He's working through a few issues with Simeon, one of our therapists. Given the nature of his discrimination, we decided, with his wife, that they should come while no one else was around – apart from ourselves, of course.'

'It's still early days for Ray,' Maggi told them, 'but Simeon is quite gifted when it comes to turning hatred into tolerance and prejudice into understanding and acceptance. So Ray is here working on himself with Simeon's help and wearing those robes is a kind of purge, at least in Ray's mind.'

Meier's eyes were on Maggi, and as she met them with her own, he smiled.

Cristy wasn't sure if they'd just witnessed an intimate moment (and who wouldn't want to be intimate with this man given how *physical* he was? Interesting, and a little disconcerting that he seemed to be having an effect on her already, or was it just her own chaotic state of mind mixing up signals?). She said, 'It sounds as though you have quite a lot of . . .' What was she trying to say? 'Quite a lot going on here. Would you mind if we record while you tell us about the place?'

'Please go ahead,' Meier invited, picking up his coffee and scooting his chair back a way to sit more comfortably.

As Connor began setting up, Cristy decided to ask her first question before the mic was on. 'We've received quite a lot of feedback since mentioning your name in our podcast and on our website. Will you tell us honestly if you were behind it?'

He laughed and put down his mug. '*Démasqué!*' he declared, clearly not minding in the least that he'd been rumbled. 'However, I need to tell you that everything we sent to you has come from our guests' messages to us. We made nothing up, but of course in most cases, we changed the names, or perhaps we didn't give them at all?' He looked to Maggi for confirmation, which she gave.

'Even the negative comments?' Cristy asked.

Meier grimaced. 'I have not seen everything you have received, obviously; maybe some of those did not come from us. Like everyone, we also are subject to bad reviews and disappointment. People come here expecting a lot, and we do our best to help, but sometimes, it is not possible.'

'They can go away angry and frustrated,' Maggi continued, 'and they find it easier to blame us rather than themselves for how they have been unable to fully open up and let go. It's important to give yourself completely to the process of healing, or it's possible you'll go away even more mixed up and afraid than when you arrived.'

'Contrary to what some people think,' Meier said, 'we cannot perform miracles.' His eyes twinkled. 'Even at weddings.'

Maggi laughed. 'No water into wine at our ceremonies.'

Meier's mesmeric eyes moved between Cristy and Connor as he said, 'Shall I tell you what really happened at Cana? I think you will be interested to know that there is a big misunderstanding of John's words in his gospel. When it's said the water was turned into wine, it's important to understand that at that time, only celibates – priests – were allowed to drink the communion wine. But at this particular wedding, Jesus told the "non-celibates", the people, to take their fill. So instead of water, they indulged in wine. No miraculous transformation – only the breaking of a tradition.' He smiled and circled a hand as though encouraging them to continue with the recording.

Having no idea what to say right now, Cristy turned to Connor, only to see that he was equally at a loss.

Apparently reading their confusion, Meier said, 'Which do you prefer? The unbelievable – i.e. the miracle – or the much less romantic, shall we say mundane, version that is more likely to be true?' He didn't wait for an answer. 'Most choose to believe in miracles, even though there is always an explanation for what might appear to be impossible.'

'So you don't believe in the Bible?' Cristy asked, hardly able to believe she was saying it.

His eyes widened a little, as though intrigued by the question, but then he said, 'Maybe that is a discussion for another time. It would certainly be a fascinating one, at least from my perspective, but I sense there are more pressing matters now. You are here to find out who I am, what we are doing here on our farm, who lives and works amongst us, how we choose our guests and what we do to help them. Most importantly though, you would like to know how I fit into Nicole's story, and whether the children were stolen or murdered.'

Cristy turned to Connor again. Where to start when her brain had suddenly emptied itself of just about everything?

CHAPTER THIRTY-ONE

CONNOR: 'Perhaps you could begin by introducing yourselves... If nothing else, I can get sound levels...'

Cristy turned to Meier, glad to have a few moments to assess him without seeming to stare or appear inappropriately interested in him as a man. She wasn't, of course; it just wasn't easy to get past his looks – or the *force* of him: gentle, yet compelling, a very real phenomenon as fascinating as it was distracting. No wonder people were so drawn to him, maybe even lost their minds to him. She was even starting to feel slightly adrift herself.

She needed to listen...

MEIER: 'My name is Jean-Claude Meier; most people call me Claude. I am Swiss by birth, and I am the proprietor of the farm where we are recording this.'

MAGGI: 'I am Magda Thomas – I prefer to be called Maggi with an i, not a y – and I expect you can tell by my accent that I'm Welsh. I live and work here at the farm. I guess you could say I'm a kind of housekeeper-cum-manager-cum-slave to my all-powerful-lord-and-master, Jean-Claude Meier.'

As Meier gave a laugh of surprise, Cristy caught Maggi's

playful wink and was intrigued to know what the actual dynamic was here. Were they a couple, as in bedmates and valentine dates? Or just friends and colleagues who knew one another well enough to rib and tease with an undertone of flirtation that didn't actually mean anything? And the joke itself – what were they meant to think of that? Maggi was clearly teasing them for suspecting this to be a cult, but maybe it was a deflection tactic. Whatever, Cristy needed to keep her mind and eyes open.

CONNOR: 'OK, all good thanks. So, do you want to take it from here, Cris? Happy to if you . . . ?'

Indicating she was ready, she addressed Meier first.

CRISTY: 'Maybe we can go straight to the heart of why we're talking to you today. Your relationship with Nicole Ivorson dates back over twenty years, continuing up to the present day. So will you begin by telling us something about it?'

MEIER: 'Yes, of course. I am willing to share all that I can . . . But you understand there are certain things I do not know – and one of them, I'm afraid, is what happened to the twins. This, I am sure, is the main purpose of your visit.'

CRISTY: 'But you knew Nicole at the time they disappeared?'

MEIER: 'I did. Very well.'

CRISTY: 'Are you the twins' father?'

If she'd hoped to wrongfoot him with the directness of the question, then his outward appearance told her she hadn't succeeded. He simply moved past it.

MEIER: 'Maybe first I should tell you about Nicole, and what a difference she made to my life. How connected I felt to her right from the start. I still do.'

He paused, and realizing he was waiting for permission to go further, Cristy gestured for him to continue.

MEIER: 'Actually, it's hard to put the depth of my feelings into words, but I am going to try . . .
'The first time I saw her, she quite literally took my breath away. It wasn't just her face – it was exquisite, of course; anyone could see that – it was the beauty that radiated from within her. We can call it an aura, if you like – a special and profound allure that drew me to her in such a powerful way that I knew from those first moments of seeing her that I always had, and always would, feel connected to her.'

He sat with the resonance of his words, his eyes unfocused and yet thoughtful, as though the strength and nature of that connection still intrigued and baffled him.

MEIER: 'Imagine this, if you can . . .'

He smiled, as though his thoughts were manifesting right in front of him.

MEIER: 'She came to me like an exotic dancer trying to bewitch me with her very sultry moves. I remember the comedy of it clearly, and how it made me laugh. I also remember feeling unsure of how close I wanted to be to her. The attraction was very strong right away and . . . déstabilisant?'

CRISTY: 'Unnerving?'

He nodded.

MEIER: 'I could tell she wasn't affected by it then – everything came later for her. She says that isn't true, that it was instant for her too, but I believe I am right. That night, she was simply feeling risqué – she was always risqué – I think she was also a little drunk. I wanted to turn away, but she was so fascinating to watch, so bold and carefree, enchanting without seeming to know it. I wanted her to understand how perfect she was . . .

'She was, and still is, like music for me – loud and passionate; gentle and romantic; complex and simplistic. She has suffered a great deal over these past years, and yet she continues to be a woman of intriguing contrasts – extrovert and shy; straightforward and unpredictable; self-contained and longing for love.

'The connection between us that began that night has never failed – at least not for me.'

He considered this for a moment, seemed satisfied he'd articulated it well, and continued.

MEIER: 'I fought it, though. It scared me; I wasn't ready for it . . . I told myself I was still traumatized by the shock of my parents' death . . . It had happened many years before but had affected me profoundly. Grief can make a person unstable, vulnerable, perhaps delusional, and the way they died . . . I suspect you already know about it. I'm sure you will have done your research before coming . . .'

As his eyes came to hers, Cristy felt a tightening in her heart, as if she'd intruded on something so private to him that she ought to apologize before going any further. She didn't, simply waited for him to continue.

MEIER: 'I had made many friends at the university in Bristol before I met Nicole. Some were students from overseas, others visiting lecturers like myself . . . She believes I was alone that night, but others were there, just not standing with me when she came to persuade me to dance. I wonder if she would have asked if I hadn't been alone? If not, we might never have met. It is painful to think that now, and yet perhaps it would have been better for her if we hadn't.'

Cristy watched him mull those words and got the feeling it hurt him even to think them. And yet why would it have been better for Nicole if she'd never met him? Did that mean he was hiding something? Or was it simply an obvious statement of fact given where Nicole was now? If their paths had never crossed it was unlikely she'd have been a mother at such a young age, and so yes, her life would have taken a very different turn.

MEIER: 'Of course, neither of us had any idea what the future held for us. How could we? Who does? We gave it no thought at all, no care for consequences. . . Once I accepted that she was going to be a part of my life, I wanted only to know her better, to bring her to an awareness of herself that, in the end, would come naturally to her.
'We were all of us unrestrained, hectic, promiscuous. We challenged our psyches, our philosophies, our hopes and ambitions as young people do. We cast off our clothes and made love with ecstatic curiosity and tender discovery. She embraced our ways as hungrily as if she had been born to them. She was as excited by us as we were by her, a shining light in our midst made all the brighter by the sheer joy of being alive. I needed to understand what was pulling us together. What kind

of forces were at work. Had we known one another for centuries? Or was this the beginning of a brand-new journey?

'I craved answers to everything about her without even really knowing the questions. I could not have expressed any of this at the time, and I probably am not doing it very well now. I simply want you to understand, if you can, that my feelings for her, the bond we share, began at the beginning, when I knew right away that it would be life-changing. I just did not expect it to devastate our hearts the way it did.'

He looked down at his hands, both elegant and workmanlike, and closed them into loosely formed fists, as though he was trying to grasp something that wasn't there.

MEIER: 'So when you ask, am I the twins' father: the answer is, it doesn't matter; I loved them anyway.'

Cristy waited, certain he was going to say more, and eventually he did.

MEIER: 'I am sure you've already heard that motherhood did not always come easily to Nicole. It was said during that terrible time that she was suffering from a post-partum depression. It wasn't recognized back then in the same way it is now, but . . . Looking back, the signs were there . . . We – she – wanted our lives to continue the way they'd been before. She found the twins restricting, troublesome . . . Sometimes, she became erratic and frightened, but she was also loving and careful, as protective as any mother could be.

'Nobody is only one thing, are they? We all experience warring emotions, differing levels of understanding and patterns of behaviour. They can even change from day to day, but it doesn't make us bad or even crazy people; it just makes us human. Do you agree with that, Cristy?'

Caught unawares, Cristy took a moment to realize that he'd just described the conflict in her own heart. Deliberately or coincidentally? The latter, of course, although he was watching her so closely that she couldn't be entirely sure.

Apparently giving her a pass on answering, he continued.

MEIER: 'When my time at the university came to an end in 2005, Nicole begged me not to leave her. I had no intention of doing so. I already had a position to go to in Lausanne; I simply needed to find us a place to live and proper help with the twins. It took longer than expected . . . I was busy, keen to make an impression on my new employers . . . I was neglectful when it came to calling her . . . I failed to visit Bristol when I said I would. I detest myself for all this now, but it is too late to turn back the clock.

'As soon as I heard what had happened, I contacted the police. I was prepared to fly straight over, but they came to Switzerland instead, to my brother's home where I was staying. In the end, I was of no help to them. I couldn't say who had taken the twins, and I still cannot, but I do know Nicole would not have harmed them.'

CRISTY: 'And yet she's now confessed to killing them?'

His face paled, and he swallowed. It was almost as if she'd struck him, and he had no idea how to fight back. It took him a while to continue.

MEIER: 'I have no idea why she would lie, but if she is being truthful, then why does she not explain where to find the bodies?'

CRISTY: 'So you don't believe in her confession?'

MEIER: 'Of course not. I think she gave it because she wants her freedom, and it was the only way she could see to achieve it. If she'd confessed sooner, it would not have shortened her sentence.'

CRISTY: 'I believe you saw her just before her last parole hearing. Did she tell you then what she was planning to do?'

MEIER: 'No. It was a shock to me, as it was to everyone else.'

CRISTY: 'You must know she was released on parole a few weeks ago—'

MEIER: 'Yes, I do, and if you are in touch with her, please tell her that I want very much to see her. I hope she will come here, to me, where she belongs. Maybe it can't happen right away; there will be restrictions . . . Is she with her mother?'

CRISTY: 'Yes, she is, but they're not at Maeve's home. Will you tell me what you believe happened to the twins?'

An air of desolation came over him, and Cristy watched as Maggi reached out to put a hand on his. His long fingers clasped gently, although absently, as if it were more a reflex than a real tenderness. His voice was quiet, hoarse, when he spoke again.

MEIER: 'I wish I could tell you.'

More moments of sadness passed as he stared at nothing, seeming almost to have left the room. Maybe he was engaging with truths, suspicions, that he wasn't prepared to share.

Cristy glanced at Connor and wondered what was going through his mind.

> CRISTY: 'Do you still have contact with any of your friends from your time in Bristol?'

Meier looked at Maggi and started to nod.

> MEIER: 'Yes, with some.'
>
> CRISTY: 'Do you think they'd be willing to talk to us?'
>
> MEIER: 'I can ask. I'm sure they would.'
>
> CRISTY: 'Do you know if any of them visited Nicole in prison?'
>
> MEIER: 'I'm not aware of it if they did. I know her parents went often – Maeve alone after her husband died – and Lauren, her cousin, was also a visitor on occasions.'
>
> CRISTY: 'Do you know where Lauren is now?'
>
> MEIER: 'I think, at this hour, she will be dropping her children at school.'

Following a moment of shock, Cristy's first thought was for Noah and Abigail, but if they were still alive, they'd be too old for school by now.

> MEIER: 'Lauren lives with her husband and family in Mineral Point, Wisconsin. She tells me the winters are hard there, but it is a very beautiful place. I would like to visit, but finding the time isn't easy, so it's good that they sometimes come here. It's how they met, while Ben was with us seeking help for depression.'
>
> CRISTY: 'So Lauren was here? At the farm?'

MEIER: 'Until she met Ben, which was quite a long time ago. Maybe ten years?'

MAGGI: 'Nearly eleven.'

CRISTY: 'When did she come?'

MEIER: 'Before my grandmother passed. Maybe a couple of years before that.'

Cristy glanced at Connor, hoping he was better at mental maths right now than she was. Bridget had said Lauren disappeared about three years after Nicole's trial, which would be 2009. Meier's grandmother died in 2012, the same year they believed he'd left Lausanne . . . She needed more time to consider this, so was grateful when Connor took over.

CONNOR: 'Do you know why Lauren isn't in touch with her mother?'

MEIER: 'I am not aware of that, but if it's true, it feels a shame to deprive her parents of their grandchildren.'

CONNOR: 'How old are the children?'

MAGGI: 'Henry ten; Lily will be eight in April.'

So both born after Lauren had left here, if he was telling them the truth. So far, Cristy hadn't got a sense of him lying or trying to mislead them in any way – more of him avoiding answers, memories, that he didn't want to confront.

CRISTY: 'Do they come too, when Lauren and her husband visit?'

MEIER: 'Of course. Children are very welcome here. There's plenty for them to do, especially in the summer months.'

CRISTY: 'Would you be prepared to put us in touch with Lauren?'

MEIER: 'I would, but perhaps I should ask her to contact you? Just in case she doesn't want to talk about things she's worked hard to put behind her. What happened affected her very deeply, especially when Nicole was found guilty at her trial. No one expected that. There seemed so little evidence, nothing they could actually convict on . . . We were all shocked and of course very upset.'

CRISTY: 'Does Lauren ever say who she thinks might have taken the twins?'

MEIER: 'Only that we must be missing something, because she won't believe Nicole harmed them herself.'

CRISTY: 'Does she wonder if Nicole was in some way involved in an abduction?'

Meier's eyes seemed to sharpen at that, with surprise and perhaps a flash of anger? Cristy immediately wondered if she'd hit on something, had opened up a possibility that he hadn't expected her to find. His answer didn't confirm it.

MEIER: 'It is quite possible that Lauren has considered the question you ask. When something so terrible happens, many dark and crazy fears go through your head. I know this from the time my parents died and from when the children disappeared. You imagine all sorts of terrifying scenarios that in cold reality make no sense at all, but in the absence of reasonable explanations, the mind can – and often does – create answers that defy logic or even sanity.'

He looked up when the door opened, and Cristy turned to see a heavy-set man in a black padded jacket, fur-lined hat and steel-tipped boots blowing in with a cascade of snow.

'*Verdammt!*' he growled, pushing the door closed and pulling off his hat. 'It's coming down thick and fast. Won't any of us be going anywhere tonight – that's for sure.'

Cristy looked at the window. A virtual blizzard was whiting out the inky dark sky. How had they not noticed the weather – or the fact that so much time had passed?

As if closer proximity might change the picture, Connor went to the window.

'Please don't tell me we can't get out?' Cristy implored.

'Not sure we should risk it,' he told her, turning back. 'In my car, maybe, but not in yours. It's already looking pretty deep.'

Maggi said, 'It comes down like that around here – so fast that sometimes you feel you've only blinked and the whole world has turned white.'

Cristy was nonplussed. She felt an irrational urge to escape but was afraid of making a fool of herself. And yet, did she really want to go? She was comfortable here, was actually enjoying his company, which was possibly even more unsettling in its way.

'There's no heating on in the pods,' Maggi told Meier. 'It'll take all night for them to warm up, so they'll have to stay here in the house. I'll go and dig out some sleepover packs. We keep them for emergencies like this,' she informed Cristy. 'You should find everything you need, but if there's anything we've missed, just say and we'll work it out.'

Cristy wondered for one insane moment if Meier actually controlled the weather and this was all part of a plot to keep them here. She said to the newcomer, 'Are you sure we can't get through? If we left now, maybe we could make it to the main road. They'll be gritting that, won't they?'

Meier said, 'You can take one of the four-by-fours, but you will need to return it in the morning, so maybe it is better if you stay here? You are very welcome, and I am sure our five loaves and two fishes can be extended to include more hungry mouths.'

Cristy blinked.

'Another "miracle" easily explained,' he said. 'Perhaps for another time. Tonight, I believe Susanna is serving her excellent homemade leek and potato soup, and some of our very own Welsh cheddar.'

Cristy looked at Connor, half-hoping he'd thought of another way to get off this mountain.

'I should call Jodi,' he said, 'put her in the picture.'

Meier got to his feet. 'You'll need the WiFi code – there's no mobile reception here, especially not in this weather.'

Feeling ludicrously lost, Cristy watched Meier leave through a door she'd only just noticed. She tried to think who she should call to let them know she wouldn't be back tonight. Aiden had returned to his father; Hayley didn't even know where she was, and David presumably didn't much care.

Nevertheless, when Meier offered her the code, she tapped it into her phone. She didn't want him to think she had no one to contact, and because he seemed to be watching her, she began a lengthy email to Clove and Jacks, letting them know that she and Connor were snowed in.

She went on to say:

Today has been interesting. He's an unusual man, very personable, hospitable – I could mention his looks, but I won't. So far, he's spoken frankly, occasionally emotionally, and he definitely comes across well, if a little secretive. Wouldn't say he's a typical cult leader, if there is such a thing, but even if there were, how would I know? We might have come at the wrong time of year for culty practices. If you're laughing at that, I'm serious. They might not happen in winter, but this could be a good venue for 'group activities' in summer. Luckily, everyone has kept their clothes on so far. Hoping it stays that way, and not just because of the cold.

She paused, considering admitting it was hard not to imagine him with his off, but she decided against it. Given her current state of hormonal chaos, it was quite possible her sense of humour was as skewed as her emotions, so that sort of joke could be a really bad choice.

She ended with:

Worried about how long we might be stuck here. C x

PS He doesn't believe in miracles.

She'd already pressed send before realizing how obscure the last comment would be for Clove and Jacks. In fact, she couldn't think now why she'd added it.

'. . . is that OK with you, Cristy?' Meier was asking.

'Yes,' she said quickly. 'Of course. I mean . . . Sorry, what am I agreeing to?'

Clearly amused, he said, 'I just offered to show you to your room. I'll come back for Connor when he's finished his call.'

CHAPTER THIRTY-TWO

After following Meier through the door he'd used a few minutes ago, Cristy found herself in a large, square inner hall that was clearly a kind of sitting-cum-games room with sofas and a tallboy, a table-tennis table propped up against one wall and a carved oak staircase climbing another.

'Through there,' he said, pointing towards a small passageway on the far side of the hall, 'is the library and music room where—'

Recalling their first visit, she said, 'We heard someone playing the piano the last time we were here. It was beautiful. Debussy, I think. Was that you?'

He smiled, seeming to find the assumption surprising. 'I'm sure it would have been Johan,' he told her. 'He is very accomplished.'

Recognizing the name from Jacks's trawl of old uni friends, she said, 'Johan Bauer, by any chance?'

'Indeed. You would have met him just now had I not failed to introduce you. We will put it right later.' He indicated a closed door beside the tallboy, saying, 'In there is the office, where we run the business side of things—'

'Do you have a website? We couldn't find one . . .'

'We made a decision not to take that route,' he explained. 'Our guests come to us through recommendation or word of mouth, and they are assessed and accepted on their particular need and our ability to help.'

'So what are you actually offering?' she asked, starting up the stairs behind him.

'Our team consists of cognitive, neuro, social, educational, sports and art therapists, and our range of programmes is extensive. It can also be tailored to suit an individual's needs, such as for our friend from Alabama, who you might also meet later. I'll be happy to show you around tomorrow, snow-permitting, and explain a little more about how we have developed the farm, which continues to be viable, into a place of spiritual and physical enhancement.'

Reaching a low-ceilinged, dimly lit landing, he pushed open the first door to the right, leaned in and flicked a switch that turned on a number of lamps.

'Here we are,' he said, gesturing for her to go ahead. 'I hope you'll be comfortable in here.'

The room turned out to be more spacious than she'd expected, with a super-king bed at the heart of it, covered by a navy plaid duvet, with two nightstands each side. An old-fashioned dressing table stood against an opposite wall with a triptych mirror, and there was an enormous armoire in one corner. The carpeted floorboards creaked underfoot as she moved forward, and two of the beams were low enough for him to caution her to mind her head.

'This is my room, where you will sleep,' he told her.

She turned to him in shock. 'With you?' she blurted.

He was startled into a laugh. 'Well, I was . . . It is an idea, certainly, but maybe when we know each other better?'

Feeling as ludicrous as she deserved to, Cristy rolled her eyes and quickly apologized. 'It's a lovely room,' she told him. In its masculine, faintly old-fashioned way, it was. 'But I can't possibly turn you out of your own bed . . . That wasn't an invitation,' she explained, in case it had sounded like one. 'What I meant was, you must sleep here, and I'd be happy to crash on a sofa, or with Connor.' Had she really just said that? She knew she had, because he was laughing again, and now, so was she. 'OK, maybe not *with* Connor . . .'

'Here will serve very well,' he insisted. 'It is a comfortable bed, and fortunately it was changed today, so everything is fresh. There is a bathroom through this door' – he went to open it – 'and you will find clean towels in the cabinet next to the tub. Maggi or Susanna will bring you a sleepover pack, but now I must take Connor to his room and then go to help settle the animals before we gather for supper. There is plenty of hot water, so please make use of everything. I will see you downstairs in an hour.'

After he'd gone, she listened to his footsteps on the stairs, still feeling faintly embarrassed and even oddly out of her depth, without really knowing why. She wondered if he was having a similar effect on Connor, who, she was certain, would not make an idiot of himself when shown to his sleeping place. There was definitely something about Meier, though, even if she couldn't put it into words. And she really couldn't, apart from to say how bizarre it felt to be staying here as his guest, in his *actual bedroom* no less, when earlier today she'd thought he was a pernicious cult leader whose charms she needed at all costs to resist.

Going to the window, she stood for a moment gazing out at the cold, wintry night. The snow was still coming down thick and fast, a silently hypnotic storm that made her wonder what chance they actually stood of leaving tomorrow. Then she was asking herself if it would be so bad if they were forced to stay longer?

Connor wouldn't like it. He'd want to get home to Jodi and Aurora . . .

Remembering she was due to speak to Kinsley in the morning, she turned back into the room and sent a brief message explaining that she'd been snowed in and might not be able to speak tomorrow. It was a relief to postpone, but the feeling was soon gone, overtaken by a horrible, sinking sense of loneliness. To distract herself, she began thinking about Nicole and all that Meier had said about her. She understood that Nicole couldn't come here because it was outside the forty-mile radius, but why hadn't he gone to her if he loved her as much as he claimed?

Did she believe what he'd told her about the depth of their connection?

Certainly, she had during the interview; she'd even wondered if anyone had ever spoken about her with so much tenderness, and had decided they probably hadn't.

A knock on the door pulled her back to the moment. 'Come in,' she called, already feeling absurdly self-conscious, but it was Maggi who entered, with a sleepover pack.

'Here you go,' Maggi said, laying it down on the bed, 'everything you'll need from toothbrush and paste, face and body wash, a hairbrush, comb, a time-of-the-month pack and pyjamas. They might be too big, but better than too small is what I say.'

As Cristy thanked her, she was recalling the several looks that had passed between her and Meier earlier. Deciding to go for it, she said, 'Did you ever know Nicole?'

Maggi seemed startled, but then she smiled. 'I was one of the students Claude spoke about during the interview, so perhaps in one sense I knew her very well. In another, maybe not at all. What matters, though, is that she has finally confessed. It's hard for Claude to accept that, but he will, eventually, and he will still bring her here if she'll come, because she is all he really wants.'

Cristy had almost stopped breathing. 'Are you saying you believe she did kill her children?' she asked, needing to be sure she'd understood this correctly.

Maggi's expression was sorrowful and yet resolute. 'Yes, that's what I'm saying. I don't know how or why, but it is what I believe.'

*

For the next few hours, Cristy watched and listened, laughed and drank Chasselas wine from Claude's brother's vineyard, all the while feeling weirdly detached from herself, or at least from the joyous nature of the evening. There were eleven of them around the table, including her and Connor, who'd clearly struck up some male-bonding thing with Bavarian Johan. (Hopefully he'd get something out of him about the friendship/orgy group back in the day. Was he someone else who thought Nicole really was guilty?)

Claude sat between Maggi and Susanna, a robust, dark-haired Scotswoman in her mid-to-late fifties, who'd dished up generous helpings of homemade soup followed by a delicious fish pie. Marko, whose Nigerian father was a naval spokesman – clearly an in-joke given how hilarious they all found it when the introductions were made – was a softly spoken, double-chinned, art therapist with a keen interest in animal husbandry. Lukas, an Italian clinical psychologist with a family background in farming, was short and wiry and anywhere between forty and sixty. There was also Simeon, a fair-haired, blue-eyed Swiss national who'd been a student of Claude's at Lausanne University. With Simeon were his 'guests' from Alabama: Milly and Ray Johnson. Fortunately, Ray had left his supremacy gear in the only pod that was open right now. He also seemed to have parked his prejudices, if his interaction with Marko was anything to go by, so maybe Simeon really did have a knack where racists were concerned.

It soon became clear that the staff around the table were both dedicated farmhands as well as professional psychologists, and apparently, they comprised only a small number of the highly specialized holistic health team that ran Bryn Helyg from March to November.

Although intrigued by the dynamics and make-up of

the gathering, Cristy's focus was mostly on Meier and how relaxed he seemed surrounded by his chosen few. Was that how he saw them? It was how they came across to her – not that they appeared fawning, or in any way in his thrall, but they were all clearly deeply attached to him. None more so than Maggi, who was curiously more maternal towards him now than she'd been earlier. Cristy wondered if Meier knew that she believed Nicole had killed the twins. It wasn't something she could ask, especially not while a guest at their table. All kinds of weird triggers might be going off in her hormone collection, but she had no desire at all to shock the room into silence, much less to alienate or upset anyone.

Funny, she reflected to herself, how concerned she seemed to be about the feelings of a group who this time yesterday she was certain she wouldn't have trusted at all. That wasn't how she was seeing them now. On the contrary, there was something about them – Meier in particular – that was making her feel . . . safe? Was that the right word? Maybe she meant welcome, or simply relaxed. Whatever, there were no negative feelings at all, and although that was strange in its way it was also really good to be in a place that was managing to make the stress of her life feel so far away.

CHAPTER THIRTY-THREE

It was close to midnight by the time she turned out the bathroom light in Meier's suite and went to open the curtains to check on the weather. Snow continued to fall, although it wasn't such a white-out now, and the violent gusts that had whistled around the house and whipped the trees for most of the evening didn't seem quite as fierce.

Leaving the curtains open, she turned and looked around the warmly lit room. There was nothing to suggest it was shared by a woman. In the bathroom, she'd found only a single toothbrush in the cabinet, some nail scissors, a roll-on male deodorant and the usual shaving-gear – she'd wondered if the two-day stubble look was achieved by design, but the absence of a special razor suggested not.

Going to open the armoire, she found only men's clothes inside, and the strong scent of him: leathery, musky and whatever it was that made it uniquely his. She inhaled deeply and felt an unexpected rush of adrenaline.

There was nothing on the dressing table that couldn't conceivably belong to him, and the several dozen books on the shelves to one side of the bed were either in French or German. From what she could tell, they were mostly academic anthologics or chronicles, although there were a few English language volumes such as the 5M farming series and some well-thumbed paperbacks specifically about lambing and calving.

No light reading for Jean-Claude before lights out, she remarked to herself as she flipped back the duvet and climbed into bed. The linen smelled of fresh laundry and faintly of him.

After turning off the lamps, she lay quietly gazing out at the stars. They seemed so bright in the night-black sky and so close that it was tempting to make a wish. She listened to the humming might of the wind, the occasional creak of the house, the gentle sound of her own breath as she wondered where Jean-Claude was spending the night. With Maggi? In another smaller room in the house? Was he already sleeping or lying awake reading, maybe going over the interview earlier and thinking about Nicole. The relationship between them, as described by both, was as intriguing to her as it was baffling. That they could still be so much in love after all this time and all that had happened . . . She might have found it unbelievable if she hadn't listened to them herself, and if its power weren't seeming to spread an ache, a sense of longing into her own heart.

She closed her eyes and tried not to think of David as she willed sleep to come. The wind continued to whoosh. A tree branch tapped against the house. Something blew over and rattled down the lane. A floorboard creaked . . . The door opened quietly, and her heart seemed to stop beating. He was here; she could sense it, as if he was already beside her. She didn't hear his footsteps or the sound of his breath, only knew he'd reached her when she felt his weight on the bed, and then on her. She wanted him with a desire that was burning out of control. His hands slipped beneath her, her legs wrapped around him and as he pressed his mouth to hers, he entered her hard . . .

She sat up with a gasp, her heart thudding wildly, her mind reeling. It was a dream; she knew that. Even so, it took her a while to turn and check that Jean-Claude really wasn't there.

He wasn't, and she sank back against the pillows in dizzying relief. The fantasy of him remained strong; the desire pulsed and ebbed. She was fiery hot all over; sweat poured from her skin until finally she flipped back the duvet and went to cool off in the shower.

By the time she'd towelled herself dry, the night sweat had passed, but her sleepover pyjamas were drenched. She rolled them into a ball and went to pull on her jeans and jumper. She was so thirsty that she could drink an ocean, and knowing she stood next to no chance of getting back to sleep anytime soon, she reached for her phone. Noticing a message from Paul Kinsley, she quickly read it.

Let me know what you think.

He'd attached two links, but seeing what they led to, she decided they could wait. She needed to quench her terrible thirst.

Using her phone torch to light the way, Cristy descended the stairs quietly and crossed the hall into the kitchen. It was still warm and was lit by a single lamp next to the hearth, where the dying embers of the fire glowed red in the darkness.

Her heart contracted when she saw Meier seated at one end of the sofa, his bare feet propped on the fender, his eyes open and regarding her curiously.

'Is everything all right?' he asked, putting aside the book he was holding and lowering his feet. He was wearing a long-sleeved T-shirt and navy joggers.

'Sorry, I didn't mean to disturb you,' she said. 'I needed a drink . . .'

'Let me,' he insisted. 'I know where things are.'

As he went to the sink, she stepped back, thankful he had no way of knowing about the dream that had woken her. He didn't, did he? She wished she could shake it, but being this close to him was bringing it back . . .

'The storm seems to have died down a little,' he said, filling a large glass from the tap.

Realizing that was true, she took the glass from him and drank deeply. 'Thanks,' she said, and feeling the need to apologize again for turning him out of his own bed, she was about to suggest they swap places when she remembered how damp the sheets were.

'Why don't you come and sit down?' he suggested, going back to the sofa.

Deciding she would, but in the chair rather than next to him, she refilled the glass and went to curl up in the down-filled cushions. 'You're having trouble sleeping too?' she asked.

'It happens from time to time,' he replied, picking up a tumbler from the floor in front of him. Scotch or brandy – hard to tell.

Suspecting their interview earlier was to blame in his case, she said, 'Insomnia's a new thing for me. I have something for it, but it's going to take a while to kick in.'

He sipped his nightcap, sat back and returned his feet to the fender. 'Lack of sleep can do strange things to the psyche,' he cautioned, 'and one of the worst is how often it makes stressful or upsetting situations seem even worse than they are.'

As his words reached her, she wondered if he could actually read her mind and wasn't at all sure how she'd feel about it if he could.

'Something is bothering you,' he told her, as if it were a normal part of an everyday conversation. Maybe for him it was. 'I have sensed it since you arrived. Don't worry; you keep it well hidden, and you were very professional when doing your job, but you're upset about something, and I'm going to guess that what you perceive as your failure to resolve the problem, whatever it may be, is causing your difficulties with sleep.'

Her eyes widened slightly. So he *could* read minds?

He smiled. 'Helplessness, frustration, indecision, confusion are almost always the drivers of stress, whether the issue is professional or emotional.' He took another sip of his drink. 'Sometimes, giving voice to the problem and listening to yourself can show you whether it's your own resistance to a situation that's blocking the answers. Often that's it, but not always.'

Wryly she said, 'You're going to tell me next that you're a good listener.'

He laughed. 'It has been said,' he responded wryly.

'You're also a professional, and I'm not sure I want to be analysed.'

'I'm also a stranger with no agenda of my own, no reason to judge or even advise, or to hold anything against you later. But that sounds as though I'm exerting pressure, so maybe we should talk about something else?'

Given how desperate she felt to talk to someone, to offload everything that was building up inside her, to release at least some of the conflict, if not the heartache, she decided to begin with Kinsley's offer.

He listened quietly, attentively, as she explained how much she wanted to seize the opportunity, how excited she felt at times about rising to the top with the backing of her old mentor. She told him how deeply she hated herself for even considering abandoning the people she cared about so much, who'd invested their loyalty and trust in her and whom she couldn't bear to hurt or betray. She covered everything, including the wonderful prospect of being close to her brother again in London, the possibility of working with Andee Lawrence, even the horror of Molly Terrance being part of the deal, although she hoped that might have gone away by now.

'I'll have to make a decision soon.' She sighed, bringing her rant to an end. 'He's not going to wait forever. He sent me an email earlier with two links – I haven't opened them yet, but I can see that one is to premises that could work for the new company, the other to a riverside apartment that his wife, who I love, thinks would be just right for me.'

She looked at Meier and almost groaned at how pathetic he must be finding her, especially after all he'd revealed about himself and Nicole today. However, his expression, though attentive, was unreadable. She started to apologize, yet again, but he got up to go and refresh his drink. When he came back, he handed a second glass to her before returning to the sofa.

'You are seeing your conscience as your worst enemy,' he told her, making himself comfortable, 'but why not turn it around and try to view it as a friend?'

She frowned, not quite following.

'I heard the change in your tone when you talked about leaving loyal colleagues and friends behind, and my thoughts, as you spoke, were that letting them down, perhaps diminishing yourself in their eyes, matters more to you than achieving an ambition you weren't even aware of until this offer was made.'

She took a moment to connect with such a rapid and clear-eyed assessment of where she was in her head. 'So, you're saying I should turn the offer down and carry on the way I am?' she countered.

He shrugged, sipped his drink and said, 'How did it feel when you spoke those words? "I should turn the offer down and carry on the way I am?"'

She thought about it, trying to isolate her reactions. 'Not bad,' she said, 'but . . . defeatist? Cowardly?'

'You're a successful woman; you enjoy what you do. Why would continuing on this course be defeatist or cowardly?'

Realizing they might not have been quite the right words, she said, 'Maybe I want to prove to myself that I can take on something that big and make a go of it.'

'But you already know you can – you wouldn't be tormenting yourself like this if you seriously doubted it, but that doesn't mean it's right for you.'

Her eyes narrowed. 'Are you talking me out of it?'

'Playing devil's advocate.'

'I'm not sure that's helpful.'

He smiled, and she decided, in that moment, that she really liked him.

'You don't want to let your old mentor down,' he said. 'I think that maybe, on some level, you feel you still owe him. On another, your deeply forged loyalties with the people you live and work with are probably telling you all you need to know. You want to stay in Bristol with the team you trust and respect, the friends you know and love and the life you treasure.'

Taking the words in, she said, 'Are you telling me that, or was it a question?'

'Take it whichever way you like. Just ask yourself how you felt when I painted that very simple picture.'

She almost wanted to laugh. 'I guess relieved was the first thing,' she admitted. 'It was like being given . . . a get-out-of-jail-free card?'

'Then you have your answer.'

She frowned. 'You're making it sound so easy.'

'Because it is, unless you want it to be complicated, and that's always an option too.'

She smiled and drank some of the brandy, allowing several minutes to pass as she continued assessing his words, testing them with her instincts and her heart, still searching for a sense of what did and didn't feel right. She was surprised, embarrassed, when she realized tears were rolling down her cheeks. She couldn't even say why she was crying or when it had started, only that sadness was coming over her in waves, and for some reason, she was unable to stop it.

'I'm sorry,' she said, using her fingers to wipe away the tears. 'I'm not sure . . . It's not like me to do this . . .'

He went to fetch a tissue and passed it to her. He didn't try comforting her, simply went back to the sofa, and she was thankful for the distance he was keeping between them when she felt so vulnerable. There was no way of knowing how a touch, an embrace even, might end.

'I don't think we have necessarily reached a solution,' he told her, 'but you can now think of the dilemma in a different way. Saying no isn't a weakness, any more than saying yes is a strength.'

'He'll offer it to Molly Terrance if I don't take it,' she said.

'Do you care? Really?'

Not sure that she did, Cristy dabbed her eyes again and thought of how refusing the offer would rob Andee Lawrence of an opportunity she didn't even know was hers. 'Nothing's ever as straightforward as you'd like it to be,' she said, almost to herself.

When he didn't answer, she looked up to find him watching her closely.

'I'm going to say something now,' he said, 'that you probably won't want to hear, but I recognize heartbreak when I see it, and I strongly believe I am seeing it now.'

Her eyes closed as a wave of emotion engulfed her. She held her breath, waiting for it to pass. 'I can't talk about that,' she told him in a whisper. 'It's . . . too new, too raw.'

'I understand,' he said softly. 'As someone who has felt it every day for many years, I still find it difficult to put it into words. Often, I don't even feel the need to try, but it can be helpful when I do. It releases a little of the pressure, allows some oxygen into my heart and somehow it keeps me going.'

'Who do you talk to?' she asked.

'Usually my brother. He is not a trained professional, but he is very astute, and of course he knows me well.'

'It sounds as though you're close.'

'We are. I see him as often as I can. He's good for my sanity, even better for my soul.'

Not sure whether it was right to ask this or not, she decided to go ahead anyway. 'He obviously knows about Nicole?'

'*Mais bien sûr.* He has been worrying since her release about the effect it is having on me, knowing she is free but not telling me where she is. It's hard, I will admit that, but I also understand that she shares my fear of what the future might hold for us. Will our love be the same now we can be together again? How much has been lost in reality while we continued to believe in our hearts that nothing could tear us apart?' His eyes came to hers. 'Have you met her? Spoken to her?'

Cristy nodded.

He swallowed and looked down at his drink. 'I won't ask again where she is; she'd already have told me if she wanted me to know.' He took a breath and put his glass down.

'She does want to see you,' Cristy told him softly. 'She asked me to tell you that.'

His eyes lifted, and she could see the hope as clearly as the pain. 'Did she also tell you why she confessed to something she didn't do?'

Mindful of Maggi's words, she said, 'How can you be so sure she didn't?'

There was a long, almost interminable silence before he said, 'You share my certainty – that's why you're helping her.'

She didn't deny it, simply watched him as he stared at nothing, wondering what he was really thinking, how much he was holding back and whether he was regretting letting her and Connor come here. Maybe there was something else entirely in his mind.

He said very softly, 'Later this year, it will be their twenty-first birthday. Grown into a young man and woman . . .' He sounded so sad, so bewildered and tormented, that Cristy almost started crying again.

'Do you believe they're still out there somewhere?' she asked.

His eyes closed, and she realized that even if he did think that, he wasn't going to tell her tonight.

CHAPTER THIRTY-FOUR

Rain came down so heavily the next morning that, by noon, much of the snow on the roads had turned to slush, making it possible for Cristy and Connor to attempt the drive home.

As soon as that was agreed, Cristy went upstairs to collect her things, still gritty-eyed from so little sleep and reflecting on her conversation with Meier last night, alongside all they'd learned about Bryn Helyg this morning. He hadn't joined them for breakfast earlier, although he'd appeared briefly an hour ago when Cristy was in the barn helping Susanna to feed the motherless calf. He'd clearly been highly entertained by her efforts, especially when Barnabus – they'd named the little beast already – had pressed his entire weight against her, toppling her back into the hay.

Since then, there had been no sign of him, although it was obviously a busy farm with much to do, hampered no doubt by the weather that had made a full tour of the place impossible. However, Johan and Maggi had organized a virtual viewing in the office, and so by the time the decision was made that Cristy and Connor were probably safe to leave, they had a much clearer picture of the farm and everything that happened there.

It was impressive; there was no doubt about that. Five purpose-built 'sanctuary' buildings housed everything from soundproofed therapy rooms to well-equipped art and music studios, a spa, a gym – there was even an indoor basketball court. There were also half a dozen staff cottages behind the farmhouse and more a couple of hundred yards down the lane apparently, forming a small hamlet with its very own ancient church. And, of course, there were the two-dozen luxury pods for guests, each with their own hot tub, fully equipped kitchen and outdoor firepit.

'I'm not sure how anything we learned today is going to fit into an episode,' Connor commented, as he drove carefully down the steeply twisting hillside, 'but it's somewhere I wouldn't mind going for a spot of R&R, that's for sure. If I could afford it, but I probably can't.'

Cristy was only half-listening, still distracted by the brief conversation she'd had with Meier when he'd turned up to say goodbye.

'Thank you for coming to see us,' he'd said, holding her hand between both of his, his dark eyes gazing deeply into hers.

'Thank you for the talk last night,' she replied. 'I think it helped.'

He smiled and continued to hold her eyes and her hand. It was hard to look away from him, although she didn't actually try. 'It's not my place to ask what happened between you and David Gaudion,' he said quietly, 'but if you do want to talk about it, you know where I am.'

She was thrown by his use of David's name when she was sure she hadn't mentioned it, and she couldn't think what to say.

He raised an eyebrow. 'You're not the only one who does their research before meeting someone.'

Rolling her eyes at herself, she said, 'Of course. And thank you.' They hadn't mentioned Nicole or the twins, had simply continued to look at one another, until she'd eased her hand free and got into the car.

'So, what are we making of it all?' Connor asked, when

they finally made it to the main road and were able to speed up a little. 'Do you believe anything he told us?'

She turned to him curiously. 'Does that mean you didn't?'

'No, not at all. He came across pretty well to me – I'm just interested to hear what you think.'

Realizing she would be too, she said, 'To be honest, I'm still trying to process it, but I can tell you this: Maggi believes in Nicole's confession. She thinks Nicole killed them.'

'Wow,' he murmured. 'She actually said that?'

'She did. She doesn't know how or why, but she said she believes in the confession, and even intimated that, deep down, Meier believes it too.'

'Holy shit. Does he know she told you that?'

'I don't think so. Food for thought though, isn't it? Unless she was messing with me, which I guess is possible, although hard to see to what end. How about you? Did you get anything out of your new BFF, Johan? I guess you realized he's the Johan Bauer who was in Bristol with Meier back in 2005?'

Connor frowned. 'He didn't mention it, but makes sense. So, he was one of the "Clifton set"?'

'As was Maggi.'

Connor's head came around. 'We definitely have to talk to those guys some more,' he declared. 'I wonder if Johan also thinks Nicole did it?'

'I've no idea, but think about this: if he was a part of that free-loving friendship group twenty odd years ago, there has to be a chance he's the twins' father.'

Connor sat with that, mulling the left-sided nature of its potential, until Cristy said, 'Going back to Meier. I find him quite . . . distracting, don't you?'

Connor nodded. 'I guess. I mean, I could see he got to you.'

Cristy's eyebrows rose as her heart contracted, but rather

than respond to the insight, she said, 'He wants to see Nicole, and we know she wants to see him . . .'

When she didn't continue, Connor said, 'So are you thinking we should make it happen?'

Was she thinking that? She had been, as far as they had any power to, but now, the more distance that opened up between them and the farm, the more concerned she was becoming about the effect Meier had had on her. She remembered someone in the feedback mentioning hypnosis without consent and that she still wasn't sure what had happened while she was under. It was hard for Cristy to believe she'd fallen victim to that kind of thing. In fact, she was fairly certain she'd had her wits about her the entire time, frayed and hyper though they might have been – and still were. Apart from the dream, of course – she hadn't been in control then – but no one ever was with a dream, and there was no doubt in her mind that it had been nothing more than that.

In the end, instead of answering the question, she said, 'We need to speak to Honey, because, as taken as I was at the time by the powerful connection he described between him and Nicole, I'm finding myself struggling with it now.' She gave herself a moment to assess that and added, 'Maybe, I'm just not a romantic at heart – or it could be that getting dumped has turned me into a cynic.'

Connor glanced at her, clearly not sure whether to engage with that. Having no idea what she wanted, she gave him no guidance.

Eventually, he said, 'Are you really just going to let things go with David?'

Sighing irritably, she reached for her phone, of course hoping for a message – and there was one, just not from him. 'If he wanted to speak to me,' she said, sending a thumbs up to her son to confirm she'd be at home later, 'he'd call. That tells me all I need to know.'

As Connor started to respond, his phone rang.

Realizing he felt awkward about answering considering what they'd been discussing, Cristy leaned forward to click on for him.

'Hey,' Jodi cried, 'are you on your way back yet? Only I've had a call from Edward Har—'

'Cristy's in the car,' Connor cut in. 'Why don't you say hi?'

'Sorry,' Jodi groaned. 'Got my mummy head on. Hi Cris. How are you?'

'I'm OK, thanks,' Cristy replied, wondering if Connor had just stopped his wife deliberately. Edward Har—? It didn't ring any bells, and maybe projecting her own secrecy onto others wasn't a good way to go. 'Sorry I kept your husband out all night,' she attempted to joke.

'I'm dying to hear about it,' Jodi responded. 'Have you come away with all the answers you were hoping to get? Like, is it a cult?'

Cristy glanced at Connor.

'Not obviously,' he admitted, 'but I think Cristy's smitten with the main guy—'

'That's not true,' she protested. 'I'll admit he's charming and attractive . . .'

'I rest my case.' Connor laughed. 'But listen to this. I haven't shared it with you yet, Cris, but something occurred to me in the early hours that I'm still trying to get my head around. I did some googling to check, and it turns out that every one of the staff at that place has a biblical name.'

Cristy blinked.

'Bear with,' he told her. 'Meier's clearly a kind of leader and all that stuff about miracles—'

'What?' Jodi exclaimed.

'Later,' he told her. 'Now here goes with the names: Johan, John. Simeon, Simon. Marko, Mark. Susanna, Susanna—'

285

'Who?' Jodi cut in, as Cristy wondered if Connor had experienced some bizarre existential event in the night.

'In the Bible, Susanna is a wealthy woman who supports Christ's ministry,' Connor explained. 'And here's another: Maggi, whose name is actually Magda, as in Magdalene.'

Incredulous, Cristy said, 'How much wine did you have last night?'

'OK, I might be overthinking it,' he conceded, apparently realizing he wasn't selling his theory well, 'but you can't deny those names are all New Testament, and you've got to have seen how followerish they all seemed. Plus, what about those "explanations" of miracles? Like he was there or something, so he *knows* what really happened. And – you're going to love this one,' he told Jodi, 'they called the calf Barnabus. You know who he was, don't you?'

'What calf?' Jodi asked.

To Cristy, Connor said, 'To be honest, I don't actually know who he was, just that he was around at that time and definitely a kind of missionary.'

'I'm worried about you, Connor,' Jodi put in.

'Me too,' Cristy assured her, 'although he's right in that they are all biblical names.'

Seeming to wish he'd never started this, Connor said, 'OK, getting back to whether we came away with any answers? Putting aside what I've just told you, we need to listen to the recording in order to give it a proper assessment . . .'

'But what about Nicole and the twins?' Jodi cut in. 'Are you any closer to finding out what really happened?'

'I wish we could give a yes to that.' Cristy sighed. 'But the best I can tell you right now is that things seem to be opening up, and the deeper into it we go, the more convinced I am that we're going to find those kids.'

Connor glanced at her in surprise. 'So you reckon Maggi was . . . what? Trying to throw us off the scent, because they're actually still out there somewhere?'

'Jesus,' Jodi muttered.

'It would be an odd way of doing it if they are,' Cristy admitted, 'but as far as I'm concerned, there's a whole lot more to that place and those people than we're even beginning to see right now.'

CHAPTER THIRTY-FIVE

The following afternoon, the whole team was in the office, working through the weekend again to put together an episode for Tuesday. The debriefing of Cristy and Connor's visit to Bryn Helyg had to wait, for now. With most of the backstory having been covered in the first three episodes, it was time to move on to Nicole's sentence and continued claims of innocence – until her sudden and so far unexplained confession. All this could be achieved without giving rise to suspicions that they were in touch with her; however, any mention of Claude Meier's and Lauren Hawkes's prison visits was proving tricky. It wasn't the right time to play in Meier's interview, since it had to be combined with Nicole's, and as for Lauren . . . Given they still didn't have a way of contacting her, there was nothing much they could say about her really.

'Obviously we can reveal, through ex-DS Patten, that the police spoke to Meier at the time of Nicole's arrest,' Cristy decided, 'and maybe we can say that he's had contact with her since she was sent down . . .' She stopped to think that through.

Connor said, 'It wouldn't cast any doubt on her confession or link us to any sort of contact with her, only mark him out as a person of interest during the initial police inquiries. So yeah, I think we can go with that, and maybe end with something like: "Next time, we'll bring you some intriguing details of Nicole's relationship with Jean-Claude Meier, whose police statement seems never to have made it to Nicole's defence team?" We won't be able to use her actual recording, obvs, but no reason not to play in at least some of his.'

Cristy nodded agreement and was about to start typing it into the script when both her and Connor's phones signalled an incoming WhatsApp from Honey.

Putting the call on speaker, Connor said, 'Working on a Sunday? Whatever next?'

'Is Cristy with you?' Honey asked sharply. 'She needs to hear this.'

'I'm right here,' Cristy called out. 'What's happened?'

'Nicole has been returned to custody,' Honey informed them.

Cristy's heart stopped.

'Why? What happened?' Connor demanded.

'Someone let it be known that she was in touch with you guys.'

'Jesus Christ!' Connor muttered.

Cristy was reeling, but shock yielded fast to fury. 'It has to have been Meier,' she seethed, and snatching up her phone, she scrolled straight to his number.

'So everything you told us was a lie,' she accused when he answered. 'You don't want to see her at all, and now you've got her locked up again—'

'Cristy, stop! What are you talking about?'

'You *let it be known* that she'd spoken to us. No one else knows that—'

'But why would you think I'd do something—'

'You tell me why you did it.'

'I am trying to tell you that I didn't—'

She wasn't listening. 'You know exactly what happened to the twins, don't you?' she cried furiously. 'You convinced – brainwashed – Nicole into confessing . . . Well, take it from me, the whole world is going to know the part you played in this, and if you think the location of your precious *compound* is safe, think again.' As she slammed the phone on the desk, cutting him off, she was shaking so hard that Clove came to put steadying hands on her shoulders.

'We fell for it,' Cristy shouted at Connor. 'We were taken in like everyone else. All that bullshit about some special connection, one true love, belief in her innocence. He did it! I'm telling you: he took those twins. Not only that – I'll stake everything I own that he knows exactly where they are now. Lying, cheating, manipulative bastard . . .'

'Cristy, there's something here you need to see,' Jacks told her.

She turned to her screen as he shared his findings.

Clove read out Molly Terrance's latest article:

Exclusive: Baby Killer Returned to Custody.
Police were called to a South Gloucestershire location early this morning to arrest Nicole Ivorson, who is said to have broken the terms of her licence. Ivorson, convicted murderer of her own children, Noah and Abigail, when they were only eleven months old, recently confessed to her crime after years of maintaining her innocence. A condition of her parole was that she would have no contact with the press, but this reporter can reveal that she has been working with Cristy Ward's Hindsight team to try and prove her innocence.

Cristy was speechless.

'How the hell does she know that?' Connor growled. 'Who the fuck told her?'

Cristy's eyes closed as the horrible, unthinkable truth dawned on her. 'I told Meier about her,' she confessed. 'It doesn't matter how it came up – it just did – and so I'm to blame for this.'

Connor stared at her, as did the others.

'I'm still here,' Honey reminded them. 'I heard all that, so at least we know how it happened.'

'I'm so sorry,' Cristy said. 'I could—'

Honey was still speaking. 'Obviously you guys can't have any more contact with Nicole, and I doubt Maeve will want to hear from you either. I'm truly sorry this hasn't worked out. I was actually starting to hope we were getting somewhere, but this . . . It's hard to see how to get past it now that Nicole could be facing an increase, rather than a reduction, to her sentence. Thanks for everything you've done – for believing in her even. It's just a shame it turned out this way.'

As she ended the call, Cristy felt herself dying inside. 'I've fucked up so badly here,' she groaned. 'I'm sorry, guys. I don't know what to tell you . . . There isn't anything . . . I've just well and truly screwed our entire series, not to mention put a potentially innocent woman back in prison . . . Fuck, fuck, *fuck*!'

Her head went back in an attempt to stem the tears, but they just kept coming, faster and unstoppable. 'Oh hell,' she choked. 'I'm sorry, I . . .'

'It's OK, shit happens,' Connor told her, trying to calm things down, 'and we're here for you – you know that. We'll sort something out. We just need to take a breather, let it all sink in and come up with a plan. We can still try to clear Nicole's name.'

Appreciating his unswerving support, not to mention blind optimism, Cristy swallowed hard and said, 'I need to make a call . . . I shouldn't be long . . .' And picking up her phone, she took it across the hall to the deserted meeting room.

*

As she scrolled to Paul Kinsley's number, she knew that any going back on the decision she'd already reached to turn his offer down was completely lost to her now. If she could make this sort of mistake, misjudge someone as badly as she had Claude Meier, thereby losing a possibly innocent woman her liberty, she had no right even to be thinking about trying to create a new empire of podcasts. She wasn't fit to continue this one, given the state of her mind, and the fact that even now she had no idea whether she was overreacting or not only went to prove her point.

Kinsley picked up on the fourth ring. 'Cristy! On a Sunday, no less. Can I assume that's good? Did you see my links, by the way? Great apartment Dinah found, don't you think?'

She still hadn't opened the links, and probably never would now, so there was no point getting into it. 'Paul, I'm really sorry,' she said quietly, 'but I can't accept your offer. I've given it a lot of thought, obviously, and honestly, I came within a heartbeat of accepting, but something's happened . . . Actually no, it's not about that – it's about my team, my life here in Bristol, realizing I'm actually really committed to what I have . . .' She didn't add *if I still have it* – there was no need. 'Obviously, I feel really honoured that you thought I was the right person, and maybe I would have been once, just not now.'

There was a lengthy silence before Kinsley said, 'So what's really going on? Is it still the Molly Terrance thing, because—'

'It's not her. I mean, I sure as hell never want to work with her, but to be completely honest, I'm going through a bit of a challenging time personally, which will make it hard for me to give a hundred percent to something as demanding as what you're proposing. Plus, as I said, I find I'm even more committed to my team here than I realized. I'm sorry, Paul, I really am—'

'Don't apologize,' he interrupted, 'just keep thinking, because I'm not giving up on you yet.'

Both touched and annoyed, she said, 'My decision is made. If you don't let me go, you'll just make it harder.'

'I'm not here to make it easier. I'm here to give you the opportunity you deserve, and no matter what you say, you *are* the best person for the job. So, go away, sort out whatever shit needs sorting, and we'll talk again in a week or two. Sorry, I have to ring off now – we have guests in for lunch.'

'Of course, I . . .'

Realizing he'd already gone, she clicked off at her end and sat with the phone between her hands, staring at nothing, while seeing images in her mind of Nicole being taken from the converted stables in South Glos, feeling frightened and confused . . . She presumably had no idea at this stage that Meier had played a part in the revoking of her licence . . .

Cristy frowned as something snagged in her mind. It was about the location. The Terrier had apparently known where Nicole could be found. The only person who could have told her was Meier . . . Except she, Cristy, couldn't remember telling him.

She reconnected to his number and was surprised when he answered.

'I was about to call you,' he told her. 'I've seen the online article now, so I have a better understanding of why you're so angry, but I can assure you I am not behind this, and nor is anyone here. I'm as upset as you are . . .'

'If it wasn't you, or anyone there, then who? Because I swear it wasn't one of us.'

'You know your team better than I do, so I'll take your word for that. I'm just sorry you felt that I wasn't to be trusted . . . I thought we'd reached an understanding . . . Well, it doesn't matter what I thought. All that matters to me is Nicole.'

As he ended the call, Cristy looked up to find that Connor had come into the room. 'Did you hear any of that?' she asked.

He nodded. 'Here's a question for you,' he said. 'If we

ever found ourselves in Terrance's position – a rival running away with a story we badly wanted – what would we do?'

Cristy frowned as she thought, until finally connecting with where he was leading her, she said, 'She had us followed. That's what happened, which means we're still to blame, for not being more vigilant, but . . .'

'She'll have used a PI,' Connor stated.

Getting to her feet, Cristy said, 'Let's give her a call, find out what she has to say for herself. And I think we'll record it.'

CHAPTER THIRTY-SIX

Amazingly, it seemed everyone was available today, in spite of it being Sunday, although it wasn't unusual when a big story had just broken. Molly Terrance was no doubt being inundated with calls, everyone wanting to know what more she had to share, who her sources were, where exactly in South Glos Nicole Ivorson had been hiding out. The questions would be endless, the attention – not to mention likes and shares – deeply gratifying for someone like the Terrier.

Cristy expected her own video call to be rejected; however, it wasn't, and after a moment of blurred connection, Molly Terrance came clear on their screens – and Cristy couldn't remember ever feeling such a strong urge to slap someone's face.

TERRANCE: 'Cristy, what a lovely surprise. How are you?'

CRISTY: 'I can tell you're extremely proud of your exclusive, Molly, and I can see what a great response you've had already, but tell me this: did you even stop to consider what you were doing to Nicole Ivorson? Did you actually see her as a person? Or was it all about making sure I didn't get the story first?'

TERRANCE: 'Oh, Cristy, you do make me laugh. The way you hold yourself up as some moral crusader, the great investigative journalist who, by the way, is apparently happy to persuade a parolee to break the terms of her licence to get a good story. So, I'd say all responsibility for sending her back to prison lies with you, my friend.'

CRISTY: 'Oh, don't worry, I'm accepting my part in it, but what I also consider myself guilty of is failing to remember how low you will stoop to get a headline. Rather than heave yourself out of London to pursue a story in person, you used a PI or maybe a local stringer to do all the legwork for you, didn't you? But all they've given you is a headline. There's no substance to your piece. Yes, she broke the terms of her licence, and yes, she's back behind bars, but what does that tell anyone about the actual case? Did you interview her? Have you made any attempt to dig into the detail of what really happened back in 2005?'

TERRANCE: 'You're making a lot of assumptions there, Cristy, we all know what happened...'

CRISTY: 'So tell me how she killed them?'

TERRANCE: 'Does it matter?'

CRISTY: 'It does if they're still alive.'

She had the immense satisfaction of watching Terrance's eyes narrow with alarm and suspicion.

TERRANCE: 'Are you saying they *are*?'

CRISTY: 'What I'm saying is: in your rush to get a headline, all you've actually achieved it sending her back to prison. And now, I won't be at all surprised if I find my own words being quoted by you tomorrow, claiming that "a source close to Nicole" has told you the twins are still alive. That's how you work. A grain of truth whipped into a frenzy of fake news, when no one's actually told you they're alive at all.'

TERRANCE: 'If they are, you realize you're breaking the law by withholding information? So maybe my story will be *Cristy Ward's* Hindsight *Team Refuses to Cooperate with Police Inquiries into the Nicole Ivorson Case?*'

CRISTY: 'Nice try, but there is no open investigation, so no requirement for us to cooperate with anyone. I don't suppose it'll stop you writing whatever suits your next narrative, but let me tell you this, Molly: if you go for *Hindsight* again, you'll end up deeply regretting it.'

As the screen went dark and the recording stopped, Clove and Jacks cheered.

'Talk about putting her in her place.' Clove laughed. 'She is such a POS.'

'The most interesting part of it,' Cristy said pensively, 'is that she didn't mention Meier.'

'So does that mean,' Connor said, 'that as soon as she found out we were in touch with Nicole, she decided she had her story and called off her guy?'

'We don't know anything for certain,' Cristy replied, 'you know how sly she is – but let's hope she hasn't cottoned on to him yet, because the last thing we want to find out tomorrow is that we were followed to Bryn Helyg.'

She checked her phone as an email arrived and seeing who it was from, she had a sudden, horrible feeling about what it was going to say. She glanced up, trying to gauge whether it had been sent to anyone else, and felt a powerful sense of relief when it didn't seem to have been.

Opening it, she read quickly:

Hey, Cristy, good talking to you. Just wondering if you've told your team about your fantastic job offer yet? You know, the one that leaves them in the lurch while you go and take over the podcasting world, making them look a bit small fry and you the goddess of all things Crime Time and beyond?

Happy to break the news for you, just say the word.

MT x

Feeling another intense urge to slap the woman, Cristy closed the email and debated quickly with herself. At least she'd already turned Kinsley's offer down, but now wasn't the right time to tell the team about it. Connor would know she'd lied to him about Vikram Rathour, and she really didn't want that level of mistrust, or suspicion, finding its way between them now, right in the middle of a series. Obviously she would tell him at some point, but on her terms and in her own time – definitely not forced there by the Terrier.

So, unable to escape the wretched woman's unsubtly sprung trap for the moment, she sent a quick email back saying:

What do you want?

It took next to no time for a response to land.

I know you interviewed Nicole – would be good to get some quotes.

Cristy's heart sank, in spite of already having guessed it would be the condition.

Leave it with me, but be aware that if you trash her, we'll be calling you out big-time.

The answer came back:

Deal.

Realizing Connor was watching her, Cristy put aside her phone and said, 'In the hope I haven't completely blown this series, shall we get back to figuring out exactly how we can take it forward now we no longer have Nicole and Honey on board?'

Still looking at her, he said, 'Provided we can come up with the right angle, I think Honey could be persuaded to carry on working with us.'

Cristy nodded, relieved that he was willing to try. 'Let's hope you're right. Meanwhile, here's what I think our next move should be.'

CHAPTER THIRTY-SEVEN

With Nicole's return to prison – not to mention *Hindsight*'s own involvement in it – being such a big story in the main news, there was a very small window available for them to re-edit the next episode in time for upload. However, it was quickly decided that this week's focus needed to be more on the effect the sudden turn in events might be having on Nicole's mental health, rather than on the licence revocation itself.

So, the psychologist who'd advised Cristy prior to their first meeting with Nicole was called in to give an account of others she'd treated in similar circumstances. She was good – concise, descriptive, certainly knowledgeable and someone they'd keep on record to use again if the need arose. Of course, the irony of Meier's expertise in this very field was lost on none of them. However, he was clearly the wrong person to speak to now.

Eventually, with some deft intercutting and useful sound overlays between the historic search for the twins and the speculative analysis of what could be happening to Nicole now, they hit the deadline on Tuesday evening, popped open the champagne and sat back to listen.

In spite of having poured herself into the series this past week, David had never been far from Cristy's mind, always there, playing havoc with her emotions and tormenting her with fears and indecision. Ten days was a long time, far too long for her to expect anything good to come of this break, so should she just accept it was over and try to get on with her life – good luck with that – or should she try messaging him again?

By the time the episode ended, thirty-five minutes later, she was no closer to making a decision, could only force herself back to her surroundings as all the usual credits and promos played. Just thank God no one knew how conflicted, how wretchedly torn apart she was inside. She didn't want anyone's pity, or advice, she only wanted this hellish separation to be over in a way that saw them back together again.

If only she could see it happening.

Her eyes went to Connor as he faded out the sound and declared them all geniuses for having got so much high value storytelling into so little airtime.

'You did brilliantly!' Meena agreed, raising her glass. 'But of course, everyone knows now that you have an exclusive with Nicole herself, so they'll have been hoping to hear at least one or two extracts from that.'

Thinking of the Terrier, who she was studiously ignoring, Cristy said, 'Honey's asked us not to use anything yet, so we're honouring the request and hoping Nicole or Maeve will give us the go-ahead to run at least something once the shock of everything has started to pass. Besides, we're keen to combine it with some of Meier's interview to get a feel for what they're saying about one another and their relationship, and there just hasn't been time these last few days to pull it together.'

'Which reminds me,' Connor said, shifting his sleeping daughter from one shoulder to the other, 'we need to send you two, Clove and Jacks, back to Wales to get Johan and Maggi on record.'

'Maggi claims Nicole is guilty as charged,' Cristy reminded them, 'but she offered me nothing to back it up, so when you go, try getting her on her own without Meier. Speak of the devil.' And, opening up a text from him, she read it aloud: '*When would be a good time to call?*'

After sending a quick message back suggesting right now, she picked up her glass to wait. 'Probably a bit soon for him to be responding to the pod,' she decided, 'so I'm hoping it'll be about the email I sent on Sunday asking . . . Ah, here he is. Actually, you guys carry on – I'm going to take it over in the meeting room.'

Leaving them all startled by her decision, Cristy quickly crossed the hall and clicked onto the line. 'Do you have some news for me?' she asked, closing the door behind her.

'I have requested a visit with Nicole,' he told her.

'Do you think she'll accept?'

'I hope so. I'm guessing you've also put in for one?'

'We have, but no idea how kindly she'll look on us, all things considered. What about Lauren? Have you spoken to her yet?'

There was a moment before he said, 'She tells me she will call you some time in the next few days, but only on the condition that you do not record anything she says.'

Disappointed, although not surprised, Cristy said, 'Please give her my word that whatever she tells us will not be attributed to her as a source. Do you think she'll be OK with that?'

'I will put it to her.' Then, after another pause, 'We listened to your latest podcast just now.'

Feeling suddenly and inexplicably nervous, Cristy said, 'You sound concerned. Did we get something wrong?'

'No, I don't think so. It was simply that . . .' He took a breath. 'It brought a lot back: the search for the twins, the fear we all had at the time . . . It was hard hearing it.'

'I'm sorry, but you understand why—'

'Yes, of course. You're doing your job, but I'm sure you realize that for us it's much more than a story or a podcast. You are talking about our lives, our experiences, the suspicions and heartache that have never gone away, and the many questions that remain unanswered.'

'Yes, I do realize that, and I—'

'Thank you for not mentioning my prison visits yet. I know you will, sooner or later, but at least I can cherish my privacy a while longer.'

She found herself picturing him at the farm, his handsome face creased, perhaps even pale with concern and for a fleeting moment she wished she could be with him. Maybe she should apologize for the way she'd torn into him on Sunday, how ready she'd been to blame him for Nicole's return to prison. In the end she decided there was nothing to be gained from bringing it up now. So speaking gently, she said, 'We don't intend to reveal where you are, only that you and Nicole have remained in touch.'

'And people will draw their own conclusions from that – as have you, I'm sure.'

'You told us your reasons when we interviewed you.'

'It was the truth. I just don't know how many people will believe it is as simple as that.'

'Is it?'

He sounded amused as he said, 'When has love ever been simple?' Then, in a slightly less melancholy tone, 'I am going to Switzerland tomorrow, just for a few days, to see my brother.'

Recalling what he'd told her about those visits, she said, 'Does that mean you're feeling the need to talk to someone?'

'Maybe.' Then, 'Would you consider joining me there?'

Her heart jolted.

'We will be at our home in Vevey, an hour's train ride from Geneva, on the way to Montreux. It is very beautiful. Unfortunately, we no longer own the vineyards, but Julien runs them, and his wife, Rula, does the marketing, so we will be happy to show you around.'

Certain there was more to this than a mere wine tour,

she said, 'Can I give you an answer when I've spoken to Connor?'

'Of course. I don't leave until tomorrow, and I plan to be there until the weekend. If you do decide to come, you're most welcome to stay with us, or there is a hotel on the lake we can recommend. I'll wait to hear from you, and meanwhile, I will contact Lauren again.'

After ringing off, Cristy took a moment to try and work out what might really be going on. Why would he invite them to his hometown when there was no obvious reason to, unless . . . ?

'If what I'm thinking is real,' Clove declared excitedly, as soon as Cristy had reported back, 'then this could turn out to be major.'

'What *are* you thinking?' Meena urged. 'What's in Switzerland that we don't yet know about?'

Cristy looked at Connor.

'The twins?' Clove answered for them.

'Is that what *you* think?' Meena asked Cristy.

'I'm not sure,' Cristy replied. 'I admit it was the first thing that came to my mind, but if they are there . . . God, it opens up so much . . .'

'Such as why he would want you to meet them,' Jodi put forward incredulously.

'I'm not sure I'm liking the sound of this,' Harry stated. 'He could be luring you into some sort of trap.'

Scoffing, Meena cried, 'That's exactly what *you* would think – although I kind of agree,' she told Cristy and Connor. 'I mean, if he's had them in Switzerland all this time . . .'

'Maybe his brother has brought them up as his own?' Clove suggested.

'I can tell you right now,' Jacks said, opening up his research file, 'that my deep dives have shown his brother, Julien, to be married to Rula, resident in Vevey with their two kids . . . Yep, here they are. Lance and Jacob, aged twenty-six and twenty-eight respectively.' He looked up to check how his news had gone down.

Connor said, 'Both boys, and too old to be Noah and Abigail anyway.'

'However,' Jacks said, 'now might be a good time for me to share the facial enhancements we've had back. It'll give you an idea of what the twins probably look like now, just in case you do happen to run into someone who could be them while you're there.'

Clove said, 'When will you go?'

'He's flying tomorrow,' Cristy replied, 'so I think we should go on Thursday, back Friday?' she said to Connor.

With an awkward glance at Jodi, he said, 'We have something in the diary for Thursday. So how about Friday, back Saturday?'

Deciding not to ask why Thursday was an issue – if her immediate suspicion of an early pregnancy scan was correct, they probably didn't want to share that with everyone yet – Cristy said, 'I'll check with Meier to see if it works. I think he's planning to come back himself on Saturday, so it might.'

'If not, I can come with,' Clove offered.

Cristy smiled, but she was immediately distracted by the images Jacks had now sent to her phone: two vibrant, super healthy-looking young people with a remarkable resemblance to one another and to their mother, Nicole. She scrutinized the faces for any signs of Meier – the colour of their eyes, shapes of their faces or mouths – but there was nothing to mark them out as being related to him. Or to Johan Bauer, come to that, although she wasn't as familiar with his features. Anyway, some children didn't resemble their parents at all, so there was no more to be drawn from this than the bewildering and even heartwarming fantasy of Noah and Abigail still being alive.

CHAPTER THIRTY-EIGHT

On Thursday morning, Cristy took the 1125 flight to Geneva, and by two-thirty – allowing for the hour time-difference – she was on a train heading along the lakeshore towards Vevey. Although it wasn't the first time she'd made this journey – she'd travelled to Montreux on a couple of occasions in the past with Matthew – the stunning landscape was even more mesmerizing than she remembered. The shimmering blue of the water, the hazy drift of sunlight and the snowy Alps on the opposite shore was so dazzling and dreamlike it was impossible to look away.

She'd come alone in the end; Clove and Jacks had gone to Bryn Helyg to take advantage of Meier not being around, and Connor hadn't been able to change his and Jodi's appointment.

'I really don't think it's a trap,' she'd protested, when Harry had tried to argue her out of it. 'For heaven's sake, you all know where I'm going, and he's made no secret of where his brother lives or the hotel he's booked me into for the night. Anyway, I'll have my phone; I'll put the tracker on so you'll know where I am at any given second of the day, and if it makes you feel any better, I'll call every hour on the hour.'

She wouldn't, obviously, nor would they expect it; she'd just wanted to make the point that she wasn't worried about this visit and they shouldn't be either. *The Quinns – honestly!*

Sometimes, it was worse than having parents, although she'd give almost anything to have hers back, so maybe Harry and Meena's fussing wasn't so bad. And fortunately, it hadn't annoyed her, which could mean, fingers crossed, that the HRT was starting to kick in.

Dream on, she groaned to herself, as her entire body, as if on cue, started to heat up – to a degree that soon made her desperate to put her head out of the window, even if it meant risking it being smashed off her shoulders by an oncoming train.

Eventually, the hot flush passed, and though she really didn't want to miss out on a single second of the stunning scenery, she found herself struggling to keep her eyes open.

She must have dozed for a while, because the next thing she knew, they were pulling into Lausanne station where she needed to change for the connection to Vevey.

It didn't take long – how smoothly everything seemed to run here, and how clean it was too – and after finding herself another window seat, she settled down to begin mentally preparing herself for what might lie ahead. Now that she was drawing closer, she was starting to wonder about the sanity of being in this impossibly romantic setting with Meier on her own, given how attracted she'd felt to him while in Wales. There was no reason to think it would be any different here, and now she was asking herself if, on some level, she'd actually wanted to come alone, and maybe it was what he wanted too. Hadn't he said, *Would you consider joining me?* No mention of Connor, but nor had he pushed back when she'd assumed he'd meant them both.

There was no doubt he was an almost impossible man to read, especially given the muddled perspective she was currently trying to operate through. Did everyone suffer with an uncontrollable and totally inappropriate libido during menopause? It didn't matter; she wasn't so far out of control that she'd allow some wild hormone rush to turn her into someone else completely, and that's who she'd be if she ended up in bed with a man she was currently investigating and who she didn't altogether trust anyway.

Didn't she trust him?

Maybe knowing he was deeply in love with someone else was what would save her from making a fool of herself with some kind of rebound affair?

For God's sake, why was she even thinking about this when it couldn't be further from the reason she was here?

Checking her mobile as it rang, her heart turned over so sharply it stole her breath and actually hurt. For a moment, she considered not answering. She was completely unprepared for this, had no idea what to say, had longed for the call so much that she was now half-afraid she was imagining it.

Clicking on, she said, 'Hi. This is a surprise.'

'How are you?' David asked. 'Not in the UK by the sound of the ringtone.'

'Switzerland. Where are you?'

'At home. Can we talk?'

'Now? I'm on a train . . .'

In a tone that wasn't readable, although definitely not hostile, he said, 'I can come to Bristol when you're back.'

It was what she wanted more than anything, had been actually praying for it, and she'd be prepared by then, would know exactly how to handle things, so why wasn't she saying yes?

'Can I call you when . . . I'm not sure how much more we have to put into the series and . . .'

'It's OK. I can wait. Just let me know when it's best for you.'

After ringing off, she stared out of the window, no longer registering the spectacular terraced vineyards cascading down the hillsides or how the train slowed going through Saint-

Saphorin station. She was waiting for a rush of euphoria or simply relief that he'd finally got in touch, and she guessed both were there somewhere, but it seemed to be worrying her too, and for the moment, she wasn't sure why.

*

An hour and a half later she was strolling along the lakeside promenade with Meier. He'd met her from the train and taken her to the stupendously grand Hotel du Lac – a shining example of the *belle époque* style that exuded all the sublime elegance and charm of its era. The uniformed staff had shown her to a lake-view room, and after giving her time to relax and freshen up after her journey, Meier had returned.

Now, with the surreal golden glow of a slowly setting sun turning the Alps on the opposite shore into another kind of wonderland, and the water into a mirror of gently changing colour, she was telling him about the call from David – only because he'd asked, having apparently picked up on some of her inner turmoil. Otherwise, she wouldn't have mentioned it.

He really was unnervingly perceptive.

'I think he wants to end it formally between us,' she said, as they approached an open-air champagne bar with several lively fire pits to warm the evening drinkers. 'He just feels it's wrong to do it on the phone.'

'Has he given you any reason to think that?' Meier asked, taking her elbow and guiding her to a tall table at the edge of the bar. 'Or is it just something you're afraid of?'

'Both, I guess,' she replied with a sigh.

After signalling for two glasses of Taittinger, he held the back of a bar stool as she climbed up, then took the one opposite for himself.

She looked at him, saw how focused he was on her issue

and felt her heart expand with gratitude that he actually seemed to care. 'I'm not here to talk about me,' she reminded him, genuinely keen to get off the subject now. 'So how about you tell me why you invited me?'

His eyebrows rose in a quixotic sort of way. 'Why did you come?' he countered.

She laughed. 'I asked first.'

'But it's important for me to know the reason you decided to accept.'

She felt a stirring of discomfort, not sure if he was expecting her to admit to her attraction or if it was the furthest thing from his mind. In the end, she said, 'I'm not sure you'll like the answer.'

Clearly intrigued, he said, 'Why don't you let me decide? But I can only do so if you are honest with me.'

'OK,' she said, drawing out the word and tightening her hands as if bracing herself, 'I – we, as a team . . . Actually, before I go there, I want to share a Connor observation with you.' She didn't really want to, just felt that she should.

Surprised, he said, 'I'm listening.'

Cristy was already embarrassed. 'He noticed when we were at Bryn Helyg that everyone there, guests excluded, has a biblical name, and he wondered if it's mere coincidence, or if it has any significance . . .' God, she felt stupid now.

Though clearly baffled, he actually gave it some thought, before saying, 'But my own name is not . . .' He broke into a smile as realization dawned. 'Ah, Jean-Claude, J.C. And Maggi?' he queried.

Cristy winced. 'Magda-lene?'

He nodded, as though conceding a point. 'OK. I'm thinking about who else was there now . . . Of course, Connor realizes you only met a handful of the staff, does he not? There are many more from all over the world, and I don't think all of their names can be described as biblical.'

'I'm sorry,' she said wretchedly.

He smiled again, and this time his eyes shone with humour. 'I am aware of the rumours of a cult,' he told her. 'They have long been circling, but I can assure you it's not who we are – unless it's how you want to characterize our community of highly qualified therapists whose only goal is the betterment of mental health.'

'I'm sorry,' she said again. She was deeply regretting getting into this now but found herself pushing on anyway. 'There's also the rationale you gave for the miracles. It seemed . . . I don't know how to put this . . .'

'Unusual?'

She nodded.

'Yes, I realize my views can be seen as a little radical, maybe even sacrilegious to some and perhaps delusional on my part?'

She could tell he was teasing her, so she met his irony with a similar look of her own.

Serious again, he said, 'After my parents' deaths, I got into reading a lot of different things, some of it about cults, I confess, and often it was quite dark, certainly not always good for me . . . I was in a difficult place, you understand. It was during this time that I went to Qumran, in Israel, to visit the caves where the Dead Sea Scrolls were found. I'm not saying this trip was a wrong thing to do; in many ways it was, as you might expect, educational, clarifying even. While I was there, I sought out translations of the Scrolls, and they led me to various works that contain more logical explanations of the New Testament stories. This is where my understanding of them comes from.'

'I see. So you don't believe you were there at the time?'

He laughed. 'If I was, I have no recollection of it. Which is to say, maybe we have all lived before, and maybe we will again, but I have no more proof of it than I do of Christ's ability to create a feast from a meal for one or turn water into wine.'

'So he didn't bring Lazarus back from the dead? Or make a blind girl see? Or rise again on the third day?'

'The first two are about excommunication and restoring sinners to the faith. The third is a more complex story of enlightenment, but a fascinating one. I'm happy to recommend some books on the subject. If you're truly interested.'

Thinking she might be, one day, Cristy said, 'You're obviously very widely read, and I imagine you could educate me in subjects I hardly even know exist, but for now, I think we're straying too far from the reasons I'm here.'

'This is true, we are, and I realize not everyone shares my interest in the esoteric; it can be quite heavy going. So, perhaps you are now going to be honest with me about why you came?'

Realizing that from her side, this didn't get any better, she braced herself again, and said, 'We – the team and I – wondered if you're going to tell me something significant about the twins. Maybe even introduce me to them?'

Although he blinked, he seemed neither surprised nor offended by her words, only reflective as he absorbed them and eventually said, 'Believe me, I wish I was able to do that, but I'm afraid it is not the reason I invited you.'

She sat back as two generous flutes of sparkling champagne and a dish of nibbles was set down between them.

He raised his glass and held her eyes as he said, 'I'm glad you came alone; it gives me an opportunity to know you better.'

Certain that he wasn't flirting, was actually quite serious about what he was saying, she waited for him to explain.

'You are already playing a very significant role in my life,' he told her, 'and in a little while, maybe a week, although it could be longer, you will probably have a better understanding of why I feel it's important for me to have this time with you.'

Not at all sure she was following, she said tentatively, 'So this visit is connected to the twins?'

He took a sip of his drink and said, 'Tell me, has Lauren called you yet?'

She shook her head.

'She will; I'm certain of it. She just needs to choose the right time. For her, I mean, and her family.'

'Does she have the twins? Or at least know where they are?'

His smile was sad. 'No, she does not.'

'But *you* know where they are.'

Instead of answering, he checked his phone and said, 'My brother is asking me to confirm if you will join us for dinner this evening at his home.'

What else could she say, apart from, 'Thank you. I'd love to.'

He tapped in a reply and put the phone away. 'This short visit to Vevey will, I hope, work two ways. As I get to know you a little better, you will also get to know me and my family. It is important, I believe, for both of us to have a deeper understanding of who the other is before everything changes.'

'Changes in what way?' she prompted, already suspecting she wouldn't get a straight answer.

His gaze drifted to the flames closest to them, and the way they reflected in his eyes made him seem as though he was somehow submerged in them. 'Much will depend on Nicole,' he said finally. 'She has agreed to see me, which is why I am flying back tomorrow, earlier than I originally intended.' He looked at her again and said, 'Now, perhaps you will allow me to tell you more about our beautiful lakeside town and why we have the world's largest fork – eight metres tall – that you see right there, seeming to hover on the surface of the water.'

*

'So the twins definitely aren't there?' Connor said when Cristy briefed him later.

'I really don't think so,' she replied, going to the window of her luxurious room to peer through the heavy silk drapes. Even in the black of night, the view was spectacular, with the hotel's pale walls, filigree balconies and outside lights reflecting like a mirage in the inky water. 'Having just spent an evening with his brother and sister-in-law, who were delightful, I think this trip really is about getting to know me better.'

'And why would he want to do that? No offence.'

'None taken. All I can tell you is what we already know: that he's gifted when it comes to drawing people out. No surprise, given his professional training – I'm just afraid I bored for England going on about my children, my time in TV, *Hindsight* and the other stories we've covered. But listen to what his brother said as I was leaving – his wife and Meier weren't there at the time, just us two, and he said: "I believe Jean-Claude is right to trust you. Please don't prove me wrong."'

'Seriously?' Connor cried. 'Did he qualify that?'

'The others joined us then . . .'

'So did anyone *not* talk in riddles this evening?'

Smiling, she said, 'It seems pretty obvious that Meier's intending to reveal something big; it's just a question of when, although I'm certain it'll be after he's seen Nicole.'

'Which is when?'

'On Saturday apparently. I've no idea how soon after that he'll be in touch with us, or what difference the visit will make, but he was keen to know if we'd heard from Lauren. Please don't ask me how it ties in; I don't think we'll have an answer for that until she does decide to get in touch.'

'OK. So what's on the agenda tomorrow?'

'More getting-to-know-you with a tour of what was once their family vineyard before I train it back to Geneva in time for the 1425 flight. He's getting the later one around seven, I think.'

'So you should be back in the office around three, given you're an hour ahead over there.'

'More like six. I flew from Heathrow, remember. Will you still be there?'

''Fraid not, but there've been some developments this end that you'll want to know about, so I'll ask Clove and Jacks to hang around. Or we can go through it together on Saturday morning.'

'Let's do that,' she said, sinking down on the bed and unwrapping one of the gift chocolates. 'But give me a heads up on the developments.'

'OK, the trip to Wales was kind of productive – Maggi confirmed she thinks Nicole killed the twins but couldn't say how or why, and nothing on where the bodies could be found. Annoyingly, she has not said this on tape. Bauer didn't seem to know anything about her suspicions; he's firmly of the opinion that the twins were taken. Are Johan and Maggi working together on conflicting stories, to throw us off the scent? I've no idea, but something else that's happened, apart from that: the supersleuths have sent through a couple of witnesses from back in the day who got in touch after hearing the pod. Interesting stuff, but I should probably go now. It's almost midnight here, so even later with you, and I think I can hear you snoring.'

Laughing, she said, 'OK, I'll let you go, just tell me: do these witnesses actually change anything?'

'Not sure yet. Let's discuss when we meet.'

It wasn't until she was finally getting into bed that she realized she hadn't asked about Jodi's pregnancy scan – although she wasn't supposed to know, of course, so it didn't matter. She hadn't told him about David's call either – except why would she do that when there was nothing to be said about it? Plenty of imaginary conclusions to draw, of course, and the one that kept coming back to her was perhaps the most likely and the most awful:

I'm sorry Cristy, I've given it a lot of thought, and I don't think things are working out between us. It's not your fault. It's just that I'm not feeling it any more. I'm sorry – really, I am – but we both know that when love dies, there really isn't any bringing it back. I think it's best if we call it a day so we can both get on with our lives.

CHAPTER THIRTY-NINE

'OK, so our first witness's name is Georgina Gould,' Clove announced on Saturday morning, as soon as everyone was settled with coffee and open computers. 'I've already spoken to her, on the record, so I'll play you what she had to say, coming in on the most relevant part.'

> GEORGINA: '... I remember seeing it, clear as day, even after all these years: a white car pulling away from the garage that belongs to number 42.'
>
> CLOVE: 'And this was on the day the twins disappeared?'
>
> GEORGINA: 'That's right. Before all the police turned up and the helicopters and everything. I was walking past with my toddler in his buggy – he's twenty-three now, so all grown up ... Anyway, I remember it because I had to stop and wait for the car to come out.'
>
> CLOVE: 'Did you see who was driving it?'
>
> GEORGINA: 'No. I mean, it was a bloke, I'm sure of that, and there was someone in the passenger seat, but I'm afraid I didn't take a lot of notice.'
>
> CLOVE: 'Did they seem to be in a hurry?'
>
> GEORGINA: 'Not especially, until they were out on the street, then they took off quite fast.'

CLOVE: 'Did you notice what kind of car it was, apart from being white?'

GEORGINA: 'Sorry, cars have never been my strong point. All I can tell you is it wasn't a van.'

CLOVE: 'Do you remember what time it was?'

GEORGINA: 'I do. It was just before one o'clock. I know because I was on my way to meet my aunt off the bus that stops – or used to stop – outside number 42. We're going back some years, of course, so I've no idea if it's still there – we moved away more than a decade ago. Anyway, I remember the bus turned up on time that day, my aunt got off and that was that – until we heard all the commotion later in the day.'

CLOVE: 'Did the police speak to you at all?'

GEORGINA: 'Yeah, they came door to door. I think it was the next day, pretty soon after anyway, so I gave them a statement, saying what I'd seen. I never heard anything back, so I decided they couldn't have thought it was important.'

Hitting stop, Clove said, 'I've been in touch with Honey. She confirmed that the statement is in the disclosure pack, so Georgina Gould is on the level, in that she did give a statement saying she saw a white car leaving the garage around one o'clock that day. What doesn't seem to have happened is any sort of search for the car. Unless there was one and lack of further witnesses and number plate details, plus all the distractions of the time, made them give up on it.'

Cristy considered this. 'OK, let's keep this in mind and maybe circle back to it later. You mentioned two witnesses had come forward.'

Responding, Clove said 'The other is a voice note from

someone called Kevin Holmes. Apparently, he used to live on the estate that more or less backs on to the other side of the woods, so about a mile from number 42, as the crow flies. He was twelve at the time it all happened, which puts him early thirties now. He says he was in the woods climbing trees with a couple of mates that day . . . Here, have a listen.'

> KEVIN: '. . . Then we saw her, large as life with all that red hair and shorty shorts – we were boys; of course we noticed something like that . . . Anyway, it looked as though she was burying something . . . She had a shovel, and she was definitely digging . . . There was something next to her. We couldn't see what it was, but yeah, about the right size for a dead cat. Or a baby, I suppose, but hers would have been bigger by then, wouldn't they? And I wouldn't have said there were two of them. Whatever it was just wasn't big enough.
>
> 'I'm afraid we didn't own up to seeing anything when the police came round asking. We were knocking off school that day and knew we'd be in big trouble if anyone found out. I mean, we talked about saying something, amongst ourselves, but then we heard they'd dug up the whole woods and nothing had been found, so what was there to say? We figured she'd either decided not to bury whatever it was or she'd come back for it before the police got there . . .
>
> 'OK, I get that one of us should have come forward a long time ago, but it's not like we were actual witnesses to anything, just three kids who didn't want to get caught bunking off school.'

'All this really tells us,' Jacks said, when the playback stopped, 'is that she was in the woods that morning, as claimed, but this guy's pretty vague, so I don't see how it helps us much.'

Cristy was staring at the rain on the window.

'Planet earth to Cristy,' Connor prompted.

Looking at him, she smiled. 'Sorry, I was just trying to work out how and where we can use these witnesses. Does Honey know about the tree-climbers?'

'She does,' Clove confirmed.

Stifling a yawn, Cristy went to pour herself a third coffee of the day. Another night tossing and turning, with way too little sleep, wasn't conducive to thinking straight this morning. Maybe a supercharge of caffeine would help. 'So tell me about Bryn Helyg,' she said, returning to her desk. 'How did you get on there?'

'I already told you,' Connor reminded her. 'Maggi repeated what she told you—'

'Sure, of course,' Cristy interrupted, the conversation belatedly coming back to her. 'What did you make of the place?' she asked Clove.

Clove's tone simmered with irony as she said, 'Definitely in need of a mental health crisis so I can book myself in. Probably a pay rise as well. Anyway, we had better weather than you guys, so we had a proper look round . . . Did you know all the animals are pets? None of them go to slaughter or get their necks wrung or brains blown out – apart from mercy killings – and half of them actually come when they're called. I felt like Dr Dolittle out there.'

'There are now two newborn lambs known as Clove and Jacks,' Jacks announced, with a roll of his eyes to hide his pride.

'Good to hear you had a great time at the petting-zoo,' Cristy remarked dryly, 'but give me more on what you made of the staff.'

Clove shrugged. 'Everyone was happy to talk, but Maggi was of course the most interesting. She didn't want to go on the record, but when I asked her why she thought Nicole had killed the twins, she told me the question shouldn't be why but how.'

Cristy's eyes widened. 'I should have thought both counted, but what answer did she give?'

'Apparently Maggie had left Bristol for Australia by the time it happened, so she doesn't *know* what went down; she's just certain that Nicole did it, and her *guess* is that she smothered them.'

Cristy pulled a face. 'Based on what?'

'I'm just repeating what she told me. She wouldn't go any further than that, although she was keen to emphasize the fact that Meier was also overseas when it happened – we know that of course – and she says he's already suffered enough, so we shouldn't try to implicate him in any way. It'll just cause more stress to no end.'

Cristy nodded thoughtfully as she took this in. 'So very protective of him,' she commented, wondering why, when she wasn't surprised, it was sitting awkwardly with her.

Jacks said, 'Bit of background on Magda Thomas. She was one of Meier's Bristol students back in 2003 to 2005 until he returned to Switzerland. After she graduated in 2006, she worked for the NHS in various posts and trusts, right up until 2014, when she went to join Meier at Bryn Helyg.'

Clove said, 'Honey checked the disclosure pack and was able to confirm that Magda Thomas was interviewed, by phone apparently, three days after the disappearance. It turns out she really was in Aus in 2005, from the beginning of June until the end of November, so nowhere near 42 Randall Lane.'

'There's also Johan,' Jacks reminded them, 'who was a fellow lecturer in Bristol the same time Meier was there. He was interviewed by the police, again by phone, two days after the disappearance, and it turns out he too was out of the country at the crucial time – at home in Germany in his case. Bear in mind the terrorist attacks in London happened the very next day, so could be why nothing was properly followed up or got pushed under a carpet, or whatever was going on back then. We just know that the entire country was in shock, and undoubtedly every force was put on high alert to find the perpetrators and anyone who could be linked to them.'

Nodding her understanding, Cristy said, 'So when did Johan Bauer leave Bristol?'

Checking, Jacks said, 'June 2005, same as Meier. In his case, he returned to Germany, where he took up a post at the very prestigious Heidelberg University, which is where he remained until 2012, when he went to help Meier start the Bryn Helyg project.'

'One last thing,' Clove said. 'For what it's worth, no one we spoke to had a single bad word to say about Meier.'

Not in the least surprised by that, Cristy finished her coffee and checked the time. She kept wondering if Meier and Nicole were together now, in a prison visiting room, discussing the changes he'd mentioned when he and Cristy were in Vevey? What were they going to be? It simply wasn't possible to know, unless Meier decided to open up when he eventually got in touch, and could they actually count on the fact that he would? Even after the short time she'd spent with him in Vevey, or maybe because of it, she was still no closer to feeling certain about trusting him. She wanted to, she knew that, and all her instincts seemed to be encouraging it. However, the skewed nature of her perception these days meant that she didn't even know if she could trust herself.

'OK,' Connor said, opening up a new screen on his desktop, 'we need to focus on the next episode and what we are and aren't going to use. At the moment, the plan is to feature the two big interviews – Nicole and Meier – no reason not to, now everyone knows we've spoken to her and she gave the go ahead via Honey. So, looking like we'll be pulling another all-weekender. Actually, I was wondering, Cris, when we set the scene for Meier's interview, maybe we could go in for a bit of me ribbing you about how attractive you found him?'

Cristy scowled. 'Will you see it as a sense of humour failure if I pass on that?' she countered, thinking of how much she'd hate it.

He grimaced. 'David. Of course. Sorry.'

'Not only him. I'd rather Meier didn't hear it either.'

'Sure, bad idea. Consider it shelved. We'll cut right to the great love story. Have you got the recordings ready to go?' he asked Jacks.

Remembering her promise to the Terrier, that she'd provide some soundbites from Nicole's interview, Cristy felt tempted to tell the team right now about Kinsley's offer just to get Molly Terrance off her back. However, knowing it would send her stress levels spiralling if Connor took it badly – and why wouldn't he? – she dismissed it. The last thing she needed right now, when her emotions were already in such turmoil, was a falling out with him especially not in front of the rest of the team who'd obviously feel just as angry and betrayed as he would that she hadn't told them about it right away.

However, there was a good chance the Terrier was planning to exert more pressure any day now, so she opened up a fresh email and typed:

> *How about an exclusive with me and Connor after the series has finished? Happy to talk you through the investigation then: an inside look on how we pulled it together. Will also allow use of quotes from the episodes if needed, obvs subject to legal oversight.*

Terrance replied straightaway.

> *I might take you up on this, unless I get to the truth first of course. How are things going with Kinsley?*

None of your business.

Closing down the thread, Cristy checked to see if there was anything new from Paul Kinsley and found that fortunately there wasn't. She really didn't want to engage with his canny methods of persuasion right now, and actually, she didn't want to speak to David either, which was why she hadn't told him yet that she was back in the UK. Of course, she'd have to deal with them both sooner or later, but for today – in fact, for the whole weekend – she needed to focus entirely and exclusively on this edit.

And the hope that Meier would get in touch again.

CHAPTER FORTY

It was past eight o'clock on Sunday evening by now, and they were all still at the office, pulling together the next episode, when an unknown US number appeared on Cristy's mobile.

Guessing, hoping, it was Lauren Hawkes (now Lauren Beagle, according to Meier), she quickly alerted the others and clicked straight to speaker.

'Cristy Ward speaking,' she said, her eyes on Connor.

'Hi, I think you might be expecting my call.'

'If this is Lauren, then yes I am,' Cristy told her.

'I hope you're not recording this. If you are . . .'

'I'm not, but you must understand that if you reveal something the police need to know, I am legally bound to pass the information on.'

'Naming me as the source?'

'Possibly. Much will depend on what you tell me, but I can't be party to covering up a crime – if one has been committed.'

Lauren's laugh was dry and sad. 'It has,' she confirmed, 'and more than one, but I'm guessing you already know that.'

Not prepared to admit to what she did or didn't know, Cristy said, 'What specific crimes are you referring to?'

Avoiding a direct answer, Lauren said, 'Tell me this, has Claude seen Nicole yet?'

'I believe he was there yesterday.'

'And he hasn't contacted you since?'

'I've left messages, but so far, I haven't heard from him.'

A low murmur of voices at the other end revealed that Lauren wasn't alone. Cristy guessed a lawyer was advising her and nodded when Connor mouthed the same thought.

Coming back onto the line, Lauren said, 'I hope he keeps to his word. If he doesn't, I'll . . . I guess I'll speak to you again, but . . .'

Sensing she was about to end the call, Cristy said, 'Is there something, anything, you can tell me now? Do you *know* what happened to the twins?'

When there was no response, Cristy felt a frisson of alarm go through her. 'Are they still alive?' she pressed.

There was another silence, before Lauren said, huskily, 'I'm sorry. I'm only calling because Claude asked me to . . .'

'But what did he want you to tell me?'

'All he said was that I had to do what I thought was right, but I know he wants to speak to you himself, so I'm going to let him do that first. If you don't hear from him by the end of the week, you have this number now; you can call me back.'

'Can I ask why you aren't in touch with your mother?'

'You've spoken to her?'

'We have.'

'How is she?'

Cristy glanced at Connor as she said, 'She's worried about you . . .'

'Did she tell you I send cards on her birthday and at Christmas?' Lauren asked shakily.

'But you never see her. She says she doesn't even know where you are, if the cards are even actually coming from you.'

'They are,' Lauren assured her.

'Does she know she has grandchildren?'

Lauren didn't reply.

'Why would you keep that from her?' Cristy urged. 'Why deprive them of a grandmother . . . ?'

Sounding close to tears, Lauren said, 'I can't see her. I can't see any of them and pretend I don't know . . .'

'Don't know what?' Cristy prompted when she didn't go on.

'It's all a lie,' Lauren cried helplessly. 'What they tell themselves, what they believe . . .'

'You mean that the twins are dead – or still alive?'

'I'm sorry, I want to help – really, I do – but not if I'm going to incriminate myself and end up in prison. I'm sorry . . . I . . . I need to ring off now.'

As the connection dropped, Cristy let go a breath and sat back in her chair, tense with frustration and bewilderment. 'What the hell . . . ?' she muttered, throwing down her pen.

After a beat, Connor said, 'One of the stand-outs for me was that she seems to have got herself a lawyer.'

'Which can only mean,' Jacks volunteered, 'that she is – or was – involved in the crimes she mentioned.'

Cristy went to take some wine from the fridge. 'Tell me none of you made a sneak recording for reference,' she warned, reaching for the glasses. 'If you did, you need to destroy it now or it could jeopardize a police investigation going forward.'

'If anyone finds out about it,' Clove pointed out, 'but promise, handwritten notes only.'

'Same here,' Connor and Jacks confirmed.

'So,' Cristy said, passing around the drinks, 'what should we take from the call, apart from the fact that she was either involved in the twins' disappearance or at least knows what happened and has kept it covered up all these years?'

'When she said she can't see her mother,' Connor said, 'or "any of them", I'm presuming she's including Maeve in that. We know she doesn't mean Nicole, because she's visited her in prison. She also said that she couldn't pretend and that what "they" tell themselves is all a lie. Who's she talking about there? Maeve and Bridget? Meier and Nicole?'

'Clove, what are you looking at?' Cristy demanded.

Reading from the whiteboard, Clove said, 'Just getting a timeline going. According to Meier, Lauren went to the farm in 2010, while his grandmother was still alive, so did she already know the old lady? And whether she did or didn't, what made it the right place for her to go? Her mother mentioned her depression, but the Bryn Helyg project wasn't up and running then, so I'm asking myself, was Meier treating her, while keeping her close?'

Seeing the potential logic of that, Cristy said, 'We know she met her husband at the farm, and they left in 2014. Remind me how old her children are.'

'Ten and seven,' Clove provided.

Connor said, 'Are you thinking the eldest might be Meier's? I know I am. The dates kind of work, and if he's let the boy go to the US with her and her husband, that gives him a pretty big hold over her.'

'In that he could take him back at any time?' Jacks asked.

Cristy nodded. 'We know, thanks to Honey,' she said, 'that he did go to see Nicole yesterday, so let's find out if Nicole, or Maeve, have contacted Honey since.' She pressed in Honey's number and was preparing to leave a message when Honey answered.

'Sorry,' she said. 'Phone in the kitchen. I'm guessing you've heard from Meier?'

'Not yet,' Cristy confessed, 'but the last time I tried Bryn Helyg, I was told he was there and would get back to me. How about you? Has Nicole been in touch since his visit?'

'No. I only know it happened because someone at the prison told me. Something's going on, I can feel it – just wish I knew what it was.'

Sharing the suspicion and frustration, Cristy said, 'We've heard from Lauren. I'll talk you through it, but basically, she admitted that crimes have been committed – didn't name any – and apparently Meier's told her he wants to speak to us himself. If he hasn't by the end of the week, she says we can call her back. No idea if that means she'll give us frank answers then, but we got the impression she's being advised by a lawyer, so I'm guessing she'll eventually end up pleading the Fifth.'

'That doesn't exist in UK law,' Honey told her, 'but I get your meaning. She'll retain her right to silence.'

'Here's what I think,' Connor said, 'if we haven't heard from Meier by the time we upload on Tuesday, we jump in the car and take a drive over to Wales.'

CHAPTER FORTY-ONE

CRISTY: 'It's Tuesday morning, and Connor and I are in the car on our way to talk to Jean-Claude Meier.'

CONNOR: 'We received a call from him about an hour ago, asking us to come, and apparently he's OK with us recording whatever he's planning to tell us.'

Hitting pause, Cristy said, 'By the time this goes out, they'll already have heard the interviews with him and Nicole, so we don't need to explain any more about who he is. I'm just wondering whether we say *where* we're going to meet him. He didn't ask us not to, but maybe we should hold back for the moment?'

'Or we can edit it in later.'

Of course. Where was her head? She didn't seem to be thinking very clearly this morning, although, distractingly, she was having no problem with feeling anxious about what might lie ahead – or with feeling bad about leaving Clove and Jacks to complete today's episode, especially when it was so nuanced in tone as well as content. However, it couldn't be helped; she and Connor had had to respond to Meier's call when it came, and it wasn't as if Clove and Jacks were incapable of fine-tuning what was mostly already there.

Apparently sharing at least some of her concerns, Connor said, 'If the guys need us, they'll be in touch, and if necessary, we can record any links they might be short of and whizz them over.'

He was right, of course, and wishing tonight's upload was the only reason she felt so on edge, she turned to stare out at the passing countryside, trying to gather her thoughts. It was hard to imagine what Meier might have in store for when they arrived at Bryn Helyg, but whatever it was, she couldn't shake the sense that it wasn't going to be good.

Unless he was planning to tell them where to find the twins.

That would be beyond good, sensational in fact.

Provided they were alive and had, all this time, been living perfectly normal lives – if anything could be described as normal in these circumstances.

Could it be possible they were already at the farm? Maybe he'd had to fly them in from somewhere or go to fetch them or send someone else . . .

'Do you have the children's age-progressed images on your phone?' she asked Connor, as they finally began the steep, meandering drive up to Bryn Helyg.

'We both have,' he reminded her. 'Although I'm not planning to whip them out if the twins are there to make sure they match,' he added dryly.

She turned to him sharply. 'Do you think they might be?' she asked, surprised that he was sharing her hopes and suspicions.

He shrugged. 'Let's just say something major must be afoot given what he said to you while you were in Vevey, and one way or another, it has to be about them, doesn't it?'

Agreeing, she opened up the app on her phone and sat staring at the movingly lifelike faces for a while, so tender and similar to each other that she wanted to imprint the lovely features on her mind so that if they were confronted by the real thing, it might not be such a shock.

Connor leaned over to switch the recorder back on.

CONNOR: 'We're just turning into the place now, going past the massive hay barn where Cristy and I thought we were about to be savaged by a cow...'

CRISTY: 'It wasn't even two weeks ago, but it feels like a lifetime, so much has happened in that time.'

She looked around, taking everything in: horses in the top field, a thin trail of smoke from one of the farmhouse chimneys, goats roaming freely...

CRISTY: 'Is it just me, or does the place feel different to you?'

CONNOR: 'I guess it seems pretty quiet for a working farm, kind of... abandoned? Do I mean that? The animals are here so...'

CRISTY: 'Look out – someone's backing out of the car park.'

Bringing his own car to a stop, Connor watched the vehicle in front, and as someone climbed down from the four-by-four, he said, 'It's Maggi, isn't it?'

Cristy watched the woman, dressed in her usual jodhpurs and boots, hair scrunched under a cap, as she came towards them.

Lowering the car window, Cristy said, 'Hi, is everything OK?'

Maggi looked pale and distracted. 'I should probably thank you for coming, but to be honest, I wish this wasn't happening. I thought you'd go away, if I told you she killed them...'

Unsure how to respond to that, apart from with the nerves that clenched her heart, Cristy said, 'Is he here?'

Maggi glanced down the lane that stretched out ahead of them. 'You need to follow me,' she replied. 'It isn't far.'

As she returned to her vehicle, Cristy said to Connor, 'Did we record that?'

'We did,' he confirmed. 'So where is she taking us?'

For the next few minutes, they kept a close tail on the Defender as Maggi led them along the narrow, winding road away from the farm, dipping through a fast-running ford at one point before rising steeply between tightly packed hedgerows. Eventually, she came to a stop in front of a large grassy bank that faced a row of old cottages. Remembering that more staff were housed in a nearby hamlet, Cristy presumed this was it and got out of the car.

It was a pretty remote spot, that was for sure: picture-book, surrounded by sky and empty fields and home to hundreds of budding daffodils. The church, at the heart of it all, was clearly ancient, and protected by a crumbling dry-stone wall.

'It looks medieval,' Cristy commented as Maggi joined her.

Glancing up at the tower, Maggi said, 'I'm told the last dragon in Wales was slain here, but they say that about a lot of churches in Wales.' She turned as Connor came up behind them, and said, 'We need to go over there.'

They followed her through a weathered stone gateway, its lintel crooked with age, into the churchyard filled with time-worn graves and centuries-old yew trees, classic symbols of immortality and eternity. The earthy scent of moss and stale water tanged the fresh, cold air, while the sound of birdsong livened the eerie stillness.

'He's over there, with his grandparents,' Maggi told them and gestured for them to go ahead.

Cristy finally spotted him, at the far side of the cemetery, squatting down in front of a grave, elbows resting on his knees. She glanced at Connor and started through the haphazardly placed obelisks, tombstones and Celtic crosses. She wondered about the ghosts they were passing, the people who'd come to lay their loved ones to rest, the passing of time and old stories long forgotten. The whole place was as emotive as it was still, as alive with the past as it was filled with the dead.

By the time they reached Meier, he was standing, turned towards them, and though no more than four days had passed since Cristy had last seen him in Vevey, she was shocked by the change in him. The light had faded from his eyes, leaving only soreness and sorrow; the colour had drained from his face.

He offered no greeting, simply looked down at the grave beside him, as if inviting them to do the same.

Cristy's heart was pounding as she read the inscription: *In loving memory of Gwyn Edward Jones 1936–2005 and his beloved wife; Marie Jones 1938–2012.*

Then she saw it: the tiny ceramic plaque beneath the engraver's simply hewn words, and her heart turned over so hard it hurt.

Marie's two great-grandchildren 2004–2005.

Tears sprang to her eyes as a flood of despair engulfed her. Their precious lives really had ended back in 2005.

She turned to Meier and found him watching her, his face deathly pale, his expression drawn with grief.

'Are they really in there?' she made herself ask.

'They are,' he confirmed.

'And you – you're their father?'

He nodded, and as he looked down at the grave again, a sudden, blinding sunray broke free of a cloud, as though to single him out in some way. Or maybe it was offering a quiet surge of strength for what had to come next.

CHAPTER FORTY-TWO

Meier led the way to an old picnic bench just beyond the church wall, perched at the edge of a steep, grassy meadow with spectacular views of the valley below. Cristy's mind was racing, still trying to get past the shock, to overcome the torrent of conflicting emotions, while feeling profoundly thankful that she and Connor had never shared the twins' age-enhanced images. They never would now, of course, and certainly not with their father, for whatever Meier had done, however his children had ended up in a hidden grave on a remote Welsh hillside, she felt certain – at least for the moment – that he didn't deserve that particular extra torment.

By the time they were seated, Meier with his back to the view, Cristy and Connor facing him with the recorder between them, she was more or less ready to begin leading them to the answers they needed.

Meier spoke first.

MEIER: 'There might be legal ramifications to consider later, about how you can or cannot use this recording, but I'm sure you're already aware of that.'

CONNOR: 'We are, although without knowing what you're going to say...'

MEIER: 'All of it will be the truth, and that's all that needs to concern us here, today.'

His eyes came to Cristy's, and as she met them, she thought she now had a better understanding of why he'd invited her to Vevey. For whatever reason, he'd decided to unburden what he'd been carrying for years, but before completely opening up, he'd wanted to be sure he was putting his trust in the hands of someone he could trust in return.

Apparently, she had passed the test.

Once again, he spoke without being prompted, this time going straight to the heart of why they were there.

> MEIER: 'Nicole has always found it hard to accept what happened... It has affected her profoundly and in ways that...'

He took a breath, seeming to fail at the first hurdle. He swallowed hard, and his unfocused gaze drifted to the churchyard, as though a part of him was still there, beside the grave.

> MEIER: 'When the twins were alive, she was a wild and beautiful spirit with no reason to hate herself or to doubt her love as a mother... It's true, she felt frustrated at times, impatient, confused – she was still young, and having two babies was... not always easy, but that doesn't mean she wished them harm...'

He wiped a hand over his mouth, almost as if he was trying to stop it from trembling.

> MEIER: 'She will tell you herself, maybe...'

He gave a dry, sad sort of laugh.

> MEIER: 'I'm afraid it is never certain what Nicole will say... She has lost a normal sense of reasoning... Not

completely, but occasionally, she will admit to things that have not happened, or she will tell you a lie that she believes in her heart to be true.

'For example, she might tell you one day that she always regretted going through with her pregnancy, but the next, she is likely to say something entirely different. She has always been . . . erratic, unpredictable; it was a part of what made me fall in love with her, but since we lost the twins, and over time, things have become much worse.'

He stopped, clearly needing another moment to collect himself, and Cristy allowed the silence to run. She didn't doubt he was going to tell them everything; he simply had to do it in his own way, his own time.

In the end, he looked at her and nodded, as if to encourage a question.

CRISTY: 'Did you always know the twins were yours?'

MEIER: 'No, not always. I didn't find out until much later, but I will come to that, if you don't mind. During their very short lives, she was afraid to do a test. She thought if I knew for certain that I was not the father, I would no longer care about them or her. I believe she understands now how wrong she was to think that.

'Perhaps you will not see my actions as proof of my love – in fact, I am sure you will not – but whatever your judgement, it will not change the fact that I did what I did to protect her.'

Cristy could sense the emotions building inside him and as he looked away, across the meadow towards a distant wood, probably back to the past, she wondered what he was seeing? Thinking? Feeling? He started to speak, but nothing came. He swallowed and forced himself on.

MEIER: 'I will tell you what happened on the morning of 4th July 2005. You understand I was in Switzerland at the time, so the first I knew of anything being wrong was when Nicole called me. It was hard to make out what she was saying. She was panicking, hardly able to get the words out, but eventually the horror of what she was saying got through to me. She had killed them, she kept telling me, and she didn't know what to do. She repeated it over and over . . . "I've killed them! Make them come back, Claude. Tell me what to do . . ."

'Eventually, I got her to explain why she was saying this . . . I didn't believe it – of course I didn't. She had made a mistake, misunderstood something . . . She told me she had put them into the bath, and because she'd had a lot to drink the night before, was hungover and sleep-deprived, she felt exhausted . . . She sat down on the floor next to the bath and played with them, splashing and making bubbles . . . She didn't remember falling asleep, only waking up and finding they . . .'

He turned away sharply, as if escaping the words, and Cristy found herself wanting to escape them too. The images, the horror of those two dear souls floating amongst toys, no longer breathing . . .

MEIER: 'She told me she had tried to revive them . . . She slapped and shook them, but she hardly knew what she was doing, so she ran downstairs for her mobile phone and called me. She needed me to tell her what to do. I said she must check again, that she had to be wrong, but she tried everything I guided her through . . .

'I was terrified for her. She kept shouting that they were going to say she'd done it on purpose . . . It was hard to make her stop so that I could think straight, but I confess I was panicking too. I could see how she would end up being accused of something she hadn't intended to do. So I took a decision that was crazy then and remains so now, but my only thought at the time was to protect her . . . I told her she needed to stay on the line with me while I used another phone to make a call.

'She was still very agitated. I could hear her wailing and sobbing . . . She begged me to come, and I would have if I had not been so far away. I kept assuring her someone was on the way . . . I thought, hoped that the friends I had called would find she was mistaken . . .

'Before they arrived, I told her she must go out of the house for a while . . . She refused to leave without them, but in the end, I made her understand what she had to do – and why.

'I had told the friends to take the twins away, if there was no mistake, so that it might look as though someone had stolen them while Nicole was not at home. Leaving them unattended would be terrible – she would receive much condemnation for that – but to us then, the fear of the authorities believing she had deliberately drowned them was so much worse.

'I didn't know about the cat until she started sobbing that everything around her was dying. She told me it had choked to death in the night and was still in the kitchen, wrapped in a towel. The idea of going down to the woods to bury it was hers. It would give her an excuse, she said, to be out of the house when the friends came. I told her to do that, and I would let her know when she could return – and then, if the babies had gone, she would need to raise the alarm.

'I know you will be asking yourselves: why didn't we call an ambulance, why were we behaving as if she was guilty when we didn't believe that she was? There are many things that can be said or doubted or condemned in hindsight, I am only able to tell you what happened. I wish it was different – of course I do; everyone does – but it is not possible to change the past or the terrible mistakes I made that day.

'Naturally, as I was not there when my friends went into the house, I can only repeat what they told me later. As soon as they realized it was too late to save the twins, they wrapped them up and carried them out to the car. One of them called me, and I gave instructions of where they must go from there. Then I rang Nicole to tell her to return to the house.

'The shock of finding them gone, even though she'd known they would be, sent her over the edge again. I insisted she must ring her mother, using the landline, then she must somehow get rid of her mobile phone before anyone else came into the house – and that if the police ever asked about it, she should say she didn't have one. I had to ring off then to make more calls. I told her I loved her, that everything would be all right and that I would be there very soon.'

CRISTY: 'Did she know the friends you sent?'

MEIER: 'Yes, but she didn't see them, and I've never told her who came, only that she can be sure the twins were treated well at the end.'

He pressed his fingers to his eyes, and it was plain to see that exhaustion and shame were coming over him in waves. Perhaps a certain amount of disbelief too, that this nightmare really had happened and that he was still living it all these years later on a remote Welsh hillside.

MEIER: 'I called my grandmother, here at the farm, hoping she would help. If you'd known her, you'd understand why I turned to her, but her character, the way she saw the world, is for another time. She told me that if I could be certain the twins were mine, she would see to things. If not, then they must be taken care of by their father. So I ordered a paternity test to be delivered to the farm and booked myself on a flight.

'The test arrived, I provided samples, and then I drove over to the house, hoping to see Nicole. The place was surrounded by press and police . . . I found Lauren in the crowd, but we had no time to talk before a detective called her over. I realized that by being there, I could end up making things worse for Nicole and for myself, so I returned to the airport and flew back to Switzerland. I'd been gone for less than twenty-four hours.

'A week later, my grandmother received confirmation that I was – I am – the twin's father. It was she who decided that we should bury them with her husband, my step-grandfather. He had passed not so long before that, so she thought it shouldn't be difficult to dig a little way into his grave. She waited for me to return to Wales, and between us we created a small casket for the bodies, then we brought them here to the church late one night to lay them to rest.'

His eyes were swimming in tears, and grief was tearing at his voice, stealing it into bouts of silence. The guilt, the shame he felt for his actions was almost palpable, and Cristy was so appalled by the scenes he was conjuring that she herself was beyond words.

A long time passed with only the chirping of birds puncturing the awful quiet, along with the distant bleating of sheep.

MEIER: 'To be sure they weren't disturbed when my grandmother's time came, her body was cremated so that only her ashes were put into the grave. And the small plaque that is there now, attached to the foot of the headstone . . . I added it after I took the farm over. As far as I know, no one has ever noticed it. Certainly no one has ever asked.'

The grave would have to be opened up quite soon, and Cristy wondered if he'd already prepared himself for it, if anyone could ever prepare for something like that. She strongly doubted it.

When it was clear he wasn't going to speak again, she said:

CRISTY: 'Did you have any contact with Nicole at all after her arrest?'

He didn't answer right away, simply shook his head, seeming to fail to take a breath when he tried.

MEIER: 'I fully expected her to tell them what had really happened. I was bracing myself for it the whole time, almost wishing it would happen, but it didn't. I found out later that she had got it stuck in her head that the twins really had been taken. It's a dissociative disorder, often brought on by PTSD, where a person cannot let go of a belief that protects them from a devastating truth. Of course they *had* been taken, if you want to look at it that way, but it was not an abduction.

'So when she was charged with their murder, she just kept saying that someone had come into the house and taken them away.

'We – I – had created an impossible situation that I couldn't see a way out of, but I was certain, if it came to it, that a jury wouldn't – couldn't – find her guilty when there was no evidence to prove she'd harmed the twins.

I was wrong, of course, because they did. That was the worst day of both our lives – apart from losing the twins, obviously.'

CRISTY: 'So why didn't you admit it then? Surely whatever came next would have been better than her being sent to prison for a crime she hadn't committed?'

MEIER: 'You are right, but although I might have been believed about the cover up, I had not been there when they died, so how could I be certain she hadn't done it on purpose? I'm sure it's what Maggi believes, but I know differently, because I know Nicole. The lies, the concealment, the use of others to carry out the most terrible crime of taking the twins away . . . The case against her would become more damning than ever, and with no way of proving the truth of what had really happened, combined with the fact that I'd made everything so much worse for her . . .

'I should have spoken up anyway, and to hell with what they did to me, but then I would have been in one prison, she in another, and she needed me. Perhaps that doesn't sound important to you, but it was to her, and to me. There was nothing we could do to bring our children back, and nor could we – or I – see a way to get her released. So all I could do was try to be there for her in every way I could.'

CRISTY: 'You mean by visiting her regularly?'

MEIER: 'It wouldn't have been possible if I'd been locked away too.'

CRISTY: 'Does she know now that you're the twins' father?'

MEIER: 'Yes, she does.'

CRISTY: 'And does she still, after all this time, believe they were stolen that day?'

MEIER: 'Occasionally. Other times, she'll tell you she killed them, so she deserves her sentence. She has said this many times over the years, but no one in authority has taken the time to believe or even to listen to her. They think she is guilty anyway, so they simply ignore her changing stories, putting them down to an unbalanced mind.'

CRISTY: 'Has she had mental health assessments during her time in prison?'

MEIER: 'I believe so, but I have no access to them. What I can tell you is that she spoke about herself so viciously at times that it has made me afraid for what she might do to herself. I've talked to her mother about it, and Maeve voiced her concerns to the prison authorities, so there were times when Nicole was on suicide watch.'

CRISTY: 'Does Maeve know what really happened to the twins?'

MEIER: 'If she does, she has never spoken about it to me.'

Mindful of how reticent Maeve had been all along, Cristy wondered if she might actually believe in her daughter's guilt, but never wanted to admit it, even to herself. There was so much to delve into here, so many emotions to explore, not least of all her own as her heart ached for all concerned.

CRISTY: 'You told us before that you didn't know Nicole was going to confess at her most recent parole hearing.'

MEIER: 'I didn't. In fact, when I saw her, a week or so before, she told me she never wanted to be free, that she had to stay locked away so she'd never have to face a world with so much shame and darkness in her heart. Apparently, she changed her mind after I left, but as I told you just now, it's not unusual for her to do so. We – she and I – have had many discussions over the years about what she does and doesn't believe. The only constant, if you can call it that, is her fear of what it would mean for me if people started to believe that it really had been an accident. If anyone knew that I had helped cover it up.

'I have told her that I am prepared to accept the consequences. In fact, I have offered many times to go to the police, but she wants us to be together again, and now, after all this time, she believes it is possible – or she did until she was recently returned to prison.

'When I saw her on Saturday, I told her I would be talking to you and so she must prepare herself for what will come next. My hope is that she will not have to serve very much longer if I, perhaps with your help, can convince the authorities that the twins' death was not murder. She has suffered too much already for a crime she didn't commit.'

Instead of asking what he expected to happen to Nicole if she was released and he was imprisoned – she'd come back to it – Cristy pushed on to the next outstanding issue.

CRISTY: 'Where does Lauren fit in to everything?'

At that he exhaled loudly, as if releasing some of the tension that had built over the last few minutes.

MEIER: 'Lauren struggled terribly after the loss of the twins and by the time Nicole's trial began she was in a very bad place, mentally. It was a lot for her to cope with. She didn't know what had really happened. Even after Nicole's conviction she continued to believe that someone had abducted them, so she was certain they must be out there somewhere... She kept begging me to help her to find them, so I did, on occasions, which was cruel – I accept that – but I didn't know what else to do.

'In the end, she began coming to Lausanne and waiting for me outside the university. I always tried to be kind to her, but she would occasionally cause scenes, accusing me of hiding the twins, of deceiving everyone. I could see how lonely and confused she was, how lost she felt without Nicole, and how much she needed me to care. So, because I couldn't think what else to do, I brought her here, to my grandmother.

'I couldn't have known then, but it turned out that working on the farm, being a part of a life that felt like a whole world away from the one she'd left, was good for her. She stayed, right up until my grandmother's death, and after, when I came to take the place over, she continued to make it her home.

'I didn't realize until recently that she'd more or less stopped contacting her family... I wasn't at the farm for long spells during her early years here, so I didn't have a clear idea of what she was doing. I wasn't even aware that my grandmother had told her about the twins, had even brought her to the grave, until long after my grandmother had gone and Bryn Helyg was up and running in the way it is now.

'To make a very long story, very short, when Ben arrived from the US, he and Lauren fell for one another, and after Lauren realized she was pregnant a decision was taken quite quickly for her to go with him when he left.

'I think, as the years have gone on, she's found it

increasingly difficult to keep things to herself, and that's why she still doesn't see her family. She doesn't want to lie to them by pretending the twins might still be alive when she knows they aren't. She will be able to see her mother after this, so to quote Nicole, there is "one good outcome".'

CRISTY: 'When did Nicole say that?'

MEIER: 'Last weekend, when I told her that I was going to meet with you in the hope that you would tell our story with more . . . compassion than judgement. I understand that I deserve to be judged harshly, but I hope you will agree that she does not. It wouldn't be right for her to serve any more of her sentence when she has already confessed. We have let it go on for too long. It is time now for her to regain her freedom and for me to pay for my part in what we did to our children.'

As he stopped speaking, he was looking past them in a way that made Cristy turn to see what had caught his attention. Maggi and a man Cristy didn't recognize were standing at the church gate.

MEIER: 'Jonathan Grant is the lawyer I have asked to come with me to the police. He will represent me going forward, but obviously I will be pleading guilty to whatever crimes I am charged with, so there won't be a lengthy trial, and hopefully all the public condemnation will be reserved for me. No more thrown at Nicole.'

He rose to his feet and held out a hand to shake.

MEIER: 'Thank you for coming here today, and for listening.'

As he walked away, clearly shattered inside, Cristy was aware of such a wrenching sadness and confusion in her heart that she simply couldn't speak.

'Are you OK?' Connor asked quietly, putting a comforting hand on her shoulder.

She turned to him and saw from his anguished eyes how deeply this confession had affected him too.

CHAPTER FORTY-THREE

'Wow,' Connor murmured quietly as they began driving in convoy along the winding lane, the Defender in front, the BMW that had come to collect Meier next, and them bringing up the rear. 'That's some exclusive we have on our hands. So why aren't I feeling good about it?'

Cristy was equally sobered by the past hour, especially the last few minutes before Meier joined his lawyer in the car. She said, 'I guess nothing good was ever going to come out of two children disappearing the way they did. Much as I wanted to believe it would,' she added, wondering how Meier was feeling now, leaving behind his children's and grandparents' grave and knowing it would soon be dug up by strangers to verify that the twins were actually there.

After a while, asserting her inner journalist – the practical, conscientious woman who needed to act on all they'd just learned – Cristy checked the time and said, 'There are still a couple of hours to go before tonight's upload, so we should send something over now. Not the interview, obviously, but the fact that we know the twins are dead.'

By the time she was ready to record, they were passing the farmhouse. The Defender turned in, the BMW kept going, and she realized they'd probably be following it most of the way to Bristol.

'I wonder who's going to run Bryn Helyg now?' she mused as they left the place behind.

'My guess is the trusty Maggi and Johan will keep things going,' Connor replied, 'until the lord and master returns. Whenever that might be.'

Deciding to leave that for another time, she pressed to record.

CRISTY: 'Hi, it's Cristy.'

CONNOR: 'And it's Connor.'

CRISTY: 'It's not often we bring you breaking news on this podcast, but that's what we're doing in this episode. By the time it reaches you, an arrest will almost certainly have been made in the case of the missing Ivorson twins. I really hate having to say this, but we can confirm that they are no longer alive, and the man who is about to hand himself in to the police in connection with their deaths is their biological father, Swiss national Jean-Claude Meier.'

CONNOR: 'We'll be telling you more about how and exactly when they died later in the episode, and you can also listen to the interviews we did with both Nicole Ivorson and Jean-Claude Meier, prior to these new developments. It's probably going to be quite different to what you're expecting, but who knows? Have a listen and let us know what you think.'

After checking it had recorded, Cristy sent the file to Clove and Jacks, and no more than five minutes later, both researchers were on the car speakerphone.

'I'll spare you our shock and how sick we feel about those poor kids,' Clove said, 'or maybe I won't. I actually feel devastated.'

'Don't we all,' Cristy responded quietly.

'So how did they die?'

'We'll play everything for you when we get back,' Connor told her, 'but today's interview isn't for public consumption until it's been vetted by lawyers. Jacks, first thing you need to do is take the age-enhanced images of the twins off the whiteboard and make sure they're erased on all devices. Cristy and I have already done it on our phones. No one needs to see them now – absolutely no one. Then can you deal with the link we just sent? Obviously it's tonight's episode opener, so over to you to get the edit sorted.'

'Clove,' Cristy said, 'we need you to go over to Patchway – Meier's being taken there now – to get a recording of the press descending when news of his arrest breaks on mainstream.'

'Does anyone else have the story yet?' Clove asked.

'No,' Cristy assured her, thinking of Molly Terrance and how she was going to respond to this exclusive. They could offer it to her, of course, but they wouldn't.

'Why don't we give it to Matthew?' Connor suggested. 'He'll put one of his top reporters on it, I'm sure, and in exchange, we'll have access to all the *News Agenda* reports going forward.'

Deciding this was a good idea, Cristy said to Clove, 'Can you make the call? Tell Matthew we're on our way back from Wales and I'll speak to him later if he wants to discuss, but for now, he needs to put Judith Evans on the story. With any luck, she'll turn up at Patchway around the same time as you, so you can record her breaking it on live TV.'

'Jacks,' Connor said, 'try to time the upload to hit all platforms ten minutes before the scheduled broadcast. I get we're not a news outfit, but no harm making out like we are when we have something like this.'

'Call us if you need to,' Cristy said. 'We should be back in a couple of hours. I'm going to try and contact Honey now to give her a heads up.'

After leaving Honey a message asking her to get in touch asap, Cristy checked the recorder and was pleased, although surprised, to see it was still running. The last few minutes would provide some great input for a future episode.

Connor said, 'There's a good chance Honey already knows Meier was going to reveal everything today. I mean, if she's spoken to Nicole since the weekend.'

Cristy nodded and let her head fall back against the seat, trying to assimilate all that had happened and was about to unfold. Meier would be arrested, questioned, probably remanded . . .

Connor said, 'There are still a lot of unanswered questions, but I guess you know that.'

'Talk me through your thinking,' she said.

'OK, Nicole's phone records for a start. We need to check with Honey, but I don't recall any mention of them, do you?'

Cristy shook her head. 'She obviously told the police she didn't have a mobile, not unusual for the time, but the fact that she did means she must have hidden it quite well, given it was never found.'

'We can ask her where she put it, if she grants our request for a visit.' After a beat he added, 'I wonder what's going to happen to her now?'

Sighing, Cristy said, 'My guess is that she'll have to serve at least the rest of her sentence, and maybe more will be added for having conspired to cover up the crime for so long.' Her eyes were once again fixed on the car ahead as she wondered what Meier might be discussing with his lawyer, what charges they were expecting to face, how much Meier was actually prepared for. He must have thought it through – obviously, he had – and she could only begin to imagine how sick and fearful he was feeling inside. He probably wouldn't show it – in fact, there was no doubt he was a master at disguising his feelings – but did that mean he was equally good at ignoring them?

'You think you read people so well, don't you?' she said, almost to herself. 'You tell yourself you have them all figured out because you have this great insight and belief in your instincts . . . Then you find out you've read them all wrong, and you realize you don't know them at all.'

Glancing at her, Connor said, 'Are we still talking about Meier?'

She nodded. 'But I guess it stands for most people.' She was thinking of David now and how different he was seeming to her after these two weeks apart. She still loved him, there was no doubt in her mind about that, but how he felt about her, how he saw their future now . . . Whatever, she couldn't let things run on the way they were. If his feelings for her had changed she needed to deal with it. For God's sake, if Meier could find the courage to face what was ahead of him, she could find it to make a call to David.

'For what it's worth,' Connor said, 'I reckon Meier's a decent guy who panicked and made a seriously bad decision. It's even possible he was still traumatized by his parents' death. No doubt, he'll be called all sorts of things when this comes out, but the truth is that none of us ever knows for certain how we'd react in a situation until we're actually in it. And boy can we get it wrong.'

'Isn't that the truth?'

'Plus, in his own way, he's been paying for it ever since – not the way Nicole has, obviously, but you can't tell me that he hasn't suffered too.'

'And now he'll suffer even more.' Cristy sighed. 'Not that he doesn't deserve it – he should have got her out of that sentence a long time ago. I just wish I could believe that locking him up would do some good, but it's hard to see how it will. Unless you call satisfying the law a good thing, and I suppose we do.'

CHAPTER FORTY-FOUR

Over the next seven days, with the main news constantly hijacked by high drama in the US, Cristy found herself torn between sadness for the twins that they were once again much lower on a scale of importance than they deserved, and relief for Meier that he wasn't, yet, as big a hate figure as he might have been if the full focus of attention were on him.

This wasn't to say the case was gaining no interest. Since last week's drop, they'd had a small avalanche of feedback, and thanks to Matthew and his star reporter, Judith Evans, *The News Agenda* was delivering regular updates on all its bulletins – all available to *Hindsight* for future use. Unsurprisingly, the Terrier was bombarding Cristy with demands for her exclusive of the investigation; however, Cristy had little trouble batting her off with the reminder that the series wasn't yet over.

It was on Tuesday morning, a whole week after Meier's self-surrender, when they were told Nicole had refused their visitor request.

'I'm sorry,' Honey said, when Cristy called her. 'We had to advise her to turn you down. She's already paying the price of talking to you – I blame myself, of course; I shouldn't have let it happen, and it's small comfort that we all went into it with the best intentions. Anyway, we can't allow her any more involvement with the press at this stage. In fact, until we know what decisions have been made about her conviction and her future custody, we'd be grateful if you didn't even try to contact her. We're pushing for her initial conviction to be deemed unsafe.'

Understanding, although undeniably frustrated, Cristy said, 'How is she?'

'I haven't seen her in person, but speaking to her on the phone . . . she sounds . . . not always as if she's listening . . . Her mother says she's not speaking to her much either.'

'So Maeve's in touch with her?'

'Regularly, but if you're about to ask if Maeve will talk to you, I'm afraid we've advised her against it too. Everything's just too delicate at the moment. However, I will tell you this: I believe Maeve when she says she didn't know what had happened to the twins until you yourselves revealed it last week.'

Cristy knew that, as Maeve's lawyer, Honey had to say that, as did Maeve in order to avoid prosecution herself. 'And Nicole's phone? Did you ask her about it?'

'She found it where Nicole told her to look – under a floorboard in the basement of the house. It was, as you suspected, a pay-as-you-go.'

'So the place clearly didn't undergo much of search?'

'Apparently not, but remember they weren't looking for a phone because she'd told the police she didn't have one. They have it now, although whether anything is still stored on it after so long, we've yet to find out. As for the service provider . . . Nicole can't remember who it was; she chopped and changed quite a lot apparently, and I don't think you can get that kind of detail from the phone itself, at least not one from that era.'

'And even if you could,' Cristy added, 'the chances of any records still existing have to be close to zero.'

'I think the point is,' Honey responded, 'that she's confirmed Meier's account of the calls that morning, and as neither of them are trying to hide anything any more, the phone and its activity isn't rating very highly on a list of priorities.'

'No, of course not. Do you know if Nicole and Meier are in touch with one another?'

'I don't, but I doubt it. There aren't really any avenues open to them for contact with the way things stand.'

Wondering how they both felt about that, Cristy thanked Honey and rang off.

She was keen to get on with the finishing touches to tonight's episode now; however, she made the grand mistake of quickly checking her messages and immediately wished she hadn't. Why had she agreed to see David at the weekend when she needed to stay focused on what was happening here?

His message said:

I'll fly over on Saturday. Shall I come straight to your place?

Since the only sensible answer to that was yes, she tapped it in and told herself she'd be ready to see him by then and hopefully in the right frame of mind to deal with whatever he had to tell her. As if she was ever going to be ready for him to finish it between them once and for all.

Connor said, 'OK, shall we record this next piece about Meier?'

Calling up the email they'd received from Meier's lawyer the day before, Cristy nodded and waited for the thumbs up to begin.

CRISTY: 'So we now know what offences Jean-Claude Meier has been charged with, and I guess you could say they've thrown the book at him. Did he deserve it? Yeah, I guess so, but, as we know, nothing's ever as straightforward as we'd like it to be – or entirely rational when it comes to decisions made under duress.'

CONNOR: 'Are we talking about you now or Claude Meier?'

CRISTY: 'You're funny. So, here goes: Two counts of Assisting an Offender, which apparently includes helping Nicole to cover up the twins' deaths, and their removal from 42 Randall Lane, which carries a maximum sentence of up to ten years.'

CONNOR: 'Next: Perverting the Course of Justice, which can result in a life sentence all on its own.'

CRISTY: 'Failure to Disclose Information – this covers his refusal to name those who helped him. For that, he could face up to five years.'

CONNOR: 'There's also Preventing the Lawful Burial of a Body – not codified in legislation, but could carry a custodial sentence of up to five years '

CRISTY: 'His lawyer was at pains to stress that, for the moment, everything is based on Nicole's murder conviction; if that ends up being overturned or downgraded to involuntary manslaughter, a lot could change. Her legal team is currently trying to establish a case for the latter, and considering how little evidence was presented at the original trial to secure a guilty verdict, they are quietly confident of achieving a better result this time.'

CONNOR: 'If they can, it's possible Nicole will be released straightaway, considering how long she's already served, but as we know, the wheels of justice turn slowly, so we'll just have to wait to see what happens there.'

CRISTY: 'Meanwhile, in spite of all the charges he's facing, Jean-Claude Meier has been released on police bail. Apparently, he's had to surrender his passport, and he's due to be fitted with a security tag sometime in the next few weeks. We can confirm that he's returned to his home in the Welsh mountains, where he'll be staying until he's summoned to court.'

CONNOR: 'Or until the press who've found him have managed to drive him out.'

Cristy said, 'Is this a good place to play in some further description of Bryn Helyg and what it's all about?'

'Possibly.' Connor made a note. 'Let's take a decision when we're done with this.'

CRISTY: 'You'll have seen news coverage of Noah and Abigail's bodies being exhumed from a grave near Meier's home. All we can add to that, at this time, is that forensic tests are still underway to establish that it really is them.'

CONNOR: 'Unfortunately for us, both Meier and Nicole have been advised against engaging any further with the podcast. However, this is not an end to the series. We'll continue monitoring the case and will bring you updates as and when we receive them, along with any interviews we are given permission to use.'

CRISTY: 'Just a quick response to the rumours that have been flying: yes, we do have a recording of Meier's full confession, but for obvious reasons, it's in the hands of the lawyers. So, we're sorry, it's not likely we'll be able to share it with you any time soon. In fact, with everything likely to be in a state of flux for at least the next couple of months, we're going to take a pause after this episode and come back to you – as Connor said – with occasional updates when they happen, until such time as we can bring the series to an end.'

Stopping the recording, Connor sat back in his chair with a groan of frustration. 'They'll be getting everything from the news long before we receive the go-ahead to use Meier's confession,' he pointed out.

'But ours will be the in-depth story,' Jacks reminded him, 'and something like this never passes its sell-by.'

'Let's be thankful for that,' Clove said wryly, 'or all of us sitting here would be out of a job.'

Cristy smiled at the truth of that, and since it reminded her of Kinsley's offer, she thought fleetingly of the counteroffer she was considering putting his way. It could wait until it was fully formulated in her mind, and that wouldn't happen until she'd had a few key conversations with the people who mattered.

Connor was saying, '. . . so it's not likely we'll ever be able to use her voice note.'

'Who are we talking about?' Cristy asked.

'Lauren,' Clove told her, 'and the message she left at the weekend.'

'I'll lay money her lawyer knows nothing about it,' Connor put in. 'He'd never have sanctioned it if he did.'

'Play it again,' Cristy said. 'Not that I think it's usable, unless we want to turn the police on her, and what would be the point of that? I'd just like to hear it one more time before we erase it.'

Calling it up, Clove hit play, and Cristy closed her eyes to listen.

LAUREN: 'Hi, it's Lauren Beagle here. I just wanted to say that I'm glad he kept his word and is now finally doing this for Nicole. He should have done it a long time ago, of course, but I'm as much to blame for not speaking out myself, so it's hardly my place to find fault with him. All I'll say in my defence is that by the time I knew what had happened to the twins, I was greatly attached to his grandmother, Marie, and didn't want to do anything to hurt her. She was an old lady with not much longer left to live, and would revealing the truth actually have got Nicole out of prison? I guess we'll never know now.

'After Marie died was another time I could have – *should* have – acted, and believe me, I wanted to, but when Claude came to take over the farm... I just wanted to carry on being a part of that world, his world... He'd always made me feel safe, *seen*, if you like, as though I mattered... You've met him, so I'm sure you know how easy it is to fall under his spell. It happens all the time, to all sorts of people. I'm not sure he means to do it; it's just how he is, and once you know him, you never want to *unknow* him.

'Anyway, meeting Ben changed a lot for me. I was more confident by then, mostly thanks to Claude's therapy. I was ready to break free of my dependence on Claude and Bryn Helyg. So, Ben and I came here, to the States, where we set up home and started a family.

'I continued to visit Nicole whenever we returned to Wales for short stays at Bryn Helyg. Each time I saw her, I tried to persuade her to admit what had really happened, but I could never seem to get through to her. She just kept saying it didn't matter if it was an accident; no one was listening to her anyway, and besides, it was her fault they were dead, so she deserved to be where she was. I used to wonder if Claude was brainwashing her during his visits in order to keep himself out of prison, but I don't know if I'm right about that.

'One thing I am certain of is that he loves her, and maybe this confession of his finally proves how much. Do you see it that way? Does she? I'm not sure what I think any more, although I expect we can agree that all this has come very late in the day, especially for Nicole.

'It's going to be interesting to see how it plays out from here. My lawyer thinks the most likely scenario is that she'll eventually be released and he'll be sentenced to a minimum of ten years. If he's right, they still won't be together, but she'll visit him, just as he's visited her all this time. They're their own tragic tale of thwarted love.

'For my part, I've been in touch with my mother, and she's coming here next month to meet her grandchildren. I wonder how it'll go? She's no Maeve, with all that saintly patience and unswerving devotion, but she's got her good points, and I've definitely missed her.

'OK, I've rambled on long enough. I'm not sure why I wanted to be in touch; I guess I just needed to get everything off my chest – my own confession, if you like – but I'd be grateful if you'd erase this once you've listened to it. There's trust for you. Please don't make me live to regret it.'

As the recording stopped, Cristy sighed and opened her eyes. 'OK, Clove, you can hit delete,' she said. 'We're not in the business of taking mothers away from their children, and that's how it could end up if this should fall into the wrong hands.' She was watching Connor and how intently he was reading something on his phone. 'Anything we need to know about?' she asked.

Looking up, he quickly shook his head and put the phone down. 'Nothing to do with this,' he assured her. 'And yes, good idea – let's get rid of the voicemail now and start working out where we want to insert further description of Bryn Helyg.'

By six o'clock, the episode featuring more of Nicole's and Meier's first interviews, together with news coverage of his charges and bail, was ready for upload, and everyone was gathered, including Iz, who'd come down specially from London. Matthew had brought Judith Evans and her researcher, Yuri, who were following the case for *The News Agenda,* and Aiden, who'd brought himself. Harry and Meena were also there. The only regulars missing were Jodi and the baby. And of course, David, who often came for important podcasts, but Cristy wasn't going to dwell on that now, especially not when the mere thought of him sent her insides into freefall.

As always, everyone sipped their drinks while listening to the episode, treating it like a live transmission, as they usually did. For the next few weeks, maybe longer, they'd be dealing with feedback and media requests for interviews, with everyone keen to know if they had more insight to share on Nicole's appeal and Meier's plea hearing. It was possible they'd be able to provide some answers; much would depend on how forthcoming the lawyers – and the police – wanted to be over that time. Certainly, Cristy and Connor were going to try talking to someone from law enforcement about the failures of the first investigation. That alone should make interesting listening and give rise to plenty of public debate; however, they had yet to pin anyone down.

'Well,' Harry declared, as the playback ended, 'a pretty sobering but fascinating story.' He raised his glass. 'You did good, guys.'

Iz said excitedly, 'As soon as you're able to officially conclude the series, I'm going to submit it for an award.'

Cristy attempted a smile, uncomfortable with the idea of gaining accolades off the back of someone's misery. However she knew Iz meant well, so she said, 'Glad you think it's worthy.'

'My mother, head of the crack squad,' Aiden declared, raising his beer.

Refilling glasses, Meena said, 'I must confess I'm intrigued, fixated on the relationship between Meier and Nicole. I just keep thinking about it. They're on another level, don't you agree? All that commitment and love over so many years . . . It's beautiful and surreal and . . . I'm not sure Harry would be in my corner the same way if I accidentally drowned our kids.'

'Definitely not,' he assured her, making everyone laugh.

'The thing is,' Meena continued, 'I find myself really keen for them to end up together. Is that wrong? I guess so, but it's how I feel.'

'I expect we'll get a lot of people saying the same,' Cristy told her. 'The world loves a love story, if they see it that way, but there'll be a huge amount of condemnation too, all mixed up with death threats and outright lies. You know what social media's like.'

'Any idea what's going to happen to the twins' bodies now forensics have confirmed it's them?' Judith Evans asked. She was a stout, round-faced woman with stunning green eyes and short, wavy fair hair – an insightful, facts-based reporter with more integrity in her soul than the Terrier could ever muster.

'I've heard they'll be returned to the grave in Wales,' Cristy replied. 'I guess Meier will arrange for a different headstone, and he'll probably have to spend a lot on security to ward off the crime tourists. It'll be interesting to see if Bryn Helyg survives in its current form after all the publicity.'

'It'll be a shame if it doesn't,' Connor remarked, starting to pack up his things. 'It does a lot of good work.'

'Aren't you joining us for dinner?' Matthew asked. 'I've booked the upstairs room at Piccolino.'

'My choice,' Aiden told them.

'Sorry to miss the last supper.' Connor grimaced. 'Although it's not, actually, is it? We've still got the final episode to do, and something's come up last minute for Jodi and me.'

Watching him closely, Cristy said, 'Is everything OK with you guys?'

'All's good,' he assured her. 'But don't forget I'm off for the rest of the week, back Saturday.'

'Going somewhere nice?' Meena asked curiously.

'To Jodi's aunt in Devon. It's her birthday on Thursday, and Jodi promised to spend it with her. Seems no reason for me not to be there too, given where we are with the series. So, have a great dinner everyone. Maybe do another after the final episode?'

After he'd gone, Cristy and Matthew exchanged glances. Something was wrong; they could sense it. In fact, it seemed everyone could, given the silence Connor had left in his wake.

'Hope everything really is OK with him,' Iz remarked, 'because he has come over as a bit . . . off, lately.'

'Isn't he always like that with you?' Meena countered.

Iz shrugged. 'Yeah, I guess so, although I'm sure that deep down, he loves me really.'

As the others laughed, Cristy said quietly to Matthew, 'I think Jodi might be pregnant again and maybe things aren't going too well.'

Matthew's concern showed. 'She's only with us one day a week so I can't say I've noticed anything, but wouldn't they confide in you if there was a problem?'

'Normally, I'd have said yes, but I've had a few things to deal with myself lately, so maybe Connor hasn't felt comfortable talking to me about personal things.'

Matthew regarded her curiously. 'Anything I need to know about?' he probed.

She should have seen that coming! However, he was the last person she wanted to talk to about David – or her hormonal chaos, come to that – so she simply said, 'I'm working things out, thanks.' And turning to the rest of the team, she announced it was time to start heading over to Piccolino's.

CHAPTER FORTY-FIVE

Cristy was able to work mainly from home for the rest of the week, sorting through feedback and continuing to find a police spokesperson willing to talk them through the original investigation's 'anomalies' – a polite word Clove had come up with to sound less accusatory. It was a relief to have some time to catch up on things she'd neglected over the past weeks, although she kept an eye on the news throughout the day in case of any more developments regarding Nicole or Meier. She didn't feel the need to stay on it herself. If anything significant broke, she was sure Honey or Jonathan, Meier's lawyer, would be in touch, and Clove and Jacks were at the office to follow things up anyway.

It was time for her to take a step back from the hold Meier seemed to have woven over her, if hold was the right word. She had certainly fallen under his spell, as Lauren had mentioned, and felt empathetic in a way that wasn't easily explained considering his crimes. Or was it? It was hard to be clear about what she was thinking when he felt like a friend, someone she wanted to know better, whose advice she trusted and whose world she wanted to be in. Of course, none of it was true. He wasn't a friend; she didn't actually want to be a part of his life or spend time with him. It was simply a hazard of what she did; getting involved with someone whose story she was telling and ending up finding it hard to let go at the end wasn't unusual.

Or maybe it was simply easier to immerse herself in the distraction than it was to focus on the one person she really did want to be with, the man who actually mattered and who she'd probably already lost.

To get herself through the more tense moments of waiting for Saturday to come round, she worked on a proposal for Paul Kinsley. Later, she'd get Connor's input, but there was no rush; they could always discuss it over dinner on Saturday night, when he and Jodi were back from Devon. Unless there was another reason they'd invited her over, and if so, she wouldn't hesitate to put the proposal aside in order to be as supportive – or as celebratory – as they might need.

Finally, Saturday lunchtime was upon her, and in an effort to stop tormenting herself over David's imminent arrival, she began going over the proposal again, carrying out further internet searches, adding more data and ideas into the mix and trying not to wish she could discuss it with him. He'd be a great sounding board and would very probably bring some creative thinking to the project that could end up making it impossible to reject.

Aware that if she looked at the clock one more time, she'd end up losing her mind, she got up from the table, abandoning her laptop and notepads to go and pour herself a drink. Even before she'd taken a bottle from the fridge, she closed the door again. Keeping a clear head and maintaining her dignity was what really mattered now. Yes, it was going to hurt a lot when he ended things, and it would probably take her a good while to get over it, but if she could survive the break-up with Matthew, she could survive this too.

She wandered over to the French doors to stare out at the garden, where snowdrops and daffodils were sharing the beds with early shooting tulips and hyacinths. Her precious camelia was going to burst into huge crimson flowers any day now, as was the rhododendron climbing the fence. Spring was coming fast. She could imagine how much pleasure Cynthia, David's mother, was getting from her garden in Guernsey, and it made her long to be there – and fear that she might never see it again.

I'm sorry, Cristy, he was going to say. *I don't want to hurt you, but you know how it goes. When love dies, you just have to let go.*

It's OK. I understand, she'd tell him, dry-eyed and dying inside. *Thanks for coming all this way to break it to me. You needn't have; I'd have been fine with hearing it on the phone . . .*

Can we stay friends? You know how crazy my family are about you . . .

I'm crazy about them too, but I think a clean break is what's needed now. With you so far away, it's not as if we're going to run into one another . . . I guess that's a good thing. I hate that sort of awkwardness, don't you? I remember it with Matthew; it's why I left my job in TV and went to start Hindsight. Then Hindsight led to you, and you led me to where we are now, and I have to admit I really wish it wasn't happening . . .

As if she was going to say all that! She cringed even to think it, although it might come bursting out if everything started going horribly wrong. Maybe she'd have a lovely hot flush right in the middle of it and start pouring sweat, so he'd think she was crying out of every pore . . . How fantastic that would be. Such a great way for him to remember her.

She started as the buzzer sounded, and her heart leapt to her throat.

She could do this.

If Meier could find the courage to hand himself in for Nicole, she could face the rejection she dreaded. And why she was comparing her situation with Meier's right now, or even thinking about him at all, she had no idea – although it was true she'd almost called him earlier, really to find out how he was but also in the hope he might ask her the same. He was such a good listener . . . And maybe this proved she was still under his spell . . .

'Hi,' she said into the entryphone.

'It's me,' David told her.

Her heart flipped again, and after releasing the main door, she went to open her own.

The instant she saw him step into the hall, she felt all that was supposed to be holding her together falling apart. How could he possibly look even more attractive than he had the last time she'd seen him? How the hell was she going to get through this without making a fool of herself?

'Come in,' she said, standing back as he reached her. 'I guess the flight was on time.'

'I drove,' he replied, hanging his coat before going ahead of her into the sitting room. 'I came over yesterday . . . A few things to sort out. So, how have you been?'

He looked so grave, so on edge, that she realized this wasn't going to be easy for him either, and it made her feel even worse. But it was OK. She didn't want it to be plain sailing for him; at least it meant he wasn't entirely indifferent to her feelings, although it was likely to make things even more awkward than they already were.

'I'm fine,' she said, attempting a smile. 'Can I get you a drink of something?'

'Sure. Thanks. A glass of wine, maybe?'

Glad to be able to have one herself, she went to pour two glasses while he settled onto one of the sofas and let go a long, unsteady sigh. 'I'm afraid I haven't heard the latest pod,' he said, as she brought his drink. 'It's been a good series so far though.'

Sitting into the opposite sofa, she said, 'Thanks. We'll

be doing another episode when we know more, but the pressure's off for a while.'

He nodded and saluted her with his glass before taking a sip. 'Have you made a decision about Kinsley's offer yet?' he asked.

He was stalling, making idle chat.

'I turned it down,' she told him. 'He's still not quite taking no for an answer, but my mind's made up. I'm OK with staying here.' She wouldn't get into anything about her new idea; it wasn't what this was about, and really, she just wanted it over with now. 'So how have things been with you?' she asked, hedging again. 'Everyone OK at home?'

He sat forward to put his glass on the coffee table and took several moments before answering. 'I've handled everything really badly between us,' he told her. 'I know that. I mean, I like to think I'm pretty good in most situations, but it turns out . . . Well, I guess this proves I'm not.'

When he didn't elaborate, she said nothing. Why make it easier for him?

'I just . . . I didn't want to burden you with what was happening,' he said. 'It came right out of the blue, and when you called that night . . .'

'I still don't know what I said,' she reminded him. 'I know I should, but . . . Well, whatever it was, it was obviously bad, so once again, I'm sorry.'

He nodded briefly. 'I'm not sure what you said either,' he confessed. 'I had such a lot going round in my head. I knew it wasn't the right time to tell you; you were obviously stressed, busy with a new series, trying to work things through with Kinsley . . . I guess I ended up thinking we needed to have some space while I got things sorted my end, and now, I'm honestly not sure how it's managed to go on for so long, or if it was the right thing to do. No, I *know* it wasn't the right thing. I've missed you, and I probably would have handled everything better if I had talked to you, but like I said, it didn't feel like the right time for you, and I was so damned angry when it happened . . .'

Realizing at last that she might have read everything wrong, her heart began racing as she found herself daring to feel hopeful. 'When what happened?' she asked carefully.

He swallowed. 'Olivia's been causing some problems.'

Her shock could hardly have been greater. 'Your sister-in-law Olivia?' she asked, needing to be sure, because Olivia to her was the woman who'd hired someone to kill his wife and tried to lay the blame at his door. Two other women had lost their lives that day, almost eighteen years ago now, and two years ago, the murders had been the subject of *Hindsight*'s most successful series to date. It was how she and David had met, when she'd gone into the case believing he was a killer who'd escaped justice, only to end up clearing his name.

'Yes, that Olivia,' he said hoarsely. 'She's been trying to block Rosie and Anna receiving their share of the proceeds from the sale of Kellon Hall.'

Knowing this was his wife's ancestral home, she said, 'But how can Olivia block anything? I mean, apart from being in prison . . . Oh God, please don't say they've let her go already.'

'No, no, she's still there, but she's instructed lawyers to challenge the inheritance. I'm told they've advised her that she doesn't have a case, but instead of backing off as any normal person might, she threatened to tell Rosie things I'd rather Rosie never knew.'

Horribly aware of what those things were likely to be, Cristy said, 'I don't understand why she would do that. What on earth could she gain from it?'

'Nothing, apart from hurting me even more than she already has. I can live with that, but not with her writing direct to Rosie.'

'Oh God,' Cristy gasped. 'Please tell me she didn't . . .'

'Fortunately, Mum saw the letter first and gave it straight to me. The things Olivia said, to her own niece, for God's sake. Olivia knows she has Down's . . .' His voice faltered as emotion got the better of him. 'She told Rosie that I'm not her real father . . . I guess we know that's true, but I've *always* considered her mine.'

Cristy knew very well how much Rosie meant to him – it was perhaps one of the things she loved most about him, the way he'd accepted his eldest daughter as his in spite of, or maybe even because of, the way she'd been conceived. She said, 'Thank God your mother got to the letter in time.'

He nodded. 'Especially considering the graphic detail she went into about the gang rape Lexie suffered. She told Rosie it was time for her to go out there and find out who her real father is.'

'Jesus Christ,' Cristy murmured, hardly able to believe anyone could be so cruel – and to her own niece.

'She's written again since, asking Rosie to come and visit her so she can explain certain things about me and why she needs to get as far away from me as she can. We intercepted that letter too.'

'She's lost her mind,' Cristy stated, feeling no doubt of it.

Not disagreeing, he said, 'My lawyer's on it, obviously. He's managed to get a restraining order to protect Rosie, but then she wrote to Anna, and that one got through.'

'Oh God, no,' Cristy muttered.

'Thankfully, there's no doubt about Anna being mine, but I ended up having to tell her everything about the rape, and you can probably imagine how upset she was to think of what her mother had been through. And she was so angry over what her aunt had tried to do to Rosie that she got in touch with her cousin, Olivia's daughter, and told *her* everything. It's been a nightmare on so many levels, but I think – *hope* – it's over now. I've just come from seeing Sam, who I'm sure you remember is Olivia's husband, and he's going to try managing things from his end.'

'Oh God, David,' Cristy murmured, going to sit with him. 'I should have been there for you . . . I would have, if you'd told me; you have to know that.'

Taking her hands in his, he said, 'Yeah, I guess I do, and I'm sorry I didn't give you the chance. I called it all wrong, and now I'm afraid I've ruined things between us . . .'

'No. Of course you haven't. Nothing like. I admit I thought you had changed your mind about me, but I never, for a minute, changed mine about you. Oh God.' She laughed, as tears welled in her eyes. 'This is what comes of us living so far apart. If we were in each other's lives every day, we'd always turn to one another; we'd *know* when something was wrong.'

His eyes were gently teasing as he said, 'Is that you suggesting we live together?'

She pulled a face she knew he'd understand.

He did, because he laughed.

'I wish we could,' she said, meaning it, 'but we both know all the reasons why it can't work.'

'Your life is here in Bristol, mine is in Guernsey. So, we're going to have to do better about communicating in future, at least I am, because I know I'm the one who was really at fault this time, and I don't want this sort of thing happening again.'

Grimacing, she said, 'I don't suppose there are any guarantees it won't, but what matters right now is that we both make a commitment to do better.'

As he wrapped her in his arms, she held him tightly, loving the way he felt against her, the familiar and wonderful smell of him, the sensations as he kissed her, long and hard, tenderly and with growing passion. It reminded her of all the ways they were so perfect for one another, and pushed away all the reasons why their relationship really might not work in the end.

'There is a certain kind of communication,' she said, when he briefly let her go, 'that we've never really got wrong.'

Reading her perfectly, he said, 'It's true, and I don't know about you, but I'm kind of ready to put it into practice again.'

CHAPTER FORTY-SIX

Cristy had always loved Connor and Jodi's Victorian semi in Southville, one street back from the canal that connected the harbour to the river, and only a few stones' throw from the office. With its typical period layout of cosy front parlour with large bay window and ornate wooden fireplace, leading to cosy dining area and equally cosy kitchen, it exuded warmth and welcome like few other places she knew. They'd done so much to make it special and characterful – and like a second home for their friends, especially her. She truly couldn't love them more if she tried, and while she appreciated she was on an unstoppable high right now (thanks to the afternoon she'd spent with David), it didn't mean her feelings were any the less heartfelt and genuine. She simply had to rein them in a little or she'd end up embarrassing them all – or, just as likely, turn herself into the target of some merciless teasing.

Nevertheless, watching how thrilled they were to see David, understanding from his mere presence that the relationship was back on, made her want to throw her arms around them in gratitude. They always had her back, no matter what, and she'd always be there for them too in every way possible.

Picking up on how relaxed they seemed – their usual selves, in fact – she dared to hope that her suspicions of a problematic early pregnancy were unfounded, and she was glad to have a few minutes alone with Connor in the kitchen to fill him in on why David hadn't been in touch.

Clearly appalled, Connor paused in the opening of a bottle. 'I never thought any of us would hear from Olivia Caldwell again,' he declared in disgust. 'Thank God he seems to have it under control. Does he?'

Cristy nodded. 'I think so. You know how "together" he is, capable, even; he just went a bit off-course with me.'

Continuing with his task, he said dryly, 'So you get to keep the diamonds?'

Laughing, she said, 'I guess so, although they're still in Guernsey, so that probably means I'll have to go over there to get them.'

He laughed too and said, 'What was it you said a few days ago, about thinking you read people so well only to find you've missed the real story altogether?'

'I was talking about Meier at the time,' she reminded him, 'but OK, point made.'

'And lesson learned – get all the facts before jumping to conclusions. I wonder who taught me that when I was starting out?'

Knowing it was her, she playfully nudged him then picked up a plate of canapés to take into the sitting room, leaving him to bring in the champagne and four glasses. No one had actually said it was a good time to celebrate; it had simply felt like breaking open a bottle was the right thing to do.

As soon as everyone had a drink in hand, Jodi declared, 'OK, so we have news!'

At the exact same moment, Cristy said, 'We have news.'

Jodi's eyes widened as she beamed. 'Don't tell me! You're pregnant!'

Cristy blinked, and as everyone laughed, she quickly caught up. 'Not me, you!' she cried.

It was Jodi's turn to blink. 'Not the last time I checked,' she assured them.

'How about you, David?' Connor asked.

'Not me. You?'

'I don't think so.'

'Enough.' Cristy laughed. 'You go first,' she told Jodi, and settled into the small sofa next to David, who was cradling the sleeping baby on one shoulder. 'Ours might take a bit longer, and no, we are *not* getting married.'

David shot her a glance that she deliberately ignored.

'Shame,' Jodi and Connor muttered in unison.

'But don't rule it out as a future date,' David advised, pushing back against Cristy's firm denial. 'I've already got a hat.'

Laughing, Jodi said to Connor, 'It's your news really, so you do it.'

Apparently agreeing with that, he took a position in front of the fireplace and said, 'You're probably not going to believe this, but I've been approached by an Aussie broadcaster to go and front their nightly news.'

Cristy started to freeze.

Jodi said, 'We'd be based in Sydney with a harbour-view apartment and everything would be taken care of, the move, visas, even Aurora's day care, provided it all works out.'

'They've put together an amazing package,' Connor continued. 'It's kind of unturndownable, the chance of a great new start Down Under, and Jodi's mother is OK about coming with.'

Cristy's mouth was dry; her heart was thudding so hard that it was a moment before she realized David had taken her hand. She couldn't be entirely sure this was really happening, and yet it was, because Connor was still talking, Jodi was laughing, and somehow, she had to make herself congratulate them when all she wanted to do was shout, *No! You can't!*

How the hell was she going to get through the rest of the evening without making her real feelings known? She simply couldn't bear the idea of them leaving, couldn't even begin to imagine running *Hindsight* without Connor.

Her own news was in pieces now, meant absolutely nothing without him.

'And now for our *really* big announcement!' Jodi cried, encouraging Connor to keep going.

Were they about to ask her to go with them? No, why would they? This was his big chance, not hers.

Was it too late to tell Kinsley that she'd changed her mind? Except, she hadn't – she really *did* want to stay with *Hindsight*.

David's hand was tightening on hers as Connor said, 'The really big news is that we've turned it down because we're totally committed to everyone and everything here, and we can't bear to be parted from you.'

As the words reached her, Cristy's mouth fell open. She tried to breathe and found she was starting to cry. 'Oh my God, that was cruel,' she scolded, too bound up in relief to get up and embrace them. 'I really thought you were going to leave me.'

Pulling her to her feet, Connor wrapped her in his arms. 'Never,' he told her. 'We're a team. Nothing – not even big bucks and heady offers – can pull us apart.'

Having no choice now but to confess to her own struggle with a dazzling offer, Cristy watched Connor's expression turn from surprise to hurt and confusion as she went through it.

'Why didn't you tell me right away?' he wanted to know when she finished. 'We could have talked it through, tried to work something out.'

Knowing she'd never admit that he hadn't been included in Kinsley's plans, she said, 'Actually, I think I *have* worked something out, and that's *my* big news. Or it could be, if we can pull it off. Much will depend on you and how you feel about it – the others too – but you are the main man.'

'Exactly what I keep telling him,' Jodi put in. 'Not.'

Clearly intrigued, Connor sank cross-legged to the floor next to Jodi's chair. 'Go for it,' he told Cristy.

'OK. So, when Kinsley first approached me, he said he was going to make me an offer I couldn't refuse. Now we're going to do the same to him, but if he doesn't go for it, David is pretty sure he can find some investors.' She glanced at him and received a nod. 'I've prepared a proposal that you can look over later,' she told Connor, 'but essentially, I've been thinking, why don't we create our own small podcasting empire – OK, oxymoron there – based right here in Bristol? That way, we get to stay put, which seems to be what we all want, and we can do a couple of things to build on what we already have.

'First – I know you're going to love this – we look into posting the pods on YouTube, something you've long been wanting to get stuck into. We could also take a look at other quality crime-casts from around the South West and consider bringing them into the fold. There are quite a few out there that might do much better with the right backing, and it would put us in a position to help develop new talent and new ideas. We could make them a part of *Hindsight Plus* or *Extra* – to be discussed – and hopefully Iz will spin her magic on the branding.'

Connor was clearly trying to take it all in. 'So our main focus stays as is,' he said, 'but we introduce video, expand to include "quality crime-casts" from around the region . . . To be fronted by us, or them?'

'By the contributors, with input from us if needed, but they would mostly run their own shows and submit to us for final sign-off before uploading under the *Hindsight Extra* banner.'

Connor was nodding his approval. 'OK. Seeing it so far, but what about us as a core team? Still you, me, Clove and Jacks?'

'Absolutely.'

'What about Harry and Meena – where would they fit in?'

Cristy turned to David. She'd spent the last couple of

hours discussing this with him, so was keen for him to take this next point.

'At the moment,' he said 'we're seeing the Quinns in much the same roles as they play now: kind of senior management, oversight gurus, legal protectors, just with a bigger organization to run. To be discussed with them, obviously, but shaping things that way would continue to allow you guys to focus on content, while they and a slightly bigger back-up team would deal with all the business stuff.'

'I think they'll go for it,' Cristy declared. 'They'll have their own thoughts and ideas, obviously, as will you once it's all sunk in, but they've long been talking about expansion, and as much as we love our old Georgian house studios, the place just isn't big enough if we do start implementing these changes. So we'd also be looking for new premises, hopefully still on the waterfront, but somewhere that will give us room to grow.'

'So exactly how many series in a year are you thinking we'd take on?' Connor asked curiously.

'That will depend on the potential investigations, and what the new players bring to the table. For us guys, we'd continue much the same as we are now, with two or three series focused on trying to solve cold cases or at least open up further police investigations. What really matters where the new crime-casters are concerned is that they deliver high-value series, none of your kitchen sink stuff or let's get pissed and talk about some unresolved case. We'll be looking for serious investigators, so journalists like ourselves, maybe lawyers, or ex-detectives such as Andee Lawrence, who we both know would be brilliant, if she's interested in taking it on for her area.'

Connor was shaking his head incredulously as his smile widened and turned into a laugh. 'You do realize,' he said, 'that Kinsley's likely to see us as a threat, albeit small time from his perspective, rather than a potential investment?'

'Which is why David is going to devise a back-up plan,' Cristy responded, 'but my guess is Kinsley will get involved, probably with an eye to buying us out further down the line, but we'll cross that when – *if* – we come to it. Who knows? We might end up buying him out or even running his global construct from Bristol instead of London or New York.'

Punching the air, Connor said, 'I need to see this proposal, but you can already take it that I'm in.' And raising his glass, he added, 'Here's to *Hindsight* ruling the world.'

'Wouldn't we all benefit from that,' David commented, with no small irony.

Laughing, Cristy got up to go and hug Connor again. 'To you,' she said, 'my other brother, my eldest son.' She grimaced at that, making them all laugh. 'My wonderful partner and very best friend.'

'This is going straight to my head,' Connor warned, 'and I'm not talking about the champagne.'

'Actually,' Cristy said, bracing herself for what had to come next, 'before we get too deep into cheering ourselves on, there's something else I have to fess up to that you're probably not going to like quite as much.'

Connor eyed her carefully, although she could see that he was so excited by the growth plans that her confession probably wasn't going to knock him off-course now – at least not as much as it might have if delivered at any other time.

Bracing herself, she said, 'I've agreed to give the Terrier an exclusive on how we pulled this latest series together. Obviously not until it's finished, but you need to know now.'

Connor stared at her in disbelief. 'You've done a deal with . . . Wait a minute . . . Why the hell would you do that? You can't stand the woman – none of us can – and we sure as hell can't trust her. So make this make sense.'

'She basically blackmailed me into it,' Cristy admitted. 'She knew about Kinsley's offer – how she knew is another story – and she threatened to tell you about it at a time when we really didn't need the distraction. So, I stalled her with the offer of a behind-the-scenes—'

'I take it you got copy approval,' he cut in forcefully.

'We don't have anything in writing yet; I've just given her my word. Obviously when it comes to it, we'll definitely want that.'

He nodded thoughtfully, clearly still not thrilled by the prospect of sharing anything with a journalist he had zero respect for. However, just as Cristy had hoped, his enthusiasm for the new-look *Hindsight* kicked in again.

'Hell, we've still got the final episode to go yet,' he declared, 'and who knows what's coming down the line with that, or where we'll all be by the time we find out.'

CHAPTER FORTY-SEVEN

FOUR MONTHS LATER

CRISTY: 'Hi, it's Cristy.'

CONNOR: 'And it's Connor. Welcome to the final episode of the series featuring the story of what happened to the missing twins, Noah and Abigail Ivorson.'

CRISTY: 'It's been four months since their mother, Nicole, was returned to prison, after violating the terms of her parole.'

CONNOR: 'And the same amount of time since their father, Jean-Claude Meier, self-surrendered to the police for his part in covering up their tragic deaths.'

CRISTY: 'A lot has happened in that time – we'll get into the detail of it in a minute, but we're starting this episode with a return visit to Bryn Helyg, Meier's "therapy farm", as it's become known in the press.'

CONNOR: 'In fact, we're just pulling into the car park behind the stables, and boy is it different to the last time we were here. It's a beautiful July day, with a clear blue sky, not a cloud in sight, and there are quite a few people milling around – I guess both guests and staff. Most of the space-age pods have their doors thrown wide-open, loungers and picnic tables on the private decks, and the field directly ahead of us is full of ewes and their few-month-old lambs.'

CRISTY: 'I'm just getting out of the car, and the scent of summer is as fresh in the air as the pungent farmyard smells, and the sounds – hopefully we're picking them up with our mics – are their own kind of chorus: a medley of baa-ing, neighing, mooing, birdsong and, yes, a few human voices carrying over from the barns and nearby stables. The whole place feels idyllic and quietly busy, suggesting business goes on as usual, although the security measures that have been stepped up since our earlier visits were pretty evident as we approached.'

CONNOR: 'No guards, as such, but a lot more cameras, apparently monitored from inside the farmhouse, as much to keep out uninvited press and unscheduled tourists these days as to prevent livestock theft, the original reason for their installation.'

CRISTY: 'OK, we're moving over towards the goat pen to dump our stuff on a picnic table in the shade of a glorious horse-chestnut . . . By the way, our arrival has been noted, and we've been told someone will be along to talk to us soon, so until they come, we'll take this opportunity to fill you in on what has happened over the last few months. Why don't you sit over that side, Con . . .'

CONNOR: 'So you get the view?'

CRISTY: 'That's the plan. Now, do you have your notes?'

CONNOR: 'Right here on my laptop. So I'm starting this, am I? OK, so here goes:

'Before getting into what's gone down with Nicole and Meier, we're going to talk a little bit about the small bodies that were exhumed from Meier's grandparents' grave.'

CRISTY: 'After the forensic analysis was complete and they were confirmed as Noah and Abigail, they were returned here, to Wales, for burial in a grave of their own, which is next to the one they were taken from. We'll be posting shots of their headstone on our website, where you'll see the engraving: *In loving memory of our beautiful twins, Noah and Abigail Meier, 2004-2005. Lost too soon. Living forever in our hearts.*'

CONNOR: 'Cristy and I were here for the committal ceremony. It was small, so actually quite an honour to be included, although we were asked not to record or post anything about it at the time.'

CRISTY: 'You'll probably be interested to know who else was there, so here goes: several of the staff from Bryn Helyg, as you'd expect; Maeve Ivorson, Nicole's mother; Lauren Beagle, Nicole's cousin; Bridget Hawkes, Nicole's aunt; Julien and Rula Meier, Claude Meier's brother and sister-in-law; and Claude Meier himself.'

CONNOR: 'You'll already know from the news that he was released on police bail following charges ranging from Assisting an Offender to Perverting the Course of Justice.'

CRISTY: 'He appeared in front of a judge two weeks ago when he pled guilty to all charges brought against him. Since then, he's been on court bail while the judge considers the submissions; apparently he's called for reports on just about everything from character and bail conduct to psychological and risk assessment.'

CONNOR: 'Meier's due to appear in court again on Thursday, when he will find out how long he will have to serve for the cover up of a crime that is itself under review and could, at any time, be reduced to involuntary manslaughter or no crime at all.'

CRISTY: 'Obviously, this is what Nicole and her legal team are hoping for, and what would probably have happened if she and Meier had not panicked on that fateful date back in 2005.'

CONNOR: 'We'll be in court for Meier's sentencing. In the meantime, something you probably already know from the news is that Nicole Ivorson's parole has been reinstated – it happened just over a month ago – and since then, she's been allowed to come to Bryn Helyg.'

CONNOR: 'She and Claude Meier have agreed to be interviewed together today, so that's why we're here, and I'm sure, like us, you're keen to find out what they have to say about everything they've been through and what is still to come.'

Meier was walking towards them, gently applauding. 'Bravo,' he said, shaking Cristy's hand first, then Connor's. 'A fair synopsis of where we are today, and I find myself feeling pleased to see you – although, of course, I continue to wish that we had never come to your attention.'

His irony was as infectious as ever, Cristy noted, and for a man soon destined to lose his freedom, he was managing to appear relaxed and in control of himself. There was, she thought, perhaps a little more grey in his hair and in the two-day beard since the last time they'd seen him, but he continued to exude the same easy friendliness that made it feel good to know him.

'How are you?' she asked, following his eyes as he turned to look over his shoulder.

'Ah, here she is,' he said, as Nicole appeared from around

the side of the stables, not unlike an apparition given her golden hair and the dazzle of sunlight behind her. He went to slip an arm around her.

The first thing Cristy noticed about her was how much more like her younger self she looked – older, of course, but it was much easier now to recognize the similarities than the last time they'd seen her. Gone were the sores on her mouth and the bruising shadows around her eyes; even her hair seemed brighter and longer, falling in a tangle of curls to her shoulders. The diaphanous flowery dress that passed her knees almost disguised how thin she was; it also made her appear close to ethereal. No wonder he was so smitten with her, Cristy thought; she truly was lovely, and what was even more remarkable was that being with him was almost certainly what had brought her back to life.

'You came,' Nicole declared, taking Cristy's hands in both of hers. She seemed both childlike and mature in her pleasure, someone who remained trapped in the past while coming to terms with who she was now. 'We thought you would,' she said, sounding almost like an accomplished hostess, 'and we've been looking forward to it, haven't we?' Not waiting for Meier to respond, she moved on to Connor. 'Thank you for being so kind to us,' she said warmly, 'both of you. Not everyone is, and we understand it – of course we do – but we like to think of you as friends.'

'Refreshments are on the way,' Meier told them. 'Susanna's homemade iced lemonade and—'

'Frozen fruit slices,' Nicole chipped in with a giggle. 'They're scrummy and perfect for when it's so hot.' She sighed ecstatically and let her head fall back. 'It's wonderful here, isn't it? I feel as though I've been dead for a long time and now I've finally made it to heaven. Perhaps I have.' She peered at Meier mischievously, as though daring him to tease her.

Clearly amused, he ran a hand over her hair and leaned in to whisper something that made her laugh.

Feeling slightly voyeuristic, Cristy glanced at Connor, who clearly felt much the same.

'So, where would you like us to set up?' she asked, deadening the moment and wishing she hadn't.

'Why not do it here?' Meier suggested.

'We'll be showered by flowers,' Nicole cautioned, 'but it'll make everything seem more romantic, won't it?' Even as she spoke, willow fluff floated in from a nearby tree, and Cristy was struck by her efforts to turn this short spell she and Meier had together into as special a time as she could.

Minutes later, as they were about to begin, Nicole suddenly sprang up from the bench, crying, 'Look! It's Maggi with Jude. I have to go and say hello.' And before anyone could react, she took off down the meadow to where Maggi was introducing a timid lamb into a small flock of curious sheep.

Meier looked at Cristy and shrugged. 'Everything is special to her, and the lambs are her favourite. This one has been sickly, so she's happy to see it gaining strength.'

As Cristy watched her, she was thinking of how interesting it would be to focus on Nicole's story another way: a free spirit crushed by the horror of what had happened to her children, then locked away for so long she felt she'd died. She was intrigued to know more about how life must look to her now. She was clearly happy to be here, filled with wonder and joy, but deep down she was surely still broken and dreading Meier leaving. There was so much Cristy wanted to ask her, and she intended to try, if she was able to pin her down.

Running back to them, Nicole came to a stop behind Meier and wrapped her arms around his neck, pressing her cheek to his. 'Sorry,' she said to Cristy, 'I hope I haven't spoiled things.'

'Not at all,' Cristy assured her, not entirely sure whether she should be addressing her as a child or a thirty-nine-year-old woman, 'we can start whenever you're ready.'

'I am now. Promise.'

Nicole remained where she was, behind Meier, and seemed to hug him tighter as Connor said, 'Take it away.'

Nicole laughed, and Cristy decided to begin with the kind of question she didn't usually favour. In this instance, however, it seemed fitting.

CRISTY: 'Tell me how it feels to be back in the world after so long in prison.'

Nicole frowned as she thought. She seemed troubled, on the brink of tears all of a sudden, until she let go of Meier and threw out her arms and let her head fall back.

NICOLE: 'It makes me want to dance, and embrace everyone, but Claude doesn't like to dance.'

She was rotating slowly, dreamily, then shrieked as he suddenly scooped her into his arms. He spun her round and round, not so much a dance as a mad, joyous whirl, with her arms and hair flying and him laughing, until he set her back on the ground. Flushed and breathless, she gazed up at him in a way that was so intense, so private, that it was easy to tell no one else existed for them in this moment.

Keeping his voice low, Connor said, 'Wish we were videoing this.'

'Even if we were, it's so *intimate* I don't think it would feel right to use it.'

Returning to the table, Meier sat Nicole down beside him and put an arm around her, as if to keep her anchored.

'Sorry,' Nicole said, 'I've spoiled things again.'

'You really haven't,' Cristy assured her. 'We're in no rush; we can take as long as you like.'

'But you did promise to answer some questions,' Meier reminded her, 'so let's try again.'

Nodding agreement, she wound her fingers through his and waited for Cristy to begin again.

She decided to take a more practical approach this time:

CRISTY: 'Did you come straight to Bryn Helyg following your release?'

NICOLE: 'Yes. Claude was waiting for me outside the prison, and we drove here together.'

MEIER: 'Your mother came too.'

NICOLE: 'Yes, and she's still here, somewhere, but we might soon be going back to the house on Randall Lane.'

A light seemed to go out inside her as she connected to how things were about to change again. So it seemed the joy, the relief and euphoria really were part of a mask to keep her in the moment, all no doubt aided by Meier's careful counselling.

Deciding to explore the post-sentencing plans later, Cristy steered them back to her release.

CRISTY: 'Were you surprised when you first saw this place?'

Nicole visibly brightened, although this time there was no mistaking her fragility as she turned to look at Meier.

NICOLE: 'Not as much as you might think. Claude had already described it to me, and I'd heard your podcast series by then, so you brought it to life for me too.'

CRISTY: 'What was the first thing you did when you got here?'

Meier laughed, and as Connor put his head in his hands, Cristy realized her mistake. She could have kicked herself.

However, Nicole didn't seem to think there was anything wrong with the question.

> NICOLE: 'The very first thing we did was go to see the twins. Claude had shown me photos of the grave before I was released, but I wanted to see it for real. So he took me there and we sat with them for a long time, didn't we?'

Meier tightened his hold on her hand and brought it to his lips.

> NICOLE: 'We go regularly. It makes us feel close to them. We take picnics and storybooks – I know they'd be older now, but we still think of them as babies, so that's how we speak to them. They'll always be babies, but sometimes we allow ourselves to imagine the kind of children and teenagers they might have grown into and who'd they be now.
>
> 'I think Noah would be a doctor or a scientist, a rock climber and skier, a farmer and a terrible dancer like his father.
>
> 'And I think Abigail would be nothing like me.'

> MEIER: 'In my mind, she is exactly like you – troublesome, beautiful, strong and vulnerable – and I wouldn't want her any other way.'

> NICOLE: 'He's only saying that because I'm sitting here. Really, he imagines her as a concert pianist, an astronaut, a gifted entrepreneur able to turn her hand to anything.'

> MEIER: 'And by the time she's twenty-five, I expect her to have sorted out the world.'

Nicole laughed, closed her eyes and seemed to fill up with

emotion. There were tears in her voice as she continued to speak.

NICOLE: 'We always know where they are, but at the same time, we don't know at all, and that's our greatest punishment.'

As the sadness and loss washed over her, Cristy allowed several moments to pass, recording only the natural sounds around them, while thinking of her own children, so close to the twins in age. How fortunate she'd been to have had them every day of their lives to love and cherish and watch grow into adults. It compounded her sadness for Nicole and made her wish she could do more to help her through what lay ahead.

Feeling Meier's eyes on her she turned to him and realized he was probably aware of what was going through her mind.

Addressing him she began again.

CRISTY: 'It must be hard for you right now, knowing you're going to be sentenced soon. Has your lawyer given you an indication of how long you might have to serve?

MEIER: 'We're hoping the sentences, whatever they are, will run concurrently. If not, I could receive up to ten years for the charge of Assisting an Offender, and they think maybe five years for Perverting the Course of Justice. That can carry a life sentence, but no one is expecting it to be so harsh. I just hope they're right.'

CRISTY: 'So the worst-case scenario is fifteen years in total – or a maximum of ten if they run concurrently?'

MEIER: 'That's right. *Donc, une éternité*, but by the end of it, hopefully society, at least, will feel that we have both paid for what happened to our children and how we kept it hidden from the world.'

NICOLE: 'It's a shame that locking us up won't ever bring them back. I just wish we'd been sent away at the same time; then we wouldn't have to be parted again.'

As Nicole's voice turned husky, Meier dropped his head against hers. He spoke so softly that it wasn't possible to hear what he was saying, but when she turned to him, the way her eyes scanned his face was a clear search for reassurance. He pressed a kiss to her forehead and pulled her in closer.

Cristy glanced at Connor, not sure whether they should continue. Their questions, their very presence was starting to feel like such an intrusion.

MEIER: 'Would you like to ask anything else?'

CRISTY: 'If you're sure you don't mind.'

MEIER: 'Please. We wouldn't have invited you here if we didn't want to speak.'

Cristy turned to Connor again and was relieved when he took his cue.

CONNOR: 'Nicole, are you planning to be in court when Claude is sentenced?'

NICOLE: 'Yes, of course. I can't let him go through it without me.'

MEIER: 'I have asked her not to come, but she is determined. My brother also intends to be there, as does Maeve, so she won't be alone. Will you be there?'

CONNOR: 'Yes. Obviously, we won't be recording, but

afterwards, we'll precis the hearing for the end of the episode.'

Meier nodded slowly, thoughtfully and as his eyes came to Cristy's, she could sense the quiet, immutable inner strength that was going to get him through this, no matter how hard he might find it, but it wasn't going to be easy – not easy at all.

Very quietly he said, 'If anyone can perform miracles, now would be a good time.'

*

Much later, as Cristy and Connor drove back to Bristol, they were silent for a long time. It was hard to put into words everything they were thinking and feeling, the lasting and deepening effect the visit was having on them both. In her mind's eye, Cristy was seeing Meier and Nicole as if they were ghosts, no longer real as they haunted the Bryn Helyg hillside, the churchyard and even the future. For one awful moment, she wondered if they were devising a suicide pact with instructions to bury them with their children.

Would they? Really?

It would mean they wouldn't be parted again.

Turning to Connor, she said, 'Tell me what you're thinking.'

He glanced at her and took his time before saying, 'Apart from all the other stuff spinning around in my head, I'm wondering how the hell we describe them to the Terrier so she won't savage them just for being who they are.'

Having almost forgotten about Molly Terrance, Cristy felt her heart sink. 'She won't be able to if we have final copy approval.'

'Maybe not in an interview with us, but separately, once she has our take on things, she can do what the hell she wants.

And if it gets her more clicks and shares . . .' He glanced at Cristy again, then turned back to the road, letting a few more miles pass, before saying, 'If she got you into this position because of Kinsley's offer, she could be feeling even more vengeful now she's out of the running for the project too.'

'That was nothing to do with me – and anyway, we don't know for certain that she is out, only that the entire thing is going to be New York-based now rather than London-based. So, Rathour gets his way, and my guess is he'd have continued to push for it even if I had accepted.'

'And you were never interested in moving to the States.' It was a statement, not a question, since he already knew the answer to that. 'Meanwhile,' he continued, 'we have Kinsley's backing for *Hindsight Extra*, plus the investors David's bringing on board, so I'm calling an all-round win for us.'

Cristy nodded and closed her eyes. 'I wonder if Meena and Harry have signed the lease on the new premises yet? Wasn't it supposed to be happening this morning?'

'Apparently it did, so the big move will be underway as soon as this episode has been uploaded.'

Feeling suddenly edgy, Cristy said, 'I don't know about you, but I might be as nervous as Meier and Nicole about next week's sentencing.'

'Dreading it,' he admitted, and neither of them spoke again until they were back in the office, where so much was going on that it would be easy to think the big move was already going ahead.

CHAPTER FORTY-EIGHT

The first they saw of Meier was when he was brought into the dock at Bristol Crown Court wearing a smart grey suit, white shirt and sombre tie. He was pale, clean-shaven, clearly as anxious as anyone could be in his position; yet at the same time, he seemed calm, almost resolute as he searched around for Nicole. Cristy knew the moment he'd found her in the public gallery simply by the increased intensity in his eyes. She looked up and saw Nicole sitting with Maeve and Julien, her own gaze fixed on Meier.

Profoundly relieved that her fears of a suicide pact had not come to pass, Cristy shifted closer to Connor to make room for someone squeezing into the far end of the press bench. They'd turned up at the Crown Court about an hour ago, minutes before Nicole and Meier had arrived at the back door, driven by his lawyer, unseen by the press. Maeve, Maggi and Johan had apparently been in the car behind; everyone else – more staff from Bryn Helyg, Meier's brother and sister-in-law, Maeve's sister Bridget and Meier's barrister – had appeared soon after. Though there was a heavy media turnout, there was no sign of the Terrier, although it was certain she'd have sent someone to cover the sentencing for her.

The room fell silent as everyone stood for the judge, solemn and forbidding in his purple robe and horsehair wig. After speaking quietly with an usher, he wasted no more time in getting proceedings underway.

The next half an hour passed so swiftly that Cristy barely had time to look up as she noted down the salient points of how the judge had come to his conclusions. Beside her, Connor was doing the same, quickly flicking over pages to keep up with the lengthy and detailed summary.

The next thing they knew, they were outside on Small Street, hugging a stunned, and tearful Nicole before she was swept away by Honey and other lawyers.

Breaking free of the crowd to start heading back to the office, Cristy took the mic Connor was passing her, and they recorded as they walked.

> CRISTY: 'Connor and I have just left the court, and I think we're both still in a state of... Confusion? Shock? How are you feeling about what just happened?'
>
> CONNOR: 'I guess same as you. I really thought, with the way the judge went on about the cover up, the loss of two children's lives, the failure to name accomplices, the burial and everything around that, that Meier was going down for at least ten – didn't you?'
>
> CRISTY: 'If not fifteen. The summation was brutal. It can't be described any other way, and you could tell that everyone in the courtroom was expecting the harshest sentence possible. I could feel myself bracing for it, so God knows what it was like for Meier.'
>
> CONNOR: 'His eyes were closed for most of it, so no idea if he was shutting it out, or taking it in. I just know I'd never want to be in his place, having my crimes, my failings, my whole damned character shredded like that.'
>
> CRISTY: 'Then suddenly everything changed. It was as if another judge took over right in front of our eyes. If Meier didn't believe in miracles before, he must be questioning that now, because the tone, the whole

proceedings went onto another plane. The judge was suddenly parroting the defence's remarks about Meier presenting no risk to the public, praising the good work he was doing in mental health on his farm in Mid Wales...'

CONNOR: 'How he was now helping Nicole to rehabilitate after the trauma of her own ordeal... His deep regret for everything he'd done... It was like Meier had managed to morph into some sort of saint, and you could see that even he didn't believe what he was hearing.'

CRISTY: 'I think we were all so taken aback by it that the sentence, when it came... Well, I'm still trying to process it, so I want you to confirm now Con, that I really did hear correctly when the judge said that, if Meier was not still holding back on the names of his accomplices, his sentence for the other offences might have been suspended. *Suspended!*'

CONNOR: 'That's definitely what I heard. As it stands, he received a three-year custodial term for Perverting the Course of Justice. So he *is* going to prison – in fact, he could already be on his way there – but from what we were able to make of the consensus before we left the court, he'll probably only serve half of it, and there's a good chance he'll find himself somewhere like HMP Leyhill, a Cat D facility in South Gloucestershire, for the last part.'

CRISTY: 'So not too far for Nicole to go to visit him, if that is where he ends up. Meanwhile, he'll probably be held in Bristol Prison – Cat B, so not the absolute worst, but still pretty grim from everything we hear. He could be there for a while before being transferred to somewhere hopefully less crowded when a place becomes available.'

CONNOR: 'You'll be interested to know that as soon as the sentencing was over, the judge called for an inquiry into the initial police investigation. He had some seriously strong words for those involved who, he said, had allowed the atrocity of a terrorist attack – shocking and terrible though it had been – to distract them from the duty of care owed to Noah and Abigail Meier.'

With that awful truth still resonating in their minds, they crossed the city centre, dropped down to the waterfront and headed towards the ferry. The only sounds being recorded as they walked were of them breathing, their hurried footsteps and the screech of gulls swooping around the harbour.

It wasn't until they reached the crossing point that Connor began again.

CONNOR: 'Clearly, a three-year prison sentence wasn't the outcome Meier and Nicole had hoped for, and yet it was so much better than they'd feared.'

CRISTY: 'I don't know about you, but I'm finding it almost impossible to imagine Meier in prison. Maybe because I don't want to.'

CONNOR: 'Can't get my head round it either, but obviously it's going to happen, so I'm trying to project to one day in the future, hopefully sooner rather than later, when he'll be back at Bryn Helyg with Nicole, amongst friends and close to their children.'

CRISTY: 'Unless he decides to name his accomplices. He might get out sooner if he did, but I can't see him doing that, can you?'

CONNOR: 'No, which makes him both crazy and I guess, honourable, the way he's accepting full responsibility for what he got someone else to do on his behalf. Amazing to me that they did it, but we've met the bloke, so perhaps it's not so amazing at all.'

CHAPTER FORTY-NINE

The following day, due to all the interest in attending the series finale, Meena ended up booking a hospitality suite on the SS *Great Britain*. Although it saddened Cristy and Connor to know they'd quite probably already celebrated *Hindsight*'s last upload at the Georgian house without even realizing it, it made sense for everyone to get together in this bigger venue. They were fourteen in all, including Paul Kinsley, who'd made a special trip from London, as had Iz. David and one of the new investors had flown in from Guernsey; Matthew and Aiden, Jodi and Aurora, and of course the core team were all there. Jacks, together with the great ship's systems engineers, had organized the tech side of things, while the Harbourside Kitchen was providing the catering.

As soon as the signal was given to begin, everyone quickly found a seat at one of the many tables and listened in silence as recaps and soundbites from previous episodes led into Nicole and Meier's recent interview at Bryn Helyg.

Seated between David and Connor, a glass of champagne in one hand, her phone in the other, Cristy found herself transported back to that remarkable day on the Welsh mountainside. She wondered where Meier was now, this minute? What he was doing? How was he feeling? Had he seen Nicole yet? He must have spoken to her on the phone at the very least.

She couldn't think why she was feeling their separation so

acutely, almost as if she was a part of it, until she realized that actually, she was in a way. She too was having to let go. She had no right or reason to continue using their lives or their heartache to search for answers that had now been found.

Next came the phone interview she and Connor had managed to snatch with Meier's barrister only yesterday. Although he wasn't providing any new information, his take on the sentencing hearing was interesting, in that he too had been thrown by the judge's sudden shift from condemnation to 'quite an astonishing level of praise'.

To close the episode, they'd decided to use Nicole and Meier's words about visiting their children's graves . . .

> NICOLE: 'We go regularly. It makes us feel close to them. We take picnics and storybooks – I know they'd be older now, but we still think of them as babies so that's how we speak to them. They'll always be babies, but sometimes we allow ourselves to imagine the kind of children and teenagers they might have grown into and who'd they be now.
>
> 'I think Noah would be a doctor or a scientist, a rock climber and skier, a farmer and a terrible dancer like his father.
>
> 'And I think Abigail would be nothing like me.'
>
> MEIER: 'In my mind, she is exactly like you – troublesome, beautiful, strong and vulnerable – and I wouldn't want her any other way.'
>
> NICOLE: 'He's only saying that because I'm sitting here. Really, he imagines her as a concert pianist, an astronaut, a gifted entrepreneur able to turn her hand to anything.'
>
> MEIER: 'And by the time she's twenty-five, I expect her to have sorted out the world.'

There was the sound of Nicole's laughter turning to sadness as the *Hindsight* theme tune began to play.

NICOLE: 'We always know where they are, but at the same time, we don't know at all, and that's our greatest punishment.'

As Jacks faded out the end link, a sober, poignant silence followed, until Meena finally said, 'They'd probably be together now if he'd named the accomplices. Do you know who they are? I mean, obviously you're not going to say in the pod, but—'

'We don't know,' Cristy interrupted. 'Our first choices were both out of the country when it happened, so it's possible it was people whose names we've never even heard.'

'So not Maggi and Johan? I definitely thought it was them.'

'Me too,' Harry agreed.

'Whoever it was,' Connor said, 'our task here is done. We know where the twins are, Nicole has been released, and Meier is now paying for his part in it all. I'm not saying we feel good about any of it – actually, we don't – but that's the trouble with truth: it's not always the most welcome guest in the room.'

In an effort to lift the moment, Harry raised his glass as he said, 'But all of you are welcome here, and this is a special moment in the *Hindsight* story. So let's get these drinks topped up, shall we?'

As soon as the champagne had gone round again, Kinsley rose to his feet. 'I know I'm the newbie around here, so I shouldn't speak unless spoken to . . .' He laughed as everyone cheered and whooped. 'But I'd like to propose a toast to you guys, Cristy, Connor, Clove and Jacks. I'm proud to be backing *Hindsight Extra*. This wasn't what I expected when I thought I was making Cristy an offer she couldn't refuse – but hey, I know when I've met my match, and you're definitely that, my old friend.'

'Not so much of the old,' she protested with a laugh.

'To Cristy!' Connor declared, raising his glass. 'Old, young, mother, partner, podcaster extraordinaire, wicked godmother and valued best friend. Let's make sure that no one – not even you, Paul Kinsley – tries to come between us again.'

'I'll drink to that,' she cheered, leaning into David as he slipped an arm around her. 'And I'm also going to drink to our new offices at the Boat Shed, starting right after we've all had a lovely summer break.'

Getting a big cheer for that, she laughed and turned to David as he said, 'Matthew took me to see the place earlier. Impressive.'

'I think it will be once it's properly set up,' she agreed, 'but I'm glad you like it.'

'I'm also liking the idea of a lovely summer break. Any thoughts on where you might like to spend it? And don't say Guernsey – I'm in need of getting away.'

She didn't have to think for long. 'My brother has already rented a place for the whole of August, and he's invited us to join them if we fancy it.'

'Sounding good so far. Where?'

'Provence.'

'Wow. Could definitely be up for that.'

'He says it will be, and I quote, "an opportunity to bring some family skeletons out of the closet."'

David's eyes widened with intrigue. 'Any idea what he's referring to?'

'Not really, but I confess I'm keen to find out. It would be good to spend some time with him and Serena anyway.'

Clearly having no problem with that, David said, '*Comment pourrais-je ne pas vouloir passer du temps avec la femme que j'aime dans le pays le plus romantique du monde?*'

The French made her think of Meier, and with a catch in her heart, she said, 'Something about the woman you love in the most romantic country in the world?'

'Exactly that, and why wouldn't I want to spend time there with you?'

Still thinking of Meier and Nicole, Cristy kissed David and wondered how long it was going to take for her to stop thinking about them at all.

'Excuse me interrupting,' Connor said dryly, 'but you'll want to see this.'

Taking his phone, Cristy read the message, and was so thrown by the unexpectedness of it that it took her a moment to realize it had nothing to do with Meier or Nicole. She looked at Connor as though he might have some sort of explanation, but all he said was, 'It's been sent to both of us, so it'll be on your phone too.'

'Are you going to share?' David prompted.

Cristy glanced at him, then read the message aloud:

You don't know me, but maybe you will – if you can find me. Plenty have tried; no one has even come close. Can you change that? I look forward to finding out.

I am The Shadow Man, and this is the gauntlet.

Acknowledgements

The lived experience of Bryn Helyg, aka Great House Farm at Builth Wells, was a joy on every level. Although there is no Claude Meier to welcome you, and no actual therapy on offer, there is much to be gained from spending time at the wonderfully cosy farmhouse, or in one of the luxury pods. It's a working farm so plenty of animals to delight and the surrounding countryside proved an endless source of inspiration. Thank you so much to Lynne Jones for making our stay so memorable.

A huge thank you also to Peter Warne for an incredible insight into how Claude's earlier life in Switzerland could have unfolded, who his parents might have been, and where the family lived, loved and worked. Vevey is one of my favourite places so it was a great joy to spend some time there with Cristy.

There are never enough words to thank everyone in my publishing team, well perhaps there are, but I'd probably fill another book trying. It is such a joy to work with Kate Elton, Roger Cazalet, Lynne Drew, Belinda Toor, Alice Brown, Elizabeth Dawson, Maud Davies, and the oft changing but still brilliant marketing team. Don't get me started on my brilliant agent, Luigi Bonomi, whose guidance and friendship mean the world, or I really will never stop! Love and thanks to you all – you make being an author a total pleasure even during the more challenging times.

**Don't miss the next gripping thriller in
the Cristy Ward series . . .**

I Dare You

Ten years ago, Keeley's husband vanished.

They were enjoying a quiet family day out on the beach when Leon left to help a stranger in need. He was never seen again.

Now, true crime podcast host, Cristy Ward, has received an unexpected message from a man claiming to be the stranger from the beach, and the case has been thrown open again . . .

I dare you to find me . . .

Could this be the beginning of a confession . . . or is it a deadly trap?

COMING SOON